About the author

Sharon Booth writes uplifting women's fiction — love, laughter, and happy ever after. Happy endings are guaranteed for her main characters, though she likes to make them work for it.

Sharon is a member of the Society of Authors and the Romantic Novelists' Association, and an Authorpreneur member of the Alliance of Independent Authors. She has been a KDP All-Star Author on several occasions.

She loves Yorkshire Tea, Doctor Who, adores Cary Grant movies, and admits to being shamefully prone to crushes on fictional heroes.

Sharon grew up in the East Riding of Yorkshire, and the Yorkshire coast and countryside feature strongly in her novels. Her stories are set in pretty villages and quirky market towns, by the sea or in the countryside, and feature lots of humour, romance, and friendship.

If you love stories with gorgeous, *kind* heroes, and heroines who have far more important things on their minds than buying shoes, then you'll love her books.

Books by Sharon Booth

There Must Be an Angel
A Kiss from a Rose
Once Upon a Long Ago

This Other Eden
Being Emerald
The Skimmerdale Collection

Resisting Mr Rochester
Saving Mr Scrooge

Baxter's Christmas Wish
The Other Side of Christmas

New Doctor at Chestnut House
Christmas at the Country Practice
Fresh Starts at Folly Farm
A Merry Bramblewick Christmas
Summer at the Country Practice
Christmas at Cuckoo Nest Cottage
The Bramblewick Collection

Belle, Book and Christmas Candle
My Favourite Witch
To Catch a Witch
The Witches of Castle Clair Complete Collection

There Must Be an Angel

Sharon Booth

Green Ginger Publishing

First published in 2015 by:
Fabrian Books
Kent, England
Published in 2020 by:
Green Ginger Publishing
Yorkshire, England

Cover design by Berni Stevens. www.bernistevensdesign.com

ISBN: 978-1-9993602-3-8

For my dad ~ my first hero.

xxx

Chapter 1

"Reader, I married him."

You know, when you come to the end of a romantic novel like *Jane Eyre*, you always think, well, that's that, she's got her hero and they'll both live happily ever after. You never think, I wonder how long that's going to last, do you? I mean, you don't close the book, pondering how long it will be before Mr Rochester is off rogering the maid and Jane is a neurotic wreck with a gin habit. Happy ever after means just that in novels, and I used to think the same was true of life. If you met a man, fell in love with him and married him, it was job done. Then I met Harry and married him, and that scuppered that illusion. Before five years were out, I'd assaulted my husband in a most unlikely manner, and done a runner in a stolen car. It just goes to show. I never imagined it would come to *that* as I stood at the altar making my vows, I can tell you.

Mrs Travers had always said I was too romantic for my own good. She disapproved of my reading so many "soppy" novels, and no one did disapproval like Mrs Travers. You should have seen her when we watched daytime television.

'Gives you unrealistic expectations of life,' she informed me, when I ventured to ask why she never indulged in a good old-fashioned love story. Mrs Travers' husband had run away with a checkout girl from Boots in the seventies, so she was quite bitter.

'He reckoned she looked like one of them dancers from Pan's People,' she'd told me. 'Looked more like Rod Stewart, if you ask me, but love's blind.'

Mrs Travers was our cleaning lady. At least, that was her official title, but she had, in her own words, "dodgy knees and clicky hips", so she couldn't bend down and she wouldn't climb stairs, and her hands were too arthritic to put in water. Basically, what happened every Monday and Thursday was that she did a bit of ironing for me — because anything I iron looks more creased and crumpled after I've ironed it than it did in the laundry basket — while I cleaned through the house, then Mrs Travers folded up the ironing, made us a nice cup of tea, and we sat together eating chocolate HobNobs and watching *Loose Women*. After all this exertion, she'd go home with the money Harry paid her for cleaning, and the extra tenner I slipped her each time, and everyone was happy.

Mrs Travers was more like family. She was Joe's cleaning lady, and more-or-less the only female in my life since I was seven years old, when a car accident had robbed me of my mum and gran. A year later, Grandad had died, leaving me in the care of Mum's younger brother, Joe. We'd moved to London when I was twelve, as he'd got a fantastic career opportunity, and he'd employed her within a month of our arrival, mainly to do general cleaning duties and laundry, but I think she kind of adopted me. She was the one who made sure I got three square meals a day, did my homework, had clean kit for PE and all the motherly attention I needed. Joe was a brilliant uncle but, really, God help me if I'd been left entirely to him, because a domestic goddess he wasn't.

When I had Amy, she came to give me a hand, and had turned up two days a week ever since, in spite of Harry. I wasn't going to refuse her help. She only had Joe and me, and a sister who lived in Margate. There'd been no man in her life since the errant husband, which I thought incredibly sad. She, however, thought she'd had a lucky escape.

'They're a waste of time,' she told me, as we sat eating biscuits, ignoring the pile of ironing and the vacuum cleaner that I'd got as far as plugging in before we decided that we couldn't do another thing until we'd had our elevenses, even though it was barely nine o'clock. 'Dirty, smelly creatures. You're better off with a budgie. At least you can keep them in a cage and cover them up when they get on your wick.'

'Not all men are a waste of time,' I protested. 'Harry's not, and neither is Joe.'

'Not Joe, obviously,' she acknowledged, picking biscuit crumbs from her plate and steadfastly ignoring the mention of Harry. Mrs Travers didn't let a little thing like Harry paying her wages influence her opinions. She'd never liked him, and the feeling was mutual.

We were meant to be getting the house ready for his return. He'd been away filming all week, and I couldn't wait for him to get home. I'd made a gateau which oozed cream and strawberries — although, as Mrs Travers pointed out, it was more for my benefit than his, since Harry rarely ate anything that wasn't low-fat, low-salt, low-sugar, wholegrain, organic and bloody tasteless. I'd dressed Amy in a new dress I'd spotted on one of our rare saunters around the shops, and I was all glammed up like, well, some glamorous thing, because that's the look Harry preferred. Determined to wow him with my appearance, I'd booked myself in for the full works at a salon I normally avoided because it looked far too posh for the likes of me.

My eyebrows had been waxed, my tortured nails hidden under acrylic talons, my roots blonded, my layers trimmed, and my face beautifully made-up with the new products that I'd been told I simply must have in order to look gorgeous. The beautician had insisted that I try false eyelashes, and, against my better judgement, I'd agreed. She'd spent absolutely ages glueing individual lashes onto my lids and nodding kindly when I said I wanted a natural look.

I'd left the salon feeling extremely glamorous and sophisticated, until I'd arrived home, when Mrs Travers, who was babysitting, took one look at me and said, 'Jesus, whatever happened to Baby Jane?'

It wasn't the effect I'd been hoping for, but then she wasn't one for make-up. Her idea of a beauty treatment was to rub cold cream on her face before bedtime and put a dollop of Vaseline on her lips if she thought they were getting too dry.

Mrs Travers looked at the clock and sighed. 'I suppose we'd better get a shifty on. His Nibs will be home in a few hours, and I want to be well out of the way by then.'

'You don't have to go,' I protested, but she rolled her eyes in horror.

'Oh, I think I do. Don't want to be around when you two start getting all lovey-dovey. Bad enough having to watch your soppy films. Don't want to see it all in real life, thank you very much.'

As it turned out, Harry was late. He'd said he'd be home just after lunchtime, but it was nearly seven when he pulled up in his treasured coupe. I watched him climb out and give it a loving pat, before he went to the boot and took out his suitcase and a large carrier bag with the name of a well-known toy shop emblazoned across it.

'Daddy's home, Amy!' I called. She glanced up briefly from playing with her dolls, and I held out my hand to her. She shook her head, grinning at me, all dimples and fine, fair hair and big green eyes.

'Come on,' I said. 'Come and see Daddy.'

She gave a big sigh, stood with obvious reluctance, and took my hand. We walked into the kitchen just as Harry opened the back door and stepped inside. I almost smothered him in kisses, and he staggered backwards, protesting at my display of affection.

'Bloody hell, Eliza, let me get through the door.'

I smiled at him. 'I've missed you.'

'Really? You hide it well,' he said. 'I've missed you, too,' he added, flashing me his gorgeous smile and handing me a small bag. I opened it and peered inside. Chanel No 5 again. It wasn't that I wasn't grateful. It wasn't even that I didn't like the perfume, because I did. It was just that, well, it was the third bottle of the stuff Harry had bought me since Christmas and it was only just May.

'Me got present?' asked Amy, staring up at him expectantly. Harry ruffled her hair and picked up the large carrier bag.

'Of course. As if I'd forget my baby girl,' he said.

Amy dived into the bag, shrieking with excitement. I saw her little hands become still, and she stared at the toy inside in some bewilderment, as well she might. We'd bought her the very same one for Christmas, just a few short months ago. She must have thought he'd bagged up her own toy.

'Isn't it super?' demanded Harry, waving at the toy laptop in smug delight. 'Now you can be just like Daddy!'

Luckily, he didn't seem to notice Amy's confusion, removing his jacket while I stared in horror at the t-shirt he revealed. God, I hoped he wouldn't wear that too often! It bore the unsavoury statement, *I'm Not a Gynaecologist but I'm Happy to Take a Look*. Why the hell had he bought that? He always did have a strange sense of humour. I took his jacket and hung it in the hall, wondering if I could engineer a "washing machine accident" and make sure he never wore it again.

I made him a coffee and tried not to feel disappointed when he merely grunted at Amy when she pointed out her new dress, made no comment on my makeover, and refused my offer of a slice of cake. It was hardly surprising, after all. Harry was very careful about his weight, so what had I expected? And really, how many men took any notice of what their children were wearing? I should have saved my money. He was only home half an hour before I'd bathed her and changed her into her pyjamas anyway. It was my fault. I expected too much.

At least he'd made the effort to buy her a present, even though it proved, if proof were needed, that he hadn't taken the slightest bit of notice of the things we'd bought her for Christmas and had obviously never observed her playing with her toys. I wondered if he still had the receipt. I could take it back to the shop and exchange it for something else. He would never know, and there would be no danger of him noticing one day that she had two identical toy laptops.

Once I'd got Amy into bed, I changed into my comfy pyjamas, with some relief, and we settled on the sofa with a glass of wine. Harry rabbited on about his trip, and the ghastly houses he'd been around, and the truly appalling couple that he'd had to be pleasant to, and how difficult it had been to pretend to care when they yakked on about wanting a whole new way of life.

'It's always the same.' He sighed. 'They tell us they want to be right out in the countryside away from neighbours. They want peace and quiet. They want to keep pigs and chickens and grow their own sodding vegetables. The minute you show them what they've asked for they start panicking and saying, "Ooh, it's a bit isolated isn't it? We'd like to be in a village, really." They end up choosing a house with a patch of garden and neighbours on both sides because it's only five minutes from the local pub. Pathetic.' He yawned and announced he was going to have a long soak in the bath. 'All I can smell is pigs and chicken shit,' he complained. 'I may be up there some time.'

Harry wasn't exactly an animal lover. I could always tell if he was showing people around a property with pets on *Twice as Nice* because, as he stood extolling the virtues of the place to them, I could see his nostrils twitching and his lip curling slightly. It was a dead giveaway to anyone who knew him well.

'Crack open another bottle of wine,' he called, as he headed to the hallway. 'I think there's a documentary about Formula One racing on tonight. May as well have some of those rice crackers, too.'

Lovely. An evening of cardboard nibbles and motor racing. Welcome home, Harry. I collected the glasses and stooped to pick up Amy's laptop from where she'd abandoned it with barely a second glance. It occurred to me that now could be the best chance I might have to get hold of the receipt. I was hardly going to trek all the way up to Cheshire, but I knew the shop the laptop came from had a branch nearby and they would let me exchange it there.

I nipped into the hallway and saw Harry's jacket hanging on its hook. Reaching my hand into the pocket, I pulled out his wallet and rifled through it, staying alert for the sound of Harry coming out of the bathroom.

I quickly found the receipt and noticed that Harry hadn't bought the toy from the Cheshire branch of the shop at all, but from our own local branch. He must have forgotten to buy Amy something and only remembered when he was almost home. Oh, well, at least it would make it easier to exchange, I thought, shoving the receipt into the pocket of my jeans.

I was about to close the wallet when I noticed another receipt with the name of an expensive florist's shop at the top. I pulled it out, curious, and felt my stomach lurch as I saw that there were several others, all for the same place, underneath it. The last time Harry had bought me flowers was the day I had Amy, so who the hell had he been buying flowers for? Expensive flowers, too, and on a regular basis.

With shaking hands, I managed to push the receipts back into his wallet and, as I did, I noticed the white edge of a photo sticking up from behind one of his credit cards. Tentatively, I pulled out a tiny passport-sized print which was face down. For a long, long moment, I stared at the writing on the back of the photograph. "For Darling H, your soul mate, M xx." Taking a deep breath, I turned the photograph over and gazed through tears at the tangled blonde curls, pouting lips and doe eyes of Melody Bird, wondering why I hadn't realised what was going on ages ago. It wasn't as if I hadn't had my doubts, at least at first. God knows, Melody had enough form. I'd been so blind, so trusting.

Melody Bird was an ex-soap star and model, forever in the papers for shagging some bloke or other, usually married ones. When I'd found out she was going to be Harry's co-presenter on his new property programme, *Twice as Nice*, I'd been horrified. Harry hadn't been too thrilled either.

'What the fuck does she know about property?' he'd demanded, storming around the kitchen in fury. 'She's just there to look sexy, while I do all the serious stuff. Why couldn't I get someone like Kirstie Allsop or Sarah Beeny? Someone who actually knows what they're talking about? I'll be a laughing stock.'

Foolishly I'd sympathised with him. Harry had built up a successful property company by the time I'd met him when he was thirty-two. That was when Joe had decided to put his house in Fulham up for sale and move to St John's Wood, and Harry had been looking for just that type of property for a client.

He'd bowled me over at our first meeting, and when he'd asked me out I couldn't believe my luck. I basically made and sold sandwiches and cupcakes for a living, so I was shocked that this hotshot businessman was interested in me. We were married two years later and, believe it or not, it was only then that I found out Harry hadn't actually built the business up himself, but had taken it on when his father died and left it to him. Still, as his mother pointed out endlessly, he was exceptionally good at it, and his father would be proud of how well he was managing it.

Initially, Harry and Joe seemed to get on well. Sometimes, I thought Joe had doubts, but he never actually said anything, so I pushed the thought to the back of my mind. Harry seemed quite enthralled by Joe's career. Joe was a successful television presenter, with his own primetime chat show, and Harry had spent a lot of time hanging around the studios, fetching and carrying, generally making himself useful, and befriending people on the set. I suppose that's how he'd been talent-spotted by a television producer friend of Joe's and given the job of fronting an afternoon show about renovating old houses. I'd been terribly proud of him, especially when he became so popular with the viewers, mostly due to what television critics called his "movie star looks". Harry had appointed a manager for his company and concentrated on his new career.

When the network decided they wanted to launch a new primetime programme, aimed at finding second homes in beautiful locations for middle class buyers, Harry was their first choice to present it, but he was horrified when they selected tabloid darling Melody Bird to co-present. Yet, within two years, he'd changed his attitude towards her, and it was all "Melody this" and "Melody that", and really, how I hadn't seen what was coming I can't imagine.

I stood there, wondering what the hell I was going to do. I thought of Amy sleeping peacefully in her Disney Princess bedroom. She had to be my priority. I couldn't risk putting her through what I'd put up with. I shoved the photo back in the wallet and stuffed it back into Harry's pocket. I would be calm and rational and behave with dignity. I would take my time to think things through and then I'd make some sensible decisions. I could do sensible. Of course I could.

Chapter 2

'Jesus, Eliza! Are you trying to kill me?'

Harry's face was white as he scrabbled round on the kitchen floor, trying to avoid the pieces of his favourite cup, which lay scattered all around him. I don't *think* I was trying to kill him but scarring him might have been nice. Or branding him? That would have been even better — a massive mark on his forehead that read *adulterer*, to match the one on mine that read *mug*.

I watched in some satisfaction as he wobbled to his feet and waved his hands at me. 'Are you having some sort of fit? Christ, look what you've done. You've marked the wall now.'

Was he serious? He was lucky the cup had bounced off the wall and smashed to the floor, because I'd actually aimed for his smug face, and he'd better shut up because there were plenty more where that came from. I had a whole cupboard full of crockery, in fact.

'Then you wonder why I turned to Melody? Look at you — you're behaving like someone from one of those ghastly soaps you lap up.'

'I swear, Harry, if you don't shut up, I'll kill you.'

'For God's sake, control yourself. Do you want to wake Amy up?'

'Don't you dare pretend to care about Amy,' I wailed, as tears welled up at the image of our three-year-old fast asleep upstairs, totally unaware that her life was about to be destroyed by her philandering father and her useless mother who had managed to keep the lid on her emotions for all of five minutes. Five sodding minutes! Honestly, I've been on diets that lasted longer than that. Just about.

I'd been so determined to keep a lid on my emotions, but as I stood there at the bottom of the stairs, something had snapped. I wanted to know what was going on, and how long it had been going on for. This was the perfect opportunity to do some investigation. The bathroom was just about the only place where Harry didn't have his mobile clutched in his hand. It was the one chance I had to dig up some evidence.

As I crept into the bedroom, I heard Harry humming some tune to himself as he scrubbed away Melody's DNA in the en-suite. It was probably something seductive by Barry White, although, to be honest, with Harry's toneless voice it might have been *The Birdy Song*. Now what put Bird in my head? How bloody ironic. His phone was in the pocket of his trousers. I had a quick root around, but there was nothing else in there. No doubt he'd destroyed all other evidence. Though, what other evidence there'd be, I shuddered to think. What was I expecting, for heaven's sake? A used condom? Crumpled tissues? A signed confession?

My hands shook as I lifted the phone from his jeans and sank onto the bed, staring at the screen as if Melody's pouting face would flash in front of me. Oh, God, what if I found texts from her on there? Well, that was what I wanted, wasn't it? But would I be able to cope with them? That was the question, and one I didn't really have the answer to. One thing knowing your husband is porking Miss-Grin-and-Bare-'Em, but quite another seeing it all in black and white, in your face, so to speak. And what would I do if I found the proof I was searching for? How would I cope, knowing my husband was shagging a blonde with boobs like a page three model and lips like a toilet plunger? Would I leave him? What would my life be without him? What would I do if I wasn't Mrs Harry Jarvis?

My fingers hovered over the keypad. Perhaps I should just put it back, live in ignorance? As I stared at the message on the screen, telling me to enter the pin number, my fingers seemed to work of their own accord, paying no heed to the voice that was telling me it would be better not to know.

The pin didn't take much guessing. It was the date that meant the most to him. Not my birthday or our wedding anniversary, or Amy's birthday, but the date he won Best Daytime Presenter at the *TV Quick* awards. So bloody predictable. I tapped the message icon on his screen and froze as Melody's name came up top of the list.

My mouth dropped open as I started to read. It was a good job that Harry was so vain and liked to smother himself in lotions, moisturisers and goodness knows what else after his bath, because I had dozens to get through, each one disgusting. She was quite shameless, and what was with all those exclamation marks and ellipses? The woman didn't know how to punctuate, that was for sure. She wasn't too original with her metaphors, either. I was so engrossed in reading about her juicy honey pot that I didn't hear Harry come into the bedroom. He was wearing a robe and was in the middle of towel drying his hair. He smelt like the Boots perfume counter and made my nose twitch from across the room.

'What the hell are you doing? Is that my phone?'

There was no denying it since my phone's cover certainly didn't bear the legend, *I'm Sexy and I Know It*. Harry grabbed the phone from my hand and stared in shock at the screen. I was in the middle of a text from Melody that left anyone unfortunate enough to read it in no doubt that, for a woman in her forties, she was certainly in no immediate danger of drying up and was positively gagging for it.

He turned a funny colour and muttered, 'Christ,' before snapping the phone shut and demanding to know what gave me the right to snoop on him. Honestly! I glared at him with such hatred I'm surprised he didn't shrivel up and die right there and then Obviously he was made of sterner stuff because he curled his lip and said, 'I hate paranoid women.'

I turned and ran from the room. He was right behind me and, as we reached the kitchen, he grabbed my wrist and said, 'It's not what it looks like.'

'Oh, please.' I shut the door behind us and pulled away from him in disgust. 'It's exactly what it looks like. You've been having an affair with Melody Bird and you spent today with her.'

'Texts can be very misleading—' he began, but I cut him off.

'The texts are just confirmation of what I'd already guessed.'

'What are you talking about?'

Trying to stay calm, I told him about finding the receipts and the photo in his wallet.

I've always wondered what puce looks like. Harry proceeded to demonstrate. 'You see, this is what I mean. This is what drove me to Melody in the first place. Do you have any idea how difficult it is to live with someone who's so insecure, so fucking needy?'

'I beg your pardon?' My voice caught, and I dug my acrylic talons into my palms, absolutely determined not to cry.

'It's true, Eliza. Sorry, but it needs saying. I've tried to be patient, to make allowances, because I know it must have been hard for you, being abandoned by your father, and not knowing anything about him. God knows, it must have had some weird effect on you, being brought up by Joe, of all people—'

'Don't you dare,' I said icily. 'Joe took care of me when I had no one else in the world. He put his own life on hold and sacrificed everything to make sure I was safe and happy.'

'Yes, yes, all very Del Boy and Rodney, I'm sure,' he said, his tone dismissive. 'But you can't say that you had a normal childhood, can you? He was incapable of providing that. And all that publicity, when his boyfriend outed him to that Sunday rag, must have been embarrassing, especially at such a crucial stage in your development. It's not your fault. I'm not blaming you.'

'Well, that's big of you,' I said, furious that he'd attack Joe. It hadn't been his fault that his one serious relationship had ended badly. Joe's partner, James, jealous of Joe's success, and seeking his own five minutes of fame, had sold his story to the Sunday papers. I'd never liked him, anyway. He ate lemon curd sandwiches and disapproved of *Coronation Street*, which said it all, if you ask me. Joe was worth ten of him.

'Don't be sarcastic. I've felt for a long time that you're rather damaged by what happened. It's too much, Eliza. Living with you is, well, claustrophobic. You want me to be everything to you, but I can't be. No one can. You made me your entire world, and it's suffocating. I'm trapped. I can't breathe. I need air.'

'I doubt you'd get much air between Melody Bird's massive boobs,' I said, but my mind was whirling. Was he right? Was I too clingy? Too needy? But look, there I was again, taking the blame, when quite obviously it was all Melody's fault.

'Don't say nasty things about Melody. She was there for me when I needed someone.'

'Melody's there for any bloke, Harry. Doesn't the fact that the press call her Miss-Grin-and-Bare-'Em alert you to the fact that she's not exactly sweetness and light? She's a scheming bimbo who's had almost as many men as she's had facelifts.'

Harry glared at me in contempt. I withered inside as I recognised the hatred in his eyes. 'Well, at least Melody doesn't look like a before photo for slimming pills. Perhaps if you'd stuffed yourself less with Maltesers and cake, I wouldn't have looked twice at her.'

That was when the cup hit the wall and bounced onto the floor. Harry began to panic. 'Look, Eliza, let's just sit down and talk about this.'

'What is there to say? You've been caught out, and now you're trying to wriggle off the hook like the slimy little worm you are.'

'Well, that's a bit much.' He had the nerve to sound indignant. 'Okay, so I'm in a relationship with Melody, I admit it. You can't help who you fall in love with.'

That stopped me in my tracks. Fall in love with? I'd been talking about a grubby affair, not *Wuthering Heights*.

'You love her?' It came out as a whisper. To be honest, I did well to get that much out. My throat felt as if it had an entire bag of Maltesers wedged in it.

He stared at me as if he'd shocked himself, then he shrugged and sat down at the breakfast bar. 'I don't know. All I know is she makes me happy. I tried not to get involved, but it just happened. She gets me. There's something irresistible about her.'

'There are two things,' I muttered, 'and they're both made of silicone.'

I climbed onto the stool next to his and turned to face him, all too aware that I was wearing my passion-killer pyjamas and huge furry Eeyore slippers. He smelt divine. His mother had bought him a new aftershave for Christmas, and it was deliciously sweet and spicy. Then it occurred to me that it probably hadn't been from his mother at all. I mean, when I gave it some consideration, what kind of mother would buy her son a fragrance called *Fetish*? I felt sick, and treacherous tears rolled unchecked down my cheeks.

Harry sensed the turnaround in my demeanour and attacked. My vulnerability made him stronger, and he was quick to seize control. As I sat sobbing, unable to comprehend how contempt for his co-star had turned to love, he informed me that I'd let myself go since I had Amy. I'd become too wrapped up in our daughter to pay much attention to him and his needs. I'd lost contact with the outside world and become clingy and paranoid. Harry had felt stuck in a marriage to someone who no longer entertained him, bored out of his skull.

'You've become so dull,' he said. 'Melody can't understand why you just sit at home all day. What happened to female equality? Don't you realise that women are quite capable of having careers these days? I mean, what's wrong with doing some work for a change?'

I glared at him, words failing me as I considered this injustice. Whose fault was it that I'd given up my business in the first place? He'd insisted that it would be better for Amy if I looked after her, rather than pay for childcare, and, although I came to love being at home with her, it hadn't been my idea. I'd dreaded being a stay-at-home mother at first, fearing I'd become isolated. I hadn't been wrong either. Three years on and I'd lost all my old friends, gaining instead thirty pounds and a Malteser addiction, which wasn't a fair swap. Anyway, bringing up a baby is damn hard work, and I'd bet Melody Bird wouldn't have been able to cope.

'How is this all my fault?' I said. 'What about you and your total lack of interest in Amy? You never want to go anywhere with us or do anything together as a family.'

'How can you say that after the sacrifices I made for you both?'

'What bloody sacrifices?' I demanded.

'My sports car for a start. I had to get rid of it because we'd never have got a child seat in there. Do you know how much I loved that car?'

'Every bugger was aware of how much you loved that car, Harry,' I said. 'You practically had an orgasm over it every time you touched it.'

'Don't be common,' he said. 'And doesn't that show how much I gave up for you, for Amy? I sacrificed my car for family life.'

'For a flashy coupe!' I said.

'Yes, but it isn't a two-seater is it?' he said. 'It's not quite the same.'

'Well, give that man a medal,' I said. 'How can I ever thank you for all you've done for us? Face it — you're more interested in being in that flaming car than being with us.'

'Do you wonder?' he said, examining the mark on the wall and tutting. 'Things haven't been the same between us since you had Amy. Why can't you have a life of your own? Go and do something useful, something interesting. It's so tedious coming home every night to hear how Amy's watched three episodes of *Peppa* sodding *Pig* back-to-back, or you've baked me yet another fucking cake.'

His words reminded me of the huge gateau sitting in the fridge. I'd kill for a slice of it at that moment — I was sure it would cheer me up. I wondered why life was never like it was in books. Fictional heroines always lost their appetites when faced with emotional trauma, but it seemed nothing was traumatic enough to put me off cake. Just my luck to be an abandoned daughter, a spurned wife, *and* a compulsive eater.

'I mean, how much cake can one man stand? Melody wouldn't touch it. You see, we have things in common like that. She has to watch her weight, too, being in television, and we like the same sort of foods. Melody's quite appalled by how much baking you do. In fact, she offered to buy you a low-fat cookbook for Christmas, but I told her you wouldn't appreciate it.'

I wiped my tears and sniffed, then lifted my head as his words struck home. 'A low-fat cookbook?' I narrowed my eyes. 'You've been discussing my baking with Melody?'

He looked uncomfortable. 'Well, er, we talk about my home life. And Melody's, too, of course. I only mentioned that I can't seem to get through to you that I simply must keep my weight down. After all, television adds ten pounds, you know.'

'And all on Melody's boobs, by the look of it.' I slipped off the stool and made my way over to the fridge. He was obviously so distracted by the mental image of Melody's humongous breasts that he didn't even notice. Had he just said she was going to get me a present for Christmas? They'd been a couple at *Christmas*? No wonder he hadn't noticed Amy's presents. He'd been too busy anticipating what he'd be unwrapping himself later on, no doubt.

'Don't be bitchy,' he said, picking up his phone as it beeped yet again. I saw him glance at the screen and smirk to himself. I opened the fridge door.

'Harry?'

'Hmm?' He looked up, and as he opened his mouth to speak, the gateau walloped him right in the face.

'Now you can tell Melody how delicious my cakes really are,' I said, half laughing through my tears.

He leapt to his feet and scooped dollops of fresh cream from his eyes. A couple of juicy strawberries sat perkily on his head, and his smug, lying face was covered in bits of sponge. It had been a perfect hit which was quite surprising, given my appalling netball record at school.

'You've gone mad.' He gasped, spitting out a fat strawberry and scrabbling around for a cloth.

'Mad? I'm absolutely furious,' I said. 'But I feel slightly better now. I guess that's what they call getting your just desserts.'

Harry glared at me. 'It's probably best if I stay at Melody's. There's nothing more to say. You're obviously overwrought and haven't considered what this will do to Amy.'

'Are you kidding me? I'm not the one who's putting her entire family at risk.'

'Carry on like this and you'll ruin her. She'll grow up bitter and twisted and disturbed, like those wretches you see on television. I don't want to get a call from some chavvy talk show in twenty years' time because you've poisoned my daughter against me. God forbid she turns up dressed in a shell suit, demanding a paternity test.' He shuddered, probably more disgusted at the shell suit than the paternity test.

'So, to protect your daughter, you're abandoning us?'

'I'm trying to do what's best for all of us,' said Harry. 'Quite obviously there are problems in our marriage we can't fix.'

'You're leaving me?' I gasped. God, what was it with me and men? None of them seemed to want to be around me. 'And you're moving in with that tart?'

Harry threw the cloth on the table and stared at me with those puppy dog eyes of his. 'I'm sorry, Eliza, but be reasonable. If I moved into a hotel, the press would be onto it in a flash. You can't trust staff, fact. Melody's place is in a very secluded mews where residents control access and, after all, we don't want the tabloids getting hold of this, do we?'

'You mean you don't. Why should I care?'

'Well, isn't it obvious? The press would hound you. It would be a massive story. Melody and I are extremely popular, you know.'

'Not for much bloody longer, mate,' I muttered.

'Well, is it really fair on Amy if everyone knows? Imagine the bullying when she started school. Be reasonable. You see, you don't use your brain.'

I was using my brain all right. It was clear that Harry's only concern was the possible damage to his reputation. If there was one thing I understood about him, it was that he loved to be loved. He wouldn't want any negative publicity. Serve him right if the newspapers tore him to shreds.

On the other hand, if I was being really honest, the one thing I didn't want to do was appear in any tabloid, admitting to the world that I'd lost my gorgeous husband to Pensioner Barbie. And he was right about Amy, too; though, if he'd cared that much about her, he wouldn't be doing all this in the first place.

'I'll have to get a shower now,' Harry said. 'Then I'm going to bed. I'm knackered. I have work in the morning, and I can't cope with a row tonight. I'll pack some things when I get home tomorrow evening. I suggest you get some sleep, too. I'll take the spare room. It's the least I can do after I've caused this upset.'

Upset? He made it sound as if I'd had the wrong fridge-freezer delivered.

He headed upstairs, and I began to clear up all the mess in a daze. Now what? Why hadn't I just kept my big mouth shut? If I'd said nothing, this might all have blown over, and I wouldn't be facing the prospect of further abandonment and, more importantly, neither would my daughter. I felt more tears hot on my cheeks and swiped them away. Crying would get me nowhere.

I rinsed out the cloth that Harry had mopped his face with, trying to quell the rising panic inside me. How could I bear to stay in this house with Harry gone? I would have to get used to the fact that I was now a single mother, and Amy would have to get used to the fact that she no longer had a father who lived with her, just as I had. Though, like me, it was a case of *what you've never had you never miss*. Harry hadn't been around much for her anyway, and my father had never been on the scene. His one and only contribution to my life had been a speedy tadpole. After that, he'd scarpered pretty sharpish, and I still had no idea why.

Now Amy was facing the same fate as me. She'd obviously inherited my tragedy gene, if there was such a thing. There had to be. All this crap couldn't be total coincidence or, even worse, down to me, surely? Was Harry right? Was I damaged? Would Amy be damaged, too? If she'd inherited my tragedy gene, then I had to start training her right now to handle it. Her future, after all, was in my hands.

I didn't want to stay in our house without Harry, knowing he was just across town with the new love of his life. The walls seemed to be pressing in on me already, the familiar rooms cold and threatening. Besides, why should I stay here while Harry set up a new home with Melody? He wasn't the only one who could walk away.

I stared out of the window into the darkness, wondering what

I should do. If only my mother were here to talk to. I wondered about my father, questioning yet again what kind of man he was and why he'd had to leave us. There had to be an explanation for his behaviour, because my mother had assured me he was an honourable man. She'd told me how happy they'd been, and even on the day she died she was still wearing the little silver and amethyst ring that he'd given her. Amethyst was her birthstone, and he'd presented her with the ring and told her that he'd always love her, always be her angel. There must have been some pretty big reason why he'd had to go.

I wished, with all my heart, that I could track him down and find out the truth. I wanted to hear his side of the story, and most of all I wanted to understand where I came from, because if I figured out who he was, perhaps I'd be able to figure out who I was, too. I didn't want Harry to be right about me, but I had an uncomfortable feeling it was possible.

But how to find my father? Where to start?

And then, all of a sudden, I knew.

Chapter 3

It struck me, as I looked down on Kearton Bay for the first time, that maybe this wasn't the best place to test the brakes of a car I'd never driven before.

Way below me, the sea sparkled in the early afternoon sunshine, and a huddle of red roofs and a distant church spire were the only manmade things visible in a landscape of rolling moorland, patchwork fields of yellow and green, and the all-embracing arms of the majestic cliffs that reached out into the North Sea on either side of the village.

I gritted my teeth. Well, there was only one way to find out. Served me right for stealing Harry's car — well, taking it without consent. That sounded a bit gentler, not so serious or scary. The whole way there, I'd been expecting to see blue flashing lights in the rear-view mirror and, frankly, I still couldn't believe I'd got this far without being pulled over and arrested at the side of the road. Could there be anything more embarrassing than that? All those people driving by, staring and pointing at me — the thought made me hot, though at least I'd have looked glamorous. Never let it be said that being dumped by my husband for a woman a whole decade older than me would have a detrimental effect on my appearance. No way was I going to let all that torture at the salon go to waste. Somehow it made me feel better, knowing that I looked just the way Harry liked. I could look as good as Melody, couldn't I?

Obeying the SatNav, I'd turned off the main moors road and

pulled up for a moment while I took in the scene, and now there I was, hoping that the brakes were up to the job. I had no idea what the car was capable of. Thank God Amy was asleep. I was going to need every ounce of concentration to tackle that road. Taking a deep breath, I drove forward and began to edge cautiously down the hill.

The road wound its way down, twisting and turning, passing cottages and a church. According to the SatNav, this was Farthingdale, and once I was through it, the next stop was Kearton Bay.

I heaved a sigh of relief as the road levelled out and drove along a little faster, passing a cluster of shops and a pub. As I rounded a twist in the road, it began to drop again, and I changed gear, my heart thudding as the car crawled down the hill. I couldn't be far away now, but the sea had disappeared from my sight, and I had no idea where I was heading.

Eventually, the road levelled out again, and I came to a crossroads. I hesitated, but the SatNav was telling me to turn right and I wasn't going to argue. I drove forward, turning right, as instructed.

'You have reached your destination.'

I jumped in alarm as the SatNav lady, whose honeyed tones had, in turn, soothed and irritated me for the last seven hours, basically told me that was that. Job done. *You're on your own now, kid.* I had no idea where I was supposed to go from that point. I looked out of the window. On my right, across the road, was a car park, and behind that a row of fairly modern bungalows. To my left was a large, Victorian pub, The Kearton Arms. In front of me, the road appeared to drop away, and I could see the bay in all its glory in the distance. So, now what?

Despite the dead weight of the false eyelashes, my eyes widened as a strange group of around five or six people came puffing up the hill, dressed in black Victorian style clothes. They all had black hair and black-rimmed eyes, and I would have suspected they were some sort of phantoms, or zombies, if they hadn't looked so knackered as they reached the top. Two of them leaned on the railings by the pub, gasping for breath. Others sank onto one of the benches and wiped their foreheads with the back of their arms. I watched them for a moment, full of sympathy. I could barely manage to walk to my car these days.

Oh well, in for a penny and all that. I wound down my window, just an inch or two, and called over to them. One of them ambled over to the car and beamed in at me. I noticed that the dress she was wearing was beautiful and not at all cheap-looking. She looked like she'd just stepped out of a gothic novel.

'You lost, love?'

A zombie ghost with a broad Yorkshire accent? That was unexpected. I saw that, despite her deathly pallor, she had twinkly eyes and crooked teeth, which was somehow reassuring. Even more reassuring was the sight of a mobile phone clutched in her gloved hand. Not the most likely accessory for a ghost really, or the most useful. I doubted there'd be much of a signal in the afterlife. I'd been trying unsuccessfully to get through to Joe and Mrs Travers since we passed Pickering.

'I don't suppose you know where Amethyst Cottage is?'

'Hmm. I think it's the one just past Station Lane. See where the road bends to the right up there?'

She stepped back as I wound down the window and stuck my head out, looking back up the road past the crossroads. 'Yes.'

'There's a little road on the left just before it that leads to Farthingdale. You can't miss it; there's another ruddy big car park at the beginning. Used to be the station, see? I think it's the first cottage, just after the lane. Mrs Lovelace's place?'

'That's right.' At least, I'd rented it from Lovelace Properties, so I guessed it must be.

She nodded. 'Yeah, that's the one. I heard it was a holiday cottage now.'

She looked at me, and I swear there was disapproval in her eyes. I couldn't imagine why, unless she was wondering how many tarantulas had sacrificed their legs to provide me with my lashes. Puzzled, I thanked her and watched as she wandered off to join her cronies. They all headed into The Kearton Arms, which looked far too grand a place to entertain such shenanigans.

I turned the car and drove back up the road. Sure enough, I

came to a small road signposted Station Lane and, underneath it, an additional sign, which read "To Ivy House Surgery". There was a car park, and I caught a glimpse of a couple of buildings as I passed, but I was too busy looking out for Amethyst Cottage which, as the zombie ghost had said, was the first cottage in a row of three just before the road twisted again. It was a pretty, stone cottage with a red pantile roof, and it looked just like the picture on the website — except the door was wide open with two people standing outside, and there seemed to be an argument going on.

I pulled up, and they stopped what they were doing and turned to look at me. I had a feeling this didn't bode well for my new start.

****

I climbed out of the car and opened the back door, then fumbled around, trying to unfasten Amy from her car seat, for what felt like forever. My stupid acrylic talons made things difficult, and it didn't help that two pairs of eyes bore into me as I struggled with the catch. Finally, I managed to release her and lifted her into my arms, breathing in the reassuring scent of baby shampoo, chocolate buttons and sleep. She whimpered softly and opened her eyes, wrapped her arms around my neck and yawned. I took a steadying breath then began to walk up the path, looking uncertainly at the people standing in the doorway.

'Am I in the right place? This is Amethyst Cottage?'

One of them, a tall, dark-haired man, probably in his late thirties, gave me a look of irritation. What the hell had I said? I noticed he had very sharp cheekbones. They looked ready to slice through his skin at any moment. He seemed rather tired. Maybe that's why he was so annoyed, though it was hardly my fault. All I'd asked was the name of the house, for God's sake. He was wearing faded jeans and a bottle green shirt, and was carrying a Christmas tree, of all things, which struck me as rather odd in May, even for a place haunted by zombie ghosts with mobile phones.

29

A middle-aged woman, with a Margaret Thatcher hairdo and a snub nose, held out a podgy hand in greeting, and I shook it, my confusion growing.

'Mrs Jarvis? I'm so pleased to meet you. I'm Mrs Lovelace. We spoke on the phone? I'm so sorry to have to tell you this, but I'm afraid we have a slight problem.'

Funnily enough, I'd already guessed that. 'Problem? What kind of problem?'

Amy wriggled in my arms, and I put her down on the path noticing, for the first time, wet footprints on the concrete. I looked at Mrs Lovelace, whose face had turned scarlet.

'Perhaps I should show you,' she murmured, leading me into the hallway. Within a second of entering the house and looking through the open door into the kitchen, I could see that "slight problem" was a bit of an understatement.

'You've got to be kidding me.'

The kitchen floor was awash with water, and it wasn't clean water, either. I looked up at the ceiling, which was minus a huge chunk of plasterboard, and watched in fascination as a rivulet of dirty brown water dripped through the floorboards above us. Droplets of water hung from the spotlights, too, like diamond earrings, and the bit of ceiling that remained intact sagged ominously, threatening to tip another torrent of water over us at any moment.

I looked down at Amy. Her left hand gripped the hem of my leather jacket tightly, while the thumb of her other hand was wedged firmly in her mouth. She peered up at the man, who'd followed us inside, her round, green eyes anxious. To my surprise, he gave her a reassuring smile, but as he looked at me the smile vanished.

'It seems the previous occupants left the bath running this morning when they left,' explained Mrs Lovelace. 'I really can't imagine how they can have been so stupid. My first tenants, too!'

The man gave her a piercing stare, and she seemed to get flustered, clearing her throat and waving her arms around. 'I mean, this was the first week I'd rented it to holidaymakers, and this is the result. I must say it's terribly inconvenient. Obviously,

I'll be getting the damage repaired as soon as possible, but it's the weekend and it may take a few days, what with re-plastering and repainting. I'm so sorry for the inconvenience. It's been a dreadful shock. My poor cleaner was almost killed.'

The man rolled his eyes at this apparent exaggeration.

'What am I supposed to do now? I'm not going back to London.' The thought was appalling. Harry would be in a foul temper with me, especially because of the car, and besides, I had business to attend to and it was important I got on with it before I got scared and changed my mind. 'Do you have any other cottages available?'

'I'm so sorry. They all have tenants in them. It's an extremely popular holiday spot.'

The man gave her a look of disgust then turned to leave.

Mrs Lovelace grabbed his arm. 'Mr Bailey, can you think of anywhere that would have vacancies today?'

He shrugged, his mouth tightening into a smile that it refused to share with his eyes.

'Kearton Bay in early summer? Hardly. You said yourself, it's a popular holiday spot. Even the locals can't move for tourists, thanks to all the second-homers renting out their properties, so she'll have no chance.'

Blimey, he was all charm. Welcome to Yorkshire.

Mrs Lovelace's eyes narrowed. 'Surely there'll be a room in a bed and breakfast, or something? You must know somewhere?'

Amy took her thumb from her mouth and pulled on my arm. 'Mummy, I'm hungry,' she said, looking at me with saucer eyes.

This was turning into a nightmare. I ran my fingers through my hair, dislodging my sunglasses which clattered to the ground. I stooped to pick them up as the man bent down to get them for me, and our heads almost collided. He caught his breath and seemed to jerk away from me, almost dropping the glasses again. He practically shoved them at me as if he'd had a shock. I raised an enquiring eyebrow as I realised he was looking me up and down as if I were a heifer in a livestock show.

He cleared his throat, obviously embarrassed. 'I, er, I was just thinking. Maybe Rhiannon would have a room free?'

'Rhiannon?' Mrs Lovelace's brow was furrowed. 'I'm not sure about that. The Hare and Moon isn't exactly a luxury hotel, is it? Still, if there's nowhere else...'

'I'd rather be on my own,' I said quickly.

'Of course you would,' soothed Mrs Lovelace, 'but I promise you, it will only be for a few days. As soon as the cottage is back to its usual standard, I'll let you know and, of course, I will pay for your room until then.'

The man sighed impatiently. 'Look, I'll take you there and talk to Rhiannon, if you want, but I have things to do, so make up your mind.'

'Don't put yourself out for me,' I murmured. I looked around as if some answer to my dilemma would materialise in front of my eyes. Amy took hold of my hand and squeezed it, as if sensing my despair.

'Of course, if you'd rather stay here ... I just hope you've brought your wellies.'

'Ah, that famous Yorkshire sense of humour,' said Mrs Lovelace with an anxious smile.

I knew all about Yorkshire humour. Joe had it in spades, and I've been known to be quite witty myself on occasion. This wasn't humour, it was plain bad manners, and he seemed to recognise that as he ran his finger round his collar, suddenly looking ashamed.

'Look, Rhiannon's not to everyone's taste, but really, I think it's The Hare and Moon, or here.'

I rubbed my forehead and almost poked myself in the eye with the arm of my sunglasses. It appeared I had no choice. 'Right, well, could you direct me to The Hare and Moon, please?'

He nodded. 'It's not far. I'll take you.'

I fought the urge to tell him to shove it. 'Thank you. If there's no room at the inn I'll come back, Mrs Lovelace, and hopefully you can point me in another direction?'

Mrs Lovelace tried to look positive but didn't quite succeed.

'Shall I follow your car?' I asked as I trailed behind Mr Bailey down the path. He was still carrying the Christmas tree. I wondered if Amy and I were safe with him. He looked a bit moody, and I wondered how he'd react when someone broke it to him that he'd missed Christmas by quite some margin. Or maybe he was just very well organised and starting to prepare for the next one?

He shook his head. 'You can't take your car any further into the village, I'm afraid.' He walked over to an ancient estate car and unlocked the boot. After shoving the Christmas tree inside he turned back to me, still unsmiling. 'There's nowhere for you to park. If Rhiannon has a room, I'll come back and help you with your things, and I'm sure Mrs Lovelace won't object to you leaving your car here, whatever happens.'

Mrs Lovelace called brightly after us. 'Not at all. Anything to help.'

I wondered how far her generosity would extend if this Rhiannon didn't have a room available. Would Mrs Lovelace be so amenable if it came to putting Amy and me up in a luxury hotel somewhere? Somehow, I doubted it.

Chapter 4

Mr Bailey led the way along Whitby Road, taking long, selfish strides as Amy and I trailed after him. We passed a hairdressing salon and a Chinese takeaway and came to The Kearton Arms. I looked longingly at its smart exterior.

'Are there likely to be any rooms here?' I called, my legs already aching with trying to keep up with him. Amy was practically running, and I was beginning to think it would be easier to find The Hare and Moon myself.

He didn't even look back. 'No chance,' he replied. 'It will be fully booked for the summer.'

We reached the top of the hill, signposted Bay Street, and I peered down in horror. From my point of view, it was practically a vertical drop. There were people walking down, tottering as they tried to keep their balance on the steep decline, and, more worryingly, there were people coming back up who looked as if they needed oxygen. I'd never seen so many purple faces and sweaty fringes. It would have been funny if I hadn't realised that I'd have to come back up at some point, too.

The left-hand side of the hill had broad steps with a handrail separating them from the road. Mr Bailey avoided the steps, probably because they were even more crowded with people than the road, so I followed him, hoping I could keep my balance.

Twisting and turning down the cliff side, the street was edged on both sides with chocolate-box buildings — some honey-coloured stone, others whitewashed, but all with red pantile roofs. At the sides of the road were narrow strips of cobbles, which I guessed were what was left of the original road, which had been tarmacked over. Tourists spilled out of every shop and café, and crowds jostled in front of me. Amy was almost wrenched from my grasp, and I bent to pick her up, deciding it was safer to carry her. Thank God I still had my flat driving shoes on. I would never have made it down here in heels.

We rounded a bend in the road. On the right was a shop selling outdoor clothing, walking boots and maps. We passed a quaint little pub called The Mermaid Inn, tucked into the corner of the bend and standing some five storeys high. It was a whitewashed building, very narrow, and had an intriguing passageway behind it and a flight of wooden steps leading to the first-floor rooms. Next to the pub was a fish and chip shop, and a little further down, on the other side of the road, was a traditional seaside store selling postcards, buckets and spades and sticks of rocks.

Halfway down the hill, a little stone bridge carried the crowds over a gurgling stream, and just before it, on the left-hand side of the road, was a short flight of broad steps, leading to an alleyway called Water's Edge. At the head of the alley was a bookshop on the left and a café on the right, which overlooked the beck. I could see people sipping drinks through the window and I envied them. My arms were aching with carrying Amy, and I was out of breath and had a stitch in my side. Mr Bailey was already heading over the bridge.

'Can you slow down a bit?'

Several heads turned in my direction, but the man himself kept on walking. I yelled this time, causing even more people to stare at me, but at least it did the trick. He turned and waited for me to catch up.

'I'm sorry. I didn't think. Would you like me to carry her for you?'

I was tempted but I was hardly likely to hand over my precious child to a total stranger, was I? And they didn't come much stranger than him.

'No thanks, I can manage. Are we nearly there?'

He nodded. 'It's not too far. The Hare and Moon's right on the seafront.'

'It's a busy place,' I said, trying to steady my breathing.

'Yes.'

'I can see why. It's beautiful.' I wasn't particularly trying to engage him in conversation, but I desperately needed a breather. Honestly, what had happened to me? Harry was quite right, I had let myself go. If I couldn't even walk down the sodding hill, how the hell was I going to get back up it? Maybe I never would. Maybe I'd have to stay down there forever or face the indignity of being hoisted back up on a sort of rope and pulley system, which the council would have to install especially for me.

We stood on the bridge, and I sat Amy on the wall, holding onto her tightly. We looked down at the beck and, gradually, I began to breathe normally again. Below us the water rushed between grassy banks, and visitors leaned on the wall, exclaiming in delight at the view, or stepping back to take photos with their phones. Mr Bailey was silent.

Well, this wasn't awkward at all, I thought, wondering if he was this anti-social with everyone. There was a faraway look in his eyes, as if he was thinking about something. He could have been attractive if he wasn't so miserable, I mused. Obviously, not gorgeous like Harry, but there was something about him. If only he could have a personality transplant, his phwoar rating would soar.

I looked back down the road. Some people were coming out of the fish and chip shop. Immediately, seagulls swooped around them, issuing loud demands to be fed.

Mr Bailey frowned. 'Idiots,' he muttered. 'They shouldn't feed the birds. Seagulls are nothing but feathered terrorists.'

I decided he was a thoroughly mean man whose phwoar rating would sadly never nudge above average. Fancy begrudging a few seagulls a couple of chips. Honestly, I hoped the rest of the residents of Kearton Bay were a bit more fun to be around than this happy chappie. Amy took advantage of my attention being distracted and pulled my sunglasses from where I'd perched them on top of my head.

'Don't even think about it, Miss,' I warned, noticing her dangling them over the water. She giggled. I saw Mr Bailey's mouth twitch in the beginnings of a smile, then he promptly turned away. Maybe he had a bet with someone that he would be a miserable sod all day for twenty quid?

'Come on. We're nearly there.'

I scooped Amy up, and we headed over the bridge, Mr Bailey walking more slowly now to keep pace with us. I breathed in the salty tang of the sea, overlaid with the delicious aroma wafting from the chip shop. We passed an old stone house, which, according to the sign on its wall, had once been the police station, complete with cells. Narrow passageways ran between little stone cottages, and I wondered where they led to. As we walked, I glanced up and saw we were walking parallel with Water's Edge, high above us. I could see more cottages, and tables with parasols, which indicated the presence of at least one more café. Then the road bent once more, and Water's Edge was lost to my view behind four-storey narrow houses, a shop selling jewellery made from Whitby jet, a small art gallery, a gift shop, and yet another café. Ahead of us, I saw the sea, and to the right of the slope which led onto the sands, an old whitewashed building with a sagging roof and big double doors. We passed a fossil and dinosaur museum, another gift shop and another pub, The Lobster Pot, before I finally caught sight of a big, white building standing to the left of the slipway, and I heaved a sigh of relief as Mr Bailey informed me we were looking at The Hare and Moon.

I nodded, too exhausted to reply. We walked the final few yards to the seafront, where a few boats were moored on the slipway and the inn itself perched high above the sands on a huge sea wall. I pulled a face as I realised that to get into the bar meant climbing a long flight of steps.

'Can you manage? Are you sure you wouldn't like me to carry her?' he offered, obviously having seen my red face and fearing I was about to keel over at any moment.

I shook my head, and he turned away, leading me up the steps to the pub door.

He pushed it open and held it for me, ushering me into the safety of the entrance porch, away from the turmoil outside. I was exhausted and placed Amy on the floor with undisguised relief.

'Thank God for that. I thought we'd never get here.'

I rubbed my aching back and looked around, my eyes adjusting to the darkness after the bright sunshine outside. 'This is pretty ancient,' I remarked, noting the thick walls and huge black beams.

'Seventeenth century. A real old smuggler's haunt — just what the tourists ordered. Welcome to Disneyland.'

I honestly tried to smile, but my lips didn't seem to have the energy to curve upwards. 'What did you mean when you said Rhiannon wasn't to everyone's taste? In what way, exactly?'

He looked uncomfortable. 'Oh, it's nothing to worry about. She just has some odd beliefs. I mean, I don't think she rides a broomstick, or anything like that. Well, I haven't seen her on it lately.'

'Ah, right.' A witch? I considered this briefly. 'Okay.'

'It doesn't worry you?'

'Why should it? Each to their own.'

Frankly, after the week I'd had, nothing much would surprise me. Besides, I knew a real witch, and I didn't think this Rhiannon person could be any more of a threat than Melody Bird.

He pushed open the heavy oak door of the bar and ushered us inside. I stepped through the door, breathing in the smell of stale beer. Straight away, I was four years old again, sitting on my Grandad's knee while he told me stories, the beery fumes from his breath wafting over me as he spoke. I felt suddenly comforted, which, given the circumstances, I suppose said a lot about me and my childhood. Maybe Harry was right about that, too? Bugger.

The bar's heavy beams, low ceiling, and latticed windows all deepened the gloom in the room, despite its white painted walls. A few men were sitting at the table nearest to the door, playing dominoes. They barely glanced at us. From an adjoining room, I could hear the buzz of other people talking and the clattering of plates, and the smell of food wafted towards me above the beer fumes.

A large black pot stood in the grate of an ancient inglenook fireplace, which dominated the room. I was aware of Mr Bailey giving me surreptitious looks, probably wondering if the fact that there was a cauldron in the bar would faze me at all. It didn't. Better a cauldron than a row of noisy fruit machines. He led me to the bar, suddenly looking anxious. A young man of about twenty was mopping beer spills off the counter, clearly absorbed in his job.

'Hello, Derry. Are you on your own?'

'Hello, Mr Bailey. Don't often see you in here.' The young man grinned. 'Were you looking for Michelle?'

My guide almost spat a denial at him. Evidently Michelle, whoever she may be, was the last person he wanted to see. Derry laughed.

'Only kidding, mate. I know what she's like. She's on the beach, organising the kids' games, so you're safe. How's Lexi?'

He nodded, obviously relieved. 'She's fine, though nervous about tonight, I think.'

'I know how she feels. I'm going to look a right pillock.'

'Well, you have to do it, for your mother's sake. Speaking of which, is she around?'

'Sure. She's in the kitchen, arguing with Jack about the food. She wants him to serve vegetarian dishes only tonight. You can imagine the ructions that caused.'

They grinned at each other, obviously sharing some private joke. I was just stunned that he knew how to smile.

Derry stepped out from the bar, pushed open the door behind him marked private and hollered for the landlady. 'Mum!'

I noticed Amy was staring wide-eyed at the cauldron and the broomstick that was resting in one corner of the room. She was all too familiar with the story of Hansel and Gretel. I hoped she wouldn't have nightmares that night.

The kitchen door was pushed open, and Rhiannon walked into the room.

I think I gasped. Mr Bailey looked round at me, so I must have made some noise. He surely couldn't blame me. Rhiannon was exquisite. This was Derry's mother? She really wasn't the middle-aged hippy I'd been expecting. She looked too young to have a son of Derry's age, with her delicate heart-shaped face, large dark eyes and rosebud lips. Her tiny frame was clothed in a cream blouse and black ankle-length skirt that looked almost Edwardian, especially as they were teamed with old-fashioned lace-up boots. Her hair was a cascade of glossy brown curls, carelessly pinned up at the sides and tumbling gloriously to her shoulders. She was beautiful.

'Darling!'

Her voice was a surprise, too. Unlike Derry, Rhiannon had no trace of a Yorkshire accent. She spoke like someone from a nineteen-forties' British film.

'Rhiannon, how are you?'

'All the better for seeing you. You don't socialise nearly enough. What can I get you?'

He shook his head. 'It's not a social call. Mrs Jarvis here…' He waved his arm in the direction where I was still standing, staring in awe at the landlady, '…finds herself in the predicament of having nowhere to stay. She's the new guest at Amethyst Cottage, but—'

'Oh, gosh, the ceiling collapsed,' said Rhiannon. She looked at Amy and me with sympathetic eyes. I wondered how on earth news had got around so fast.

'You're welcome to stay here, of course,' she said, with a wide smile that showed beautifully even teeth. 'We only have two guests staying, at the moment, and they leave tomorrow. I don't really take guests, as a rule, but if they come to us, I always think it's for a reason.'

'Thanks so much.' I was grateful, even if she was a bit odd.

'Why don't you sit down, and I'll bring you both a drink,' she said. 'You must be exhausted. Then I'll show you to your room, while Gabriel fetches your things.'

His name was Gabriel? Now it was my turn to look shocked. Maybe it was another sign. I fished in my bag and brought out Harry's car keys, which I dangled in his face.

'If you don't mind that would be fantastic. There's only one suitcase and a bag,' I informed him, sinking wearily into one of the plush benches in the corner of the bar. He looked at me, obviously astonished that I'd given him the keys so easily.

'I trust you,' I said simply. 'You have the name of an angel. How can I not? Besides, I doubt very much that I'll be able to get back up that hill today. It nearly killed me coming down it.'

Gabriel swallowed and glanced at Rhiannon, who was positively beaming at him.

'There's a darling. Now, Mrs Jarvis, what can I get you and your daughter?'

I watched, quite amazed, as Gabriel turned and left the pub. Blimey, what power did Rhiannon have over him to make him obey her like that? He was hardly the most obliging of chaps, and I doubted he did favours for many people. I wondered if he was romantically attached to her? I wouldn't be surprised. She was so lovely. Mind you, she could do a lot better for herself. Anyone who smiled would be a result after his charms, frankly. Some angel.

I tried to concentrate on what Rhiannon was saying, but all I could hear was Joe's voice in my head, as if he'd only spoken the words yesterday, not all those years ago.

'The name of an angel and the heart of a devil.'

I didn't think Gabriel Bailey was the devil, but I had to admit it was a weird coincidence. Kearton Bay was full of surprises. I wondered what I'd let myself in for.

****

Lexi's smile died as she saw Gabriel's face, and she sat beside him, concern evident in her eyes.

'Are you okay?'

He tried unsuccessfully to smile, nodding at the Christmas tree, which was standing, rather incongruously, in the corner of the living room. 'I got it.'

'You went back there? I told you I'd go.'

'There wasn't time. The next tenants were arriving, and Mrs

Lovelace said if I wanted to get into the loft I had to make it fast.'

'Well, of all the nerve! It's our stuff!'

He looked at her indignant face, and this time his smile came easier. 'She'd had a bit of a disaster when I got there. The tenants had flooded the bathroom. Water everywhere. Made a real mess of the place.'

'Good.' She was silent for a moment then asked, 'How bad?'

'Bad enough to make it uninhabitable until the workmen have been in for a couple of days.' He hesitated. 'The new tenant turned up. Woman of about thirtyish, I should say, with a little girl. I had to take them to The Hare and Moon, get them a room there until the cottage is ready again. She's booked it for four weeks, believe it or not. More money than sense, obviously.'

Lexi frowned. 'Did she upset you, Dad?'

'Upset me? Of course not. Why would she?'

'Dunno. Just thought — oh, never mind.'

There was an awkward silence, and Gabriel sighed with relief when he heard the back door open and the sound of his sister Sophie's voice ringing through the kitchen.

'I'm telling you now, Archie, if that flaming woman starts any of her spell-casting, I'm out of there.'

'You say that every time. You know you'll enjoy it, so why moan?'

'I'm just saying. And did you notice the weirdos from Whitby have arrived? Talk about the living dead. Bloody *Zombie Apocalypse* round here, half the time.'

Lexi met Gabriel's eyes, and they grinned at each other.

She stood up, patting his shoulder. 'I'll make us all a cup of tea. I don't know about you, but it sounds like poor Archie could use one.'

He waited until she left the room then leaned back in his chair, his eyes closing as he tried to clear his mind of the scent of roses, jasmine and vanilla. It had been so vivid, so strong, it had brought it all flooding back. Even the sunglasses and the Chloé handbag were savage attacks on his memory. He shook his head and took a deep breath. She wasn't Zoe. The past was done with.

He wondered which cruel twist of fate had decided that he, of

all people, would become entangled with the new tenant of
Amethyst Cottage.

Chapter 5

The little room that Rhiannon showed us to was at the back of the building, overlooking the sea.

'I do hope you'll be comfortable here. It's small but cosy, and if you need anything, you only have to ask.'

'Thank you, Miss, er?'

'Bone, but, please, just call me Rhiannon.'

'I'm Eliza, and this is Amy.'

'Delighted to meet you.'

Having helped me with our cases, Rhiannon didn't seem in any hurry to leave us to it. She looked at me, her deep brown eyes thoughtful.

'So, what brings you to Kearton Bay, Eliza?' she asked.

'Just fancied a holiday with my daughter.'

I jumped as the sound of sleigh bells rang out around the room, and grabbed my bag, rooting around inside it. Why was it that, no matter how often I pulled out that damn mobile phone to check it, when it rang, it was always hidden at the bottom of my bag under a pile of junk? I found it eventually and read the name that flashed up on the screen. A range of conflicting emotions shot through me, and Rhiannon watched, her eyes curious, as I dropped the phone, unanswered, onto the bed.

'Goodness, it's a bit early for Santa!'

I blushed. Buggery bollocks. Why hadn't I done what Mrs Travers had been nagging me to for the last four months? Sodding sleigh bells in May! And there I was, mocking that

Gabriel bloke for carrying a Christmas tree!

'Amy likes it. I put it on for her at Christmas and never bothered changing it. I suppose I ought to get around to it.'

'Not at all. Why should magic be reserved for December? It's around us all the time. If the sound of sleigh bells helps us to remember that, then why not?'

She smiled, and I found myself smiling back. She had a way of making you agree with her, whether you did or not, if you see what I mean.

'Perhaps you'd like to come to a little gathering I'm hosting tonight? It's for Beltane — May Day. We're a few days late but we postponed it till the weekend. There's going to be a bonfire and lots of food, and there'll be a short ceremony. It's up at the paddock behind the new bungalows, opposite The Kearton Arms. Mr and Mrs Gray are very kind and let us use it for events such as this. You'd both be very welcome.'

'Perhaps. I'll think about it, thanks.'

'There was a ceremony this morning — the crowning of the May Queen, then a maypole dance.' She clapped her hands, obviously delighted at the memory. 'Total chaos, as usual, but marvellous fun. What a pity you came too late to enjoy it. There are some games on the beach right now for the children, if you'd like to take the little one, but I suspect you're a little tired at the moment?'

'I am, yes. Sorry.'

'Not at all. Well, I hope you have a lovely stay here. It's been a bit of a strange start to your holiday, hasn't it? Still, everything happens for a reason, you know. Maybe you're already on the path to finding what you seek, even if you don't know that you're seeking it.'

'O-kay.'

Rhiannon laughed. I guess she was used to people thinking she was a bit weird. 'There's a dining room downstairs but if you'd prefer to eat in your room, just let me know,' she said. 'I'll leave you to unpack. I do hope we'll see you tonight. Seven o'clock in the paddock. It will be a special experience, I promise you.'

I hadn't intended to go to the Beltane celebration, but after Rhiannon had been so kind and welcoming, offering us shelter in our hour of need, it seemed churlish not to.

The walk back up that dratted hill nearly killed me, but I consoled myself with the thought that I must be burning off masses of calories and, after all, I wanted to lose weight, didn't I? No way would I usually have taken that much exercise in a day. In fact, I'd been known to watch an entire Zumba DVD while sitting on the sofa with a custard doughnut and a can of Coke, and somehow managed to feel exhausted at the end of it, so this had to be an improvement. Carry on like this, and I'd be sylph-like in no time.

Following the crowds, I trudged wearily up the hill, Amy easily keeping pace with me, despite her tiny legs, which was a bit embarrassing. The hordes walked cheerily towards an archway between the row of bungalows opposite The Kearton Arms, and I wheezed along behind them, the strong smell of smoke curling round my nostrils, making me think, and not for the first time that evening, that I might need an inhaler before much longer, and I wasn't even asthmatic. I arrived at the paddock to find dozens of people gathered round a crackling bonfire, chatting and laughing with each other as if that mountain that they called a street wasn't much more than a speed bump.

Feeling conspicuous, I perched Amy on the top bar of the fence next to the gate and hovered just outside the paddock, reluctant to go any closer. I could see enough from my viewpoint and I wasn't sure I wanted to venture further, particularly when I heard drumbeats and everyone started to cheer, as, from the gate opposite mine, a mock throne was carried into the paddock by four young men. Sitting on it, looking rather regal, was a pretty young woman, perhaps in her late teens, or early twenties. She had the most glorious waist-length red hair and was wearing a long white dress and a crown of flowers. After climbing down from the throne, she approached the bonfire and stood waiting. I knew enough about May Day to guess that this was the May

Queen, but I wasn't sure what on earth the creature that appeared next was.

From out of the trees a strange apparition, dressed entirely in green and wearing a huge mask of leaves and foliage, and with what looked like deer antlers on his head, came forward and pointed at the May Queen. It was almost sinister.

I watched in fascination as she gave a nervous giggle and began to run. The drumbeats set up a steady rhythm, and the crowd began to clap along to it as the creature gave chase, following the girl as she ran around the bonfire, threading her way between the watchers. For some reason, I couldn't get the image of Edward Woodward in *The Wicker Man* out of my mind.

I hoped there weren't going to be any human sacrifices. You never knew with these remote moorland villages. I'd seen enough old movies to know the secrets these people could keep. And, now that I came to think of it, what kind of name for a pub was The Hare and Moon? I mean, surely it should be The Hare and Hounds, or something normal like that? And then there was Rhiannon with her cauldron and broomstick. Jeez, what had I got myself into?

The drumbeats were getting louder, and I started to feel a bit panicky. What if they all turned on us? Now that I looked, I could see all those weird zombie ghosts were standing nearby, too, laughing and pointing at the poor May Queen. I was about to make a break for it, and was wondering how far I'd get before a group of baying villagers with pitchforks caught up with me, when I heard a young girl in a cropped t-shirt snap at a spotty boy beside her.

'Don't be a prick, Darren. Gizza Pringle, you fucking tightwad.'

My bubble of panic burst immediately and, reassured, I took a deep breath and turned back to the bonfire.

I noticed Gabriel Bailey staring into the bonfire as if his life savings were burning in the flames. The May Queen ran past him, and I watched in surprise as she caught his hand briefly, and he looked up and smiled at her. Bloody hell, two smiles in one day? I wondered if she was his girlfriend, but if so, where did Rhiannon fit in? The redhead was a bit young for him, but then, women often went for older men, and, of course, most men would love a younger girlfriend. Only Harry was contrary enough to go for a woman ten years older than his wife. Just my sodding luck.

Eventually, the creature caught the May Queen, and they embraced briefly. He gave her a chaste peck on the cheek, and then they separated, laughing. He headed off to a group of young men, who were jeering and obviously filming him on their phones. He would probably feature on Facebook within minutes.

The girl headed towards Gabriel, who was standing with a middle-aged couple — a tall man with grey hair, who had his arm around a short, plump woman with a blonde bob and treacherously high heels.

As I watched, I saw Rhiannon approach them, together with another young woman with dark hair. Gabriel looked away, and I could see by his body language that he was distinctly uncomfortable. It was fascinating, like watching a soap opera.

The creature took off his mask and I was surprised to see that beneath it was Derry Bone. No wonder he'd said earlier that he was nervous. His mates were going to torture him about this for years.

Rhiannon stepped forward and clapped her hands. The murmuring stopped, and everyone turned to face her. Amy shifted on the beam of the fence, entranced by the whole thing, staring especially wide-eyed at the zombie ghosts in their dramatic black Victorian costumes and dark make-up.

'With the union of the Green Man and the May Queen, this village is ensured prosperity for the coming year,' Rhiannon announced. There was a great deal of clapping at this news.

'Be nice to make a profit for once!' shouted someone, and everyone cheered.

'There's food laid on back at The Hare and Moon, if you'd all like to make your way down there in a moment,' she continued. 'First, though, may I ask for a moment's silence as we give thanks to the god and goddess.'

I saw several people shuffling awkwardly and there was a bit of muttering and nudging. Eventually, heads bowed, and most people, if not all, were silent as if in prayer.

I watched from a distance. The May Queen was looking down at the floor so had no idea that she was being watched by two people. One was Derry Bone, who was being very disrespectful of his important role in the proceedings and had lit a cigarette, which he was sharing with a couple of his mates. The other was a rather odd-looking young man, tall and skinny with thick brown hair and a long face, who was gazing at her in naked adoration.

Beside Rhiannon, the dark-haired girl was ogling Gabriel. Honestly, there was no other way to describe it. She was practically drooling. If he was aware of this, he showed no sign. He had his arm through the May Queen's and was staring up at the evening sky, which was illuminated by a silvery moon. I had a sudden strong feeling that he was praying, although his eyes were open, and he wasn't speaking, so I don't know where that idea came from. All this hocus-pocus was obviously getting to me. Time to get back to the pub before the crowds descended.

I was just about to lift Amy off the fence when, to my horror, I heard sleigh bells. Every single head turned in my direction, as I made a grab for the phone from the top of the fence next to Amy, where I'd stupidly placed it. I hadn't brought my bag, seeing no reason to drag more weight up that wretched hill, but my phone was something I couldn't bring myself to leave behind. Now I was cursing my decision, as the sound shattered what had been for some, not least Rhiannon, a very spiritual moment.

In my haste I fumbled, and not used to the acrylic nails, misjudged my distance. I dropped the phone onto the grass, where it continued to ring out those bells, for all the world as if Santa was on his way. I finally managed to pick it up and paled as I saw Harry's name flashing on the screen. I meant to press "end call", but in my panicked state I pressed "answer" instead.

I stared at the phone in dismay as the ringing stopped and I distinctly heard Harry demanding, 'Eliza? Eliza is that you?'

'Oh, no!' Hastily ending the call, I looked up, relieved to see everyone had turned away. Well, almost everyone. Gabriel caught my eye, and for a moment I saw a look in his, a strange look that I wasn't quite able to work out.

We stared at each other for a long moment, then I grabbed Amy, as she seemed about to topple off the fence. As I stood her safely on the ground I saw Rhiannon stop her murmuring and look directly at me. Her face broke into a smile, then she looked up at the moon and resumed her prayer.

That was enough for me. They were all barking mad, and trust Harry to draw attention to me in his usual clumsy fashion. What did he want anyway? To tell me how sorry he was and to admit he'd made a terrible mistake and beg me to come home? Or, as was more likely, if I'm honest, to demand to know where the hell his car had gone and to tell me to bring it back immediately or he'd have me arrested on sight. Oh, sod him.

I grabbed Amy, and we set off back down the hill before the hordes could overtake us. Except that most of them did. Even allowing for our head start, before long, crowds of people were passing us and went pouring into The Hare and Moon before us. I thanked my lucky stars when I finally found an empty seat and managed to plonk myself down with Amy on my knee and a pile of food before us, hoping that no one recognised me and mentioned the embarrassing ring tone.

The bar was heaving with people. While I'd been unpacking and hiding away in our room upstairs, someone had, presumably because of Beltane, decorated the bar with a wide variety of flowers. They were on every available surface, and the scent mingled most uncomfortably with the smell of beer. Beautiful as they were, they made the bar feel even more cluttered, and I began to feel claustrophobic.

At least the food was good and there was plenty of it. I piled up our plates and tucked in, encouraging Amy to try some. I looked around me in interest at the other guests, who were picking at the buffet and chatting to each other over drinks.

Just behind the zombie ghosts, who thankfully turned out to be Goths left over from the nearby Whitby Goth Weekend, I briefly glimpsed Derry, still in costume as the Green Man. He grabbed a hotdog — obviously, Rhiannon had lost the argument with

Jack — then dashed off somewhere, possibly to change. The tall, skinny man who had also been mesmerised by the May Queen was nowhere to be seen. The girl herself was sitting with a group of people around her own age. There was no sign of Gabriel Bailey. I wondered what their relationship was. He'd seemed quite arrogant when I first met him, but he'd sort of made amends by bringing me to The Hare and Moon and then collecting our bags for me. He may have the name of an angel, but it didn't seem to be making him happy. On the contrary, he seemed quite sad, somehow. Maybe the May Queen was playing away, and he knew it? The girl seemed to have a few admirers. That's what happened when you dated a younger woman. They were bound to go off with someone more their own age at some point, although I could see the attraction of Gabriel. He wasn't handsome in a conventional way, but he was quite striking with those well-defined cheekbones, their sharp edges softened by his dark, gently curling hair.

Then I remembered Melody Bird's wild, blonde curls, and my heart sank. No doubt Harry had run his fingers through those many times. I suddenly felt quite sick as tears pricked my eyes. I was tired, that was the problem. Beside me, Amy was yawning. It must be time for bed. I glanced at my watch. Ten-thirty. No wonder I was knackered, and poor Amy should have been asleep hours ago.

I stood up, taking Amy's hand, and led her to the bar, where Rhiannon was chatting to a sandy-haired man in a checked shirt.

'We're going up, Rhiannon,' I said. 'I just wanted to say thank you for putting us up, and for tonight. It was an amazing experience.'

Rhiannon beamed at me. 'I'm so glad you enjoyed it. Remember, breakfast will be available between seven-thirty and nine-thirty tomorrow morning. Sweet dreams, Eliza. And you, Amy.'

The landing was quite dark even with the lamps lit, but I'd expected that. The pub was so ancient — one of the oldest buildings in Kearton Bay, apparently — and upstairs, the ceilings were even lower than in the bar, and the windows smaller. Our room held nothing more than two single beds, a wardrobe, a small television set and a chest of drawers. Most importantly, though, the beds looked soft and inviting with thick duvets and plump pillows.

Having washed and changed Amy and cleaned her teeth, I tucked her up in bed, and within ten minutes, she was sound asleep. I wandered over to the window. It was late, and I was on the point of collapse, but I was sure I'd find it impossible to sleep. The moon cast its gentle light over the sea, and I stared up at it, wondering if my mother was watching me now.

What if I was wrong? What if all this was some dreadful mistake? I rubbed my arm and stared at the dark water lapping on the sands, then peered out as a movement caught my eye. What was a girl doing out walking alone at that time?

In the moonlight, I could see she wore a long dress and carried something in her hand. As I watched, she looked around her in a furtive manner and then rounded the bay, disappearing from sight. I was almost certain that she was the May Queen. Maybe she'd noticed the skinny man, after all.

I wandered over to my bed, yawning. I may as well deal with what I'd been avoiding all day. I leaned over and reached into my handbag, searching for my mobile phone. I lay back on the bed, holding the phone in the air as I scrolled down, wrinkling my nose as I counted the number of missed calls and texts. Poor Joe had tried to contact me quite a few times. He would be frantic. I would have to tell him we were all right. I couldn't face talking to him, not tonight, but I would text him. It was the least he deserved.

I had four texts and eight missed calls from Harry. He'd be terrified that I'd acted so out of character and worried that I was about to blow the whistle on his sordid affair. He would also be furious that I'd pinched his precious car. Well, I would deal with all that tomorrow. I needed to get a shower and get into my pyjamas, but first I must text Joe. I just needed five minutes to get my mind clear and think about what I should tell him.

Within two minutes, I was fast asleep.

Chapter 6

I woke at five-thirty, shivering with cold and astonished to realise that I had slept through the night. I remembered with some guilt that I hadn't sent Joe a text, after all.

Climbing under the duvet and snuggling into the warm, soft bed, I resolved to call him at six, only to fall asleep again and finally wake up at seven-thirty, when Amy's voice stirred me from my slumber, demanding the toilet. After I'd taken her to the bathroom, I rang Joe, determined to get it out of the way before breakfast.

I could hear the relief in his voice as he answered the phone. 'Oh, thank God! Where the bloody hell are you? You do know I've had Harry calling nonstop, all day yesterday? What the hell's happened? He wouldn't tell me anything — he was convinced you were staying with me.'

'He's been porking Miss-Grin-and-Bare-'Em,' I said. 'He's leaving me. I couldn't just sit there and wait for him to go, so I left him instead.'

'You *are* joking?' It took my painful recounting of the whole sorry episode for Joe to finally realise I was deadly serious. 'What a prat. I always knew it. Well, you'll be fine, love. A fresh start. Your life will be better without him in it, trust me.'

He seemed unable to grasp the fact that life without Harry in it was unthinkable. I mean, take Harry away and what was left? Well, Amy, of course, but take Amy out of the picture and what was left then? Zero, that's what. I was so used to thinking about what Harry wanted, what Harry needed, what Harry liked, that I'd totally lost track of what I wanted, needed and liked. So, I could hardly be blamed for thinking that all I wanted, needed and liked was Harry, now could I?

'I don't know how I can bear it,' I whispered.

'Eliza, listen to me. It's his loss, not yours,' said Joe, almost fiercely.

'It's Amy's loss, too,' I said, feeling tears on my cheek and wiping them away with the back of my hand.

'Amy's got us. She'll be fine. Where the hell are you, anyway?'

'I'm in Yorkshire. I'm sorry I didn't call earlier, but—'

'Yorkshire? Have you gone home?'

Joe always called Knaresborough home, even though we'd left there twenty years ago when I was twelve. I wished I could tell him that was where I was, but I had to be honest. He was appalled, as expected.

'Kearton Bay? Oh, God, Eliza, please tell me you're not doing anything stupid.'

'It was meant to be. You know all that stuff Harry said about my father? Well, it occurred to me that maybe he was right. I need to get it clear in my head and find out the truth for myself. So, I'm here.'

'But, love, you hardly know anything about him. All right, he came from Kearton Bay, but so what? It was thirty odd years ago. He'd already left there by the time he met your mother in Leeds and he may never have gone back. The chances of you finding him are practically zero.'

'But at least here there is a chance.'

'What if you find him and he's married with more children? Do you think he'd be happy if you turned up on the doorstep to rock the boat? I'm sorry, love. I don't want to upset you, but you've got to think about these things.'

'And you think I haven't? I'm not stupid. I'm going to make discreet enquiries, but, come on, with a name like Raphael, someone must have heard of him. How many can there be in a place like this?'

There was a loud sigh. 'You should have come to me, or at least given me some warning. I've been frantic since Harry called.'

'I tried calling you yesterday afternoon, but I couldn't get a signal, and once I got here, it just went out of my head. I'm sorry, but if I'd told you before, you'd have tried to talk me out of it.'

'You're not wrong there,' he said. 'You're making a big mistake. Kearton Bay's the last place you want to be. Come back to my house. If you want to go away, I'll pay for you and Amy a lovely long holiday. Anywhere you fancy, just take your pick.'

'But it's not about a holiday, is it? I need to know about my father and this is the only place I can find out who he was. I honestly think it's what I'm meant to do, Joe. When Harry went to bed, I went online to look for some accommodation, and the search brought up the name of a holiday let called Amethyst Cottage. You've got to see that was a sign from Mum?'

There was a silence while he digested this information. I knew he had to see the significance of that name, given her devotion to the little silver ring that I now wore on my right hand. When I'd realised that the cottage had only just been advertised and was available for as many weeks as I wanted, right up till the end of August, I'd been convinced that I was meant to go there and find my father. Joe didn't sound so sure.

'I hope you're not expecting miracles, love.'

'It just feels like it's the right time. Maybe it was mum directing me here?'

'So, is that where you are now, then? Amethyst Cottage?'

'Well, no. When I got there, the ceiling in the kitchen had collapsed, so I've had to move to a room in a pub till it's fixed.'

'Oh, dear God!'

'No, listen, it's fine. Everyone's been so kind and welcoming. I'll only be here for a few days, and then the cottage will be fixed, and everything will be okay. Please stop worrying and let me do this.'

'I don't seem to have a choice. I should warn you, though, Harry's panicking. He was on about calling the police.'

'Huh, and risk publicity? Anyway, he's only worried because I stole his car.'

'You did what?' Joe started to laugh. 'Well, that's cheered me up. Why did you do that?'

'I didn't plan it, but when I got the email from the landlady to say the cottage was empty, I just knew I had to get here straight away before I changed my mind, but my car had a flat battery.'

'Oh, hell. Really?'

I sighed and uncrossed my fingers. 'No, not really. I was pissed off at him and I wanted to hit him where it would hurt most, so I stole his precious car.'

Joe could barely speak for laughing, which was a relief, though really, my impulsive decision had bitten me in the bum. I'd hated driving the damn thing all that way, and it wasn't the most practical car, especially in a hilly area like this.

'Jesus. No wonder he was in a state. Well, serve him right. He can drive around in your Fiesta for a while. It will kill him — hopefully. How long are you planning on staying up there?'

'I'm not sure. I didn't really think things through,' I admitted. 'I just wanted to get away. I've booked the cottage for four weeks, then we'll see.'

'How's Amy?'

'She's fine. She's already asked for you, and she's been whingeing about seeing Jeeves and Wooster.'

Joe laughed. Once, he'd owned a little dog called Bertie, who'd been almost as popular as he was, appearing regularly on his show with him. After he died, Joe didn't feel ready to get another dog, but his agent had rewarded his success at a television awards night with two micro pigs. They now appeared on screen with him, and the public adored them, but not as much as Amy, who had begged endlessly for one of her own. Fat chance. Harry wouldn't even keep a pet goldfish. He considered pets too much of a commitment and he wasn't big on commitment, obviously.

'That'll be right. Never let it be said that her old uncle is more important than two bloody pigs. Look, I'm going to call Mrs Travers, love, convince her that you're not in a hospital bed, somewhere. Promise me that if you change your mind, you'll come to my house and let me look after you.'

'I promise, but honestly, Joe, I'm staying here. I'm going to find out who my father is, even if it turns out he doesn't want anything to do with me. At least then, I'll know who I am.'

'I'll tell you who you are, Eliza,' said Joe. 'You're Eliza Hollingsworth, my niece, Amy's mum, and the loveliest young woman on God's green earth. And you don't need any man to prove that.'

I blinked back tears. Dear Joe. If he could have seen me sitting there with the waistband of my trousers digging into my rolls of flesh and my feet crammed into huge, furry Eeyore slippers I doubted that he'd have thought me so lovely, but it was terribly kind of him to say so.

****

'Bacon sandwich for you, Gabriel, and for you, miss, an egg sandwich. Though how you can resist my bacon, I'll never know.'

Gabriel took the plate being offered to him and smiled his appreciation at the old lady who'd brought it. 'Thanks, Hannah. I really shouldn't, though. I'm doing this far too often, and it's not good for my health.'

Hannah sniffed. 'Rubbish. I've eaten bacon every day of me adult life and I've lived to tell the tale, haven't I?'

'More than the poor pigs did,' said Lexi. She took the egg sandwich, biting into it with relish, then looked up in alarm. 'You didn't fry this in lard, did you?'

'Would I dare? After the rollicking you gave me that time? Vegetable oil, and before you ask, no, I didn't cook the bacon with the egg.'

'Good.' Lexi continued with her feast, her conscience apparently clear.

Gabriel watched her in amusement. 'I wonder where you put it all. You've already had a huge breakfast this morning.'

'And, just like you, not a pick on her. She must be burning it off, somehow.'

'Walking up and down all day with the donkeys will do that.' Lexi looked up at the sky and smiled. 'At least we've got sunshine again today. Should be busy. We'll get ready and head off in half an hour.'

'Aye, we've been lucky with the weather the last few days,' Hannah acknowledged, looking round the farmyard and smiling fondly at her hens, which were basking in the warmth of another fine May morning. She nodded over at the paddock, where her donkeys grazed. 'Are you on the sands today, or is Eddie taking a turn?'

Gabriel shook his head. 'Eddie's going. I'm going to mend that fence behind the barn, and then I've got a rabbit hutch to build for the Smithsons.'

Hannah patted his shoulder. 'Well, at least you've got an order.'

Gabriel sighed. 'Barely keeping the wolf from the door. I suppose it's going to take time.'

'Seems like a waste of time to me.' Hannah was watching him steadily, her faded blue eyes sharp as ever, despite her eighty-eight years. 'Are you sure this is what you want? It's not too late, you know.'

'We've been through all this. It's what I want — for now at least. The bacon sandwich was lovely, thank you. A cup of coffee would be perfect to wash it all down.'

'Cheeky bugger.'

Hannah laughed, but Gabriel knew that she wasn't convinced.

'I'll put the kettle on, but it'll have to be tea. I've run out of coffee. You can make yourself useful later and pop to Henderson's for some. Can you give Eddie a shout and tell him his butty'll be ready in five minutes?'

'I'll go,' said Lexi, handing back her empty plate. She headed off towards the barn where Eddie, who looked after Hannah's herd of donkeys, was checking the tack.

Hannah turned her gaze back on Gabriel. 'Well?'

'Well, what? Hannah, I'm fine here, honestly. Business is picking up slowly. I'm heading off to Helmston and Whitby tomorrow, to have a chat with all the pet shop managers, see if they'd be willing to take some of my stuff on a sale or return basis. It will be okay.'

Hannah looked down at the empty plates and shook her head. 'It's all wrong, this! I'm sorry, but someone's got to tell you. You're throwing your life away, and for what? There's people suited to this life, like Eddie and my Albert, but a man like you? It's not right, Gabriel. I've known you all your life. I wouldn't be standing here now, if it weren't for your grandfather, and you played on this farm when you were just a little lad. I've watched you grow up and I've seen what you made of yourself. You may say it's none of my business but — well, it breaks my heart.'

Gabriel touched her wizened apple cheek gently. 'Of course it's your business, Hannah. You're the one who gave Lexi and me work, for a start. And I do appreciate your concern, honestly. But this is right for me now. It's peaceful and undemanding. I feel—'

'Invisible?'

He didn't answer, and she sighed. 'Aye, I know. I do understand, honest, but it's a bloody shame, there's no getting away from it. Any road, I'll leave you to it and put the kettle on. Come in for your tea in five minutes.'

'I will. Thanks.'

Hannah shuffled off across the farmyard, and Gabriel watched her, his spirits sinking. He hadn't been in the mood to hear all that. Not today, when he'd been feeling so low. He supposed it had been the stress of moving yet again, and landing back on Sophie's doorstep, that had made him feel that way, and, of course, there was the anniversary. It had been two years since he'd last seen Zoe. He remembered her bruised face, as she lifted her bags and headed for the door. He remembered grabbing her arm, begging her to stay, the look of fear in her eyes and the sound of a car horn outside blasting. He remembered the door slamming and Lexi's anguish. They'd been in Kearton Bay a year now, trying to rebuild their lives, but how far had they really come? He took a deep breath and steadied himself. Everything would be all right. One step at a time.

Chapter 7

Now that I'd reassured Joe that I was okay, I decided it was time to begin my mission. I needed to start making enquiries — discreet enquiries, of course. The last thing I wanted was to upset anyone or cause any upheaval in an innocent family's life.

The question was where to start? You didn't get many Raphaels to the pound, and if he was still in the village, someone would surely have heard of him, but how to make enquiries without arousing suspicion? I needed to be careful who I asked. Anyone with a long history in the village could be a relative, so I needed to find people who were new here and not connected, but how?

I decided to try Derry. Rhiannon was too wily, too clever. Derry was young and probably didn't take much notice of what was being said to him.

Heading downstairs to the bar, I found Michelle stacking the coolers with bottles of alcopops and juice. I eyed her uncertainly. I'd only discovered this morning at breakfast that Michelle was the dark-haired girl who had been ogling Gabriel last night. No wonder he'd looked so wary when he'd entered the pub yesterday. The woman obviously fancied the pants off him, and there was no way the feeling was mutual.

'Oh, morning. You look a bit different today.' She straightened up, sneering at me.

'Do I? In what way?'

'You were all tarted up yesterday. Didn't recognise you without the slap on. Not so glamorous today, even with them false lashes.'

Flaming cheek. I flushed with embarrassment. I'd just spent ages in the shower scrubbing yesterday's make-up away. I'd forgotten all about putting more on. I'd have to dash back upstairs and get ready before I inflicted myself on polite society. Thank God there were people like Michelle in the world, who would stop us mere mortals going outside looking like shit.

'Is Derry around?'

'In the kitchen, washing up. Why?'

Quite honestly, I didn't see what business it was of hers but, being me, I couldn't bring myself to say that. 'Just want a quiet word about lunch.'

'Jack'll be in soon. It's him who deals with the food. Why, are you on a special diet?'

'No!' Bloody hell, she was a gobby mare. No wonder Gabriel wanted nothing to do with her.

Michelle waited, evidently expecting more information. When none was forthcoming she tutted and went back to stacking the bottles. I pushed my way through to the kitchen, trailing Amy behind me, since Michelle obviously wasn't going to call Derry out for me. He was standing at the sink, up to his elbows in bubbles.

'Hello. Can I get you something? Tea, coffee?'

'Just some information, please.'

'Sure. There's a tourist information centre at the top of the hill near the ice cream bar.'

'I think *you* could help. This village is so ancient, it's really caught my imagination.' I was becoming as good at lying as Harry. If I'd ever been bright enough to go to Cambridge, there was no doubt MI6 would have recruited me. 'I was wondering who knew the most about it around here? I suppose everyone has lived here all their lives, right?'

Derry laughed. 'You must be joking! Half the buildings in this area are owned by strangers, since the Boden-Keans sold most of their properties. It's full of holidaymakers in the summer, and half empty in the winter. Not many true locals left.'

'Who are the Boden-Keans?'

'Sir Paul and his son, Will. They own Kearton Hall, which is between here and Farthingdale. It used to be a massive estate, and they were the major landowners in the area, but, you know how it is.' He shrugged. 'Times have changed. They had to sell a lot of properties to preserve the house. Still quite substantial, though. Put it this way, you wouldn't struggle to build a shed in their garden. Not like this place. No garden here.'

'But you have an entire beach,' I pointed out and he laughed.

'Yeah, fair point.'

I had to admit, I quite liked the sound of the Boden-Keans. I wondered if I could possibly be related to them? I rather fancied the idea of a stately home, and, of course, it would explain why my father couldn't stick around. He was probably expected to marry Lady Parker-Farquhar, or some such person, and had reluctantly had to leave my mother to her fate, despite his broken heart.

'But you're local?' I asked. 'You and your mum?'

'I am, but Mum's family are from Cornwall, originally. She's lived here since she was about eighteen. Although, she kind of has family roots here, too. It's complicated.'

He wasn't kidding. All I needed was a list of people who weren't from the village. 'There must be someone who's lived here all their lives?'

'Yeah, 'course. Let me think.'

He screwed up his face and began to reel off a list of names, but Amy began to whine. I stopped him in mid-flow. 'What about all the local businesses around here? Are any of them run by locals?'

'Most of them, except for Cyril Goodall at the art gallery. I remember him moving here when I was little. Then there's Henderson's Store. Marty and Milly own that and the land opposite Water's Edge, on the other side of the beck. That's a car park for locals. Nowhere else to keep the cars, see? Oh, and there's Pinky's, the café on Water's Edge. The MacLeans have run that for two years. Other than those people, you could talk to any of the other shopkeepers.'

Finally, I had a few leads. 'Okay, that's great. Thank you. I'll have a browse around and see what I can dig up about the place.'

'Dig up?' Derry grinned. 'Head to the dinosaur centre, then. All sorts of fossils and bones up there.'

'Cheers, Derry. Sorry to have bothered you.'

'No problem. Good luck with the history lessons.'

After dashing back upstairs, to prepare to face the world with half a ton of make-up and a can of hairspray in place, I told Amy we were going out. She didn't seem too impressed. She was sulking. She was fed up with being cooped up in the room and was missing her *Peppa Pig* and Disney DVDs. She missed her Uncle Joe, too, and didn't even have her favourite pyjamas with her. I felt like the worst mother in the world.

Taking her hand, I led her downstairs through the bar and onto the seafront. After the darkness of the bedroom in the pub, the daylight was dazzling, and we both stood blinking in the sunshine for a moment. Overhead, seagulls swooped and screeched, scouring the decks of the boats for fish. Amy was thrilled, and it was a full ten minutes, while she admired the boats and laughed at the gulls, before I had the heart to drag her away and we finally headed up Bay Street.

I walked slowly, telling myself it was because of Amy's little legs. To be honest, she could probably have beaten me to the top, which was humiliating, to say the least. I kept having to stop and pretend to be looking at things in shop windows while I got my breath back. Still, at least it gave me a chance for a proper look around.

The street was ancient. Little cottages, with the dates carved above their front doors, told their own story. One of them said sixteen eighty-seven, another seventeen ten. I noticed that many of the cottages had brochures in little racks outside them, advertising that they were holiday lets, which seemed a bit of a shame.

I walked over the little stone bridge and came to Water's Edge. Wasn't that where Derry had said the MacLeans had their café? It may be a good place to begin enquiries. It seemed a narrow little thoroughfare, with tiny cottages and businesses all crammed together, but it was packed with tourists already.

As we stood watching the water bubbling below us, I became aware of the sound of hooves and an excited buzz from the crowd. I turned to see eight donkeys clattering down the hill towards us. A man, probably in his late fifties, was leading the first one. Bringing up the rear, a little grey donkey was being led by a girl with long red hair. There was no mistaking the May Queen. Well, whatever she'd been up to last night, at least she was alive and well.

Amy was ecstatic, and I had to pick her up to stop her rushing towards the donkeys. I promised her a ride later, as they were obviously heading to the beach. We watched as they passed us, much more sure-footed on this steep hill than any human.

When they were well out of the way, I led Amy up the steps to Water's Edge, keeping a tight grip on her hand. The café at the beginning of the beck was called The Copper Kettle and seemed to be heaving already. Opposite it, the tiny bookshop's door was open, and an elderly gentleman stood on the step, drinking tea or coffee and soaking up the sun, while his customers browsed the shelves. He smiled and nodded at us as we passed, and Amy giggled and waved to him.

I soon found Pinky's, mainly because of the yelling that was coming from inside it. I hovered uncertainly outside the door, as the sound of a bitter argument floated out of the open window and into the passageway. Several people looked at the café as they passed, their faces showing either amusement or disgust at the heated exchange that was obviously taking place inside. I had a feeling that now wouldn't be a good time to question the MacLeans. I would try Henderson's instead. Shopkeepers always knew everyone and everything. It was time to begin my mission.

****

We strolled down Water's Edge which, for the most part, consisted of crooked little cottages, many of them with the brochures outside. Where the passageway came to a bend stood a larger, more modern café called New Waves. Opposite most of the cottages were little patio gardens, overlooking the beck. The gardens opposite Pinky's and New Waves had several tables and chairs, but only the latter one's was occupied with customers. Just round the bend, there was a little shop selling plants and flowers, and then the passageway continued to King's Row.

As I came out of Water's Edge, I looked around. To my left, the street stopped dead, where iron railings fenced it off for safety reasons, as beyond was a sheer drop down to the beach below. I could see the back garden of New Waves, with more customers sitting at tables looking out over the sea. To the right of me, the street ran steeply down to the beach, with The Hare and Moon just visible at the bottom. There were more old houses, with little alleyways and passages running between them. The cottages down those were separated by narrow cobbled paths, and I reckoned you could lean out of the bedroom window of one and shake hands with someone in the bedroom of the house opposite. You'd certainly need thick curtains if you were living in one of those. And a thick skin, too, now I came to think about it. After all, it could get quite embarrassing if things got a bit, er, noisy. The sound drifting down these narrow alleyways on a clear night would be mortifying. How could you look your neighbour in the eye the next morning?

King's Row was less touristy than Bay Street. It consisted mostly of cottages, with a few shops. The Lobster Pot ran the full width of both streets, and a couple of men were sitting on the back step outside it, having a crafty smoke. There was a post office, a chemist's shop, and a fishmonger's. They all looked like something you'd see in a museum, a mock-up of an ancient village for the benefit of tourists. It was as if Kearton Bay was in a time capsule.

Next to the fishmonger's was Henderson's General Store. Outside, a board was advertising the headline for the local paper. Several people were coming out of the shop carrying provisions.

Squaring my shoulders, I pushed my way through them and walked into Henderson's, just as a middle-aged woman with a blonde bob came rushing out, carrying a cardboard box piled high with fruit. She almost collided with Amy and looked horrified.

'So sorry, darling,' she said.

Amy blinked, thought for a moment, then said 'Ouch.'

I rolled my eyes. 'She didn't touch you,' I said, nudging her gently. 'Don't worry,' I told the woman. 'She can be a bit of a drama queen sometimes.' I had no idea where she got it from.

'My fault. Couldn't see her over all these apples and oranges, and stuff. For my class, you see. Got to encourage them, haven't I? Sorry again!'

I stared after her for a moment, as she trotted up the street, full of admiration for the easy way in which she kept her balance in her treacherously high heels. If I remembered correctly, she'd been standing with Gabriel and another man at the bonfire last night. The shoes were what jogged my memory. I turned my attention back to the present and pushed Amy gently forward into the shop.

Taking off our sunglasses, I headed to the counter, where a woman was standing with her back to the door, rearranging some notices on a board on the wall.

I waited, trying to ignore the display of sweets in front of me. I couldn't possibly have some Maltesers, could I? Not after the huge breakfast I had troughed earlier. The woman turned around and smiled at me enquiringly.

My mind went blank. I really hadn't given much thought to how I was going to get any information out of Mrs Henderson. It hadn't occurred to me that I'd have to actually make up some lies. The Famous Five made it look easy. Surely, I was just as capable as four posh kids and a dog? I opened and closed my mouth before impulsively asking for the Maltesers and an Aero for Amy. We could eat them back at the pub. We were bound to get peckish later. Harry would have been disgusted if he'd been with us, but of course he wasn't with us. Not any more. It made me wince, thinking of his reaction, if he knew how much I'd already eaten that day.

'Good job Sophie's gone,' said the woman, who I assumed was Milly Henderson. She was short and plump, with shiny black hair and a round face. She had black eyebrows drawn on with a pencil, and they were rather too high and a little too curved, giving her a permanently surprised look. 'She would have given you a ten-minute lecture on the sin of eating chocolate.'

'Sophie?'

'The woman you just passed in the doorway, the one carrying all the fruit.'

'Oh, the teacher?'

The woman snorted. 'She's not a teacher. She runs Lightweights.' She pointed to a poster on the wall behind her that advertised a slimming club, which apparently held its meetings every Wednesday night at 7pm in Farthingdale Village Hall. 'Gets on my flipping nerves. Every time she's in here and someone wants to buy anything nice she gives them the whole flipping talk about calories or units, or whatever it is that daft club count. I wouldn't mind, but she's not exactly stick-thin herself. I mean, I'm the soul of discretion, but I can tell you she's not averse to the odd Walnut Whip.'

Crikey, I thought, did the food police get everywhere?

The woman took my money and handed over the chocolate. 'Are you on holiday here?' she enquired.

'Yes. I'm staying at The Hare and Moon, at least, for the time being.'

She raised one of her strange eyebrows. 'Hmm, Rhiannon's place? Rather you than me. Spooky building that one. Mind you, it's not surprising with that witch in charge. There's a lovely pub up at the top of the hill, you know. They do rooms, and there's a great restaurant there. I'm sure you'd be more comfortable in those surroundings, though there may not be any vacancies. It's very popular. Not like The House of Bone. Or there are plenty of holiday cottages, if you'd prefer self-catering. God knows there are enough of them.'

'It's no problem. I'm actually booked in at Amethyst Cottage for a month,' I said. 'I'm only at Rhiannon's for a few days.'

'Really? That's a long time for a holiday. Most people are only here a week or two.'

I faltered. She seemed suspicious already. I shrugged in what I hoped was a nonchalant manner, already sure that this was not the right woman to confide in. 'I suppose it is.'

'Is it just a holiday, then? Just you and the little one?'

Blimey, were all the locals this nosy? I hesitated, then remembered what the woman had just said about holiday cottages. A lightbulb flicked on above my head just like they do in cartoons. 'I'm here to look at property for sale. I was thinking I may get a second home up here.'

'Oh, right.' The woman nodded. 'I might have guessed. Well, there may be a few left, but you'll probably find they're more expensive than you imagine.'

'That doesn't matter,' I said. 'We live in London and we want our daughter to have somewhere she can spend her summers. You know, run around and have some adventures while she's still young.' God, the lies were tripping off my tongue now. I was quite impressed with myself.

'Talking of your daughter, did you know she's taken her shoes off?'

'What?' It took me a moment to register that Amy had sat down on the shop floor and removed her socks and shoes through sheer boredom, a habit she'd got into lately. I groaned and crouched down beside her, as the woman surveyed us, a thoughtful expression on her face.

'Well, you may find not everyone's as open-minded as me about your plans, love. I mean, nearly half of the properties around here are holiday lets now. Second-homers aren't popular with everyone, although no one can deny that they bring a lot of money into the village. Now, let me think, where would it be best for you to look? There are some estate agents in Whitby and Helmston who deal with property in this area, and I'm sure I've seen a couple of for sale signs.'

I rolled my eyes at Amy, who beamed up at me. It served me right for telling fibs. I was just wondering how long it would be before the woman stopped talking, when the shop door opened, and Gabriel Bailey strolled in. He was wearing faded blue jeans, and a white shirt which emphasised his broad shoulders. He looked down at me in surprise and then nodded politely. I noticed he had the most extraordinary blue-green eyes. Really, they were intense. I could imagine them piercing through darkness like rays from a lighthouse. I felt like they could puncture my soul with one glance.

I concentrated on fastening a wriggling Amy's shoe, my fingers suddenly finding it impossible to operate a simple buckle. Dratted acrylics.

'There's Beck Cottage, I'm sure of it. 'Course, it depends what you're looking for. I mean, did you want small and cosy, or were you looking for something grander? Like the ones Up Top?'

'I'm sorry, Mrs Henderson?' Gabriel said, as I struggled desperately with a reluctant toddler and an impossibly complicated shoe buckle. 'Do you need a hand with that?' he asked, and before I could answer, he crouched beside me, deftly fastened Amy's buckle and smiled at her, as she beamed back at him like he was her new best friend.

'Oh, I was talking to this lady,' said the shopkeeper. 'She's here hunting for a second home.'

'Really?' Gabriel's smile faded. He fastened the second shoe then straightened and turned back to the counter.

'I was just saying, I think Beck Cottage is up for sale. Do you know anything about it? Or can you think of any others around here?'

'I think,' he said, as he fumbled around in his pocket before counting out some change, 'that I should be the last person to answer that question.'

'Oh, come on, the lady just wants somewhere for her kiddie to spend the summers.'

'How nice for her.'

I stood, pulling Amy to her feet. Was that a flicker of disappointment I saw in his eyes? Why should he care what I was here for, anyway?

He slammed the change onto the counter beside a jar of coffee and glared at me. I decided he looked quite sexy when he was angry.

'If I had my way, second homes would be illegal. This place is dying, and the houses are getting more and more expensive to buy. What future is there for our children if they can't afford to live here? If you want a second home so badly, buy a caravan.'

Grabbing his jar of coffee, he stormed out of the shop, banging the door behind him. I realised my mouth was open and snapped it shut.

'I'm so sorry about that, love,' said Mrs Henderson. 'You don't want to take any notice of him.' She frowned, her pencilled eyebrows knitting together in a perfect curved letter M. 'I've never seen him like that. It's the second home thing, you see. Told you not everyone's as open minded as I am about it.'

I felt more rattled than I cared to admit. There was no need for him to go off like that. I'd done nothing wrong. I wasn't even interested in second homes and had no intention of moving up here — though, of course, he didn't know that. I was, after all, working undercover. The thought stirred something in me. This was turning into a real adventure. Having spent the last three years as a stay-at-home mum, where the most important decisions of the day were which recycling bin the chocolate wrappers should go into and whether to buy top-brand disposable nappies, or be really radical and go for the supermarket's own brand, the thought of my secret mission was unexpectedly thrilling.

'Thank you,' I said, deciding that it was time to be a bit more daring. 'He obviously has strong views about second homes. I take it he's a local?' Smoothly done, I thought, proudly.

Mrs Henderson considered. 'Sort of. Well, his parents live in Whitby, but his sister and her husband live in the village. That was her who you bumped into — Sophie. Her husband's a solicitor. They live at The Old Vicarage, Up Top. Did a lovely renovation on it, by all accounts, though I didn't know it when the church owned it. Only been here a few years meself. Gabriel, well, he arrived here about a year ago. Lived with Sophie for a few months then moved into one of Mrs Lovelace's cottages. Oh! Well, there's a coincidence, now I come to think of it. It was the one you've rented. The one she's renamed Amethyst Cottage now. Turfed him and Lexi out on the streets and turned it into a holiday let, 'cos it brings in more money, so now they're back at

Sophie's. No wonder he's fed up, really, is there?'

'Hell, I don't blame him for being angry.'

'Well, it's not your fault, is it? I mean, you didn't turf him out. It was that Mrs Lovelace. Four cottages she owns here now. Anyway, I'm sure he'll find somewhere else to rent soon enough, although he may have to go nearer Whitby. Trouble is, him and Lexi work locally so they won't want to move too far away.'

'I'd better get this one home before she takes off her shoes again,' I said, deciding that since Gabriel's family hailed from Whitby, there was no point in pursuing that line of enquiry. I led Amy to the door, and fixed her sunglasses in place before we went outside.

'See you soon,' called Mrs Henderson, 'and keep your chin up. I'm sure we'll be able to find you somewhere. I'll ask around.'

I gave her a feeble smile and led Amy out of the shop. 'Well, I've dropped myself well and truly in the doggy do there, haven't I?' I muttered, as we headed back to the pub. 'You see, Amy? This is what you get when you start telling fibs.'

She beamed up at me, and I bent down and kissed her, overwhelmed by a huge surge of love for her. 'You're so good,' I told her, 'even if you do take your socks and shoes off at the most inconvenient times.'

As I looked up, Gabriel stepped out of the chemist's shop. For a split second, he stared at me before crossing the road, no hint of an apology in his face.

'Looks like I've made an enemy there,' I muttered, putting my sunglasses on. 'Well, with any luck, we won't bump into him again.'

Chapter 8

With a big sigh, I leaned back in my chair and undid the button of my trousers. I was absolutely stuffed. First a full English breakfast, fish and chips on the bench outside the chippy for lunch, and now a huge tea of crab salad with some delicious local ice cream to follow. Harry would have been appalled, which cheered me up a bit. Thinking of Harry, I automatically reached into my bag and pulled out my mobile phone, my heart sinking as I saw there were no messages or missed calls.

I looked at Amy, whose face was now covered in melted ice cream. She even had some in her hair. I laughed, despite my depressed state. 'Did you enjoy that?'

Amy beamed and nodded. 'Like stwabewwy.'

'I think we'd better go upstairs and get all that washed off, don't you?'

Amy leapt off her chair immediately, and I could only marvel at her energy. After that long hike up and down the hill, and the amount of food I had shovelled down today, I had to force myself to my feet. I picked up my bag and stuffed my phone back inside it.

As soon as we got upstairs, I washed Amy and dressed her in clean pyjamas, then we flopped on the beds in exhaustion. Amy stared hopefully at the blank television screen. Eventually, with a monumental effort, I managed to stand up and switch the TV on. Dropping back down on the bed, I pointed the remote at the television until I found something that Amy would tolerate watching.

'I'll buy you some DVDs tomorrow,' I promised her, having spotted that the television had a built-in DVD player. I was just wondering if there was anywhere in the village that sold them, or if I'd have to drive to Helmston or Whitby, when I heard a muffled sound coming from my handbag. Sleigh bells. My stomach churned as I reached into my bag, for once managing to locate the phone before the sound stopped.

As I lifted it up, I felt a wave of nausea as I saw Harry's name on the screen. 'Hello?'

'Eliza! Thank fuck for that. I've been ringing nonstop for two bloody days.'

Funny that, since I'd checked my phone like someone possessed just about every hour on the hour, and there'd been nothing from him all day.

'Where the hell are you? Have you got my car?'

Surprise, surprise. The precious car. Not are you all right? Is Amy all right? I'm sorry for being such a complete ratbag and breaking your heart. Just, have you got my car? I tried to keep my voice steady.

'Yes, it's here. It's fine.'

'What do you mean, fine? Why did you take it? Is this your way of paying me back?'

'How could you say such a thing? What sort of person do you think I am?' I demanded, staring up at the ceiling and mouthing "sorry" to whichever deity happened to be listening to my outrageous lies.

There was a heavy sigh. 'Look, this has all got rather out of hand. Why did you do it?'

'Because I needed to get away, and my sodding car had a flat battery. It wasn't deliberate.' I was going to hell, no doubt about it. I was doomed to spend all eternity with murderers, tyrants and Melody Bird.

'Well, where are you? I'll bring your car to you and take mine back. Are you at Joe's? He's not picking up his phone now, either. He denied you were there, but he would, wouldn't he?'

'I'm not with Joe.'

'Well, where are you? I'll come and see you. Talk things over properly.'

'I'm up in North Yorkshire. Doubt you could spare the time.'

'North Yorkshire? What the fuck are you doing up there? Are you in Knaresborough?'

'No.'

'Well, where then? Why are you being so cagey?'

I was silent for a moment. 'I'm in Kearton Bay.' Huh, so much for keeping him guessing. I was such a pushover where Harry was concerned.

'Kearton Bay? Where the hell's that?'

I bit my lip. I should have known it would mean nothing to him. He never listened to a word I said. 'It doesn't matter. I'm not coming home, anyway, so you'll have to drive my car for a while.'

'What do you mean, you're not coming home? I need my car!'

'Tough,' I said. Why did he think I would give a damn what he needed?

His tone changed. 'Eliza, I know you're hurt and I'm sorry for that. Can't we at least try to keep it civil?'

Keep it civil? He'd broken my heart. Didn't he understand that?

His voice was wheedling. 'Please, darling. We can't just leave things like this. We need to talk; to discuss where we go from here. You must see that? We have Amy to think of, after all. We owe her that much.'

I closed my eyes. He was right about that, at least.

'I'm sorry for the things I said to you. I was angry and I just lashed out. I always attack when I'm under pressure. I'm not perfect.'

'You don't say?' I said. 'Who knew?'

'I mean it. I was cruel, I see that now. I should never have spoken to you like that.'

I took a deep breath. 'Harry, do you still love me?'

There was a long silence. 'I'm very fond of you. I'm just not in love with you any more. Do you see?'

Oh, I saw, all right. I ended the call and sat staring at the phone. It was only a few days ago he'd told me he loved me, and I'd had no reason to doubt it. When had he fallen out of love with me? What had I done wrong? I curled up on the bed and hugged the pillow, trying to hold back my tears, at least until Amy was asleep. It was going to be a long night.

****

The next day, I decided it was time to make the acquaintance of the MacLeans. Maybe things would be less fraught at the café this morning.

Rhiannon suggested that she look after Amy for half an hour, while she had her breakfast. 'It will be fun to have her, and I think you could do with a little time to yourself. Plus, the weather's not so good today. I think we may have rain before long.'

I nodded gratefully. I saw the look in Rhiannon's eyes and was almost certain that she knew the kind of night I'd had. Harry's phone call had stirred up too many painful emotions. After sobbing quietly into my pillow, I'd fallen asleep at one o'clock, only to wake at five. I'd stayed in bed, unable to turn on the television as I would disturb Amy and cursing myself for forgetting to pack a book. Desperate to take my mind off Harry, I'd reached into my bag for my mobile, thinking that perhaps I could play a game to pass the time, and my hands had closed around the bag of Maltesers. I'd forgotten all about them after my nasty encounter with Gabriel. Stomach rumbling, I'd opened them and eaten them all, ignoring the voice in my head, which kept telling me it was hardly a healthy breakfast and no wonder I was still trying to lose two stones of baby fat three years after giving birth.

At seven o'clock, after showering and dressing, I'd switched on the television, turning the volume down low, and found myself lying on the bed, guiltily breaking off chunks of the Aero that I'd bought for Amy. Now I felt sick, and the thought of eating any breakfast made me want to heave.

'Thanks, Rhiannon. If you don't mind that would be great.'

Although it wasn't yet nine and was quite overcast, the bay was already bustling with life. Derry had mentioned that there were still some locals who made a living fishing; many of them had turned to lobster catching, and dozens of lobster pots were stacked up against the side of the old lifeboat station, which stood opposite the pub and was now a museum. Some ex-fishermen made a living from taking people on fishing trips, while others had turned their boats into pleasure cruisers, taking sightseers for a tour of the bay and as far as Whitby and back.

Pinky's windows were wide open, and I could hear someone's dulcet tones long before I reached the café. 'You're a sodding waste of space, and you can either help me out today, or piss off and find some other mug to sponge off!'

I stopped dead in my tracks. They were still at it then? Whoever it was didn't sound in the mood for a cosy chat. Having said that, this was the second day running I'd heard arguing. Maybe if I waited for a lull in hostilities, I'd be waiting a long time. I decided to risk it.

I pushed open the café door and looked around me in astonishment. Blimey, this was the place to go if you wanted to know what a migraine felt like. I should have guessed from the name of the café. Bright pink painted walls glared at me, a vivid backdrop for the white plastic tables and chairs, and the pink and white checked tiled floor. Canvases of pale pink Cadillacs, strawberry milkshakes and pink iced cupcakes lined the walls. I would have guessed that the proprietor of this place had a bit of a thing for pink, even if I hadn't seen her standing behind the counter, wearing a pink T-shirt and sporting vivid pink streaks in her slightly frizzy dark hair. She obviously hadn't noticed me, as she was leaning in a doorway, shouting into the hallway behind it, which I guessed was probably part of her living quarters.

'I mean it, Fuchsia. If you don't get your lazy arse down here in five minutes, I'm gonna go up there and drag you out of that flaming bed.' She turned back to the counter with a sigh and started as she saw me standing there. 'Oh, shit! Sorry, bad day.'

'Obviously,' I said with a wry smile.

'Can I get you something? Stupid bloody question. You wouldn't have come in here if you didn't want something, would you?'

'Don't worry about it.'

For an awful moment, I thought she was going to cry, but to my relief she merely shut the door behind her and turned to a stack of menus at the side of the till. 'Haven't even had time to put these out on the tables yet,' she confided. 'Here, take one. Let me know when you've decided what you want.'

'Just a coffee would be fine,' I said. 'Why don't I put the menus out, while you fix my drink?'

'Oh, God, would you? Cheers,' she said, handing me a bundle of menus and giving me a grateful smile. 'Seriously, I'm not usually this fucked up. You've just caught me on a bad day.'

Five minutes later, we were both sitting at a table, drinking hot steaming coffee from — unsurprisingly — pink mugs. To my astonishment, she'd pulled up a chair and joined me. She was wearing denim shorts, thick black tights and Doc Marten boots, and obviously wasn't a conventional café owner, but at least her sitting with me would make it easier to strike up a conversation with her. My secret mission was back on.

'I'm sorry about that,' she said.

I noticed she had a north-eastern accent. I shook my head. 'Don't worry about it. It's nice to know I'm not the only one with problems.'

'Oh, trust me. I've got problems, all right. Bloody kids. You got any?'

'Just one. She's three.'

'Aw, lovely age. Pity they don't stay that way. You on holiday here, then?'

I nodded. 'Sort of.' Hell, was I going to get a lecture from this woman, too? Should I risk it? Well, no pain, no gain. 'I'm staying at Amethyst Cottage. At least, I will be, when the ceiling's fixed.'

'Oh, yeah.' The woman took a sip of her drink and laughed. 'Lydia Lovelace's big flood. Serves her right.'

'She doesn't seem to be popular.'

'Not in this village. Heard all about you. Mrs Jarvis isn't it?'

'Eliza.'

'I'm Rose. Rose MacLean. Heard you were a bit posh,' she

added frankly, looking at my diamond engagement ring and designer watch meaningfully.

'Hardly!'

'Swanky car, apparently. What are you doing in this café? You'd be better off at The Kearton Arms.'

I stared at her. It was hardly a way to attract customers, was it?

Rose laughed. 'I'm only joking, pet. You seem all right, to me. People here just love to gossip. You can't help having a swanky car. Well, I suppose you can, actually. Scrap that.'

'It's not my car.' Even as I said it, I was wondering why. Did Rose really need to know the embarrassing truth?

'Don't tell me. You pinched it!' Rose cackled at the thought, but her face dropped when she saw my expression. 'Away, man! You've nicked a bloody car? You don't look the type.'

I looked around, horrified. Luckily, there was no one else about to hear of my criminal behaviour. 'Not intentionally,' I whispered. 'It's my husband's car, and he wasn't around to ask. He'd, er, had a lot to drink the night before and, well, my car had a flat battery and I didn't have time to wait around.'

Rose squeezed my arm, suddenly brimming with sympathy. 'Did you do a runner? Was he beating you, pet?'

'No, nothing like that. I just had to get away.'

'Sodding men. Don't you worry, love. I won't ask questions. Nobody's business but your own. You said he'd been drinking? Alcoholic, is he? Nobody can blame you for getting away from that one.'

I blushed, wishing I'd never lied. 'No, he isn't an alcoholic. Honestly.'

'It's okay. My ex was a waste of space, too. I mean, he wasn't an alcoholic, or anything. He was a used car salesman.'

My confusion must have shown in my face.

'The bugger was a complete liar,' explained Rose. 'I didn't notice at first. It was quite flattering. He was a laugh, and it was all good for a few years. I thought we'd cracked it.' She sighed heavily.

'What happened?' I asked, enjoying listening to someone else's life story for a change, instead of dwelling on my own.

'He ran off with a librarian. I mean, honestly! A fucking

librarian! I don't think he'd ever read a book in his life. She was moving to Spain, and he moved with her.'

'God, I'm so sorry,' I said, genuinely.

'Oh, no, don't be.' Rose shrugged. 'Truth is, he was a big mistake. After I had Cerise, he practically kept me tied to the kitchen sink, and he was about as trustworthy as an MP, so it was a relief when he buggered off. Mind you, he could have done it sooner. He'd just sold the car business and bought this place. Said it was his dream to run a seaside café. Bloody librarian turned his head, and that was that. Still, at least he left me this place. The librarian was a rich widow, and he felt guilty about me and the kids, so he signed it all over to me. He was really getting on my wick by then, and God knows I'd flaming earned it. Besides, he was fucking ginger. Can you imagine how much that orange hair clashed with all the pink? It was never meant to be. So, you see, I do understand. Whatever your fella's done — and it's absolutely none of my business — you're probably better off without him. Was it drugs?'

I hid a smile. 'No. It wasn't drugs.'

'You probably did the right thing. I mean, I had to think about my kids. You've just got the one did you say?'

'Yes, one. Amy.'

'Aw, lovely name. So, you know what I mean. You have to protect them, don't you?'

I nodded, saying nothing.

She watched me thoughtfully. 'You don't have to discuss this, you know. It's no one else's business but your own. Too many busybodies around here. Keep yourself to yourself and don't feel obliged to talk about your private life to anyone. I learned that the hard way. I mean, if he was shagging around, that's not something you want to talk about to just anyone, is it?'

Something in my face must have betrayed me.

'Aw, I thought so.' Rose patted my hand kindly. 'Guessed straight away but didn't like to say. No need to look so terrified. It doesn't take a genius to work it out. Besides, no offence, but your eyes look like pissholes in the snow. You've been crying — a lot. Bet he worked with her, didn't he? They always shag the people they work with. Don't tell me she was his secretary? Bloody men. So predictable.'

I buried my head in my hands.

Rose sighed. 'Is it his secretary? It usually is.'

I shook my head, angrily blinking away tears. 'If only it were that simple.'

Rose tilted her head to one side, her brain apparently trying to compute all the possibilities that would make screwing his secretary seem simple.

'Jesus, is he shagging a bloke? It's okay, love. I won't tell a soul.'

I couldn't help laughing. 'No. It's not a bloke. It's — oh, hell. Have you heard of Melody Bird?'

Rose was silent for a moment, her face screwed up in concentration. 'Melody Bird? Rings a bell.' Her eyes opened wide as realisation dawned. 'You don't mean Miss-Grin-and-Bare-'Em? Her off that telly programme? The one with that gorgeous bloke, where they go around finding posh houses for rich numpties with more money than sense?'

I stared at her. Rose stared back. Then her mouth dropped open as the penny finally dropped. 'No way! Don't tell me you're married to — Harry Jarvis?'

I felt tears on my cheek. How embarrassing. 'Yes. At least, I am for the moment. I don't think I will be for much longer, though.' My voice caught.

'Oh, I'm sorry, pet. Don't cry. You shouldn't have told me if it upset you. I can't believe it. I'm in shock. It's like finding out that Kirstie and Phil have been at it on the set of *Location*. Not that they would. I mean, Kirstie's a nice girl, you can tell that just by looking at her, whereas Melody Bird is a well-known trollop. I don't know, there's no accounting for taste. I'll get you another coffee.'

She walked to the counter and busied herself pouring two more drinks. I rubbed my eyes and sniffed. Then I remembered the make-up and dabbed gently instead. The last thing I needed was black kohl down my face and dislodged eyelashes. What the hell was I doing confiding in a total stranger? More to the point, what the hell was I doing crying over Harry? He'd made it quite clear he no longer loved me, and if he was pathetic enough to succumb to that bimbo's dubious charms, why would I waste another tear on him? If only it were that easy.

'So, Miss-Grin-and-Bare-'Em,' called Rose. 'Strictly between you and me, of course — implants?'

I probably shouldn't but I began to laugh. 'Too right they are,' I confirmed. 'And she's had a nose job, and regular Botox injections.'

'I knew it,' said Rose triumphantly. 'She must be pushing forty, and a face like a fifteen-year-old.'

'She's forty-two,' I said smugly. 'If you watch each episode back-to-back, you can distinctly see her getting younger.'

Rose snorted and added milk to the coffees. 'If that programme keeps going for much longer, she'll look like a foetus.'

My smile dropped. 'It won't be long before she's got Harry getting fillers and God knows what else. He's paranoid about ageing. He'll be dyeing his hair next. That's the thing about television, you see. The hint of a grey hair, a wrinkle, or an extra pound is just the worst thing that could ever happen to you.'

I paused, the reality of what I'd just said sinking in. 'I really don't fit in with his world. Not like Melody. I'm probably the most unsuitable person ever to be married to a celebrity.'

Rose shook her head. 'I can't believe it. You married to Harry Jarvis. I mean, he's a good-looking bugger and he must be loaded, too. That programme's really popular. What's it called again? *Twice as Nice*, that's it. Fancy being married to him, of all people!'

'Well, that explains your interest in local property, I suppose.'

I froze. I knew without turning around that Gabriel had walked in. Fan-bloody-tastic.

'I'm sorry to disturb your scintillating conversation about second homes and property prices and celebrity husbands,' he continued, 'but would you mind if I cut in for a second? Lexi would like a vegetable quiche,' he said to Rose, who was glaring at him, 'if it's not too much trouble?'

'Who's rattled your cage?' she demanded.

'It's fine, Rose, honestly,' I said, jumping up and scraping back my chair. 'I was just going, anyway.'

'No, you weren't,' said Rose. 'Stay where you are.'

'Don't leave on my account,' said Gabriel. 'I've no intention of hanging around longer than necessary.'

Well, that put the tin hat on it. I'd just about had enough. Rose was right. Why the hell should I leave because of him? I strolled over to the counter and took the mug of coffee from Rose's hand like a true middle-class rebel.

'Not common instant, surely?' he asked smoothly.

I flushed. He seemed to really dislike me, and I couldn't think why. I was a nice person – apart from being a car thief and a spy, of course. It couldn't just be because I was staying in his old home, surely? It was hardly my fault his landlady had evicted them.

He raised an eyebrow as I turned to him, smiling sweetly, hoping he couldn't hear my heart pounding in my chest. I noticed he had some fine lines around his eyes, and a rather well-shaped nose. I imagined many women would find him extremely attractive. There were quite a lot of ridiculous females who fell for the brooding, moody look. Personally, those turquoise eyes, dark curls and chiselled cheek bones had no effect on me, whatsoever.

I suddenly realised I was staring, and blushed. His expression changed, somehow, as he watched me, seeming to take a mental photograph of me. I shifted uncomfortably, tugging my dress down a little in the vain hope of covering my knees, which Harry constantly assured me were on the podgy side. I wished I'd just walked out when I had the chance. Thank God I'd put my make-up on and done my hair. At least he couldn't criticise my appearance. Well, apart from the weight obviously, but I was working on that — eventually. There was a pause for what felt like forever, until Rose broke the silence.

'Are you paying for that, or what?' she demanded.

He paid and took the quiche from her hands, then strode towards the door. He paused and turned back to the counter, which I was now leaning on for support, my anger gone and my legs feeling like they'd had the bones removed.

'I almost forgot, Sophie asked me to remind you to bring your booklet tomorrow night, if that means anything to you. Apparently, you've forgotten for the last two weeks,' he said.

I looked round at him and swallowed nervously. Was I seeing things, or did his eyes keep straying to my behind?

'Oh, bugger,' said Rose. 'Yeah, I'll try to remember. Cheers.'

He nodded, his gaze flickering momentarily over to my rear again, then he turned and left the café, leaving me rather stunned.

'Did you see that?' I demanded. 'Did I imagine it, or was he—'

'Checking out your arse,' finished Rose. 'Totally.'

'I doubt it!' I spluttered. 'He looked stunned by the size of it. Did he have to make it so obvious?' I walked back to my table, mortified. So, I had a fat arse. Did he have to draw attention to the fact?

'Er, Eliza?' Rose bit her lip as I looked round. 'I hate to say this, but I think I know why he was looking. You appear to have chocolate smeared all over your bum. Jesus, I hope it *is* chocolate!'

I glanced over my shoulder and felt my face begin to burn with embarrassment. I must have sat on some of that flaming Aero. Oh, God, how humiliating. I stared at Rose in dismay. 'I will never, ever live this down,' I said. 'Of all people! He and I seem destined to cross swords for some reason.'

'Oh, never mind him,' said Rose, waving her arm impatiently. 'I want to hear all the goss about Melody Bird. And I mean all of it!'

****

Gabriel handed Lexi the quiche and sat down on a rock, suddenly weary.

'What's up with you?' she asked, putting the bag down beside him and pushing Cilla, one of the bossier donkeys, away from her, as she attempted to nudge inside her pockets.

'Nothing. Just tired.'

'Tired? It's only nine-thirty! Blimey, I know you're getting on a bit, but come on. We've got a full morning to get through yet!'

Her laughter died as she took in his expression. 'Are you sure you're okay, Dad?' she asked, scooping up the bag and sitting beside him.

'Yes, of course.' He looked at her and smiled. 'I'm fine, honestly. Stop worrying about me.'

'Can't help it,' she told him with a nudge. 'It's my job.'

'I think you'll find it's supposed to be the other way around.' He laughed. 'Oh — customers.'

He nodded as a young woman with two toddlers walked towards the donkeys. Lexi jumped up and began to busy herself, sitting the children on the backs of Freddie and Blackberry, two of the smaller donkeys. Gabriel watched as they began to walk along the sands, the children squealing in excitement.

He really had to get a grip. He couldn't believe how much Eliza's arrival in Kearton Bay had unsettled him. The smell of Chanel No 5, the immaculate hair, the thick make-up, the expensive jewellery and Chloé handbag — it was all frighteningly characteristic of Zoe.

He'd hoped coming back here, starting again with a new job, close to his family and with less pressure on him, things would ease, and for a while there, he'd thought it was working. Pottering around Hannah's farm was easy, compared with his previous work, and no one pointed at him or judged him there. He'd thought that he and Lexi could settle in the cottage and begin to heal. Then Mrs Lovelace had dropped her bombshell, and now Eliza Jarvis was swanning around the place, reminding him of things in his past that he'd really rather forget. He wondered what had upset her. He'd noticed the swollen eyelids and realised she'd been crying. It had quite unnerved him, and he hadn't known what to say after that. If she thought she had problems, she ought to try living his life.

He stood up, as a plump woman, with a child of around six, wandered up to him, an anxious look on her face. 'The donkeys, are they tame? They won't gallop away with him, or anything?'

'These little fellas? No, don't worry about that. They're plodders,' he assured her.

Like me, he thought as he hoisted the little boy into the saddle.

Plodding through life, doing the same thing day after day and getting no further on. This wasn't him, Hannah was right. He had to do something — and soon.

85

Chapter 9

That afternoon, as predicted, the heavens opened, and Kearton Bay was subjected to torrential rain. Luckily, I'd remembered to bring Amy some of her favourite books, which kept her occupied as I paced restlessly round the room, pausing occasionally to peer out of the window, to stare up at the bleak sky and wonder what the hell Harry was getting up to.

Joe had called me, but the signal was terrible, and he kept getting cut off. He was obviously in a hurry, too, as his show was live that night and he was busy with rehearsals. When he finally admitted defeat and yelled, 'See you when I can, love!' before hanging up, I felt even more lonely and wretched. I missed him. I missed Mrs Travers, too, and even the thought of Jeeves and Wooster made me ache for home.

What was I doing here, anyway? I'd come here chasing after a father I'd never met, running away from a husband who'd broken my heart. It was depressing to realise that my whole life was a reaction to the dishonourable actions of the two men who should have cared for me most, but if I went home, things would be just the same as they ever were. The fact that Harry had asked after his car, and not his daughter, made that pretty clear.

With no sign of the rain stopping, Amy and I had our evening meal in the pub and then wandered back upstairs, where I got her ready for bed. After reading her a story, I tucked her under the duvet and then, as she drifted off to sleep, put the television on at low volume and settled down on my bed to watch the soaps until Joe's show came on.

My mind drifted over the events of the last few days, and I wondered what I was going to do about finding my father. For all I knew, he was walking around Kearton Bay right now. I could well have passed him on the street or had a meal in the dining room of The Hare and Moon, while he sat at a table next to me or drank a pint at the bar. I had so little to go on.

My parents had met when Mum was a student at Leeds University. Joe knew little about their romance, as she had been reluctant to discuss it when she finally came home, pregnant and heartbroken. He said my grandparents wanted to find my father and "beat the living crap" out of him, but Mum wouldn't give them any information. She'd confided in Joe that his name was Raphael. She'd called him her angel and said he came from Kearton Bay but had left there after an argument with his father. I had no idea what he did for a living, what his surname was, or if he'd ever gone back to Kearton Bay. I knew it was a real long shot and my only cause for optimism was his unusual name. Surely, someone would remember him?

I thought about Rose. She'd said that she came from an inner-city estate and had only lived in the village for two years. She didn't appear to have any emotional attachment to anyone from here. If I confided in her, I wasn't likely to hurt her or cause any problems. Plus, she ran a café and was bound to know lots of people. Surely, if there was a Raphael still living in the area she would have heard of him?

I decided that she was the person to confide in. She already knew about Harry and Melody, so she may as well know the whole lot. I would visit her again tomorrow and start the ball rolling. That decided, I felt much better by the time *The Joe Hollingsworth Show* started at nine o'clock.

Joe looked tired, I thought. He worked way too hard, always filming, promoting, or making guest appearances on panel shows and other people's chat shows. He was also writing his autobiography and had a looming deadline for that. He was under a lot of pressure, and I wished he would ease off. Yet, he was ever the professional, cracking jokes and making everyone feel at ease. Judging by the clapping and whooping coming from the audience at the end of the show, he'd done his usual fantastic job, even pretending to admire the crap band Tuna Sandwich, who made my ears bleed when they performed their latest song. I was so proud of him, not least for his acting skills. I sent him a text, telling him what a fabulous show it had been and how much I'd enjoyed it, and then I tried to settle down to sleep.

I'd almost succeeded, when I heard whispering outside my door and the sound of another door creaking open. I recognised Rhiannon's voice, but the other one didn't sound like Derry and there were no other guests at the moment. After twenty minutes, there was some giggling and then a very different kind of noise. My eyes opened wide. Rhiannon obviously had a guest of her own, and their meeting wasn't something I wanted to eavesdrop on. I wrapped the pillow around my head, trying to muffle the sound. These walls and doors were ancient, and not exactly thin. Whoever Rhiannon was with, they weren't being quiet about it.

I must have bobbed off eventually, but I slept fitfully. I kept waking up every couple of hours, checking my phone. Eventually, I realised I needed the loo and climbed carefully out of bed, hoping not to disturb Amy. As I gently opened the bedroom door, I almost leapt back in fright as I made out two figures creeping along the landing. It was Derry, who appeared to be fastening his jeans, and the May Queen who was padding behind him, her shoes in one hand, stifling a giggle. I waited until they'd crept down the stairs and then rushed to the bathroom. Had it been Derry that the May Queen had been meeting secretly on the beach the other night?

After climbing back into bed a few minutes later, I checked my phone again. Five-thirty. They all had more energy than I had. What with Rhiannon and her mystery lover, and now Derry and the May Queen, it was like living in a *Carry On* film, only I wasn't in the mood for laughing.

****

Rose was thrilled to hear all about my secret mission. She'd fussed over Amy, made her a banana milkshake and poured us both a coffee, then sat down at the table beside us. I looked around in surprise. There were no other customers — again. Maybe the rain was putting people off, although, quite honestly, I doubted many people could cope with the decor.

Rose spent ten minutes telling me all about Fuchsia's surly behaviour and her reluctance to go to college that morning.

'I wouldn't care,' she said, 'but she'll be bloody lucky to get a job at all. Round here, they're as rare as rocking horse shit. Most people have to try Helmston or Whitby to find work. The least she can do is attempt to get some decent qualifications. Can't even be arsed to walk to the bus stop Up Top, never mind go to college.'

I'd learnt that Kearton Bay was a village of two parts. The part that straddled down the cliff and huddled round the bay itself was known as Old Town, due to its great age, and the part that sat at the top of the cliff and bordered Farthingdale was known as Up Top. This consisted of more modern buildings, mostly Victorian villas built when the railway came to the area, although Derry had told me that there was no train line here now and the old track was used as a bridle path and footpath, with the old station turned into a restaurant. The Kearton Arms had been constructed during that golden era. Apart from the twelfth century church and Elizabethan Kearton Hall, most of the other buildings Up Top were fairly modern.

The village was larger than I'd realised, and I knew it was going to be even harder than I'd imagined to find my father without help, so when Rose finally paused for breath in her rant against her errant daughter, I broke the news to her about the real reason I was in Kearton Bay.

'Fancy not knowing who your father is! Mind you, Fuchsia's never met hers, either, although she knows his name and she's looked him up on Facebook. Took one look at his ugly mug and never bothered again. At least she knows who he is, and how to find him if she wants to. Imagine not even knowing that.'

I reached into my bag and brought out a tissue, mopping up the milkshake that Amy had managed to slurp over the table. She'd discovered that if she blew into a straw, rather than sucked on it, she could make a mountain of bubbles that would rise up in her glass and flow over like lava from a volcano, which seemed much more fun than actually drinking the stuff. Rose darted over to the counter and grabbed some serviettes to mop up the rest.

'So, what do you know about him, then?'

She ran her hand through her thick hair, unwittingly dragging half of it across her parting and leaving one of her pink streaks standing up like the crest of an exotic bird. She looked at me with excited grey eyes that were rimmed with smoky black kohl. She was wearing massive hoop earrings that must have felt like rocks hanging down from her lobes. I thought how pretty she was, in a rather individual way.

'Do you have any family in the village at all, Rose?' I just wanted to check, to be absolutely certain that I wasn't going to hurt her. 'I mean, apart from the girls, obviously.'

Rose shook her head. 'Nope. All my family are from Oddborough. Told you.'

'Well, all I know about him is that he was from here and left after an argument with his father. He met my mother in Leeds. She was a student, but I've no idea what he was doing there, and his name was Raphael.'

She was silent for a moment, dipping her little finger in her coffee and tracing patterns in the liquid as she thought. Slowly, the pink crest peeled down into its rightful position. I waited, wondering if she was mentally going through every resident she knew, trying to recall anyone of that name. Then she raised her eyes to mine and I saw they were quite troubled.

'Eliza, do you remember the bloke that was so rude to you here yesterday?'

I nodded, a feeling of dread suddenly upon me. 'Gabriel Bailey? Of course. Why?'

'Well, yeah, Gabriel — the name of an angel. And the thing is, Eliza, the thing is, I think he may be your brother.'

Chapter 10

It was Saturday when I got the call that I could move into Amethyst Cottage.

Rhiannon seemed sorry to see us go. 'I'm going to miss you. It's been lovely having you to stay.'

Now that I thought about it, I realised I would quite miss The Hare and Moon, even though the nightly shenanigans were proving to be a bit much. If it wasn't Derry and his redheaded girlfriend sneaking around, it was Rhiannon and her mystery lover hammering the headboard. Thank God Amy was a heavy sleeper. It was a pity my own problems kept me awake so much, otherwise I might have been able to sleep through all the comings and goings in the pub.

Night after night, I had lain awake, trying to untangle the mess that my life seemed to have become. Mrs Travers had reluctantly called me, all too aware that I'd want information about Harry, and sure enough, I'd demanded to know what was going on back in London.

'Getting on my nerves,' she informed me. 'He's moping around and keeps checking his phone every five minutes and sighing a lot.'

'He hasn't moved out?' My pathetic heart had leapt in hope.

'Says it's a security risk, leaving the house empty.' There was a silence, and then she confessed, '*She's* been here.'

I'd almost thrown the phone against the wall, but then remembered that if I did I'd never know what happened, so controlled myself.

'Don't worry, he wouldn't let her in. Though that could be 'cos I was there. Said she was giving him a lift to a meeting, 'cos he couldn't face driving your Fiesta. She had a face like thunder. All's not rosy there, if you ask me.'

'Really? What was wrong with her?'

'Who am I, Miss Marple? All I know is, they were talking in very unfriendly tones, and he's snapping at me like a blooming alligator. I've had enough. I'll be glad to go to my sister's, for a rest, truth to tell.'

Joe had also rung me, sounding weary. 'I'm coming to see you next week,' he promised. 'Just getting the last show out of the way and then I'm free — well for a few days anyway. Is there a spare room in that cottage, or will I take the sofa?'

'There's a room, don't worry. It will do you good to get away.'

'Any progress with the mission?'

'Actually, yes. I'll tell you more when I see you,' I told him mysteriously.

'Oh, hell, sounds ominous. All right, if you insist. Just don't get your hopes up, and be careful, love. Promise?'

'Promise.'

And I *was* being careful, sort of. Rose had taken complete charge and had come up with a plan of action, while I still reeled from the possibility that the man who I seemed destined to keep running into may, in fact, be my brother. Well, half-brother, at any rate.

'But, how do you know?' I'd demanded as Rose took a sip of coffee and studied my face for signs of hysteria. 'I mean, this is crazy.'

'I know. Good job he wasn't really checking out your arse, eh? Think how disgusting that would have been.'

I had to concede that things had worked out well on that score and thank God I hadn't fallen for that brooding look. How embarrassed would I be feeling right now?

'It's the name, Raphael. I mean, come on, it's not exactly common, is it? I only know 'cos of Sophie. She runs the slimming club in the village. Lightweights. That's what Gabriel was on about, when he said I'd forgotten my booklet. It's my weight record booklet. I forget it on purpose sometimes, hoping she'll forget what I weighed, but she never bloody does. Anyway, she's a chatty sort. We were all on about families one night, and she couldn't wait to brag about hers. Archie, he's the husband, he's personal solicitor to Sir Paul at Kearton Hall, no less, and her dad used to be the doctor here, Dr Raphael Bailey. Apparently, all the men in her family were named after angels until Archie put his foot down. Her dad and his dad were both Raphael, and her poor great-grandfather was Uriel, can you believe? Anyway, like I say, her dad's Raphael, and to be honest, Eliza, I can't imagine there being two of them in this village, can you?'

I felt a bit sick. 'No. Not likely. So, this Raphael — I think Mrs Henderson said he lived in Whitby?'

Rose nodded. 'I think Sophie mentioned that they live there now, yeah. I can't really recall 'cos, obviously, it didn't seem important at the time. It's her you need to talk to. It shouldn't be difficult. She loves bragging about her family.'

'And how do I do that without arousing suspicion? I've only met her once, very briefly.'

'She's chatty enough. Tell you what, why don't you join Lightweights with me? Come along on Wednesday. It's a bit pricey, and it's full of bonkers women who think dieting is the most important thing on earth but at least you'll get to meet her.'

'What about Amy?'

Rose frowned. 'I suppose I could ask Fuchsia. Mind you, I wouldn't even trust her to look after Cerise. It's usually the other way around. She's only twelve, but she's got more brains than Fuchsia.' She thought for a moment then her face brightened. 'Bingo! You could ask Lexi!'

'Lexi?' Vaguely, I recalled Gabriel asking for a quiche for someone of that name. A horrible thought occurred to me. 'She's not tall, red headed? The village May Queen?'

'That's her. Have you met her? Nice girl.'

'Really? Is she his girlfriend?'

'Whose girlfriend?'

'Gabriel's?'

Rose snorted. 'Course not! She's his bloody daughter.'

I almost choked on my coffee. 'His daughter! He's — he's married?' Funny how the thought hadn't even occurred to me.

Rose shrugged. 'Not sure, to be honest. If he is, they're not together any more. He arrived back in the village about a year ago with Lexi, and they moved in with Sophie and Archie. No sign of any wife.' She looked thoughtful. 'Come to think of it, he's a bit of a black sheep.'

'Meaning?'

'Well, come on. His father's a doctor, his brother-in-law's a solicitor. They live in this swanky house, and Sophie can't brag about them enough, but Gabriel — well, he builds rabbit hutches, and walks up and down the beach, taking kids for donkey rides.'

'He does what?'

I couldn't believe it. Gabriel was so commanding. He was intelligent, well-spoken and quite intimidating at times. I couldn't imagine him doing such menial jobs for a living. Not that there was anything wrong with doing menial jobs. I mean, I greatly admired a man with a well-stocked toolbox, but it just didn't seem like him, somehow. I suppose I should have guessed, seeing that he was always dressed in jeans when I saw him, but for some reason I'd always imagined him behind a desk, or something. He just struck me that way. Not that I thought about him much.

Rose obviously read my thoughts. 'I know. Odd. I don't know where he was living before he came back here, but he can't have had a decent job there, either. I mean, he's looking for rented accommodation. You'd have thought Sophie's brother would, at the very least, have been able to buy his own place. When you meet Sophie, you'll know what I mean.'

'So, how can I ask Lexi to babysit? Won't it look a bit odd? I've never even spoken to her. Is she trustworthy?'

I doubted it, remembering the girl sneaking around the landing at The Hare and Moon, but Rose was certain she was a decent person.

'Lovely girl, Lexi. Says what she thinks. I like that. She's got a card in Henderson's window, advertising a babysitting service. It would be perfectly reasonable for you to call her and ask her to mind Amy while you go to Lightweights with me. What do you say? And, if you think about it, you can possibly wangle more information from her, too. Get friendly with her, get chatting over a coffee. Who knows what little gems she may be able to tell you?'

It had sounded shamefully devious, but I'd had to admit, it was a good plan, so I'd called the number on the card, and Lexi had confirmed that she would indeed be able to babysit on Wednesday evening and would be at Amethyst Cottage at six forty-five.

So, with all those plans and plots swirling around in my head, I was quite relieved to be in the cottage. I needed space to think, and away from the crowded Old Town, I may finally get it.

****

You wouldn't know anything had been amiss in Amethyst Cottage. The floor was dry and clean, the ceiling re-plastered and painted and the kitchen immaculate. Amy was thrilled to have her own bedroom again, and I was pretty pleased about it, too. It was also wonderful to have a kitchen. It's funny what you take for granted. I opened and closed the fridge door and ran my hands over the gas hob, thinking of all the things I could buy and cook.

I'd contacted Sophie who'd been delighted that I wanted to join Lightweights. 'How disciplined of you to start dieting on your holidays! We're a friendly bunch here, nothing to worry about.'

Rose showed me her booklets, revealing that she hadn't even studied them properly herself. I wasn't sure why she was going to the club, because she didn't seem to care about losing weight and she certainly wasn't counting units.

'It's a night out,' she said, when I asked her why she bothered. 'Sod all else to do around here unless you can afford to go to the pub, and I need at least one night away from this bloody building.'

I suppose it was hard for her, living above the café. She never really got to go anywhere, and I got the distinct impression that money was tight. Pinky's was never busy, even on the sunniest days when the other teashops were heaving. I reckoned the decor was too much to cope with and, to be honest, the food wasn't the best either. I'd braved some of Rose's scones, and they were pretty vile, though I would never dream of saying so. She'd been so good to me, and frankly, if her idea of a night out was a meeting at the local slimming club, she needed all the support she could get. It wasn't my idea of fun, but beggars couldn't be choosers, and neither, apparently, could undercover agents.

****

'And you must be Amy?' Lexi shook Amy's hand solemnly. Amy grinned and that was that. They'd bonded. I could see my daughter was going to be quite happy being looked after by her.
'There's food in the fridge if you're hungry,' I told her. I wasn't joking. I'd driven to Sainsbury's on the Saturday afternoon and loaded the boot of Harry's car with all my favourite food. Now I was panicking because it was Wednesday and my diet started tonight, and I still had lots of tempting stuff in the fridge. Hopefully, Lexi would scoff some of it and get it out of my way, but looking at her, I doubted it.
She was undeniably pretty, with beautiful, glossy red hair, falling almost to her waist, a slender figure, creamy skin and large turquoise eyes. She also had long, long legs. It was quite sickening, really. I felt like a Pug standing next to a Red Setter.
'So, you're going to Lightweights?' she asked, plonking herself down on the sofa and putting her feet up as if she was at home, which I suppose she was, sort of. I'd forgotten she used to live in that very cottage. I felt a sudden sympathy for her. It couldn't be easy losing your home and having to live with relatives.
I nodded, and she rolled her eyes.
'Sophie — the group leader — is my aunt,' she informed me. 'I warn you now, she takes losing weight very seriously.'
'Really? Well, I suppose it's her job.'

96

'Yeah, bit much, though, when you live with her. She bangs on about units during every flipping meal.'

'You live with her?' I said, trying to sound surprised.

'Yes. Well, for now, at least. She's lovely really. She'll look after you.' She frowned. 'Bit weird, though, isn't it? Joining a slimming club on your holidays?'

'Well, look at me. I have to do something about this,' I said, indicating my podgy stomach.

She looked. 'Yeah, I suppose so,' she said.

Charming. She had some of her father's personality, then, as well as his eye colour. I wondered what her mother was like. What sort of woman would Gabriel Bailey fall for?

'Sorry. That sounded rude,' she said. 'I didn't mean it to come out like that. I was just agreeing with you. Always speak before putting my brain into gear. It's a family trait, I'm afraid.'

I wondered if she was talking about her father, her aunt, or both. Amy was all ready for bed in her new polka dot pyjamas, bought in Whitby on Saturday.

'Is she okay to stay up for a while?' asked Lexi.

'Well, yes, I suppose. Wouldn't you rather I put her to bed?'

'No, it's cool,' said Lexi. 'We've hardly had chance to get to know each other, have we, Amy?'

Amy shook her head. 'Can I watch a DVD?'

Lexi eyed her suspiciously. 'Hmm. Depends. Which DVD are we talking about?'

'*Ice Age*?' suggested Amy, hopefully.

'Fabulous,' said Lexi. 'My absolute favourite! Do you want to find it for me?'

Amy didn't need telling twice. She scrambled down from the sofa and shot over to the television cabinet, where I had put the handful of DVDs I'd purchased on Saturday. I smiled. My daughter would be in safe hands while I was away from her.

'I'd get off now while she's occupied,' Lexi whispered, obviously a seasoned babysitter. I nodded and headed for the door, my stomach fluttering as I prepared to meet the next member of my family.

****

'Hell, is this for real?'

We were inside Farthingdale Village Hall, which was an old stone building down Station Lane. I'd never been down there before. Rose told me the lane led to Farthingdale, and that if we went a little further, we'd see Sophie's house on the left-hand side and behind it the church of St Hilda's, whose vast churchyard bordered Sophie's garden. The lane apparently narrowed after The Old Vicarage and was surrounded on both sides by tall trees, but Rose told me the surgery was tucked away down there, closer to Farthingdale's centre than Kearton Bay really.

The village hall lay between the station and the vicarage, so it was quite a hike to get there. It had been bad enough struggling up that sodding hill again, arriving at the doors of the hall with my hair plastered with sweat, my make-up no doubt smudged where I'd rubbed my face to wipe the perspiration away, but now I was faced with a group of women who wouldn't look out of place in a Victoria Wood sketch.

'Who the hell's that?' I asked, nudging Rose and nodding at an extraordinary looking young woman who was wearing — inexplicably — a hat with woollen plaits attached. She was peering at a booklet in her hand and telling anyone who'd listen that she'd just been weighed and had lost four pounds that week.

'Clarissa,' whispered Rose. 'Compulsive liar. To my knowledge, she hasn't lost an ounce since she started.'

I looked round the hall, trying to avoid eye contact with my fellow fatties. We all stood, waiting to be weighed like naughty schoolchildren. I could hear them nervously joking that they'd cut their toenails and plucked their eyebrows ready for the scales. I wondered if I could plead that the hairspray and make-up weighed half a stone alone?

When I finally reached the desk where Sophie was sitting beside another woman, I was sweating so much I'd probably lost that half a stone, anyway.

Sophie smiled up at me. 'Eliza? So glad to see you here. Now, let's see what the damage is, shall we?'

I stepped reluctantly onto the scales and waited while Sophie peered over at the screen. She looked up at me and nodded sympathetically, wrote something inside the new member's booklet I'd been handed when I'd arrived, and passed it back to me.

I looked at her writing and gasped. 'Are you sure?'

'It's always a shock, but the scales are accurate, honestly.'

'It's not a shock. It's a surprise. I've lost five pounds since I came here.'

She peered at me. 'Really? Well, that's lovely. Still, more work to be done yet, eh?'

Rose grinned, and I picked up my bag and moved along to pay the woman sitting beside Sophie, who was taking the membership fees. I didn't understand it. It was the first time in years I hadn't watched every mouthful I ate and just stuffed down what I fancied. How the hell had I managed that?

The woman taking my money wasn't much of an advertisement for Lightweights. She was fat, to be blunt, and didn't look as if she'd dieted in her life. She had a round, smiley face and sparkling brown eyes and a dark bob, and her face dimpled when she spoke.

'Welcome to Lightweights, Eliza. I'm Meggie. Have a look through the booklet, which will explain the diet to you, and after the meeting, Sophie will sit with you and go through it all properly.'

I smiled faintly and paid my money, then hunted for a couple of empty chairs. I plonked myself down on one and flicked through the booklet till Rose arrived.

'How did you do?' I asked her, as she sat down next to me.

'Eh? Oh, stayed the same,' she said casually. I got the feeling she didn't give a monkey's, one way or the other.

After an interminable half hour, during which the door opened and closed endlessly and a parade of women of all shapes and sizes traipsed into the hall to be weighed, Sophie finally clapped her hands and announced that she was ready to begin the meeting.

'Now what happens?' I whispered.

'Oh, watch and learn, kid,' said Rose, rolling her eyes.

Sophie went around all the members individually, pointing out their weight loss or gain, and we all had to clap or commiserate, depending on the circumstances. When all the smugness or hand-wringing was over, Sophie introduced me to the group.

'This is Eliza. She's a new member and she's here on holiday from London.'

There was a muttering, and everyone turned to stare at me as if she'd informed them I was from a newly-discovered tribe in the Amazon rainforest.

'I went to that there London once,' said one woman. 'Wouldn't go again. Filthy place.'

I opened my mouth but then closed it again, remembering I was undercover. Undercover agents always kept their cool.

Sophie then began to talk about the diet, and my eyes glazed over. How did they all do this week after week? It was boring as hell. I stifled a yawn as some woman moaned that she couldn't resist buying boiled sweets every time she went to the shops.

Sophie nodded sympathetically. 'I can imagine it's difficult. I don't have a sweet tooth myself, but I'm sure it's a tough one to deal with,' she said.

I remembered what Mrs Henderson had said about the Walnut Whips and pursed my lips just like Mrs Travers. Sophie was telling fibs.

'Has anyone got any suggestions that would help Faith?' she enquired, beaming round at the group. Everyone shrugged and stared at the floor. Then Clarissa, the woolly plait woman, stuck her hand up.

'Yes, Clarissa?'

Clarissa looked primly round at everyone. 'When I have a sweet craving, I freeze some grapes. If you suck them one at a time they taste just like boiled sweets.'

I stared at her, wondering if she was taking the mickey. Beside me, Rose snorted.

'What bollocks,' she said.

Sophie glanced over at her. 'Sorry Rose? Did you say something?'

Rose sighed. 'Let's face it, life's too short to freeze grapes, Clarissa.'

'Well, if it works for Clarissa then we shouldn't knock it,' said Sophie. 'Each to their own. What about you, Eliza?'

I started. 'Eh?'

'Have you got any tips to stop Faith from buying boiled sweets?'

I thought about it. 'Er, make your own?'

Rose snorted again. She was beginning to sound like *Peppa Pig*. Sophie frowned. 'Make your own?'

'Make your own sweets?' asked someone, suddenly interested. 'What kind of sweets?'

I shrugged. 'All sorts,' I said. 'Toffees, chocolates, marshmallows, boiled sweets — it's not difficult when you know how.'

'Really? Do you make them, then?'

They were all looking at me now, suddenly interested.

'Well, yes. I used to make them all the time. Not so much, these days. Still trying to lose baby weight.'

They looked at me sympathetically, obviously able to relate. All except Clarissa, who was staring at me as if she would like to sprinkle me with holy water, and Sophie, who looked distinctly uneasy, sensing rebellion in the ranks.

'Yes, well, that's lovely. Has anyone else any tips for treats that won't pile the weight on?'

'Do you make fudge?' asked Meggie suddenly.

'Oh, yes, fudge is easy,' I said.

'Would you make me some?'

'Meggie!' Sophie sounded close to meltdown. I winked at Meggie and tried to give her a subtle nod, but when I turned back to the front of the room, Sophie was glaring at me. I'd already blotted my copybook with my possible half-sister. Better start getting into her good books.

'What about you, Sophie?' I asked. 'You obviously know what you're doing. What would you recommend?'

She looked thrilled.

'Nicely saved,' whispered Rose, as Sophie began to rabbit on about — well, rabbit food. Cucumber sticks and low-fat dips and bloody melon balls. It was too late, now. All I could think about was fudge.

Eventually, the hour was over, and we all scraped back our chairs after promising to stick to the diet all week. The rest of the class filed out, and Sophie called to me to wait a moment and she would be there to give me "the talk".

'I'll wait with you,' said Rose. I think my secret mission had given her something to look forward to at last.

Sophie and Meggie faffed around a bit, sorting money and packing stuff away, and then Sophie sat with me, while Meggie started heaving boxes of Lightweights' products into Sophie's car. Guilt got the better of Rose, and she went to help her, while Sophie began telling me all about the diet.

She yakked on about traffic lights and units and other dreary stuff, and I nodded and smiled and tried to sound interested, but all I could think about was how to get any information about her family from her. Rose had assured me that Sophie was inordinately proud of her relatives and it didn't take much to get her started.

Eventually, she stopped talking and asked me if I had any questions.

'Not really,' I muttered, having gone blank on the subject ten minutes ago. I looked up in relief, as Rose returned with Meggie and sat beside me.

'All clued up now, then?' she asked.

'She certainly is,' said Sophie. 'I'm sure she'll do well and have an excellent weight loss next week. Such a shame she has to go back home after that. How are you enjoying your holiday?'

'Oh, it's been fun,' I said. 'Kearton Bay's a lovely place.'

'Isn't it?' she said proudly. 'Of course, it's changed a lot in the last few years. Far too many holiday-lets, nowadays, and not enough locals, no offence. Still, we've managed to retain the character of the place. You won't find any kiss-me-quick hats or dreadful amusement arcades here, thank God.'

Rose winked at me. 'Eliza's staying at Amethyst Cottage, Sophie. Used to be Gabriel's place, didn't it?'

Sophie scowled. 'It did, though it didn't have a name then. What that woman did was outrageous. Please don't take this as an attack on you, Eliza, but that was my brother's home, and he was thrown onto the streets, so she could make more money renting it to tourists. It's disgusting. He was devastated.'

'I know,' I said. 'I've met him.'

Her face lit up. 'You've met Gabriel? When?'

'Several times, actually. I think we got off on the wrong foot. He doesn't approve of my staying at Amethyst Cottage.'

'Oh, don't take it personally. Gabriel's a darling,' she assured me. She looked at me, seeming to see me properly for the first time. 'So, are you married, Eliza?'

Well, that was a change of subject. 'Er, yes, I am,' I said, looking at my wedding and engagement rings and wondering how she'd missed that huge, ugly rock. Subtle it wasn't.

'Oh.' She looked downcast for a moment then stood up. 'Well, I'd better be getting off home. Archie will be wondering where I am.'

Rose and I looked at each other. She'd obviously lost interest in me.

'Actually, Sophie,' said Rose suddenly, 'Eliza's married to Harry Jarvis. You know, the television presenter from *Twice as Nice*?'

I glared at her. What the hell had she said that for? The last thing I needed was people banging on about Harry, especially with the way things were between us. Sophie sat down again and stared at me in delight.

'Really? Harry Jarvis? Oh, my God, he's divine! I love that programme! And isn't Melody Bird lovely? Such beautiful hair. I voted for it at the National Television Awards, you know. The programme, I mean, not the hair. Is Harry going to be joining you?'

'I'm, er, not sure. He may come up for a brief visit. He's very busy.'

'Oh, I can imagine. It's hard being married to a successful man, isn't it? My husband, Archie, is personal solicitor to the Boden-Keans, up at Kearton Hall. Of course, the benefits are enormous, but it's difficult to be alone so much. I can relate.'

'Sophie lives at The Old Vicarage,' said Rose, as if I didn't already know. 'It's a beautiful place, isn't it, Sophe?'

Sophie looked at her in undisguised delight. 'Thank you, Rose. Of course, we had to do a lot to it. It was a bit of a wreck when we bought it, just the sort of thing your husband would appreciate, Eliza. He used to do that programme about renovations, didn't he? We found him so inspiring. You must come over and see what we've done with the place one day.'

'Oh, I'd love to,' I said quickly. 'It sounds amazing.'

'Bring your daughter, too. How old is she?'

'Three,' I said. 'Lexi's babysitting for her right now.'

'Oh, of course she is. Well, she's in good hands. Lexi's a lovely girl. She was the village May Queen, you know.'

I nodded. 'Hard not to recognise her with that gorgeous hair.'

Sophie sighed. 'Yes, it is quite striking.'

'She didn't get it from her father, though,' I said, pushing it all I could. 'He's quite dark, isn't he? Are your parents red-haired?'

'Oh, no. She got that from her mother,' said Sophie.

'Really?' Rose sounded genuinely interested. 'Who *is* her mother, Sophie?'

Sophie stood up. 'She lives abroad now,' she said, packing her leaflets into her bag and looking round for Meggie, who was putting on her coat and stifling a yawn. 'Anyway, do give me a ring, Eliza, if you get stuck with any of the diet rules, or need any motivation. I'm sure you'll do well and will have a great weight loss next week. We'll sort out a visit before you leave — maybe next week?'

She rushed off, and Rose and I stared at each other.

'Touched a nerve there,' I said. 'Couldn't get out fast enough, once you mentioned Lexi's mother.'

'I know,' said Rose. 'Funny thing is, I wasn't that bothered before, but now I really want to know. Who was she, and what the hell happened to her?'

Chapter 11

Amy and I soon settled into the cottage. It was small — too small to be a permanent home, really, with a living room and kitchen, two tiny bedrooms, and a bathroom, and a square yard at the back. It was simply but elegantly furnished and had a rustic charm, but it was about a quarter of the size of home, and I couldn't imagine how people could live there all year round. I couldn't picture Gabriel and Lexi squashed into it.

It was, however, lovely to be Up Top, and to be able to walk along country lanes, winding our way between fields of early summer wheat and yellow oilseed rape. From certain places, you could look down and see the sea sparkling below, just visible between a cluster of red roofs and crooked chimneys. It was a world away from the Old Town, where all those buildings huddled together, and the salt tang of the sea filled your nostrils, and the mocking cry of seagulls and chattering of tourists assaulted your ears all through the day. It really was like two separate villages and, much as I was enchanted by the ancient streets and coastal charm of the bay, it was nice to wander around in the peaceful open air and take Amy for walks without meeting a soul.

It was also good to be able to walk around without fear of assault by a deadly seagull. They were the greediest creatures I'd ever met, and God help you if you were strolling along with an ice cream or a bag of chips in your hand, because they would dive bomb you and terrify the life out of you. Sometimes, I'd seen them on street corners, standing there in gangs, scanning the area for potential victims. They were a sodding menace. I couldn't think why no one had warned me about them.

Being in Kearton Bay was certainly doing Amy some good. Her skin glowed, she ate heartily, and slept well. She never mentioned Harry. Not once had she asked where he was, although she'd frequently whined for Joe and Mrs Travers. Her silence spoke volumes.

I hadn't even glanced at the diet sheet since the Lightweights meeting. I wasn't interested in following the diet, or any diet, to be honest. I was eating well, apart from the odd bag of Maltesers, and I felt miles healthier, probably due to the walking.

One day, I got an unexpected visit from Lexi. She popped in with some fresh eggs from the farm where she worked.

'Oh, yummy,' I said. 'Omelette for tea, I think.'

'And totally free range. You ought to bring Amy to the farm one day, Eliza. She could meet the hens and the donkeys. We have some that have retired from work and are there all the time. She'd enjoy it.'

I wasn't sure at first but, after all, I did need to get to know Lexi better, so I agreed to take Amy up there one afternoon.

'It's not far from here,' she told me. 'Just go farther up Whitby Road, and on the right, you'll see a sign for Clover Lane. It takes you to Whisperwood Farm, which is Hannah's place. More of a smallholding now, but still worth a visit. Hannah would love to meet you. She's a fan of *Twice as Nice* and she's sort of my honorary grandmother, though don't tell my real one that, for God's sake!'

Well, look, she'd given me an opening and I had to take it, didn't I? 'Do your grandparents live nearby?'

'Whitby. They used to live here, though. Grandad was the village doctor, but he liked living away from the village, so he wouldn't be bothered by people pestering him to deal with their ailments, when all he wanted to do was grow marrows and watch *Hollyoaks*.'

'Is that true?' My possible father was a *Hollyoaks* addict?

She laughed. 'Not entirely. He mostly grows peas. Anyway, I

must get back to work. Hope you enjoy the eggs. Don't forget to pop round. Hannah would love to see you. She gets quite bored now that she can't do much physical work.'

I promised her I would. It occurred to me that if Hannah had lived here all her life, she would be just the person to wangle information from about Lexi's grandfather. Plus, I could chat some more to Lexi and maybe even bump into Gabriel. It was even possible that I may get a civilised conversation from him, though really, in my wildest dreams I couldn't imagine it.

****

Apart from the odd cloudy day, May was turning out to be a glorious month. Looking out of the window that morning, I peered up at the cornflower blue sky and sighed in contentment. I hadn't felt so relaxed in ages and, given what was going on in my life, that really said something.

Mrs Travers had rung me the previous night.

'Fun and games here,' she told me. 'He came storming in yesterday morning, banging doors and chucking his stuff around. I reckon she's nagging him to move in with her, and he's not budging. I heard him say something on the phone about not wanting the house left empty, but if you ask me, he's stalling.'

'Really? Can't you get any more information for me than that?'

'Well, there's gratitude,' she said. 'I'm not Poirot, you know. I'm doing my best, but he's not daft. He knows I talk to you and he's not going to tell me anything about that tart, is he? I do know he's proper peeved about the car, though. He hates driving your Fiesta. He's started getting cabs everywhere.'

'Good. Serves him right,' I said. It served me right, too. I missed my little Fiesta, which I suppose was karma. It may not have been as grand as Harry's car but at least it didn't draw attention everywhere it went. You should have seen the crowd of teenagers that gathered around the flashy coupe in the car park of the Whitby Sainsbury's when I did my shopping. It was positively cringe-making.

'What about you?' she asked. 'How are you getting on?'

I told her I was five pounds lighter and had joined a slimming club, then I started rabbiting on about my other mission and how I thought I may have found my father.

She didn't exactly sound thrilled, giving me the same warnings Joe had issued about being careful and not forgetting he had a family to consider, as if I were about six years old and not the mature, responsible adult I actually was.

'Look, just take care, love,' she finished. 'Not just for their sake, but for yours. I don't want to see you hurt again.'

'I will,' I said, wondering why they thought me incapable of fulfilling my mission. If they'd seen me making my discreet enquiries, they couldn't fail to be impressed. I was born for this undercover lark. 'How's Joe? I haven't heard from him all week.'

She hesitated, and I could almost hear the cogs of her brain whirring. 'Not sure,' she admitted eventually. 'Not himself.'

'What do you mean? He's okay, isn't he?'

'He looks very run down, if you ask me.'

'Haven't you asked him what's wrong?'

'Of course I have, but do you think he'd tell me? You two are a nightmare. Why you can't just be normal, I don't know.'

As I looked up at the sky over Kearton Bay, I realised that was the reason I felt so relaxed. Here, I *was* just normal. I wasn't the niece of Britain's top chat show host; I wasn't the wife of a television presenter; I wasn't dreary Eliza, who could never quite measure up to the standards of Harry's colleagues and acquaintances. Here I was a normal mum, going for walks with my daughter, breaking my diet, sharing a coffee and a moan with a friend and heading off to the supermarket to do the weekly shop — even if it was in a ridiculously flashy car. I loved it. It felt as if, bit by bit, I was beginning to discover who Eliza really was.

If I went back to London would I lose her again? It was a worrying thought, and I realised I was chewing my acrylic nails as I considered the possibility. They would have to come off, no doubt about it. They were looking much the worse for wear and, besides, they really got on my nerves. The eyelashes had already gone, thank God. Never again.

'So,' I said, turning to Amy who was eating her Weetabix at the kitchen table, 'what shall we do today?'

Amy had no hesitation. 'Donkeys!'

I'd been promising her all week that I'd take her to the beach. I couldn't keep avoiding it. Besides, I wanted to pop into The Hare and Moon to see Rhiannon. I'd had a call from her to tell me that I'd left one of Amy's books behind. I may as well go there first, then take Amy for a donkey ride, and then visit Rose before heading back up Bay Street.

Plans made, I finished my cup of tea, cleared away the breakfast dishes, and got us both dressed. I pulled on faded blue jeans, a printed tunic top, and a pair of flat sandals that I'd bought from the supermarket the other day, having realised that, at some point, I was going to break my neck if I insisted on wearing heels round here.

I smothered us both in suntan lotion and tied my newly-washed hair up in a ponytail, then I found our sunglasses, and we were set. It was only about a ten-minute saunter to the top of Bay Street, and then we began the steep decline down towards the sea. It was heaving with people. I tried to imagine what the village must feel like in the winter months, when the tourists deserted it, but it was hard to picture. What happened to all those businesses? The local population couldn't possibly sustain all those cafés and gift shops out of season. No wonder Gabriel was so fed up with the situation.

Amy started pulling on my arm the minute she spotted the sea, but I managed to persuade her to head into The Hare and Moon first. The dining room was already busy, and I glimpsed Derry through the open door, carrying plates to an elderly couple in the corner. I watched them enviously as they tucked into their full English. I missed the breakfasts here. Cereal might be healthier, but you couldn't beat a greasy fry-up, let's be honest.

Michelle was in the bar, wiping the tables. She straightened up as I walked in, and smirked at me, no doubt thinking I looked a mess, but I was past caring. She didn't look so fabulous herself, truth to tell, being half evil troll.

'Bit early for a drink,' she remarked. 'What can I get you?'

'I've come for Amy's *Gruffalo*,' I said. She looked bemused, and I explained that it was a book and I'd been told that I'd left it behind in my room.

She shrugged. 'Well, Rhiannon's still upstairs. Go and get it, if you like.'

'Are you sure it's okay?'

'Sure. She won't mind,' she assured me and returned to wiping down the tables. I led Amy upstairs and into Rhiannon's living room. There was no sign of her, and I hovered outside the door of my old room, not sure if she had new guests booked in. I couldn't hear anything, but that wasn't proof it was unoccupied. It was best to check with Rhiannon. She'd probably removed the book from my room, anyway.

I walked down the landing to her room and tapped gently on the door, a split second before it opened, and a sandy-haired man stood there in his boxer shorts, a look of horror on his face.

Rhiannon was in bed and she merely adjusted the sheet when she saw me. I dragged Amy into the sitting room and waited, feeling sick. It wasn't just the sight of the man's hairy beer belly and spindly white legs that were making me nauseous. I'd seen him before. He'd been in the bar on a couple of occasions, and I'd seen him in Henderson's Store. Unless I was very much mistaken, he was Marty Henderson, husband of Milly. So that was the mysterious — and noisy — lover that Rhiannon had been entertaining in her room late at night. How could she? I felt ridiculously disappointed in her.

The door opened, and she stepped inside. She didn't look anywhere near guilty enough, if you ask me. If I'd just been caught doing the horizontal tango with a married man I'd have crawled into the room, ringing a bell and moaning "unclean", but apart from her face being a little flushed, she looked the same as usual. In fact, she smiled at me quite warmly as she tightened the belt on her robe and sat on the chair opposite me.

'How lovely to see you. I expect you've come for *The Gruffalo?* It's in the drawer in the sideboard, Amy, if you'd like to fetch it?'

Amy obliged, unaware of the tension that was building within me. I glared at Rhiannon, infuriated on behalf of Milly

Henderson.

'Would you both like a drink?' Rhiannon asked pleasantly.

I shook my head. 'I don't think so.'

Her smile dropped. 'Oh, dear, I appear to have offended you.'

'It's nothing to do with me,' I said. 'I should think it's Milly you're offending.'

'Ah.' Rhiannon sighed. 'I see.'

'Do you?' I couldn't help myself. I was furious. I was so sick of women like her, who just took what they wanted with no regard for anyone's feelings but their own. 'Have you ever loved someone and found that they've been cheating on you?' I demanded.

She looked at me, her eyes sad. 'No.'

'Then, you're lucky, because it's the most painful experience ever. How could you do that to Milly? Women like you are the lowest of the low, and I thought better of you than that. I hope one day you know what it feels like.'

She adjusted her robe and smiled at Amy, who was staring at me with some concern. I tried to smile at her, too, aware that I was causing a scene, and it really was none of my business.

'I would never want to hurt anyone, Eliza, I assure you.'

'Then, why do it?' I demanded. I could feel hot tears pricking my eyes and I blinked them away, furious with myself.

'I don't see marriage the way most people do,' she admitted. 'I don't understand how any human being can claim ownership rights over another. Relationships go through difficult times, and sometimes men turn to me for comfort. I always make it clear to them that I don't want them to become emotionally attached and I don't want their marriages to suffer because of me. I find that a little dalliance restores their spirit and they find renewed happiness in their marriage. I can't see what's wrong with that.'

I was stunned. Talk about deluded. 'Well, congratulations. You've come up with a whole new therapy. Have you thought of volunteering for Relate? For God's sake, those men made a commitment. If they didn't want to honour it, they shouldn't have made a promise to be faithful. Because that's what marriage is, a promise to be faithful to one person for the rest of your life.'

'If he chooses to break that promise, that's not my fault—' she began but I cut her off.

'It's not the wife's fault, either,' I said, my voice cracking with emotion. 'She made that promise, too, and she made it in good faith. Women like you are poisonous.'

I stood up, shaking. She stood, too, reaching out to me, but I moved away and more-or-less pushed Amy out of the sitting room and down the stairs. I grabbed her hand and led her out into the sunshine, taking deep lungfuls of air. Bloody Rhiannon. Bloody Marty Henderson. Bloody Harry!

****

The sand was still damp from the outgoing tide, as we headed onto the beach. It was crowded with people, and the donkeys were already plodding along, carrying young children on their backs.

Lexi waved. 'You came! Ready for a ride, Amy?'

Amy dropped *The Gruffalo* on the nearest rock and ran towards her. Lexi scooped her up and laughed. 'Just wait for them to come back, and then you're first in line. You can take your pick of the donkeys,' she told her. 'On the house,' she added with a wink.

Amy watched them eagerly, trying to decide which one she favoured. I picked up the book and sat down, my mood completely ruined.

Lexi raised an eyebrow. 'You okay, Eliza?'

I nodded, remembering Lexi's shenanigans with Rhiannon's son. Just like his mother, obviously. I wondered if Lexi knew what she was letting herself in for. No doubt, he'd told her to keep their relationship secret. He was probably off porking God knows who behind her back.

Amy looked at me anxiously and then up at The Hare and Moon. I smiled at her, trying to reassure her. Luckily, Lexi's colleague walked up with the donkeys in tow and a whole crowd of pushy parents and chattering children, and she was quite distracted as Lexi hoisted her onto a little grey donkey called

Smokey, who Amy had declared to be her favourite.

I watched as Lexi adjusted the stirrups, and her colleague started collecting money from the next bunch of parents and hoisting more children up into the saddles. I felt totally out of sorts, and all the joy had gone from the day. I flicked sand off my jeans and rested my chin in my hands, watching as Amy and the other children were led up the beach, Lexi keeping her arm around Amy's waist. The donkeys looked as if they could do the walk in their sleep. I didn't know how they stayed awake, frankly. I was nodding off just watching them.

When Amy had finally returned and been lifted off Smokey, she trotted back to me and asked if we could make sandcastles. Since we didn't have a bucket and spade, we settled on making sand hills instead. We moved nearer to a little rock pool and began scooping wet sand into small piles, patting them into shape and writing our initials on them with our fingers.

It was lovely on the beach, with the sun on our backs and the gulls calling, and the distant sparkle of sunlight on the sea. The gentle lapping of the waves was almost hypnotic, and I couldn't stop yawning. Amy was splashing in the rock pool, looking for crabs, and I lay on the drier part of the sand and watched her, smiling. She looked like a different child, her fair hair bleached blonde by the sunshine and her skin golden and glowing with health. She found a shell and held it up to me, her eyes bright with excitement. I felt utterly contented and smiled to myself, closing my eyes and breathing in the fresh, salty air.

I don't know what happened next. I must have fallen asleep, but if I did, it could only have been for a couple of minutes. I thought Amy was beside me. I could hear gentle splashing in the pool and a child's giggle, and I honestly thought she was right there. When I opened my eyes to look at her, it wasn't Amy at all, but a dark-haired little boy who was dangling a starfish in his fingers and staring at it in amazement.

I half sat up, propping myself on one elbow as I looked around, wondering where she'd gone. When I couldn't see her, I scrambled to my feet and looked frantically along the beach, my hand shading my eyes against the fierce sun.

Lexi was just coming back with another load of kids when I ran to her, calling frantically.

'What's up?'

'Have you seen Amy?' For one, glorious moment I thought that maybe she'd given her another donkey ride. Lexi shook her head, and my stomach turned over in dread. I began to run, asking everyone if they'd seen a little blonde girl in a white T-shirt and pink leggings. They all looked at me as if I'd gone mad. I turned around in blind panic, to find Lexi behind me.

'Don't worry,' she said, gripping my arms, 'we'll find her. Where was she, when you last saw her?'

I looked at her blankly for a moment then pointed in the vague direction of the rock pool we'd been sitting beside. The sand hills were still visible, and *The Gruffalo* lay abandoned beside them. I wiped away a tear.

'Would she have gone up the slipway?'

I looked at the concrete slope that led back up to the street and The Hare and Moon. I thought about Amy's anxiety over my argument with Rhiannon. Could she possibly have headed back there? There was no sign of her on the beach, anyway, and I was too terrified to contemplate the idea that she might have walked into the sea.

'Eddie and I will keep checking along here,' she said, taking charge in the face of my hopelessness. 'You go up there and see if you can see her. She can't have gone far with those little legs.'

I nodded, trying to swallow down the panic, and began to run up the slipway, past the little boats that were moored there, and dodging my way through the crowds, my eyes scanning frantically for a glimpse of blonde and pink. I couldn't see her anywhere, and the longer she was alone, the more bad things could happen to her. The streets were full of strangers. My little girl could be in mortal danger, and it was all my fault.

Chapter 12

Gabriel put the hutch into the boot of his car and set off to deliver it to the Walker house. It was down Vanity Yard, a tiny little alleyway tucked away off King's Row. He almost crawled down Bay Street, grumbling at the milling crowds who seemed in no hurry to make way for a car, and was about to round the horseshoe and head back up King's Row, when, out of the corner of his eye, he saw a flash of pink opposite him at the edge of the pavement. It was a lone child, running along the kerb scarily close to the road.

He pulled over and climbed out of the car, heading across the road towards her. He recognised her all right. The question was, where was her mother?

The little girl looked up at him, her face scarlet with exertion and her cheeks tear-stained.

'Where's Mummy?' she said, her voice fearful. Gabriel scooped her up, thanking God that she hadn't been on the other side of the road. He'd been driving very slowly, but even so...

He searched his memory banks and, from somewhere deep within them, recalled Lexi telling him the child's name. 'Amy?'

She sniffed and threw her arms around his neck, shuddering with exhaustion. Gabriel patted her back and looked around him in confusion. Where the hell was Eliza?

'Let's find your mummy. She'll be worried sick,' he said, turning just in time to stop Eliza hurtling into him.

'Oh, God, you've got her! Oh, thank you, thank you!'

She was obviously beside herself, her face as red and her cheeks as tear-stained as her daughter's. 'I thought maybe she'd gone to see Rhiannon. I was just in the pub looking for her but there was no sign of her. I thought — I thought someone had...'

She broke off, sobbing. Gabriel felt stunned as she leaned against him, trembling as she reached for Amy's hand.

'It's all right, she's fine. She was near the road and, luckily, I saw her.'

Her damp blonde head pressed against his chest and he caught the scent of apple shampoo. He breathed it in, relieved that she wasn't wearing her usual perfume, and had a sudden strange urge to comfort her. She must have been terrified, imagining all kinds of scenarios, each as horrifying as the next.

'I'm so sorry.' She pulled back and took Amy from his arms. He felt a pang of regret as they moved away from him. 'It was the relief and the shock.'

'That's understandable. Don't worry,' he assured her, noticing for the first time that she had much less make-up on, that her nose had a dusting of freckles, and her eyes, without the spider-leg lashes hiding them, were a beautiful soft green.

'Come on, monkey, let's get you home. Oh, I need to let Lexi know she's okay.'

'Lexi?'

'And the man she works with — Eddie? They were looking on the beach, while I came up here.'

'I'll take care of it.'

Eliza nodded, smiling faintly, and turned to walk away from him. He shook his head, trying to clear it of the strange thoughts that were suddenly swirling around in his confused brain. He wondered what had just happened. He supposed it was the realisation of what could have happened to that little girl that had shocked him and brought out his protective side. Frowning, he pressed the button on the remote to lock his car door and headed to the beach to reassure Lexi and Eddie that all was well.

****

The following Wednesday, I was stunned to find that I'd lost another two pounds.

Rose was suspicious. 'Don't tell me you're following this sodding diet?' she demanded. 'How can you even understand it? It's clear as mud.'

'I'm not following it,' I whispered. 'I haven't even looked at it since last Wednesday. No idea what's going on.'

'Well, when you figure it out, let me in on the secret,' she replied, looking at her own weight chart, which showed that she'd managed to gain a pound.

Sophie was all smiles and full of congratulations. I felt pretty rotten as she told everyone what an example I was and how well I'd done on my first week. 'So, what did you find particularly useful?' she asked, as we all sat in our little circle, our hands sore from clapping every achievement.

I felt the colour drain from my face. I had no idea what to tell her. I hadn't even thought about it. I scrabbled round in my memory, trying to recall last week's conversation.

'Er, I froze some grapes,' I said feebly. 'They were delicious. Just like boiled sweets.'

Clarissa looked smug, as Rose stared at me open-mouthed.

'She'll be even more insufferable now,' Rose complained, as we began to put our chairs away at the end of the meeting.

Sophie approached us as we were leaving. 'I was wondering, would you like to pop round tomorrow? You can see what we've done to the house. I'd value your opinion.'

'I'd love to,' I assured her.

Rose cleared her throat, and Sophie flushed. 'You, too, Rose. I meant both of you, obviously.'

'Oh, cheers, Sophe. Sadly, I can't 'cos I've got the café to look after, but thanks for the invite.'

'You are mean,' I told her, as we walked out of the village hall.

'Bollocks,' she muttered. 'Been here two years, and she's never asked me to have a look round in all that time. I've been dying to have a nosy round that house for ages, but no. What's your flaming secret?'

I nudged her. 'I'm family,' I teased.

Rose laughed grudgingly. 'All right, I'll give you that. You seem to be fitting in with them, anyway, being invited into the inner sanctum, and Gabriel doing his knight in shining armour act and rescuing your child.'

'Don't,' I said, still traumatised by the whole episode. 'I can never thank him enough. God knows what would have happened to her, if he hadn't spotted her.'

'Well, that's what big brothers are for,' she pointed out with a wink.

Meggie had managed to duck out of packing away, somehow, and she and some of the other members were clustered near the gate, casting furtive looks around and keeping an eye out for Sophie.

'Have you got the stuff?' Meggie whispered. I reached into my bag, my hands trembling. If I got caught, I'd be for it. I brought out a tin and prised the lid off, as they all leaned forward and peered in. There were lots of oohs and aahs, and Meggie reached in and pulled out a piece of the contraband. She bit into it, and everyone held their breath as she chewed.

'Oh, my God! That's the best fudge I've ever tasted!'

Everyone stared at me in amazement. Evidently, that counted for a lot.

'Could you make me some?' demanded another woman.

'Did you say you made marshmallows? Can you make some for me?'

I shrugged. 'Sure. What flavour?'

'Flavour?' she looked at me in bewilderment. 'Don't they just come in one flavour?'

'Yeah,' Meggie said. 'Bland.'

'Not at all,' I said. 'I can make you salted caramel flavour, or lemon meringue, or raspberry ripple, or —'

'Marshmallows?' They all looked at me as if I'd finally discovered the cure for a common cold.

'Can you make me some lemon meringue ones?'

'Can I have some of the fudge?'

'Do you make toffee?'

'Hell's bells,' Rose said. 'Give her a bloody chance. Here, Eliza.

Use this.'

She handed me a notebook and pencil, and I began to jot down the orders.

'Let's get out of here,' said Meggie. 'Sophie will be out in a moment and, if she sees us, we're done for.'

They scarpered, and I tried not to feel guilty about my part in this latest criminal caper.

'You'll be making sweets all sodding week,' Rose said. 'Doesn't it bother you?'

'Nope,' I said, shoving the notebook in my handbag. 'I enjoy it. Harry would never eat them at home, so it seemed pointless, but I find it relaxing. I enjoyed myself this morning, making Meggie's fudge and a couple of cakes, just for the fun of it.'

'Fun? There's nothing fun about baking.' Rose shuddered.

'Have you ever thought you may be in the wrong business?' I laughed, and she nodded.

'Frequently.'

We parted at the end of the path, and she headed off towards Bay Street, while I walked back to Amethyst Cottage.

Lexi was just finishing reading a story to Amy when I walked in. 'How did you get on?'

'Two pounds off.'

'Excellent. I'll put the kettle on,' she said, heading into the kitchen.

Five minutes later, she handed me a cup of tea and sat down next to me on the sofa. Amy leaned against me, watching *Winnie-the-Pooh* and sipping milk.

'So, what have you got planned for tonight?' I asked Lexi, thinking that now I'd been weighed, I could risk having something to eat.

'I'm having supper with my friend, Georgia. We're just going to get a Chinese and chill out before I go home to Dad. I need to spend some time with him tonight.'

'He doesn't mind you going out, surely?'

Lexi laughed. 'God, no! He's always telling me to socialise more, but I can't be bothered. I'm going out on Saturday though,' she said with uncharacteristic coyness.

That sounded interesting. 'Oh?' I asked. 'Anywhere special?'

Lexi sipped her tea quietly, thinking for a moment. Then she put her mug down and looked at me earnestly. 'If I tell you something, promise you won't tell anyone else?'

'Of course.' I had an awful feeling I knew what was coming.

'I'm spending the night in a hotel,' Lexi said, 'with a man.'

'Really? How lovely. Who's the lucky fella?'

'Derry Bone from the pub in the village. He and I are, well, you know.'

Oh, I did. Each squeak, moan, and giggle had imprinted on my mind. 'In love?'

'In love? Don't be daft! We're what they call friends with benefits. You know, fuck buddies.'

I nearly spat out my tea. 'That's not very romantic!'

'Oh, God, not you, too. You're as bad as Georgia. Love sucks big time.'

'You're a bit young to be so bitter!'

Lexi sighed. 'If you'd seen the marriage my parents had, you'd have a pretty dim view of it, too.'

I did try to stop myself from taking advantage but I'm only human. 'I hope you don't think I'm prying, Lexi,' I said carefully, 'but how come you live with your dad? Where's your mum?'

Lexi gulped down the rest of her tea. 'She lives abroad. Probably won't ever see her again.'

'I'm sure that's not true. She is your mother after all. I can't imagine—'

'Trust me, Eliza. She's never coming back. My mum was a fool and paid the price. I can't say I have much respect for her at all, and I really wouldn't want her anywhere near my dad again.' She stood up. 'I must be going now. I've got a lot to cram in tonight. So many people want to see me!' She laughed.

'Oh? What's so special about tonight?' I enquired, still trying to make sense of her previous comment but realising that she didn't want to discuss her parents any further.

'Just my birthday. I'm nineteen today,' she said. 'That's why Derry's taking me away on Saturday, to celebrate. He's such a sap, sometimes.'

'Your birthday! And you're stuck here with me? Why the hell didn't you say?'

'It's no big deal,' said Lexi. 'Although, I'd better be going. Like I said, I'm going to Georgia's, and then Sophie and Archie want to give me my present. Haven't seen them all day, what with work and babysitting.'

She headed to the kitchen door, and I followed her.

'You won't say anything, will you? I mean, about Derry? Only, Dad thinks I'm staying at Georgia's overnight, and I wouldn't want to disillusion him.'

'Why is it a secret?' I asked, confused. 'Is Derry telling you to keep it quiet?'

'No way. He wants to tell the world I'm his girlfriend,' she admitted. 'I just don't see the point in anyone knowing. People are so keen to label you, aren't they? If they see we're together, they'll assume we're in a relationship, and that's the last thing I want. Or they'll decide I'm some kind of slapper, which I'm not. And I really don't want my dad to be disappointed in me. It's best he doesn't know what I'm up to.'

She winked at me, as I promised I wouldn't say a word. As I closed the door, I reflected that I'd totally misjudged the situation between Lexi and Derry. I'd thought he was using her, when it seemed she was actually using him. But what she'd said about her father really worried me. Why wouldn't she want her mother near him again? And what did she mean by paying the price?

I sighed as I realised that, despite all my best efforts to be a cool and detached undercover agent, it was all beginning to matter a bit too much.

Chapter 13

Amy's little face was tight with concentration as she watched *Winnie-the-Pooh*, while I sat in the armchair opposite and considered Lexi. I wished I'd known it was her birthday, so I could at least have got her a birthday card, but Henderson's would be closed now, and I wasn't sure where I'd be able to buy a card so late. Nor did I fancy driving around looking for somewhere.

Then I had a rare brainwave. I'd made a sponge cake that morning and, miraculously, it was still untouched. I didn't have any candles, but there were a few tubes of Smarties in the top cupboard stored away for Amy. I could stick some of those on top of the cake to brighten it up a bit. It wouldn't be the classiest of cakes, but it would taste good, I was confident of that.

'Pretty, Mummy.' Amy stared at the cake in admiration, and I smiled down at her. There was nothing in the world that could be more beautiful than my daughter. She was definitely my masterpiece and far prettier than any cake, which was ironic really, considering that it had taken me a couple of hours to create this particular work of art, whereas Amy had been all conceived within, oh, let's be honest here, five minutes maximum. Well, Harry was always in a rush and he wasn't big on foreplay.

I lifted Amy up, so she could get a better view of the cake. 'Shall we take this to Lexi? It's her birthday today.'

Amy nodded. She was usually in bed by seven-thirty, so this was quite an adventure. I glanced at my watch. Eight-forty. They should have had their Chinese by now. Once I'd helped Amy into her coat, I turned off the television and grabbed the car keys. After strapping her in her car seat, I collected the cake which was safely inside one of the new tins that I'd bought in Whitby. I hadn't been able to resist. Knowing that Meggie wanted me to make her fudge, I'd invested in all sorts of cooking paraphernalia and now had almost as much here as I had at home. With it placed carefully on the passenger seat, I set off on the short drive to The Old Vicarage.

Sophie's home was a large Victorian brick building, just before the lane narrowed to Farthingdale. It was mostly hidden from view by a hedge of conifer trees, but as I parked in the drive, I saw that it had a beautiful front lawn, edged by flower beds, which were a riot of colour, and a variety of shrubs. There was a clear view across the enormous churchyard to the beautiful Norman church of St Hilda's, which served both Farthingdale and Kearton Bay, and to the fields beyond.

I'd supposed it would be eerie, living so close to a load of graves, but it was actually a really pretty view with a tranquil feeling, and I thought how peaceful it must be. According to Rose, some years ago, it had been decided that a more modest house was better suited as a vicarage, and the grand old house had been sold off and replaced by a three-bedroomed cottage on the other side of the church in Farthingdale. Eventually, the Crooks had purchased it and restored it to its former glory.

I hoped Sophie wouldn't be annoyed that I'd turned up unannounced that evening, ahead of tomorrow's grand tour. I wasn't stopping. A quick drop-off and I'd be gone.

There were two cars already in the drive – Gabriel's old estate and Sophie's bright red Mini. I pulled up behind them and parked, telling Amy that I wouldn't be a moment, then collected the cake tin and carried it up the path to the front door.

Standing on the step, I knocked tentatively, and it crossed my mind that this was a bad idea. What if Gabriel answered? I could imagine the look of scorn on his face when he saw the home-made cake. It wasn't the grandest thing I'd ever made. What if he laughed at it? Oh, bugger it. Why was I bothered what he thought, anyway? I stood up straight and vowed not to let his attitude bother me. The cake was for Lexi, not for him, and if he sneered, I would push the whole damn thing in his face. I had form, after all. As I contemplated this image, I felt considerably cheerier, and by the time the door opened I was smiling.

'Oh. It's you.'

'Nice to see you, too.' I was disturbed by how much his cool greeting bothered me. I suppose I'd hoped that since he'd rescued Amy, things would be warmer between us. Evidently, they weren't. He looked quite shocked to see me. He was holding a phone to his ear, and for a moment, he seemed to forget that fact as he stood there staring at me, while I waited, wondering if I would pass inspection. Then he blinked, finally remembering that he'd been in the middle of a conversation.

'Sorry, Flynn. Someone's just turned up. Can I call you later? Thanks. Bye.' He ended the call and put the phone in his pocket. 'Eliza Jarvis,' he said. 'To what do I owe the pleasure?'

To my intense irritation, I found I could barely speak. Instead, I thrust the tin into his hands.

'For me? You shouldn't have.'

Smug git. I repositioned my shoulder bag strap, which was slipping down my arm, and tilted my chin defiantly. 'It's a birthday cake for Lexi. I didn't know, you see, and there wasn't time to buy her anything. I know it's not much, but I wanted to do something. She's been so good, and I didn't want to just let her birthday pass without ... oh, hell!'

He was staring at me intently, probably thinking I was a lunatic. I closed my eyes waiting for the sarcastic comment.

'That's so kind of you.'

I opened one eye suspiciously. Bloody hell, was he smiling? I opened both eyes and found myself smiling nervously back at him. I noticed that he had dimples in his cheeks and his turquoise eyes crinkled in the corners. He looked rather nice. Well, human, at least.

'That's such a lovely thing to do. I'm afraid Lexi's not in at the moment but she won't be long. Come in and wait. You can give it to her yourself.'

'Oh, no, honestly, I wouldn't want to intrude.' Hell's bells! I couldn't be alone with him. I was bound to put my foot in it and piss him off, somehow. It was inevitable.

'Not at all. She'll be pleased to see you, and I'm afraid it's quite a long time since she had a birthday cake. I never even thought...' His voice trailed off and he looked down at the tin and sighed.

'I have Amy in the car,' I said awkwardly. I felt a bit unnerved, to be honest. Gabriel being nice was trickier to handle than I'd imagined.

'Bring her in, please. It would be good to see her again. We quite bonded the other day.'

He smiled again. Damn. He'd played the trump card. He'd saved Amy, and I owed him. I nodded and collected her from the car, wondering how long he could keep up the friendly act. Well, as soon as Lexi got back, and I could hand over the cake, I'd be out of there.

Carrying a half-asleep Amy into the living room of the house, I was attacked from all sides by images of Sophie and her family. Photos hung on every wall, and there was a large framed portrait of her with the tall, white-haired man I'd seen her with at Beltane, surrounded by three young children, all smiling widely. Rose wasn't kidding when she'd said Sophie was proud of her family — that much was obvious.

In front of the fireplace, a huge German Shepherd dog sprawled on a cream rug. It barely glanced at me as I walked in, obviously too comfortable to move.

'Useful, isn't she?' Gabriel said, nodding fondly at the dog. 'Tessa, you're supposed to alert us to the presence of strangers.'

Tessa merely yawned and put her head back on her paws.

'As you can see, she's well trained,' said Gabriel, motioning me to sit down on the armchair opposite his. 'Still, she's an old lady now. We have to make allowances.'

I sat down nervously, Amy on my knee, not sure if I was warier of him or the dog.

'Would you like a drink? I think there's some of Sophie's wine somewhere, or I have a couple of beers in the fridge?'

'If you don't mind, I'd prefer tea?'

No way was I risking alcohol. I was so nervous that God knows what I'd blurt out while under the influence. He went through to what I presumed must be the kitchen. I stared at Amy, who blinked sleepily in response. Okay, what just happened? Where had Shrek gone? He seemed to have transformed from an ogre to a — well, human being. Maybe rescuing Amy had been the breakthrough. Maybe he'd taken pity on me at last and realised that I wasn't the monster he seemed to think I was. Or maybe he was just past caring. Whatever the reason, it was a relief.

As Amy snuggled into my arms, her thumb firmly in her mouth, I cast my eyes round the room, squinting at the bookcase to see what lurked on its shelves. Books were such a giveaway. Harry never read anything except lads' magazines and anything featuring him. The Crook/Bailey collection was quite a mixture of reference books, horsy books, and a wide range of fiction titles. I was surprised to see that beneath a shelf full of crime novels were *The Complete Works of William Shakespeare* and a whole section of nineteenth century classics. I wondered if they belonged to Lexi. I couldn't imagine Gabriel reading *Pride and Prejudice*, somehow. There was a long row of Jilly Cooper books, too. They had to be Sophie's. I'd bet fifty quid she had a raunchy side to her.

By the time he brought through two cups of tea Amy was sound asleep on my knee.

'Let me,' he offered, putting the cups on the coffee table and taking her from me, gently laying her on the sofa. I remembered the sight of him as I'd turned the corner into King's Row the other day and found him standing there, Amy in his arms. My hero. Like Rose said, that's what big brothers were for. I frowned, watching him as he carefully moved a cushion away from Amy and made sure she was comfortable. I couldn't see any resemblance between us, but then, he didn't really look like Sophie, either, so I supposed that didn't prove anything.

'Where is everyone?' I asked, thinking there was no way I could make conversation with him without other people to share the burden. What the hell would I talk to him about? Everything I said and did seemed to annoy him, and his good mood surely couldn't last much longer.

'Sophie and Archie have gone to pick Lexi and my nieces up from the stables. Sophie's children are horse mad, and Lexi is best friends with the owner of the place. And Oliver, my nephew, is upstairs. He's doing 'A' levels and he's meant to be studying, though I'm pretty certain I heard the theme tune to *The Big Bang Theory* ten minutes ago.'

I gave a weak smile, wondering how long it would be before reinforcements arrived. I was feeling hot and increasingly flustered. Did he have the heating on or something?

'I really wanted to speak to you before Lexi gets back,' he said, handing me a cup of tea and sitting down. 'I'm sorry I've been a bit, well, abrupt with you.'

I swallowed some tea and nearly shrieked in pain as the hot liquid scalded my throat. Well, if that didn't wake me up, I really couldn't be dreaming, so what the hell had got into him?

'I do have a bee in my bonnet about second homes,' he admitted. 'I worked in a village a few miles south of here for some years. It was a real picture postcard place — duck pond, village green, the works. It was a huge draw for holiday-makers and, eventually, almost everything that made it a proper working village closed. First the school, then the post office, then even the pub. It went from being a thriving community to a handful of occupied houses, surrounded by a vast number of empty buildings. Local families, people I knew and cared about, had to move away because they couldn't afford to buy in the area, and any rental property was let to holiday-makers.'

I wasn't sure what to say. He was under the illusion that my sole purpose for being here was because I wanted to buy a second home in Kearton Bay, and I could hardly put him straight.

'I've lived here almost all my adult life,' he continued. 'I've had brief spells in other places, but this is the village I call home. It's the village Lexi calls home. I can't stand by and see it end up like Thornley Beck. Can you understand that?'

'Okay, you've convinced me,' I said. 'I admit defeat.'

'I'm sorry?'

'I won't buy a holiday home here. Hey, you're my knight in shining armour. You saved Amy. I owe you.'

Gabriel laughed. I stared in fascination at his dimples. I wondered if his father had dimples, too.

'You're joking of course?'

I put down my cup with a sigh. 'No, I'm not joking. Honestly, I do see what you mean, and I don't want to buy one of the little places around here, just for it to sit empty most of the year. It's a terrible waste. You're absolutely right.'

He was staring at me as if he couldn't believe it. Not surprising really. It was the fastest turnaround in history, from his point of view. Bet he was wishing he could convince everyone to change their minds that easily.

'What about your husband?'

I'd forgotten all about him, actually. Just for a short while, obviously. 'What about him?'

'Well, second homes are his career, aren't they? I've watched that wretched programme with Sophie. No offence but it makes my blood boil.'

'Mine, too,' I murmured. He raised an eyebrow, and I shifted in my chair, rather embarrassed. 'Harry was never bothered about it in the first place. He's got other fish to fry.'

He gazed at me for a moment, but as I didn't offer any further information, he picked up his cup and stared into it for a moment, seeming to find the tea quite fascinating. Finally, he looked up, his eyes locking onto mine.

'Can we put all this behind us and make a fresh start? I know you're not here for much longer, but if we do bump into each other again, it would be nice to be friendly. Especially since my daughter seems to be very fond of you both.'

I nodded. 'Believe me, Mr Bailey, I have enough to deal with, without falling out with people. Lexi is a lovely girl.' I grinned up at him. 'Hard though it may be to imagine, I'm quite sure you can't be all bad with a daughter like her.'

He laughed again, the dimples puckering his cheeks quite endearingly. He looked totally different when he wasn't being all grumpy and serious. In fact, I'd go so far as to say he looked rather nice. Maybe he wouldn't be such a bad brother, after all. 'Fair point,' he said.

Our heads turned as the front door opened, and chattering voices filled the hallway.

'Welll'

Sophie, Archie and Lexi stopped in surprise at the sight of us. Behind them, two teenage girls stared at me curiously, probably wondering who the hell I was and what exactly I was doing with their Uncle Gabriel.

'Well, this is a surprise,' Sophie said, rushing forward to hug me as if we were suddenly best friends. 'I wondered whose car that was! What are you doing here? I wanted to show you around properly tomorrow. It's all spoilt now!'

'Hardly,' said Gabriel. 'Eliza just came round to bring something for Lexi.'

Lexi looked enquiringly at me, as I lifted the tin from the floor and passed it to her. Oh, buggery bollocks! I hadn't expected an audience. How stupid the little Smartie cake seemed now.

Lexi opened the tin and grinned. 'Birthday cake!'

She passed the tin to Sophie, who peered eagerly inside and then nodded approvingly.

'I know it's not much, but I just think everyone should have a cake on their birthday, no matter how old they are. I haven't had one since I was seven, which is the great tragedy of my life.' What was I saying? I was babbling. How embarrassing.

'It's lovely,' said Lexi. 'Thanks, Eliza. I can't remember the last time I had a birthday cake...'

Archie clapped his hands. 'Well, I don't know about you lot, but I could really fancy a nice fat slice of that cake. Stop being greedy, Lexi, and start sharing!'

Lexi laughed and took the tin into the kitchen.

Sophie called out to her, 'Just a tiny slice for me, darling.' She sat down gently on the sofa, taking care not to wake Amy, and leaned towards me. 'I got weighed tonight before class started,' she confided, 'and I've gained three pounds! Three flipping pounds! It's a constant battle, isn't it? Bloody weight. Now, mind, that's in confidence. Don't you go telling any of the others, for

God's sake.'

'Of course not. It's easily done. I suppose it would help if I could stop eating Maltesers,' I said. 'They're my main vice. I just can't resist them.'

'See, I'm not one for chocolate. Maybe the odd Walnut Whip, but really nothing that warrants a three pounds gain. I can't think why it happened because I'm extremely disciplined, aren't I, Archie? Oh, I'm sorry, this is my husband, Archie,' she said belatedly.

'Oh, yeah, yeah, you are, darling,' he confirmed, squeezing next to her on the sofa. 'You were exercising hard all weekend, as well.'

'Archie!' She nudged him violently in the ribs, and he chuckled.

The cake was a huge success. Sophie couldn't get over how light and delicious it was. 'So much better than the stuff they serve at Pinky's, though don't tell Rose that, or I'll never hear the end of it.'

I didn't want to agree with her, for poor Rose's sake, but I couldn't really deny it, either, so I kept my mouth shut.

'It really is delicious,' agreed Gabriel. 'You have hidden talents, Mrs Jarvis.'

'Thank you, Mr Bailey,' I smiled. 'It's just about the only talent I do have.'

'I'm quite sure that's not true,' he murmured.

Sophie, who had been about to take a bite of cake, paused for a moment, her eyes wide. She started to say something, but Archie clapped her on the shoulder and announced it was time for Lexi to open her presents.

'Poor little bugger's been working all day. We haven't even seen her. Go and fetch the stash, Tally.'

The younger girl ran upstairs, and we heard her rummaging around. There was some muttered conversation, then she came back, followed by a tall young man, who I presumed was her brother, Oliver.

'I hope you haven't spent too much,' said Lexi, who looked mortified by all this fuss. I didn't blame her. There's nothing more embarrassing than opening presents in front of people, especially people who've bought them for you, and even more especially when you hate all the gifts and you've got to pretend they're lovely. I should know. There's only so much excitement you can fake when presented with yet another box of lavender bath salts and flower-shaped soaps. I'm sure Harry's mother had bought a whole cupboard full of them on special offer and just doled them out to me each year. I'm convinced it was a plot to make me smell like an old lady and put Harry off me. She should have saved her money. Harry appeared to be rather drawn to old ladies.

Gabriel looked distinctly uncomfortable. I wondered if he'd bought her anything himself, or if he'd left it to Sophie to choose something for her. I couldn't imagine him whipping round Marks and Spencer looking for girly gifts, somehow, although, to be fair, Lexi didn't seem the girly gift sort.

Lexi began to open the presents, and I leaned forward curiously, wondering what she'd got. Amy slept through it all, which was amazing, considering the sound of tearing wrapping paper and the shrieks coming from everyone. And when I say everyone, I mean Sophie. She really was excitable, like a puppy with a new toy.

The younger girl, who was called Tallulah but was known as Tally, had given her a thick, glossy book on art history, illustrated with some amazing photographs of paintings. Lexi was thrilled, which surprised me, considering she spent her days working with donkeys. It hadn't occurred to me that her interests may lay elsewhere.

Tally looked quite embarrassed by her profuse thanks. 'It's for your course,' she muttered. 'Thought it might help.'

'It really will!' said Lexi. 'It's fabulous.'

I must have looked a bit baffled, because Sophie explained that Lexi had started a degree with the Open University and her next course was art history. People were full of surprises.

Pandora more-or-less threw a present at her and then cleared off into the kitchen. Lexi opened it and revealed a DVD of "Britain's top comedian", Charlie Hope, live on tour.

'Fabulous!' she said, her eyes shining. 'I love him!'

Oliver had bought her a box of chocolates and demanded that she give him all the ones with nuts in. Sophie and Archie handed her a box with a well-known jeweller's name embossed on the top. Lexi looked at them warily, and Archie laughed.

'Don't worry, we're not proposing. Open it.'

She flipped off the lid and revealed a lovely watch. As the one she was wearing was scratched and battered, it was obviously welcome.

'And don't go wearing it around the farm,' warned Sophie. 'Look at the state of your old one.'

'Too right,' said Archie. 'It's too good for work.'

'It's lovely,' I said admiringly. 'Really pretty.'

Sophie looked at my watch and blushed. 'Well, obviously, it's not as grand as yours. I mean, look at that! You shop in posh places, don't you?'

'A Christmas present,' I said. 'It's a bit grand for me. I was hoping for a Kindle.'

Gabriel stared at me, and I reddened. Now he probably thought I was an ungrateful madam. Why couldn't I just keep my big mouth shut?

'Go on, Gabriel, give her your present,' said Archie.

Lexi looked up at her father, and he looked back, suddenly awkward. I was sorry to be there, sure I was contributing to his embarrassment. He obviously didn't have much money and may not have been able to buy her much of a gift. Now he was going to feel shown up in front of a woman with a bloody designer watch on her wrist. I would have left to make things easier for him, but I wasn't sure how to do that now, especially with Amy still asleep on the sofa.

He walked over to an oak sideboard and opened the middle cupboard, taking out a small box and handing it to Lexi with a mumbled, 'Happy birthday, darling.'

Lexi carefully unwrapped the gift, while I watched through my fingers, my stomach churning with nerves for him. Oh, I hoped she liked it, whatever it was.

'Oh, Dad!'

I could tell from her voice that she did, and I put my hands down, suddenly realising that I'd been holding my breath. I leaned forward and looked at the present, my mouth dropping open in awe.

It was a jewellery box and obviously something he'd made himself. Every little detail spoke of his care and love for his daughter. It was beautifully fashioned from solid wood, and on the lid was a delicately carved picture of a long-eared hare, gazing up at the moon.

'Home,' Lexi murmured, looking up at him tearfully.

He nodded and smiled. 'Home.'

She passed the box to Sophie and threw her arms around him, sharing some secret message, the meaning of which I had no idea. There was a hush as we all watched, and I wondered if I was the only one who felt like an intruder.

Oliver broke the silence. 'For God's sake, Lexi, open those bloody chocolates. I've been dying for a nut cluster all day.'

Lexi laughed and handed him the box of chocolates, and then Amy woke up and, after an initial moment of shock at all the strange faces around her, relaxed upon seeing Lexi and accepted a chocolate. She rapidly became the centre of attention with everyone making quite a fuss of her. Gabriel made her a cup of cocoa, and Tessa finally woke up and moved from the rug, wandering over to say hello to her and receiving an adoring hug in return.

It was a delightful evening, and no one could be more surprised about that than me. I was quite sorry to announce that I'd have to take Amy home, as it was so late and way past her bedtime.

'It's been lovely,' I told them, realising I meant it. 'Thanks so much for having me.'

'Not at all,' said Gabriel. 'Thank you for Lexi's cake. And,' he said quietly as he showed me to the door, 'thank you being so forgiving. I really am sorry I was such an arse.'

I couldn't help laughing. 'Please don't mention arses, Mr Bailey. Not after I'd managed to decorate mine so nicely with mint Aero.'

His face lit up and those dimples made a welcome return. 'I was going to tell you,' he admitted, 'but I thought it best left to another woman. And my name's Gabriel,' he added. 'Like the angel, remember?'

My heart sank. I'd forgotten all about my mission and, for a while there, I'd felt like a normal person with a normal life, again. 'Well, thank you, Gabriel. It's been quite an evening. Not what I expected at all.'

He looked at me, no longer smiling. 'Me neither,' he said.

There was a silence for a moment, then Sophie called, 'Gabriel, your bloody dog's just been sick on the rug!'

Gabriel rolled his eyes. 'She's been your dog for the last six months, remember!' he yelled back.

I grinned, screwing up my nose, as Archie yelled, 'Bugger that, I think there's half a sodding cake in that lot.'

'Yuk, you'd better go and see to your patient,' I told him.

His smile faded a little, and he nodded. 'Goodnight, Eliza.'

'Goodnight, Gabriel.'

As I lay in bed half an hour later, staring up into the darkness, I thought about what a fabulous evening it had been. The Crooks and Baileys were such a lovely family. It had been a privilege to be part of Lexi's birthday celebrations. I finally nodded off at around midnight and, for the first time I could remember, Harry wasn't my last thought before I drifted off to sleep.

Chapter 14

I woke up surprisingly early the next morning and lay for a few moments, luxuriating in the warmth and comfort of the big bed, seeing the sunlight peeping round the edges of the blind, and remembering with contentment the lovely evening I'd had.

I was quite looking forward to getting Amy and myself ready and heading back to Sophie's for her grand tour. She'd refused to let me set foot out of the living room last night, insisting that I had to see the house properly. I smiled, realising that I was already quite fond of Sophie. I had a warm, unfamiliar feeling lately that I realised was happiness. I loved it at Kearton Bay. I could easily get used to this way of life.

Just as I was contemplating this, the sound of sleigh bells rang out. I reached for my phone, which lay on the bedside table, my stomach doing its usual little jig when I saw Harry's name.

'Eliza? I'm sorry I haven't been in touch for a while, it's been absolutely manic here.'

I could well imagine. I wrapped the duvet around me, already subconsciously protecting myself as I waited to hear what he had to say.

'Are you there?'

'I'm here. How are you?'

'Fucking stressed, if you must know. It's crisis time here. You won't believe this, but Martin called us into his office yesterday and dropped a real bombshell on us.'

I wished he'd dropped more than that on them.

'He reckons that people are getting sick of seeing rich people looking for beautiful houses, what with this recession, or whatever it is, and that maybe it's time we wound up *Twice as Nice* and focused on the less well-off trying to get on the property ladder.'

So, did that mean he wouldn't be working with Melody in future? I was about to ask but didn't get chance.

'Well, we weren't happy about that, I can tell you. I told him, if you think we're going to be trailing a load of chavs around backstreet terraces and council estates, you can think again. It's ludicrous. As Melody said, in a recession, people want taking out of their dreary lives. Seeing all those lovely houses we view helps them forget their own miserable circumstances and dream for a while. We all need to dream, don't we?'

I gripped the phone. 'Personally, I seem to be stuck in a recurring nightmare.'

He wasn't even listening. 'Things are really bad here, and Melody and I are having to lobby the powers-that-be. They must be made to realise that no one wants to watch such dismal programmes. We have to fight for *Twice as Nice*. You can imagine we're having a terrible time of it.'

Gosh, yes. The poor darlings.

'Anyway, I was wondering if you'd call Joe and ask him to drive your car up to you and bring mine back? I'm lost without it, and I simply can't bring myself to drive that ancient Fiesta. You really must get a new car, Eliza. It's positively embarrassing. What will people think? So, will you ask him?'

'How do you know he's coming up here?' I demanded.

'Mrs Travers let it slip the other day. Not that it was any great surprise. I mean, we couldn't sneeze without Joe being there to say God bless you, could we? He couldn't go too long without seeing you.'

Unlike you, obviously, I thought. 'I'll ask him,' I said, my voice dull. 'Is that it?'

'What do you mean, is that it?'

'Is that why you called? To ask me about the car?'

'Well, and to tell you about work, of course. It's been a hell of a week. I'm so stressed I can't tell you, and Mrs Travers is buggering off to Brighton, or somewhere, and I'll have to sort the house out, as if I haven't got enough to do.'

'Margate.'

'Pardon?'

'She's going to Margate.'

'Oh, well, whatever. They're all the same, those places,' said the property expert. 'So, if you could call Joe, it would be terribly useful. I'll give the car keys to Mrs Travers to pass onto him, and he can post mine through the letterbox when he gets back. I shouldn't think he'd want to drop in for a cosy chat.'

He laughed, and I realised I was clenching my fist and tried to relax. 'Amy's fine, by the way,' I said.

'Is she? Oh, good. Do give her my love. I've missed her so much.'

I'd had enough. 'I'll have to go, Harry. Amy's calling for me,' I lied.

'Oh, right. Well, okay. I'll speak to you soon.'

'Don't bother,' I said.

'What?'

'I said, don't bother. I don't want to talk to you. I don't give a shit about *Twice as Nice*, or Melody or Martin, or anything else that's going on in your poxy life. I'm too busy sorting out my own and looking after Amy. Remember her? Don't call me again!'

'Eliza, you don't mean that—'

Oh, I bloody did. I ended the call and bit my lip to stop the tears from falling. What a doting father he was. I thought about the present Gabriel had handcrafted for Lexi and remembered the duplicate laptop Harry had bought for Amy. The difference between the two men was staggering.

I sent Joe a text, putting Harry's proposition to him, as it was too early to wake him with a phone call, then I lay there for a moment, tempted to pull the duvet over my head and cry myself back to sleep, but as I thought about my plans for the day I sat up, suddenly determined. Harry had spoilt enough of my life. He wasn't going to spoil another day of it.

****

You'd never have known how chaotic the scene had been last night in the living room of The Old Vicarage. When I arrived the place was immaculate, and Sophie showed me round her home, obviously bursting with pride, while Tally sat with Amy and endured one of her seemingly endless conversations about *Frozen*, donkeys, Jeeves and Wooster, and why George Pig was so much more delightful than his big sister, Peppa.

I dutifully admired Sophie's bespoke kitchen units and granite worktops, the spotlights in the ceiling and the slate floor. I cooed at her grand bathroom, with its Jacuzzi bath and power shower, and aah-ed at her conservatory and utility room. I could tell it all meant a great deal to her, and, to be fair, it was a lovely house.

As we toured the bedrooms, she told me about her family. She and Archie had been together for over thirty years. They'd met when she started work as a typist at the law firm in Helmston, where he was a junior solicitor.

'I made a joke about him having the wrong name for a solicitor, being called Crook, and all the other girls gawped at me as if I was going to get sacked or something, but he just laughed and agreed with me. Next day, he asked me out, and that was that.'

They'd lived in Helmston for some years but, when they decided it was time to start a family, they'd moved back to Kearton Bay where both had lived as children. The twins had arrived eighteen years ago, and Tallulah a year later.

'So, you've always lived here, apart from Helmston?' I felt bad playing the innocent, but I had a job to do. Sherlock Holmes didn't waste time with guilt.

Sophie smoothed the duvet cover on Oliver's bed and shook her head. 'No. I moved to Whitby when I was twelve, and mum and dad had Gabriel the following year.'

'So, Gabriel was born in Whitby?'

'That's right. The first Bailey man not born in Kearton Bay for generations.'

'Why did they move to Whitby?'

'Dad had a disagreement with Grandad about the way the practice was being run. Grandad had fixed ideas, and Dad wanted to try new things, so he decided to strike out on his own.'

Joe said that my father had left Kearton Bay after a disagreement with his father, so that fitted, but where did Leeds come into it?

'So, he went to Whitby?'

'Yes. Joined a practice there, and we stayed there for a while. Then Dad had a falling out with one of the partners and he went to Wetherby.'

My heart leapt into my mouth. Wetherby was pretty close to Leeds — that much I did know. Was that how he'd met my mother?

'And then?'

Sophie frowned, as she noticed a pile of clothes stuffed under Oliver's bed and pulled them out for inspection.

'What? Oh, he didn't like it. Moved back to Whitby, made up with Grandad, and went back to work here at Kearton Bay till he retired. Look at the state of these clothes! They're not even dirty. Bloody kids.'

She began to fold them up. 'That reminds me. I meant to ask you, do you want to borrow my iron, some time?'

'There's one at the cottage,' I said, puzzled.

She looked me up and down, her face a little flushed. 'Oh. Sorry. Just thought I'd ask.'

Oh, bugger. I would never get the hang of this ironing lark. I glanced down at my rather creased dress, which I'd spent absolutely ages trying to get right, before giving up and hanging it on a coat hanger with a vague hope that the creases would just drop out themselves overnight.

Sophie obviously decided it was time to change the subject. 'Anyway, enough of the family history. Amy must be bored stiff.'

'Amy will be fine,' I assured her. 'It's Tally I'm worried about.'

'Oh, Tally won't mind,' Sophie said. 'She's got a way with children. She's such a good girl. I'm very lucky. Are you hungry?'

We sat down at the kitchen table, and Sophie pushed a selection of low-unit snacks at me, then it was my turn to be pumped for information.

'So, whereabouts in London do you live?' she enquired, nibbling on a prawn, as I tried to look enthusiastic about the rice crackers I was munching. In the living room, Amy and Tally were tucking into roast chicken sandwiches. I tried not to feel jealous. I could always get a takeaway later.

'Chiswick,' I said.

'Oh. I'm not familiar with London. Only went once, to visit Gabriel when he lived there. I wasn't too impressed, to be honest.'

'Gabriel lived in London?'

'Oh, yes. Got a job there — only to please Lady Zoe, of course. Not 'cos he wanted to be there. He and Lexi hated it, and I can't say I blame them. Relief all round when he put his foot down and moved back home.'

This was all news to me. To think he'd been in London! But why? And when?

'I suppose everyone's different,' she continued. 'You obviously like it there. Is Chiswick nice, then?'

I nodded. 'Yes, it's lovely. Lots to do, and not far from my uncle's house.'

'Oh, where does he live?'

'St Johns Wood,' I told her.

She raised an eyebrow. 'Classy. What does he do for a living?'

I flushed. 'He, er, he's in entertainment.'

'Really? What sort of entertainment?' She looked at me suspiciously. Blimey, she'd be thinking Joe was a high-class pimp, if I carried on being so evasive. I decided to come clean. 'He's in television.'

Her face lit up. 'Like your husband? Does he do property shows, too? Would I have heard of him?'

I sighed. 'No, he's a chat show presenter, and yes, probably. Joe Hollingsworth?'

Sophie's face was a picture. Honestly, I thought she was going to explode.

'You're Joe Hollingsworth's niece?' She could barely manage to whisper the words. Talk about awestruck. I wasn't too surprised.

Joe had been voted "The Housewives' Favourite" in *All the Goss* magazine for the last four years.

He'd howled with laughter when he first won it. 'Poor bloody housewives. Barking up the wrong tree there, aren't they?'

Sophie shook her head. 'I just can't believe it. You've no idea how much I love that man. Archie gets quite jealous, sometimes. Of course, I know he's a celebrity and wouldn't be interested in me.'

'Well, not romantically,' I admitted. 'You're the wrong gender, I'm afraid, but as a person, Joe's interested in everybody. He gets on well with all sorts.'

Except Harry, obviously.

Sophie wanted to know all about Joe and what his house was like, and if Jeeves and Wooster were really his pigs or just "actors", and did he think he'd ever get another dog after losing Bertie?

I held my hands up in the end. 'You can ask him yourself in a few days,' I told her. 'He's coming to stay with me. Just for a couple of days, but I'm sure I'll find time to introduce you.'

Sophie's mouth dropped open. 'Really?'

I nodded. 'Sure. Why not?'

She was speechless for a moment, then she grabbed the dishes of carrot batons and rice crackers and prawns and tipped the whole lot in the bin. I stared at her in surprise as she marched over to the fridge and pulled out a large plate.

'Bailey's cheesecake,' she whispered, putting it down in front of me. 'Bugger the diet. This is a special occasion. But for God's sake, don't tell the others!'

****

Joe arrived two days later, greeted by an ecstatic Amy.

'Hello, Sweetpea.' He grinned, scooping her up into his arms and whirling her round. It was hard to say who looked the happiest.

I patted my trusty old Fiesta. 'She made it, then.'

'She did, though, God knows, I held my breath most of the way here. How we got down those hills, I don't know. Like a bloody slalom course round here.'

I laughed, linking my arm through his, and led him inside, where he looked round approvingly.

'Thank God for that. I was expecting all sorts after you told me the ceiling had collapsed. Nice little cottage. Bit small, though.'

'You're taking Amy's room, and she can come in with me, for now. Good job Mrs Travers didn't come, after all, or you'd have been on the sofa.'

Mrs Travers had refused point blank to visit, despite my pleas. She didn't agree with the north and wouldn't believe my assurances that she would still be able to watch *EastEnders* and buy *All the Goss*. She'd tolerated Joe's broad Yorkshire accent and my faint one, because we'd been sensible enough to make the effort to become honorary southerners by moving to London, but she wouldn't entertain the idea of being surrounded by a whole lot of people whom she could barely understand. Instead, she'd gone off to stay with her sister in Margate. They were always arguing but seemed to enjoy it, and Mrs Travers always returned from her jaunts to the town with a smile on her face and a renewed energy.

It was probably for the best. She would take a dim view of the fact that my acrylic talons had already gone. I'd had them removed as they'd ended up looking almost as bad as my own chewed stumps. Denise, the hairdresser at Klassy Kutz, had offered to replace them, but I'd declined. They got on my nerves. She was quite disappointed, but I'd appeased her by letting her touch up my roots. She'd been quite thrilled that someone from "that London" had graced her salon, and we'd got on well, so she got over her disappointment quite quickly, especially when I left her a generous tip.

Joe asked to be excused from looking around the village that evening, pleading exhaustion. He looked drained. He had dark shadows under his eyes and his skin had an unhealthy pallor.

'Are you okay? You don't look well,' I said, squeezing his hand in concern.

'Packed in smoking,' he confessed. 'Reckon it's going to finish me off. Never felt less healthy in my life.'

'You've stopped smoking? About time! What made you finally quit?' I asked, remembering how many times I'd begged him to do it in the past, even buying him special chewing gum, to no avail.

He shrugged. 'Getting on a bit, now. Fifty, after all. Time I looked after myself, I suppose.'

'You're all right?'

'Me? Right as rain. Just been a busy few weeks,' he said.

'And now the series has ended, are you planning a holiday?'

'Eventually. I've still got my autobiography to finish, remember? Deadline's not far away.'

'You could write on a beach, as easily as at your house.'

'I'm filming a panel show next week, and I have a few other bits and bobs in the pipeline.'

I groaned. 'Joe, when will you ever slow down? You should be taking some time to enjoy yourself. Life isn't all about work, you know.'

He sighed. 'So I keep being told.'

'Good. I'm glad other people are trying to persuade you.'

He smiled at Amy. 'Shall we have a nice quiet evening in? I haven't seen *Frozen* for a while. What do you say?'

'I haven't brought it with me,' I whispered. 'For God's sake, don't start her off!'

Joe winked. 'Have a look in my bag,' he told her. 'You might find a present in there for you.'

Amy scrambled off her chair and rushed over to where Joe had put his laptop bag. Unzipping it, she exclaimed in delight as she found, tucked in beside his laptop, three Disney DVDs, including *Frozen*.

'Mrs Travers snaffled them for me from yours,' he explained.

I smiled. I could always rely on Mrs Travers and Joe. Where would I be without them?

Chapter 15

I'd promised Rose that she would be the first person in the village that I'd introduce Joe to. She'd been stunned when I told her that I was his niece and that he was coming to stay for a couple of days.

'Bloody hell, Eliza, are there any more secrets you're keeping?'

Joe was used to being gawped at everywhere we went, and so he took little notice as the murmuring of tourists began, and people began to stop and stare at him as we passed. I still found it all very embarrassing, all too aware that people would also be looking at me, wondering who I was and how I came to be with him.

'Dear God, how are we supposed to get back up here?' Joe asked, as we made our way down Bay Street. 'They should install a stairlift.'

'We only have to go halfway down to Pinky's,' I promised. 'It's not much further. At least it's not too warm today. You ought to try coming back up here in the heat.'

'Don't think I'd bother,' he admitted, sighing in relief, as we climbed the steps to Water's Edge and the path finally levelled off.

'Welcome to my humble café,' said Rose, bowing low as we entered Pinky's. 'Plonk yourself down and I'll bring you a coffee over,' she added, as Joe looked around him in undisguised horror.

'Jesus,' he whispered. 'Wish I'd brought my sunglasses.'

Rose brought us coffees and handed Amy an ice cream before cutting three slices of quiche for herself, Joe, and me.

'So, Joe Hollingsworth, eh? In my café. Who'd have believed it? What do you think to the place, then?'

'It's very, er, unusual,' said Joe. I watched him take a bite of the quiche and saw his eyes widen, but he was far too polite to say anything and chewed valiantly.

'Yeah,' Rose conceded. 'I may have made a bit of an error of judgement with the decor, but hey ho. Too late now. I guess, when Jimbo buggered, off I wanted to show the world that this place was all mine. Stamp my identity on it. Might have been a bit of an overreaction, to be honest. Have you taken him to meet Sophie yet?'

'Of course not! I promised you'd be first. Sophie's popping round to see us later this afternoon.'

'There you go, Joe. Proper treat in store for you there, pet,' said Rose with an evil grin.

'She sounds fascinating,' said Joe, putting his half-eaten quiche back on the plate. 'But you don't really think she may be your half-sister, Eliza?'

I shrugged. 'It's possible, but not definite.'

I filled Rose in on what Sophie had said about her father's falling out with her grandfather and the move to Wetherby.

She nodded. 'Sounds like an open-and-shut case to me.'

'I wouldn't go that far,' I said. 'There are still big fat question marks. I mean, Wetherby's not Leeds, and we don't know how long he was there, or even which year, exactly. It may all be a coincidence.'

'I agree,' said Joe, 'You can't go jumping to conclusions.'

'Bollocks,' said Rose. 'How many other sodding Raphaels do you think there are around here?'

I folded my arms, suddenly quite annoyed with her. 'You can't know that. We need to be absolutely certain, and I'm not — far from it.'

Rose was obviously puzzled by my attitude. 'I thought you'd be pleased? I thought this was what you wanted? Why are you being so offhand about it all?'

'I'm not. I just don't want to get my hopes up and find it's all rubbish, that's all.'

I felt really out of sorts, and it wasn't just Rose's quiche that was making me want to cry. I'd no idea what was wrong with me. I felt like howling.

'I think it's all been a bit much for you,' said Joe. 'All this stuff with Harry, and now this cloak-and-dagger business. It's too big. Maybe you should back off, go somewhere else for a while and forget all about this.'

'No chance,' I said, blinking back tears. 'I've come this far. I need to find out the rest.'

'Well, you seem to have taken to them all, at any rate,' he admitted. 'You're obviously getting on well with Sophie. What about the others? Gabriel, did you say? And Lexi?'

'Lexi's lovely,' Rose said. She put down her half-eaten quiche and sighed. 'This is shit. I don't know how you can eat it. It's like bloody rubber.'

'It's fine,' Joe said. Rose's eyes met his, and he grinned sheepishly. 'Okay, it's not the best I've ever tasted, but it's not the worst, either.'

'You liar,' she said, and they both laughed.

'What about the brother, or whatever he is?' Joe asked.

'Ah, our black sheep. I have an update on that for you, Eliza. Been doing some digging of my own.'

I sat up, curious to know, despite my sudden nerves. 'You mean about his wife?'

'No. About him,' she said. 'Had a chat with Rita from the post office. Don't worry,' she added, obviously noticing my worried expression, 'I was subtle. I just told her about being invited to Sophie's for lunch and said it was weird about her brother having to live with her again. "Oh, I know," she said. "It's all very odd. I can't think what Dr Bailey is playing at these days." I was like, "No, not Sophie's father, her brother, you know, Gabriel." "I know who you mean," she says, "Dr Bailey, her brother." Well, you could have knocked me over with a feather, so I starts to question her, and it appears that, until fairly recently, Gabriel was working in Helmston as a GP. So, I went down to see Walter, who runs the dinosaur and fossil place, and I was like, "Walter, is this right about Gabriel Bailey once being a doctor?" and he was like, "Yes, absolutely. And a good one, an' all, by all accounts," and I was like, "So, what happened? Why is he giving donkey rides on the beach now?" and he was like, "No one knows. And if they do, they're not saying." There you have it. What do you make of all that?'

Joe and I were both sitting there with our mouths open, and it took a few moments to make any sense of what she'd said, but eventually Joe gave a whistle and said, 'Well, the mystery deepens.'

'I knew it!' I said. 'I never saw Gabriel as an odd job man giving donkey rides. I knew it was all wrong, but why would he give that up?'

'Maybe he didn't have a choice,' Joe said. He saw my expression and shrugged.

'Maybe he was struck off,' he continued. 'Don't look so shocked, love. It happens. And why else would a man with a well-paid job like that end up doing that sort of work?'

I couldn't think of a reason, but I couldn't believe he'd been struck off either.

'Well, we've obviously got some more detective work to do,' said Rose, gleefully.

I said nothing. It didn't seem like such a thrill any more. These weren't just names to me now. They were real people, and it was their lives we were digging around in. It seemed wrong, and I didn't feel proud of myself for doing it. Somehow, I felt that I was letting them down, and I wasn't so sure, any more, that finding my father was worth it.

****

Sophie arrived at Amethyst Cottage that afternoon, bringing with her a bottle of wine and a copy of the *Radio Times* with Joe on the cover, which she begged him to sign for her. He duly obliged, the crinkles in the corner of his eyes revealing that he didn't mind and found her quite amusing — especially when she begged to take his photo and then couldn't figure out how to work the camera on her phone.

'Sodding thing!' she wailed. 'Honestly, why do they make them so complicated? I'm ever so sorry, Joe. Can you just hold on a minute?'

She peered at her phone in frustration and, in the end, I took pity on her, taking it from her hands and snapping the two of them together. Sophie couldn't have smiled any wider if she'd tried.

'I can't believe it, I really can't. Fancy you being Eliza's uncle. I voted for you in the television awards, you know. Bloody Ant and Dec! You should have won both awards, not just one. Anyway, get some glasses out, and we'll have a toast to your success.'

We got out the glasses and toasted Joe being an award winner, and sipped our wine and listened to Sophie prattling on about how much she adored *The Joe Hollingsworth Show*, and how much she enjoyed *Twice as Nice*, and how wonderful Harry was and how she couldn't wait to meet him, and I sat there with gritted teeth thinking there wasn't enough wine in the bottle to get me through much more of that conversation. I decided it was time to steer Sophie off course and began talking about Lexi.

Sophie was obviously proud of her niece. 'Studying humanities, but she's specialising in history and history of art. Always liked that sort of thing. She's such a good girl.'

'Why didn't she go to an ordinary university?' asked Joe.

Sophie looked decidedly shifty. 'She moved around a bit and never really settled at school. She was bullied for a while, and it put her off. It was only last year that she decided to go for it. She always liked history. I just know she'll be a big success. It runs in the family. They're all clever — except for me,' she admitted with a sigh.

'You seem bright enough to me,' Joe said, and Sophie's eyes lit up.

'Oh, thanks. Mind you, I'm not really. Just a typist, whereas all my family are doctors and nurses, and Archie's a solicitor and my kids are all doing so well. Oliver and Pandora will be heading off to university in September. I feel quite stupid, sometimes.'

'But if you hadn't been a typist, Sophie, you'd never have met Archie,' I pointed out.

She thought for a moment then nodded. 'Yeah, you're right. Everything happens for a reason.'

'What about Lexi's mum?' I asked casually. 'What did she do for a living?'

'Zoe?' Sophie snorted and took another mouthful of wine. 'All she ever did was spend money. Designer this and designer that. No offence, Eliza,' she added hastily. 'Thing is, she didn't earn a penny in the whole time they were together, and the way she spent, you'd have thought she was loaded.'

'Liked her luxuries, did she?' asked Joe, topping up her glass with the last of the wine and giving me a sly wink.

'Oh, Joe, you have no idea.' Sophie sighed, apparently not noticing that she was now on her fourth glass, while Joe and I were still sipping our first.

'She sounds appalling,' he said, patting her hand comfortingly. Sophie nodded.

'Terrible woman. Trapped him into marriage, you know. Got pregnant deliberately. Oh, Gabriel will tell you different! He always did stick up for her. Kept telling us that she couldn't help being depressed and that shopping was some sort of therapy for her. Huh! Expensive therapy. My God! Anyway, was depression her excuse for having an affair?'

'She had an affair?'

Sophie stared at me and seemed to realise what she'd said. 'What must you think of me? Prattling on like this about something you have no interest in whatsoever.'

She took a deep breath and pushed her glass away, turning to Joe with a slightly lopsided smile. 'Now, Joe, you must tell me all about those sweet little pigs of yours. I was so sorry to hear about poor little Bertie, by the way. They become like family, don't they? Such a shame.'

I realised that I'd got all I was going to get from Sophie that day, but I'd heard enough. Gabriel must have loved his wife very much, to have put up with all that. I knew it had nothing to do with me and nothing to do with my mission to find my father. What the hell was wrong with me? Nothing had changed, yet for some reason I felt more miserable than ever.

****

Joe stayed for two nights, as promised, then had to say goodbye. I cried, and so did Amy. I think I even saw tears in his eyes, but he had no choice. He had work to do and he didn't like to let anyone down.

'Are you sure you don't want to come back with me?' he asked, carrying his bags to the door and staring in some dismay at Harry's car. He wasn't looking forward to driving that any more than he had my ancient Fiesta.

'To what? Harry and Melody?'

'Come to my house. Stay with me for a while. Get your breath back and forget all this private detective stuff. You don't seem to be very happy with what you've discovered so far. Are you really sure you want to go on with it all?'

Quite honestly, I wasn't, but everything was so messy in my life and I wanted some loose ends tying up. As for finding my father, well, that was becoming ever more confusing. What's that quotation from *Marmion*?

Oh! What a tangled web we weave, when first we practice to deceive.

Yep, Sir Walter Scott had pretty much summed it up. The whole Bailey family tree was becoming ever more baffling by the day and I was increasingly worried that I was only going to cause an even bigger mess.

Yet, if I walked away, how would I ever know why my father had to abandon me and my mother? There had to be a reason and I needed to know what it was. All my life, I'd fantasised that he'd had to leave us against his will. If Raphael Bailey was my father and had been married to Gabriel's mother at the time then that helped to explain some of it, but I wanted to know why he'd felt unable to make any contact with me at all. Surely, he knew my mother would be discreet? She'd loved him so much, she would never have caused trouble for him.

150

I felt depressed when Joe left. I wasn't sure if I was going to stay on at Amethyst Cottage or not, and he'd promised that if I decided to, he would come back and stay again, but I missed him and felt quite lonely. I rang Rose for sympathy, only to find that she was as fed up as I was, if not more.

'Bloody Fuchsia! She's practically finished at college now and she's decided that she's bored with office work and might look for something else to do. Two years studying office practice, and she's on about doing hair and beauty! Beauty! She's got a face like a smacked arse half the time. Nothing beautiful about that. I need a drink. Do you fancy coming out tonight?'

I wasn't sure. 'Lexi's already babysitting for tomorrow's class. Doubt she'd want to babysit two nights running.'

'You can ask, can't you? She'll probably be glad of the money.'

She was, and I rang Rose back to inform her I was free, after all. 'Not The Hare and Moon, though,' I said.

'Oh? Why not?'

I hadn't told Rose about my run-in with Rhiannon and I didn't want to. The fewer people who knew about her affair with Marty, the less chance there was of Milly being hurt. 'I'm just bored with it. There are three other pubs in this village, and I haven't been in one of them. What about The Kearton Arms?'

She sounded doubtful. 'Dunno about that. It's a bit pricey, Eliza.'

'My treat,' I said. 'Honestly, you're doing me a favour. I just want to get out and forget all about everything for a while.'

Eventually, she agreed, and we arranged to meet outside the pub at half-past seven.

Having never been in there before, I wasn't sure what to expect, but I liked the interior of the pub as soon as I stepped inside. It wasn't as old as The Hare and Moon, and its rooms were much larger and brighter. It had thick carpets, cushioned seats, and highly polished woodwork. The bar was big and heaving with customers, and the dining room looked even busier. As Rose and I stood waiting to be served, we scanned the room, hoping that there were a couple of seats empty.

We were served by a ruddy-faced man who introduced himself

as Clifford. 'And what can I get you lovely ladies?' he enquired.

'Just an orange juice, please,' I said.

Rose pulled a face. 'Boring,' she said. 'Vodka and Coke please, Clifford, and make it a bloody large one.'

'That kind of day was it?' He grinned. 'Take a seat, and I'll bring them over.'

'Over where?' I asked, looking round and seeing no empty tables.

Rose nodded to the far corner, where two people were sitting, deep in conversation. 'Over there. Meggie and Ben won't mind,' she said, leading me to the table through the crowds.

Meggie looked up as we approached their table, and smiled in welcome.

'Would you mind if we sit here?' Rose asked. 'We don't want to shove in, but there are no other empty seats.'

'No problem,' replied Meggie's husband, who introduced himself to me as Ben English. He seemed a pleasant enough chap, perhaps in his early fifties, with light brown hair and hazel eyes.

'Ben, this is Eliza,' Meggie said. 'You know, the one who made that fudge.' She leaned over and patted my hand appreciatively. 'Never tasted anything like it,' she said. 'Is it too late for me to ask for some marshmallows?'

I shook my head. 'No. I've got half the orders done already and I'll do the rest tomorrow, ready for the meeting.'

'What's the point of going to this slimming club if you're all secretly eating sweets?' Ben asked, not unreasonably, to be fair. It was a question I'd asked myself, too, pangs of guilt attacking me as I thought about Sophie, and also wondered if I was right to jeopardise all those women's attempts to lose weight.

Meggie spoke slowly and clearly as if explaining to a child. 'We're not going for the diet. It's just a night out, that's all. A chance to catch up with everyone. Anyway, it keeps Sophie in work,' she added. I tried to smile, but I couldn't help feeling I was sabotaging poor Sophie's attempts to help everyone and undermining her position as group leader.

'Meggie works at Ivy House Surgery,' Rose said, looking hard into my eyes. 'She works for Dr Pennington-Rhys now, but she used to work for Dr Bailey, isn't that right, Meggie?'

Meggie nodded. 'Yes, that's right. Lovely chap, he was. Not that Dr Pennington-Rhys isn't lovely, too. I've been very lucky with my bosses, I must say.'

Rose leaned towards her, her expression eager. 'But when you say Dr Bailey, you mean old Dr Bailey? Not young Dr Bailey?'

Meggie frowned. 'Well, sort of. It depends what you mean by old Dr Bailey. I wasn't around when old, *old* Dr Bailey was working, of course. I'm not quite fifty yet, I'll have you know.'

By now, I was thoroughly confused, and when Clifford brought the drinks over, I wished I'd gone for the vodka, too.

'Cheers, Clifford,' said Rose, and he nodded and headed back to the bar, as she continued her investigations. 'So, there were three Dr Baileys?'

Ben yawned. 'Bloody hell, Rose. What does it matter?'

'There have been quite a few,' said Meggie, nudging Ben. 'The one I worked for was Dr Raphael Bailey, although I suppose that doesn't help much since his father was Dr Raphael Bailey, too. But I never worked for young Dr Bailey, you know, Gabriel. He worked in a practice in Thornley Beck, a few miles south of here, and then London for a while, before working in Helmston.'

'Why did he never work with his father?'

Meggie looked surprised at the question. 'Well, I suppose he wanted to prove he could be a success on his own, without family influence. I dunno.'

Ben looked thoroughly bored, and I decided it was time to change the subject, murmuring something about how lovely The Kearton Arms was, but Rose was like a dog with a bone.

'So, why isn't Gabriel still a doctor? What happened, Meggie?'

'What do you mean, what happened?' She was decidedly cagey.

'Well, what made him give up medicine?'

Meggie glanced at Ben, who took a sip from his pint and said nothing. 'Well, I don't know, really. None of my business,' she said.

I felt sorry for her, and ashamed of myself for being party to all this prying. 'What flavour marshmallows would you like,

Meggie?' I asked, desperate to steer the conversation away from the Bailey family. 'The salted caramel is popular.'

She looked at me gratefully and seemed about to say something, when another voice chimed in from behind me. 'Got struck off, as far as I know. And not surprising, either.'

I turned and saw an elderly woman with short, platinum blonde hair budging her seat towards us. To my surprise, she pushed in between me and Rose without even asking.

'Oh, hello, Maureen,' said Meggie wearily.

'Evening, Meggie, Ben.' The woman turned to Rose and held out her hand in greeting. 'Maureen Evans. You run Pinky's Café, don't you?'

'That's right, and this is my friend Eliza. She's staying here for a few weeks.'

The woman barely glanced at me, eager to fill Rose in on the situation with Gabriel Bailey. I didn't like her, and I didn't know what made her think she had the right to butt in, anyway.

'I used to work with Meggie, didn't I?' said the woman, as if reading my thoughts.

Meggie nodded, not looking too thrilled about it.

'I started back in the days of old Dr Bailey, who was a proper gentleman, I must say, not like his son, or his grandson, for that matter.'

Ben must have seen the look of pure bewilderment on my face because he tried to clarify. 'Maureen worked for old, old Dr Bailey, the first Raphael,' he explained. I'd just about managed to work that out.

Maureen nodded. 'That's right. He was old school. He'd have had a fit if he knew how things would turn out. Anyway, like I said, I worked for him, and very nice it was, too. Then his son joined the practice. Just about the same age as me, he was, and thought he knew it all. Kept bossing his father about and trying to change things. Flaming nuisance, truth be told. I was glad when they had a falling out and he cleared off to work in Whitby. 'Course, they didn't get on with him for long, either, and he ended up going to Wetherby. Huh, soon realised which side his bread was buttered there and came back. His father was too soft, if you ask me, giving him his job back. Anyway, I stuck at it, even when his father retired, and it was just me and him. Grumpy old sod he was. Pretended to be upset when his father died, but I don't think he really cared a jot. And then Meggie came to work with us, too, didn't you, Meggie? And eventually I'd had enough of him and left. Don't know how you coped with him, Meggie, really I don't.'

Meggie took a sip of her drink and said nothing.

Rose was practically bouncing on her chair. 'Yes, but what about Gabriel? You said he was struck off.'

'She said, as she far as she knows, and the truth is, none of us know,' said Meggie firmly.

'Oh, do I not? Well, it hardly takes a genius to work it out, does it? One minute he's a doctor with a posh house and a flash car, and his wife's swanking around like Lady Muck with her designer handbags and posh frocks, and the next he's on his own, wife walked out on him, and he hasn't two pennies to rub together. You know that house on the Farthingdale crossroads, just a bit up the road opposite here? The big Victorian one with the walled garden? That was his. Oh, yes,' she nodded, seeing my eyes widen in disbelief. 'When he'd been working in Thornley Beck for a few years, he bought it, to please Lady Zoe, no doubt. Except, that wasn't good enough for them. Kearton Bay was too dull, so they upped sticks to that London. He was another one who thought the grass was greener elsewhere, just like his father. Well, when he got back from London, he bought a smaller house in Helmston — cheaper there, see? And look at him now. I ask you! Now, in all honesty, can you see any other reason why a man with all that training, and a job that paid enough to buy a house like that, would end up working on Hannah's farm, feeding donkeys, and living with his sister, if he didn't have to? Can you?'

The awful thing was, I couldn't. It didn't make sense, unless Maureen was right, and Gabriel had been forced to give up the medical profession. But what could he have done that was so bad?

Maureen looked around, apparently satisfied that we were struck dumb with shock. 'Well, I'll be off,' she said, standing up and pushing her chair back to its original position. 'Nice to see you, Meggie. Not often we bump into each other, these days, is it?'

'No,' said Meggie, and we waited as the woman pushed through the crowds towards the door.

'And there's a bloody good reason for that,' she added when Maureen had finally exited. 'Listen, you two, take no notice of that woman. She knows nothing. She's got an axe to grind with the Baileys, because Dr Bailey — Gabriel's father — sacked her for unprofessional conduct. She had no idea what confidentiality meant and still doesn't, by the sound of it.'

'But if Gabriel wasn't struck off, Meggie,' said Rose, 'what would make him give up such a successful career?'

Meggie looked at Ben, and he gave her a look as if to say, "don't ask me". She had no answer to that one, and that's what I'd been afraid of.

Chapter 16

There followed two days of heavy rain, which meant Amy and I spent most of our time in the cottage, playing games and watching DVDs, baking together and reading.

I'd been racked with guilt, thinking about Sophie and the other Lightweights ladies. The meeting on Wednesday had revealed I'd lost another two pounds, but the delight of that revelation was spoilt when I handed out the contraband after the meeting, feeling that I was encouraging the others to break their diets. Some of them really did go to the meetings just for the social side of things, but I knew many, not least Meggie, really needed to lose some weight.

I spent hours after Amy went to sleep, scrolling through the internet pages on my phone, searching for low-calorie versions of the sweets I'd been making for them. I spent two afternoons experimenting with different types and flavours, with Amy perched on the stool beside me, helping me to decide which of the samples worked and which didn't. We quickly realised that the low-calorie versions weren't as good as the real thing, but they weren't bad, and I came up with a plan I wanted to put to Sophie.

Finally, the clouds cleared away and the sun came out. Amy was delighted, itching to get outside in the fresh air again. I considered going to visit Rose, but I didn't really want to go down to the chaos and crowds of Old Town. I wanted to be up here in the peace and quiet. I stood by the gate, looking down the road, as Amy skipped up and down the garden path, delighted to be outside at last. The verges were bright with buttercups, daisies and wild poppies. The sky was clear and, apart from the occasional rustle of the trees and the noise of insects in the grass, all was still and quiet.

'What would you like to do today?' I asked her.

She grinned, and I knew what she was going to say before she even opened her mouth. 'Donkeys.'

I groaned. I really couldn't face the beach. Then I remembered Lexi's invitation to the farm. She'd said there were donkeys and chickens there, and that Hannah would be welcoming. I looked down at her hopefully. 'Would you like to see some chickens, too?'

She clapped her hands and nodded, so I took her back inside and got her ready, noticing as I fastened her shoe buckles that my nails were looking awful. The acrylics had done them no favours whatsoever.

I didn't take the car. Lexi had said it was just up the road, so I locked the cottage and took hold of Amy's hand and we began to walk along the road, keeping to the edge as there was no footpath. After about ten minutes, I saw the lane on the opposite side of the road as Lexi had said, and we carefully crossed over. Whisperwood Farm. I thought it sounded lovely, like something from an Enid Blyton book. I imagined a whitewashed farmhouse with hens in the yard, beautiful stables with heavy horses looking out over the loosebox doors, a barn full of hay with a tractor parked outside, the sound of cows mooing in the fields and the clanking of buckets of milk being carried to a dairy to make creamy, yellow butter.

The lane was long and uneven, twisting and turning between fields and going on for much longer than I'd expected. There were little lanes leading off the main one that looked appealing and ripe for exploring. We passed other buildings, cottages and villas with smart cars parked outside, where washing on lines blew in the gentle breeze and the sound of lawnmowers and hedge trimmers broke the silence. I felt a pang of envy for the people who lived in these tucked-away homes. How peaceful it was. What could they possibly ever worry about living here?

Finally, up ahead, I saw some barns and outhouses and a five barred gate, which had a sign tacked to it reading "Whisperwood Farm". I realised I may have been slightly optimistic in my vision. At the end of the yard sat a big stone house. It had the familiar red roof and pretty gables, but it seemed a bit run down. The window frames looked as if they were rotting, and paint was peeling off the door. It looked a bit sorry for itself, to be honest.

I opened the gate and led Amy inside, keeping a tight hold on her, as she immediately wanted to introduce herself to the chickens, which were strutting around the barn. I closed the gate after me. The last thing I wanted was to let them out into the road. Amy and I crossed the yard, and I tried to stop shaking as the hens came over to have a look at us. Amy wasn't worried at all, and there was I trembling like a first-class wimp!

Two plump white ladies, obviously top of the pecking order, were particularly demonic-looking, strutting around us and staring unblinkingly at us with evil, beady eyes. Did chickens smell fear? Their beaks came perilously close to our ankles, forcing me to stoop to despicable levels.

'Bugger off! I have Paxo!' I threatened. They stared at me disdainfully, but didn't attack, so I assumed they were reconsidering their behaviour. Then, just as I was feeling safe, from one of the outhouses, a high-pitched whirring started. I looked at the chickens in horror, fearing a stampede.

'Pluck off,' I commanded. That seemed to do the trick. They strutted away, obviously sensing a woman on the edge, and totally unfazed by the noise, which I supposed must be a regular occurrence. Then I remembered that Gabriel did his woodwork there. It was probably him with some sort of electrical saw. I turned Amy towards the farmhouse, desperate to get indoors before I humiliated myself even further and told them to get stuffed.

I had to knock three times on the shabby door, and I'd just decided no one was in, when it finally opened, and an old lady stood there. She stared at me for a moment, her faded blue eyes taking in every detail of me, as I stood squirming under her scrutiny. I hoped she hadn't seen my shameful behaviour towards her chickens. Then she looked down at Amy and her gnarled hand reached out and stroked her blonde hair.

'Well, you must be Eliza and Amy,' she said.

Thank God, Lexi must have told her about us. I'd wondered if she would think it a cheek when two total strangers turned up, asking to see the animals, but obviously she'd been expecting a visit. I nodded, holding out my hand in greeting.

She took it, placing her other hand over mine and squeezing it gently. 'I'm Hannah,' she said. 'Hannah Lang. Come in, and I'll put the kettle on.'

She led me inside, and I found myself in a large kitchen. It was dominated by a huge old range and a massive scrubbed pine table with eight chairs around it. There was an ancient flagstone floor, and the units were rather shabby, but it was clean. To my surprise, Tessa was lying in front of the range. Gabriel and Lexi probably liked to keep her close.

Hannah filled the kettle with water and beamed down at Amy. 'Now, me and your mummy are going to have a nice cup of tea, but what about you, eh? What would you like? I've got milk and fresh orange juice in my fridge.' She looked up at me. 'What does she usually drink?'

Amy was staring in awed silence at the old lady, so I decided milk would be fine, and Hannah poured her a cup and set it down on the table, before going to the cupboard and producing a tin of biscuits. 'There you go. They're Lexi's, but she won't mind.'

Amy climbed onto a chair and reached for a ginger biscuit.

Hannah poured the tea and passed me a cup, setting a sugar bowl beside me, which I left untouched. 'So,' she said, sitting opposite me and taking a sip from her tea, 'you've come to see the animals, eh?'

'I hope you don't mind,' I said. 'Lexi thought it would be a treat for Amy and she didn't think you'd object.'

'Of course I don't. Why should I?' she asked. She gazed at me again, those eyes of her thoughtful. 'From London, aren't you?'

'Yes, Chiswick. Well, I'm originally from Yorkshire.' I hoped that if I told her we came from the same county, she might think a bit more of me. Northerners didn't seem to set much store by London, in my experience.

'Oh, aye? Whereabouts?'

'Knaresborough,' I said.

She nodded approvingly. 'Lovely place. So, why leave?'

'My uncle had to move to London for his work, so I went with him, obviously, since I was only twelve. He was my guardian,' I explained.

'Oh. What happened to your mum and dad, then?'

'My mum was killed in a car crash with my gran, when I was seven. Grandad died not long after, so Joe took care of me after that.'

She was silent for a moment, probably digesting the tragedy that had been my early life and wondering if I was about to burst into tears. She seemed to decide that it was safe to continue with her enquiries. 'No dad?'

I shook my head. 'No. Never knew him. Joe was my dad, to all intents and purposes. He was amazing.'

She smiled. 'Aye. I like him. Watch him every week. Couldn't believe it when Lexi told me he was your uncle. Small world, eh?'

I nodded, relieved that she liked Joe and didn't seem fazed by the fact that I had a celebrity for an uncle. I helped myself to a chocolate digestive, suddenly feeling more at home.

'I hear you're married to a celebrity, an' all? From that *Twice as Nice*?'

I sighed. So much for getting away from it all today. 'Yes. I am.'

There wasn't a lot else that I wanted to say on the subject, but Hannah was quite persistent. I must say, for an old lady, she was all there with her cough drops. She obviously sensed by my attitude that all was not rosy in that particular garden.

'But he's not on holiday with you?'

'He works very hard.'

'Don't they all? Long time for a holiday, a whole month.'

'I suppose so.'

'Be about time for you to go home. Shame that. We've only just got to know each other.'

'Well, yes, I suppose so.'

'So, why Kearton Bay?'

I nearly choked on my biscuit. Blimey, she wanted to know everything. What was with the interrogation? 'Why not?'

'Seems a bit out of the way from Chiswick, that's all. And there are plenty of places to visit down south, if you like that sort of thing,' she said.

'Maybe I don't like that sort of thing,' I suggested. 'And, anyway, you're forgetting I'm Yorkshire born and bred. Where else would I go but God's own county?'

She considered me for a moment then her face broke into a big smile. Her skin dissolved into a thousand wrinkles and she began to laugh. I smiled, glad I'd apparently won her over, then my eyes widened as her laugh turned into a cough and eventually ended on a wheeze that sounded like the air being let out of a set of bagpipes.

'Are you all right?'

'Oh, aye. Right as rain, me.'

She looked over at Amy, who was sipping her milk, watching her over the cup with concerned eyes. 'She's beautiful,' she murmured. 'How old is she?'

'Three,' I said with some pride. 'And I know she is.'

'And does she behave herself?'

'She's an angel,' I said. 'Apart from the occasional strop, and the fact that she takes her socks and shoes off when she's bored.'

She began to laugh again, and I found I was holding my breath, hoping she didn't launch into another coughing fit.

'My son was good as gold at three,' she admitted finally. 'By hell, he made up for it later on, though.'

'Does he work here?' I asked.

'Who, Albert?' she shook her head. 'You must be joking. He hated the farm. Hated Kearton Bay. Buggered off to Australia and married some glamour puss over there with false titties and big hair. You know the type.'

Oh, I did. I really did. Bloody men were all so shallow. I gave a big sigh and sipped on my tea.

'Any road, you came here to look at the animals. Now, I can't take you around the farm myself, on account of my pins being a bit unsteady, but Gabriel's in the workshop, if you get stuck.' She smiled at me, her old eyes sharp as tacks. 'He's a lovely man, Gabriel, don't you think?'

I nodded, my face burning. I really didn't want to get onto the subject of my possible big brother.

'Wasted around here,' she said. 'Deserves a hell of a lot more, I can tell you.'

I couldn't help myself. 'I've been told he used to be a doctor? Is that true?'

She nodded. 'It's no secret, aye.'

'So, what the hell is he doing working here? No offence, Hannah, but it takes a lot of studying and hard work to become a doctor. Why did he give it up?'

I waited for her answer, hardly believing how long she was taking to reply. She was looking into her cup as if tea leaves could reveal the answer. Maybe they could, but she'd used teabags. The longer she hesitated, the more my imagination ran riot.

Eventually, she looked up at me. 'Why don't you ask him?'

'Ask him?' Funny, the idea had never even occurred to me.

'I think that you've already heard other folks' version of events, but I'll tell you this, you don't want to listen to gossip. Ask him, and then make up your own mind.'

The one thing I was certain of was that I'd never feel able to ask Gabriel Bailey why he was no longer a doctor. I knew my face was still red, because it was burning, and the more Hannah studied me, the hotter I felt.

She reached over and patted my hand. 'In the paddock behind the house are three donkeys. They're retired now, but I bet Amy would enjoy meeting them. And, don't forget, if you get stuck or want to know anything, Gabriel's just in the barn. I'm sure he'd love to show you round.'

She gave me a huge smile again, and I tried to smile back. I couldn't agree with her. I was sure he was far too busy to bother with me, and I sure as hell wasn't going to interrupt his work.

'Oh, Eliza,' Hannah called, as I led Amy to the back door. I turned to find her pointing at a cupboard next to the fridge. 'There's an iron under there if you ever want to borrow it, lovey.'

Chapter 17

'I'm sorry, but I'm afraid it's quite impossible.' The lady was not for turning. 'I have new tenants arriving tomorrow, so I'll need you to vacate the premises by ten o'clock, as agreed.'

'But, Mrs Lovelace, you said I could have it for as long as I wanted,' I protested, overwhelmed at the thought of going back to London so soon.

'Yes, four weeks ago! A lot can happen in that time. I'm astonished by how many bookings I've taken for the summer. All four of my properties are fully booked. I think I'm undercharging. I may have to up my prices.'

I put the phone down, scowling at the receiver as if she'd be able to see me. In all fairness, she couldn't be blamed for my predicament. When I'd booked the cottage, it was newly advertised, and I'd had the pick of the available weeks. It wasn't her fault I'd thought that four would be long enough, nor that she'd let it to other tenants in the meantime.

I sat down at the table, my head in my hands. Now what? I wasn't ready to go back to Chiswick. I still had things to do. I tapped my fingers on the table, my mind whirling in confusion. Did I really, though? I'd got as far as discovering that my probable father was Raphael Bailey. I'd met his son, his daughter and his grandchildren. I knew roughly where he lived and a bit about his past. I knew he'd fallen out with his father and that he'd been in Wetherby at some point when Gabriel was young, which meant it was quite possible that he'd met my mother in

Leeds. It was all pointing in one direction and I wasn't sure what more I could do.

I guessed that the only thing left to find out was the exact date that he'd lived in Wetherby. If it was thirty-three years ago then the chances were, he was really my father, but did I honestly want to know? I stared into space, trying to decide what to do. If I did get the proof I needed, what then? What about poor Sophie, finding out her father wasn't the hero she thought he was? What about Lexi? She seemed to have enough upheaval in her life. Finding out her grandparents' marriage wasn't the perfect relationship she assumed would be yet another blow. And what about Gabriel?

I stood up and headed to the kettle, which I flicked on automatically. Mrs Travers always said, "When in doubt, have a cup of tea", and I seemed to be following her advice more and more. I wondered how she was getting on in Margate. She'd sent me a brief text, to tell me her sister was still a sour old boot and the house was a disgrace, as usual, and she'd spent an entire day cleaning it, as she always had to, in spite of her clicky hips and dodgy knees, then ended by saying, "Having a lovely time, see you soon."

I smiled to myself. I did love Mrs Travers, and I was missing her, not least for her ironing abilities. Should I cut my losses and head home? To what? Normal life? I found my heart sinking at the prospect. The truth was life would never feel normal again. Harry had tried calling me three times since our last conversation, but I'd refused to answer the phone and ignored the messages he'd left. Even if he eventually stopped seeing Melody and wanted me back, how could I ever trust him?

I looked up at the ceiling, knowing that Amy was sound asleep in bed upstairs, and had to admit the unsavoury truth. The future without Harry in it seemed scary to me, but the trouble was, the more I thought about it, so did the future with him in it. I just didn't know what to think any more. All I knew for certain was I wasn't ready to start living it. I'd put my marriage on pause by coming to Kearton Bay, and I wasn't ready to press play just yet.

Rose was furious that I'd been turfed out of Amethyst Cottage. 'Bloody woman. Good at chucking people out of there, isn't she!'

'She's hardly chucked me out, Rose. I only hired it for a month, and the month is up. Not her fault that she's let it to other tenants. That's what it's there for.'

'No matter. I guess you'll just have to go back to The Hare and Moon,' she said.

I stared gloomily at the slice of chocolate cake she'd handed me and shook my head. 'No way. I'm not going back there.'

'What do you mean? What's wrong with The Hare and Moon?' She leaned forward, her eyes bright with excitement. 'Did you see a ghost? They always reckoned that place was haunted. Not surprising when you think about it, with all that history. Smugglers and pirates, and God knows what in there, I reckon. Still, not like they harm you, is it? And better than going back to London before we finish our mission.'

'It's not that. I just...' I hesitated, but there seemed no way round it. I took a bite of the chocolate cake and chewed bravely, though it was probably even worse than the quiche she had foisted on me last time I came here, and that was saying something. 'Thing is,' I said eventually, lowering my voice so the couple of customers she had in the place wouldn't hear — after all, such rare creatures shouldn't be scared off — 'I caught Rhiannon doing something she shouldn't, and we had words, so now we're not speaking.'

Rose grinned. 'Caught in flagrante? Who was it this time?'

I put down the rest of the cake and gave her a horrified look. 'This time? So, it's true? She does put it around a bit?'

She gave a nonchalant shrug. 'So what if she does? Does it matter?'

'Of course it matters! He's a married man. What about his poor wife?'

Rose sighed. 'Look, I know you've been to hell and back with Harry and Miss-Grin-and-Bare-'Em, but don't let that cloud your judgement, okay? Rhiannon's not as bad as you think. She just has a different mindset to most people. I don't think she agrees with marriage and can't get her head round it at all.'

'That doesn't make it right!' I spluttered. The other customers turned to look at me, as did Amy. I cleared my throat and handed her a glass of lemonade to distract her.

'Just because Rhiannon doesn't believe in marriage, doesn't make it okay for her to wreck other people's.'

'Strikes me, she's not the one wrecking it,' Rose said. 'Look, I don't know who she's at it with at the moment, but I do know Rhiannon. She's a decent person and she wouldn't set out to hurt anyone deliberately. I think you should look at the husband, if anyone. He's the one who made the promise to another person. He's the one who's broken the vows, not Rhiannon. It's always the other woman who gets the blame, but if he wasn't willing, she wouldn't have a chance, would she?'

I thought about Harry. We'd been happy enough till Melody Bird came along. If she hadn't batted her eyelashes and flashed her ridiculous boobs at him, he wouldn't have succumbed, I was sure. It was Melody's doing, I had no doubt about it. All right, Harry was wrong to fall for it, but if Melody had played fair, none of this would have happened, and Harry and I would be fine.

'I still think she should leave him alone,' I muttered sulkily. 'And I'm not going back there.'

'Right. Well, what are we going to do, then?' Rose asked. 'I'd happily put you both up myself, but we've only got two bedrooms. Fuchsia and Cerise share as it is.'

'It's okay. I'll ring around, see if I can come up with anything. There must be somewhere available?'

She didn't look convinced. 'It's nearly June. I doubt it very much, but hey, anything's worth a try, right? I'll get you the phone book.'

Twenty minutes later, I'd rung every agency, every bed and breakfast, every other pub in the village, and there was nothing available. 'I guess I'll have to try Whitby,' I said. 'Maybe there'll be something there.'

'Probably a bed and breakfast somewhere,' she agreed. 'Short notice, though, if you have to be out tomorrow.'

I looked at the clock. Half past ten — less than twenty-four hours to go. I was in real trouble.

The door to the café swung open, and Rose stood up as Lexi walked in, her long red hair plaited and her pretty face free of make-up.

'Coffee, Lexi?'

'Please.'

Lexi smiled gratefully at Rose and slid into a chair beside Amy, who looked delighted to see her.

'What are you eating?' she asked her.

Amy showed her the fairy cake that she'd been half-heartedly chewing on for the last twenty minutes.

Lexi pulled a face. 'Rather you than me,' she whispered. She looked at me and frowned. 'Wow, you look happy. Not. What's up?'

I explained about my dilemma, and she looked quite shocked that I may be leaving. 'So soon? Has it really been four weeks? God, that went fast,' she said.

'If I don't find somewhere soon, I'll be heading back to London,' I said gloomily.

She looked appalled. 'Fate worse than death. I hated London.'

'How long were you there?' I asked. It wasn't part of my investigation. I was genuinely curious.

She considered. 'About four years, I think. Every moment felt like months, I was so miserable. So was Dad. He used to tell me that one day we'd come home.' She smiled, her eyes soft at the memory. 'When I'd had a really bad day, he'd take me outside, and we'd look up at the moon, and he'd tell me that the same moon was shining over Kearton Bay, so really we weren't so far away, after all.'

'What about when the moon wasn't visible?' Rose asked, as she brought back her coffee and sat down at the table with us.

Lexi grinned. 'He'd tell me that Sophie must have been particularly annoying that day and the moon was hiding.'

That explained the carving on the jewellery box. I couldn't imagine Harry being so understanding and creative, if Amy had felt homesick. Is that what fathers were supposed to be like? I

168

felt a sudden pang of loss at the thought, for myself and for Amy.

Lexi tried, unsuccessfully, to stifle a yawn.

'Are we keeping you up?' I asked.

She blushed. 'Had a late night.'

Rose nudged her. 'Up to no good with Derry Bone, no doubt.'

Lexi looked at me in horror.

I held up my hands. 'Don't look at me. I never said a word,' I said.

Rose laughed. 'I've known for ages. You're not that discreet, Lexi. Fuchsia and Cerise have seen you meeting up with him loads of times. You really need to be more careful, if you want things kept secret around here.'

Lexi's skin was clashing wildly with her hair. 'Jesus, as long as my dad doesn't find out. He'd be horrified.'

'Why? I'm sure he's aware that nineteen-year-old girls usually have boyfriends,' Rose said.

'Boyfriends, yes. Casual shags, I doubt he'd be so thrilled,' she whispered.

'Is that what Derry is? Aren't you in love?'

'Nope. Who needs that millstone around the neck?'

'You sound like Rhiannon,' I said, unable to help myself.

'Rhiannon! 'Course. You can go back to The Hare and Moon,' she said. 'There's only one guest there at the moment, and they're only there till tomorrow. Bags of room.'

I shook my head. 'Not going back there, Lexi. Sorry.'

She looked surprised but didn't ask questions. She was silent for a minute, sipping her coffee. Then she looked up and smiled. 'Problem solved. I'll ask Hannah.'

I didn't think so. 'Hannah? I barely know her!'

'So? Look, she can't get upstairs at all so sleeps on a pull-out sofa in the front room. She's got four flipping bedrooms upstairs, all empty. She'd be glad of some money, truth to tell, and I'd be glad if she had company at night. She's a stubborn old stick. Not been that well lately, and I hate leaving her alone. We all do. Eddie had a phone put in for her last year, so she could contact us if she needs us, but she's so pig-headed she probably wouldn't, anyway. It would be great to know she had someone there with her, after we've all gone home, even if it's just for a few weeks. What do you say?'

I glanced at Rose who was nodding and smiling. 'Sounds perfect,' she said.

I looked at Amy. I had no doubt she would enjoy herself. She'd loved it at the farm and had made firm friends with the three retired donkeys. She'd also got on well with Eddie, and Hannah seemed to have really taken to her. It seemed pointless to refuse, if it was all right with Hannah herself.

'Shall I ring her?'

'I suppose so, if you're sure she won't mind. I mean it, Lexi,' I added, as she stood up and headed outside, unable to get a signal on her mobile from the café. 'If she doesn't sound happy about it, don't push her. I don't want to force her into anything she doesn't want.'

She nodded and stepped outside.

Rose leaned forward, her eyes shining. 'Brilliant. Now we can make that final push on our secret mission and get definite proof that Raphael Bailey is your dad. Thank God for Lexi. Didn't I tell you she was a great girl? Mind you, bitter and twisted, or what? Poor Derry. She ought to open her eyes and give Will a chance.'

'Will?'

'Will Boden-Kean, up at the big house. Aw, he's lovely, and he's absolutely mad about her. Has been for ages, but she doesn't even seem to know he exists.'

I thought back to Beltane night. 'Is he tall, skinny, unusual looking?'

She grinned. 'Yeah. He's not conventionally handsome, I'll give you that, but he's got a heart of gold. Oh well, one day maybe she'll notice him, and then fireworks will explode and all that crap.'

'You sound as cynical as Lexi!'

'I've got cause to. She hasn't. You have to earn your stripes in this sodding world.'

Lexi was back within two minutes, a huge smile on her face. 'She's thrilled to bits,' she said. 'I told you she'd be fine about it.'

Rose clinked her cup against mine. 'Cheers,' she said. 'Here's to a long and successful stay in Kearton Bay.'

I knocked my cup against hers, returning the toast, but secretly wishing that I could make up my mind, exactly, what it was that I was hoping for.

****

'Come in, come in. Look at you, miss, with your hair in bunches. Don't you look bonny?'

Hannah beamed at Amy, as we entered the farmhouse the following morning. Amy held up her toy laptop for inspection.

'Well, look at that,' said Hannah in amazement. 'A blooming computer at three. I don't know. Proper clever clogs, you are,' she said, to which Amy nodded in agreement. I smiled and looked up, my heart thudding as I saw Gabriel sitting at the kitchen table. I felt my smile falter as I saw the expression on his face. Was that suspicion in his eyes? Then his mask was back in place and he nodded.

'Hello, Eliza. How are you?'

'Fine, thanks. And you?'

'Fine.'

There was an awkward silence, and Hannah shut the kitchen door. 'Well, we've established you're both fine,' she said, 'so that's summat, any road. I'll put kettle on. Gabriel, would you do me a favour and show Eliza upstairs, while I get little 'un a drink?'

I hardly dared look at him, imagining how well that suggestion had gone down, but he stood, and I followed him through to the hallway. He invited me to go first but I was horrified at the thought. No way did I want him staring at my enormous behind as we went up the stairs.

He showed me into a small room, painted pale blue. It held a single bed and a chest of drawers, and I was surprised to see posters of *Tangled* and *Frozen* adorning the walls. I looked at him enquiringly.

'Lexi got them yesterday and put them up for Amy. Thought it would help her settle in.'

'Bless her. How many girls of that age would think of that?'

His dimples reappeared, making him look a whole lot friendlier. 'I know. She's always been that way.'

'You must be very proud of her. I hope Amy grows up to be so thoughtful.'

There was another silence, then Gabriel said, 'I'll show you to your room.'

He led me through another door into a large room with a double bed and an ancient wardrobe and chest of drawers. It was decorated with wallpaper that must have been up for years, judging by the faded blue of the forget-me-knot motif, and the green carpet was thin and a little threadbare.

'I know it's a bit shabby,' said Gabriel, 'but it's clean. Lexi worked really hard in here yesterday, and there's fresh bedding.'

'It's lovely,' I said. 'I'm so grateful.'

'It used to be Hannah's son's room,' he said. 'Hasn't been occupied in a long time.'

'He's in Australia, isn't he?' I asked, glancing out of the window at the farmyard, where the killer chickens lurked like hired assassins by the barn. He didn't answer, and I turned, surprised to see him watching me, his eyes narrowed.

'Yes, and good riddance to bad rubbish,' he said.

'He was that bad?'

'He was a selfish swine,' said Gabriel. 'I don't know what went wrong with him, to be honest. Hannah and Albert were such good parents, and he had a loving home here. Some people are never happy with what they've got. They always want more, what they can't have.'

He shrugged, and I wondered what he was thinking. 'Anyway, he left home pretty young, kept coming back when he needed money, broke his father's heart, and finally cleared off abroad. Hannah always said he killed Albert. Not strictly true, though the stress may well have been a contributing factor.'

I couldn't help myself. 'You sound like a doctor,' I said, hating my slyness. I saw the colour drain from his face.

'Do I? Well…' He gave a feeble laugh and held up his hands. 'I just make rabbit hutches.'

I wanted to ask. I could have, it was the right moment, but I just couldn't make myself do it.

'I'll leave you to unpack,' he said, then turned and left the room before I could change my mind.

I sank onto the bed and stared unseeingly through the window. If I hadn't known better, I would swear that Gabriel was onto me. I'd seen undisguised suspicion in his eyes. He didn't trust my motives, and I was angry at myself for how much that upset me. After all, he was right, wasn't he? I wondered why being undercover no longer seemed any fun at all.

Chapter 18

It was amazing how quickly Amy and I settled into life at the farm. Everyone fell over themselves to make us welcome, and Amy loved being in such close proximity to the donkeys. She got quite possessive of them, introducing them as "her" donkeys and changing all their names to suit herself.

Hannah, who I quickly realised wasn't as well as she made out and rarely ventured beyond the yard, had definitely taken to Amy, and the feeling was mutual. They were always together, and Hannah had taken over preparing Amy's meals, read her a story at night, and even watched DVDs with her. I felt quite redundant. I suppose Hannah was making up for losing her own son, Albert, and having no grandchildren of her own. Eddie told me he hadn't seen her looking so lively and happy in a long time.

Lexi and I grew closer. After much persuasion, and a fair amount of mockery, she finally shamed me into feeding the chickens and collecting eggs, and I even started grooming the donkeys.

I saw Gabriel around the farm quite a bit. He was often to be spotted doing odd jobs around the place and sometimes helped tack up, or groom, the donkeys. Mostly, though, he was in the workshop, and I always knew when he was inside by the banging and whirring and clatter that came from there. He didn't come into the house much. Sometimes, Hannah would make him a bacon sandwich in the morning and ask me to take it out to him. It seemed churlish to refuse and I'd no good reason to, so I'd cross the yard and deliver it to him. He would take it with thanks, and I'd leave and return half an hour later to collect the empty plate.

I felt an awful sense of guilt and shame around him. I was here undercover, and he'd no idea that I'd been prying into his personal life. It was a horrible secret to carry around with me, and every time I saw him, I was reminded of the underhanded way I was behaving. I had the power to blow his world apart and destroy his entire family. I didn't want to hurt him. I didn't want to hurt any of them.

Then there was this other thing — this vague, uneasy feeling eating away at me that I couldn't quite understand. There was so much mystery and so many secrets around Gabriel. He could be so cagey and evasive about himself and his life, yet, sometimes I would catch him looking at me, and there was a questioning look in those amazing eyes of his, like he was the one trying to figure *me* out, not the other way around. It made my stomach flip and the little butterflies that often appeared and fluttered in there whenever I was around him morph into pterodactyls. And I didn't understand any of it. I only knew that I needed to hurry up and complete my mission fast, find out one way, or another, and then head back to London, as far away from Gabriel Bailey as I could.

If I didn't have all the undercover stuff to worry about, life at Whisperwood Farm would have been blissful. The house was basic but clean — thanks, I discovered, to Lexi's hard work. She'd taken over cleaning duties, as Hannah's health deteriorated, and fitted in the housework between looking after the donkeys, babysitting and studying for her degree. I was happy to take over the housework from her, and she seemed relieved, though Hannah decided, after the first few days, that she was more than capable of doing the ironing and it was probably best if I concentrated on the cleaning side of things.

Hannah showed me how to use the range and, after a few dodgy starts, I managed to get the hang of it and was soon turning out the orders for the sweets from the Lightweights members. I'd come clean to Sophie about my illegal sugar-dealing, and we'd put our heads together to come up with a plan.

Every week I was going to bring a low-calorie dessert to class for all the members to try, as well as bringing recipes in for them to have a go at themselves. I would continue to provide them with low-calorie versions of the ever-popular marshmallows and, as an incentive, the member who lost the most weight each week would get a bag of the proper marshmallows as a special treat. As Sophie said, once a week wouldn't harm them, and at least marshmallows were extremely low in fat. I felt much better about myself now that I'd come up with a more helpful plan, and Sophie seemed to really appreciate my honesty.

I'd also started doing all the cooking. Hannah showed me how to make a delicious chicken stew, and no one could say the ingredients weren't fresh. It took me a while to get my head around the fact that I could be feeding a chicken one day and eating it the next, but it was just one of those things that I had to get used to. At first, I'd been quite smug, thinking that the hunted had become the hunter, but then I felt sorry for them because, let's face it, there was no way it was a fair fight. I was a bit hesitant about eating them for a while, but the plain fact was they tasted good and, as Hannah said, you couldn't let emotional attachments to livestock rule you when you lived on a farm, though Lexi had a very different view of that matter.

Eddie obviously adored Hannah and loved working on the farm. He was a widower, now in his late fifties. He had no children, and from what I could gather, he spent most of his time either at work or propping up the bar of The Hare and Moon with his best friend Bernie, who was the estate manager at Kearton Hall. He took it upon himself to show me around and fill me in on the history of Whisperwood.

'When I were a lad,' he said, sounding like something from a Hovis advert, 'there were nigh on a dozen people working at this place at the busiest times. We had hundreds of acres and a thriving dairy herd. It's a crying shame to see it in this state.'

Eddie had come to work for Hannah when he was only fourteen and he considered himself family. 'She and Albert were a lovely couple. Couldn't do enough for me. I don't know where

I'd have been, after me wife passed away, if it hadn't been for them two. Then me an' Hannah, we helped each other through after Albert died. It were a tough time, and after that, well, things started to slide, an' bit by bit Hannah sold the land off. Now there's no more than five acres here, all told. Bloody shame.'

'Didn't their son help out at all?'

'What, young Albert? He never helped anyone but himself. He were about the same age as me, and we got on fine at first. I dunno what happened to him, honest I don't. The older he got, the more restless he were. Seemed to resent being stuck on the farm and wanted more from life. I ask you...' He waved his arm around to take in the vista of fields before us, '...what more can life offer than this? Any road, I was glad when he finally buggered off for good. I think Hannah had reached that point, an' all.'

'Did they only have the one child?'

'Aye. Shame that. Hannah and Albert were lovely people and they would have suited a big family, but there were complications at the birth. Even then, he were causing problems for her, see. Truth is, she nearly died, and she would have if it weren't for Dr Bailey. He saved their lives, bless him.'

'Dr Bailey?'

'Gabriel's grandad. Brilliant doctor. Hannah wouldn't be here now if it weren't for him. Mind you, I often wonder if he should really have bothered to save young Albert.' He shook his head. 'Nah, that's a wicked thing to say. Ignore me. Shouldn't think such things. I'm just protective of Hannah, that's all. She had one of them there heart attacks last year. Proper poorly. Frightened the life out of us. I wouldn't want to see her under any more stress, you understand?'

He looked at me, his eyes suddenly serious. I blinked, not sure that I did, but he held my gaze, as if waiting for an answer.

'Hannah's been good to me,' I said at last, not sure what he wanted me to say. 'I wouldn't want to cause her any harm.'

He hesitated then nodded. 'Aye, I reckon you've taken to her. She's had enough hurt in her life. She doesn't need any more, and that's all I'm saying on the subject.'

He walked away towards the stables, and I stared after him in bewilderment, wondering what the hell that was about.

I'd telephoned Joe to let him know that I'd moved into Whisperwood Farm, and he hadn't sounded keen at all. 'Why have you moved there?'

I explained that the cottage wasn't available, and I hadn't been able to find other accommodation.

'What was wrong with The Hare and Moon? Thought you liked it there?' he demanded.

I frowned. Why was he in such a bad mood? 'I didn't want to go back there, and Hannah offered. Don't worry, Joe. I know she's a stranger, but she's been kindness itself, and she and Amy have really bonded.'

Joe was silent. He seemed to say nothing for ages, which wasn't like him. 'I was going to visit. Will it be okay for me to stay at the farm, or should I book into the pub?' he said eventually.

I was surprised he was coming back so soon. 'You should be fine here. Hannah's a massive fan of yours and she has two spare bedrooms. Bet she'd love to have you.'

'You think?' There was another silence before he said, 'I'll be there tomorrow. Should be about six-ish.'

'Tomorrow? Really? What about your work?'

'Nothing I can't put off,' he said.

I nearly keeled over. 'Blimey,' I said. 'I'll get your room ready before you change your mind. See you tomorrow.'

****

Joe was as good as his word, arriving at ten to six the following day. Amy was delighted to see him and screamed in delight as he whirled her round, their antics sending the hens scattering in fright.

Eddie, Gabriel and Lexi had all hung around to meet him and shake his hand. Lexi bombarded him with questions about Jeeves and Wooster and commiserated with him about the loss of Bertie, but Eddie and Gabriel seemed to be hanging back, watching him and weighing him up. I guessed they were wondering if he was going to be a bit of a diva, but they needn't have worried on that score. To be honest, I was surprised they'd waited to meet him. They didn't seem the type of people who set much store by television or celebrities.

Hannah came shuffling out into the yard, and she and Joe stared at each other.

He held out his hand. 'You must be Hannah. I've heard a lot about you.'

Hannah shook it and nodded. 'Aye, I've heard a lot about you, an' all.'

'Have you indeed?' Joe looked tired, his mouth tight with tension.

Hannah smiled. 'You're in the magazines enough, "Mr Housewives' Favourite". Hard to miss you, really.'

Joe laughed, and she took his arm and led him inside the kitchen. We all followed, and I poured tea and dished out the chicken stew, which I'd made that afternoon especially. Even Gabriel had some, and Eddie pronounced it delicious and a credit to Hannah's teaching. Tessa took to Joe straight away, lying at his feet while he fondled her ears and chatted to his audience. They seemed surprisingly enthralled by him and in no hurry to leave. I watched him with some concern, though. He definitely wasn't his usual self.

As Lexi put the kettle on to make yet another cup of tea, I led Joe upstairs to show him to his room and he began to unpack.

'They're treating you all right?' he asked. 'You're happy here?'

'Of course,' I said in surprise. 'You've met them. They couldn't be nicer, could they? And really, when you think they hardly know me, it's amazing.'

'So, you'd be happy to stay on here a while?'

He looked deadly serious and I had a sudden feeling of dread. 'Joe, what is it? What's going on?'

He sank onto the bed and put his head in his hands.

I sat beside him, my mind racing. 'What's happened? You're scaring me. Is Mrs Travers all right?'

'She's fine, love. Oh, Eliza, I'm sorry, I really am. That it should be me who has to tell you this.'

I was silent, chewing my lip. 'It's Harry, isn't it?'

He nodded, unable to meet my eyes.

I took a deep breath. 'Is it to do with Melody?'

He looked up at me and there were tears in his eyes. 'Eliza, you're going to have to be very strong now, love. I got a call from Barney Murray. You remember Barney?'

Of course I remembered Barney. When James Sinclair had ended their relationship and publicly outed Joe, it had been Barney who looked after Joe and turned the whole situation around so that public opinion swayed in his favour. He was a PR man at the top of his game, and the one many celebrities turned to in their hour of need. I felt sick.

'The thing is, love, he wanted to tip me off. There's going to be a story in one of the tabloids tomorrow. They've found out about Harry and Melody.'

I closed my eyes, as Joe reached over and squeezed my hand. 'Harry and Melody got wind of the story. They've buggered off to the South of France to get away from it all. She's got a second home there, ironically. I'm so sorry, love.'

I felt numb. Seeing it in black and white would make it real, final. How could there be any going back from that? Now the whole world would know what a fool I'd been, and that the glamorous Melody Bird had lured my husband away from the drab, dreary wife who simply couldn't compete.

'I thought it best you stay up here for a good while. It must be fate that you got out of the way. It's going to be in all the papers and the reporters are going to want to talk to you. At least they won't have a clue where you are, and let's hope it stays that way. You can hide out here till the fuss dies down. Harry and his tart can't stay away forever, they've got work to do. Let them deal with the fall-out when they get back.'

I nodded, frozen. I knew what he was saying but the reality of it all just wasn't sinking in.

'Are you all right?'

'Would you mind going downstairs alone, Joe? Make my apologies? I feel like being on my own for a while,' I murmured.

He nodded. 'Of course, love. I'll go and tell them what's happened. Best they know all about it. You have a lie down.

Don't worry about Amy, we'll see to her.'

I hardly heard him. I left the room and wandered into my own, gazing out of the window over the farmyard. My marriage was over. There was no way back from this. It was odd but, somehow, the fact that it was going to become public knowledge made it official. While it was just a secret shared by a few, I'd thought, somewhere in the back of my mind, that maybe there was a way through it. That was impossible now. I'd had so many conflicting emotions about my marriage for so long, not sure what it was I was hoping for, what I'd wanted. Now, it had all been taken out of my hands, and all I could think was that downstairs was a little girl who was going to grow up without her father, just as I had, because I knew Harry too well, and I knew that Amy was way down on his list of priorities.

I felt tears pricking my eyes and squeezed them shut, refusing to let them fall. If I started to cry now, if I let the grief out, it may never stop, and I was too scared of what would come tumbling out.

****

Gabriel and Lexi walked slowly home, their arms linked, their heads bowed deep in thought.

'Poor Eliza,' said Lexi, 'and poor Amy. What a tosspot. And to think, she knew he was at it all this time. Kept that bloody quiet, didn't she?'

Gabriel said nothing. So, she'd come to Kearton Bay to escape her treacherous husband? It hadn't been what they'd thought at all. When Eliza had moved into the farm, he and Eddie had been very concerned. What was wrong with The Hare and Moon, if Amethyst Cottage was unavailable? She'd stayed there before and seemed happy enough. And, anyway, what was she staying on for? She'd already had a month here, a long holiday by anyone's standards. All right, she'd told Gabriel she wasn't looking for a holiday cottage any more and he'd believed her, but the farm was a different matter. It was run down and needed investment, but it was in a prime location, and with all those outbuildings and land...

'You don't think she's scouting out property for that husband of hers?' Eddie had asked, his face lined with worry, and Gabriel had been unable to answer, his spirits sinking at the thought. Surely, she wouldn't stoop so low? But the outbuildings would make wonderful conversions and the farmhouse could be renovated to a high standard. He'd seen *Twice as Nice* at Sophie's and he knew what could be done and how much money could be made. Had that been Eliza's plan all along?

Hearing the truth about Harry's affair with his co-presenter, he'd felt a deep sense of shame at his mistrust, and, looking at Eddie, he knew it was shared.

'But why Kearton Bay?' Hannah wanted to know.

Joe shrugged. 'She wanted to come back home to Yorkshire. She Googled holiday accommodation and saw Amethyst Cottage advertised.'

He'd then explained about her mother's ring, which made Gabriel feel even worse.

Lexi had been in tears. 'Poor Eliza. She's far too nice to be treated like that. What a bastard, and to go with Melody Bird, of all people! She's just a walking pair of boobs.'

Hannah had said nothing, seemingly deep in thought.

'I was wondering if it would be okay for her to stay here a while?' Joe had asked. 'The press will be hanging around her house, trying to get information. No one knows she's here, except for me, Harry and Mrs Travers, and none of us will say anything. I just want her kept away from it all until the fuss dies down, and there's no doubt they'll look for her at my place, too.'

'Of course,' said Hannah. She looked at Joe, her eyes suspiciously bright. 'I think me and you need to have a little talk, Joe,' she said. 'Private, like.'

He stared at her for a long moment then nodded.

Eddie, Gabriel and Lexi had said their goodbyes and left them to it. Eddie shook his head as they parted at the end of the track.

'I dunno. Seems we got the lass all wrong,' he mumbled. 'Feel proper bad about it all now. Fancy all this just being a coincidence, an' all. Weird, eh?'

Gabriel nodded. Fate. More and more, he felt that's what it was. She'd been brought here for a reason. He remembered Beltane evening, standing by that bonfire, deep in thought, his mind in turmoil.

He'd looked up at the moon and thought, in his despair, that if there was a greater power out there, call it God, the Universe, whatever, he hoped that it could hear his silent pleas for help. His life was at yet another low point, and he didn't know what to do any more. Rhiannon had sensed his misery and confusion. She'd told him that this was Beltane, a magical night of new beginnings and fresh starts.

'Listen for the sound of bells, Gabriel,' she'd said, a mischievous smile playing on her lips. 'But beware, for if you don't turn away from them, the fairy queen will make you her slave forever.'

He'd thought she'd lost her mind, and Sophie was certainly of the same opinion, yet within minutes, he'd been stunned to hear the sound of sleigh bells. While Lexi had giggled that Santa had arrived, he had, despite all his scepticism, found himself looking for a fairy queen. And Eliza had been standing at the gate, desperately trying to turn her phone off. And their eyes had met. And he hadn't turned away.

He listened in silence as Lexi continued her tirade against Harry Jarvis and his silicone-enhanced lover. Above them, a sliver of moon peeped down on him, her body cloaked in darkness, a mystery she would only reveal when the time was right.

Chapter 19

The papers had a field day. One of the tawdry tabloids broke the story, as promised, with the headline "Harry's Bird", which was quite subtle, really. I was dismayed to see that, as if the humiliation of Harry's affair being made public wasn't enough, they'd printed a photo of us, taken at an awards night a few years ago. I was pregnant with Amy at the time and looked like a space hopper. The dress I was wearing had been bought for me by Audrey and was more suitable for a woman of her age group than mine, and it was before I'd been persuaded to bleach my hair, so I still had my dark chestnut locks. The overall effect was to make me look old enough to be Melody's mother rather than her "love rival".

I, apparently, was being "comforted by friends".

By Sunday, the other tabloids had caught up with Harry and Melody, tracking them to her "love nest" in the South of France. I switched on the television on Sunday morning, to see the presenter of a national news programme going over the front pages of the tabloids and wincing at headlines such as "A Bird in the Hand", "Twice as Vice", and "Cor, What a Lovely Pair!" accompanying a photograph that had made the covers of them all. It showed Melody standing on the beach, wearing a miniscule white bikini, and standing behind her, his head nuzzling into the crook of her neck and his arms wrapped around her tiny waist, was my treacherous git of a husband.

Everyone at the farm was kind and polite around me which,

frankly, made me feel worse. Eddie kept shaking his head and telling me that Harry was a pillock, leaving a lovely lass like me for that floosy. Hannah informed me daily that no good would come of it, and Joe assured me I was better off without him. Lexi said nothing. She just gave me little hugs every time she passed. It was all rather wearing.

Gabriel seemed to be keeping out of my way. Quite honestly, I was glad about that. The space hopper photo of me was being reprinted in almost every newspaper, and I didn't think I could face him, knowing he'd seen me looking such a state. Even I could have found a better picture and I'm my own worst critic. I even briefly toyed with the idea of anonymously posting the editors a different one, but Joe said they would probably keep using the one they had as it provided a better contrast between myself and Melody. Funnily enough, that didn't cheer me up.

The one good thing was that Joe had cancelled all other engagements to stay with me. He didn't like letting people down, but he said I was his priority. It wasn't so much that I needed him there, although that was lovely, but that he got a break at last. He seemed to really relax after the first couple of days, and he and Hannah were as thick as thieves. I got used to walking in on them and seeing them clam up immediately, obviously having been discussing me. I supposed they were just trying to decide the best way to handle the situation, but it was a bit insulting. Still, at least they were getting on and Joe was finally unwinding, so it wasn't all bad.

He loved sauntering round the farm with Amy, chatting to Eddie about the vegetable patch, wandering round the orchard, helping with the hens and the donkeys. There was some colour back in his cheeks, and he was sleeping well. The dark shadows were fading. I hadn't seen him look so well in ages and, apart from his constant worrying about me, I don't think he'd felt better in a long time.

I'd been avoiding Old Town, not wanting to risk tourists recognising me. Joe said it wasn't likely, as I'd changed a lot since that picture was taken, but I didn't care. If even one person connected me with the space hopper woman, I'd be devastated.

I didn't want the sympathy of the locals, either. I could imagine Milly Henderson wanting to know every detail and I really couldn't face it.

Rose had been fabulous, coming up to the farm a couple of times in the evening, after a long day at work, bringing vodka and making me laugh as she dissected the picture of Melody on the beach and found fault with just about every square inch of her.

On Wednesday night, she popped round after the Lightweights meeting, which I'd missed, and brought me a huge basket of flowers, which all the members had clubbed together to buy. I was so touched that I burst into tears, and Rose said she'd never seen anyone so pathetically grateful for a few yellow roses, orange gerberas and a bit of gypsophila.

She also gave me a card from Sophie. It was obviously a marketing device from Lightweights, as it bore their logo on the back. The cover showed a smiling face and the words "When times get tough, keep your chin(s) up!" I wasn't sure how that was supposed to make anyone feel better, but I suppose the thought was there. Sophie had written inside. "You deserve better. We're all thinking of you xx", which made me cry.

I rang her to thank her, and she couldn't have been more sympathetic. No, really, she couldn't. You'd have thought someone had died. In the end, I was the one consoling her and assuring her that, really, things weren't so bad, and I was positive I'd come through unscathed eventually.

Between her sniffles, she managed to invite me round for dinner. 'It's my wedding anniversary — twenty-five years. I'd love it if you and Joe and Hannah would come. Saturday night?'

I promised her I'd let her know when I'd spoken to them, which I did. Both agreed, although Hannah was a bit overcome at the thought of leaving the farm, which she rarely did these days.

Rose offered to babysit Amy, although she was a bit put out that I'd been invited for dinner and she hadn't.

'Charming,' she said. 'Obviously, I'm not good enough for Princess Sophie's posh house.'

'Don't be daft,' I said. 'Firstly, she's doing it because she thinks

I'm a sad loser and feels sorry for me, and secondly, it's a great excuse to get Joe round to her house. Can you imagine how much she's going to brag about that to her pals?'

Rose cheered up after that.

On Thursday, I was shocked to get a visit from Rhiannon.

'Eliza,' she said, hesitantly, 'I'm sorry to just drop in on you like this but I really wanted to see you.'

I waited, not sure what to say. The truth was, I wasn't so angry with her any longer, and I'd been feeling guilty about our falling out. What she was doing was wrong, but really, what business was it of mine? And who was I to judge, anyway, given how sneaky and duplicitous I was being about Gabriel and his family? At least with Rhiannon, what you saw was what you got. She was true to herself, even if her truth was a little skewed compared with most people's version.

'I'm so sorry to hear about your problems,' she said. 'Really, I do realise how awful you must be feeling, and I expect that I'm the last person you want to see in the circumstances. If it helps at all, Marty and I don't see each other any longer. He's rebuilding his relationship with Milly, and they seem happy. I don't expect things to go back to the way they were between us but if there's anything I can do—'

It was too much. I shook my head, full of shame. 'Rhiannon, honestly, there's nothing to forgive. It's none of my business, and I'd no right to speak to you the way I did. I'm not exactly whiter than white,' I admitted. 'I apologise. I've — I've missed you, actually.'

She gave me a huge smile. 'I'm so glad because I've missed you, too. It does get rather lonely at the pub without you. There are only men to talk to now, which isn't quite the same.'

'And Michelle,' I reminded her. She gave me a wry look and we laughed. It was good to see her again. Whatever the rights and wrongs of Rhiannon's private life, I'd grown to like her and hated falling out with her. Besides, I'd an uncomfortable feeling that she'd be a lot more understanding about my secrets than I'd been about hers.

∗∗∗∗

Sophie wrapped her arms around me and held me to her, patting my back as if I were a baby who needed to get its wind up.

'How are you feeling? You're looking well,' she said, surveying me critically, like she was examining me for signs of decay. 'It must have been such a dreadful shock to you when you found out. I couldn't get over it, could I, Archie?'

Archie ushered us into the living room and gave her a knowing look. 'No, you couldn't, could you?'

'And the minute your back's turned they're off on holiday. Disgusting — like he couldn't wait for you to be out of the way.' Sophie plumped up the cushions on the sofa and motioned to us to take a seat.

I helped Hannah to sit down, and she gave me a look as if to say, *What the bloody hell have you got us into?*

'Beer, Joe?' asked Archie, obviously trying to head his wife away from the subject. Joe nodded, and Archie disappeared into the kitchen, but Sophie wasn't swayed.

'Is it true,' she continued, 'that you knew all about it, and that's why you came here?'

'Er, yes, that's right.'

'I can't believe it. And you never said a word!' She looked at Archie, who had walked back into the room carrying two bottles of beer and was now rolling his eyes at her.

He handed a bottle of beer to Joe. 'Be reasonable, Sophe, she's hardly going to put an announcement in Hendersons' window, is she?'

'You know what I mean. How brave you've been. Well,' — Sophie's eyes were full of sympathy — 'it's his loss. You're worth ten of that Melody blooming Bird, hair or no hair. They'll get their comeuppance, you mark my words. People always do. What goes around comes around, doesn't it, Archie?'

He shrugged, obviously not sure. 'Are you going to offer the ladies a drink, Sophie?'

'Oh, yes, in a minute. I just know there's someone else out there for you,' she continued. 'Someone who knows how to treat a woman like a lady. Who knows? He may be in this very village. Maybe you've already met. That would be funny, wouldn't it? What do you say, Hannah?'

Hannah looked at Archie for help, and he shook his head. 'Leave her alone, Sophe. I'm sure she hasn't come here to talk about this. Thought we were supposed to be cheering her up, for God's sake?'

'Oh, yes. You're quite right. Would you both like a glass of wine? Then I'd better check on the lamb. I hope you all like lamb? Oh, dear, I should have asked. But it's Dad's favourite, you see.'

I felt my insides plummet like a broken lift. 'Your dad's coming?'

I daren't look at Joe. On top of everything else, I was going to meet the man who was probably my father. I felt cold with shock.

'Of course,' said Sophie. 'Didn't I mention that? Flynn was invited, too, but he dropped out at the last minute. Not surprising, really. He's not one for socialising. Sorry, do you know Flynn Pennington-Rhys? He's the local doctor. Worked with my father, until Dad retired, and now he's at Ivy House Surgery on his own. He and Gabriel are best friends. I must get you both a glass of wine, but first, can I have a photograph of you, Joe? No one will ever believe you were here at my house if I don't.'

Joe took a gulp of beer, and Archie patted him on the shoulder. 'Go with it, mate. It'll be quicker in the long run.'

'Oh, Archie, how do you work the camera on this stupid phone?' demanded Sophie.

'Are the kids back from the stables yet?' asked Archie, pretending he hadn't heard her.

'Not yet,' said Sophie, peering at her phone in frustration. 'I'm sure they won't be long.'

'Where's Lexi and Gabriel?' enquired Hannah. I'd been wondering that myself.

Sophie looked up from her phone, and I saw her cheeks were

distinctly pink. 'Er, they've gone to the supermarket. I forgot something.'

Archie grinned. 'She had a mishap with dessert,' he said.

Sophie looked appalled. 'Fancy telling them that! All right, I admit it. I made a slight miscalculation. I've sent them out for a substitute. Dessert will be shop bought, so shoot me!'

Archie laughed and assured her it was hardly a crime, although he did think it was a bit much that poor Gabriel and Lexi had been sent out to scout round for an alternative.

Sophie gave up on her phone and rushed into the kitchen to check on the lamb and pour Hannah and me a glass of wine. I was feeling so nervous by then that I was tempted to tell her to forget the glass and just hand me the bottle. I couldn't believe that I was going to meet the man who may well be my father. I hadn't had time to prepare. Mind you, maybe that was a good thing. I'd have been a nervous wreck if I'd known in advance.

I took a huge gulp of alcohol as I heard the back door open and a whole cacophony of voices assaulted my ears.

Archie sighed. 'Sounds like they're all back. Here we go then.'

Within a few minutes, the living room door opened, and Sophie ushered her parents in. She didn't have to introduce her mother to me. It was obvious who she was from her eyes. They were the same almond shape and identical shade of blue-green as Gabriel's. She was accompanied by a stocky, rosy-cheeked man, with navy blue eyes and a head of thick, snowy white hair. I tried not to stare at him, but goosepimples stood up on my arm as his own brushed against it, when he reached over to hug Hannah.

'Keeping well, Hannah?' he enquired.

Hannah nodded. 'Not so bad, you know. How are you?'

'Very chipper. Working the allotment keeps me fit. Got to keep the pounds at bay, haven't you?' He patted his stomach and sighed.

Hannah nodded. 'So they tell me.'

'And who is this lovely young lady?' he enquired, fixing me with a wide smile. I tried to decide if he looked mean enough to abandon my mother without a second thought, but he looked way too kind. Maybe there really had been a good reason for his behaviour, as I'd always suspected. Or maybe looks were deceiving. Look how gorgeous Harry was. Devious little shit.

'This is Eliza. She's staying with me for a while,' said Hannah, offering no further information.

Mrs Bailey turned to look at me immediately. I wilted under her scrutiny.

'Eliza, eh?' said Dr Bailey. 'Delighted to meet you, my dear.' He shook my trembling hand, while his wife appeared to be assessing me for faults as if I were a horse she was considering purchasing. 'We've heard all about you,'

'No, we haven't,' muttered his wife.

I swallowed. They'd obviously been reading the papers, then. Well, what did I expect? There was an awkward silence, then Archie introduced them to Joe, which was a relief as they watched his show and immediately switched their attention to him, thank God, giving me the chance to gulp down the rest of my wine and try to steady my nerves.

Not that I had much chance. I'd just stood up, intending to head to the kitchen to beg another glass of wine, when the door flew open again and Lexi bounced into the room, followed by Sophie's three children and a rather hesitant Gabriel. They'd obviously all been upstairs getting cleaned up and changed.

'Grandma, Grandad! How are you?' Lexi threw her arms around her grandfather, while Tally hugged her grandmother and the twins hovered between them.

'Same as we were last Sunday,' said Dr Bailey. 'Unless you know something we don't.'

'Oh, shut up, Raffy,' said Mrs Bailey. 'Honestly, is it any wonder they hardly ever visit us when you're so anti-social?'

Sophie had obviously tuned into my psychic demands for alcohol because she was standing at the door holding a bottle of wine. 'Quite right,' she said. 'This is an important day for me. I mean, for us. Our anniversary and the twins' good-luck-at-university-party.'

Mrs Bailey gave her a withering look. 'Are you mad? They haven't even found out their results yet.'

'It's a foregone conclusion,' Sophie assured her, handing

Gabriel the bottle. 'Can you pour Mum and Dad a drink, please? And I think Eliza's glass is empty,' she added, nodding in my direction.

Gabriel looked at me, and I held out my glass. My hands were shaking so much, if I'd been holding a glass of milk, I'd have turned it into butter.

'It's nice to see all my grandchildren,' said Mrs Bailey, 'seeing as they so rarely visit these days.'

'Sorry,' said Lexi. 'Just been so busy. I work terribly hard, you know.'

'So I hear,' said her grandmother, pinching my seat beside Hannah. 'Mrs Lang, how are you? Lovely to see you, after all this time.'

I felt faint. I was suddenly aware of Gabriel's hand on my elbow.

'Are you all right? You don't look well,' he murmured.

'What?' I shook my head, trying to pull myself together. 'Oh, yes, sorry. Just a bit hot.'

He poured my wine and told me to sit in the armchair, which I did with relief. While drinks were served, and small talk made, I sipped my wine and watched Dr Bailey.

So, that was the man who may be my father? I studied his face intently, looking for any trace of physical resemblance. I could see a little of Sophie in him, perhaps. She had his round, dark blue eyes and his rather wide nose. There wasn't much of Gabriel in him, though. He definitely took after his mother. I'd seen her fixing me with the same piercing stare as her son, and she shared his fabulous bone structure. Dr Bailey had a round face. He was probably in his mid-seventies, which meant he'd been a good twenty years or so older than my mother, which was a bit creepy, given she'd have been a student, and he must have been around fortyish. It just didn't feel right. I didn't see any physical likeness between him and me, and I hoped that was a good sign and not just wishful thinking.

After half an hour or so, when everyone was complaining that they were starving and wondering exactly what Sophie was doing in the kitchen, she announced that dinner was ready, and we all made our way to the dining room. She'd made bruschetta with tomato and basil for starters.

'One of Jamie Oliver's recipes,' she said. 'I did try to find vegetarian dishes, because of Lexi, but I really wanted to do the lamb.'

'Why are you still vegetarian?' Dr Bailey enquired, as we all tucked into the bruschetta. I was appalled to find I was sitting between him and Gabriel. Never mind vegetarianism, I suddenly felt like the meat in a very scary sandwich.

Lexi shrugged. 'Because I love animals,' she said simply.

'Why shouldn't she be?' demanded his wife. 'Might do you some good to cut down on the meat. You're getting quite a tummy on you. At this rate, I'll have to sign you up for Sophie's slimming club.'

'I'd rather die,' he announced, which I thought was a bit harsh on Sophie, although I took his point.

The bruschetta was very good, and even Mrs Bailey approved.

Sophie beamed as she collected the plates, refusing all offers of help. 'Of course, we'll have to cut down for the next week to make up for all this food, won't we, Eliza? Goodness knows how many units are in tonight's meal, and you should see the dessert Gabriel brought in.'

'Oh really, Sophie, I'm sure Eliza doesn't want to think about that wretched diet tonight,' said her mother. 'Give her a break, for goodness' sake.'

'That's not what you say to me!' said poor Sophie.

'Well, it's different for you. You're the leader, for one thing, and for another, you're obviously giving yourself too many nights off. I mean, Eliza doesn't have much to lose, whereas you ... and, of course, you're older. You'll find it hard to shift, at your age.'

'I'm only bloody fifty-one!' spluttered Sophie. 'My God, I do love the way you boost my confidence, Mother.'

'Take no notice,' Dr Bailey told me with a wink. 'They're always like this.'

Sophie headed into the kitchen, muttering under her breath, followed by Tally, who I suspect had gone to soothe her nerves.

Mrs Bailey seemed totally unfazed. She looked around the table at us all and smiled. 'Well, this is pleasant, isn't it? So, how did you two get on with your exams? I know your mother thinks you'll get top marks, but what do you think?'

Oliver and Pandora looked at each other and shrugged.

'I probably did better than her,' said Oliver, with no trace of modesty. 'I'm naturally brighter.'

'Bugger off,' said Pandora.

'Charming,' said Mrs Bailey. 'What about you, Lexi? How's your studying going? I do wish you'd gone to a proper university.'

Lexi rolled her eyes. 'It's going well, thanks. I'm enjoying it, and this way, I get to fit the work around my job.'

'Oh, yes, the donkeys. And is this the career you've chosen? I don't mean the donkeys, but animals in general?'

Lexi shook her head. 'I'd like to do something that involves history. I like old buildings, and art and stuff. Maybe work in a museum, or something?'

'Really?' Mrs Bailey looked stunned. She wasn't the only one. It was a bit of a departure from working on Hannah's farm, that was for sure. There was a lot more to Lexi than met the eye. She was a girl with many layers, and I suddenly realised how fond I'd become of her.

Sophie and Tally returned with the main course which was slow-cooked lamb. Tally carried a vegetarian meal for Lexi. Dr Bailey clapped his hands in delight and announced that lamb was his favourite dish, and Sophie's ruffled feathers appeared to be smoothed a little as she sat down and invited everyone to tuck in.

Joe and Dr Bailey were soon deep in conversation about some of the guests that Joe had interviewed on his show. Dr Bailey was adamant that Jeeves and Wooster were "actors", and, in the end Joe had to take out his phone and show him pictures of them in his garden to prove that they were genuinely his pets.

'Who's the little girl holding them?' Dr Bailey enquired, finally convinced that they were, in fact, amateur pigs and not members of Equity.

'That's Amy, Eliza's little girl,' said Joe, smiling proudly. 'She's three now. Loves those pigs almost as much as she loves her Uncle Joe.'

Mrs Bailey leaned across to look at the picture. 'She looks like her father,' she announced.

There was silence for a moment. Mrs Bailey looked around. 'Well, now I've mentioned the elephant in the room, I suppose there's no harm in saying I'm terribly sorry to hear of your troubles, Eliza. It's rotten bad luck having such a rogue for a husband. I know what I'd have done if Raffy had ever strayed.'

I glanced at Joe, who shook his head slightly. I hoped my face wasn't too red. Poor Mrs Bailey. If she only knew.

'Maybe Eliza doesn't want to talk about it, Gran,' said Tally, looking at me with sympathetic eyes.

'Well, she can hardly avoid the subject,' said Mrs Bailey. 'Especially with all the fuss the papers are making. I must say, I don't think much to your husband. What a rotter.'

'He always was,' said Joe. 'She was always too good for him.'

'Yes, all right, Joe,' I murmured.

Hannah tutted. 'I never met him, but I tell you this. He doesn't deserve a lovely lass like Eliza. She can do better. And she will, one day.'

'Oh, I couldn't agree more!' said Sophie eagerly. 'There's bound to be someone much better suited to you. You're so much prettier than Melody Bird. I can't think what he sees in her.'

'I can.' Oliver snorted, earning himself a smack on the arm from both his sisters.

'Joe, tell Grandad about that interview you did with the *Hollyoaks* cast. He's a big fan,' said Lexi.

Dr Bailey's face lit up, and he turned to Joe, who immediately began to regale everyone with his very funny story about that night. I could have kissed Lexi.

Just as I was beginning to relax again, Gabriel leaned over and murmured in my ear, 'I'm sorry.'

He smelt of patchouli, sandalwood and mandarin oil. I breathed him in, nearly dropping my knife and fork as I tried to steady myself. 'For what?'

'My mother and Sophie. They're not really known for their tact. They don't always think before they speak. It must be so upsetting, all the stuff in the papers.'

It was the first time he'd mentioned what had happened since the story broke.

I gave him a weak smile. 'That's not the worst thing that's happened to me lately. Don't worry about it.'

'I can imagine. It must be very difficult for you.'

He looked awkward, and I tried to make light of it to ease the sudden tension. 'You're not kidding. Have you seen that God-awful photo they keep printing of me? I should point out that I was seven months pregnant at the time. It wasn't cake. Well, not all of it,' I admitted. 'It's so bad, I was thinking of anonymously donating a better one. I mean, couldn't they have found a more flattering picture?'

He smiled. 'Oh, yes I saw that picture. You looked—'

'Like a space hopper.' I sighed. 'I know.'

'Beautiful,' he said at the same time, and I stared at him in amazement. 'I mean, I thought you looked lovely. So pretty. Dark hair suits you.'

'Does it?' I was astonished. 'Harry always said it was dull and boring. He has a thing for blondes. Obviously.'

He shook his head slightly. 'Never try to change into something you're not, just to please someone else, Eliza,' he said. 'It never works. Trust me.'

I didn't quite know what to say to that.

He looked a bit embarrassed, as if he'd revealed too much of himself. 'The lamb's very good, isn't it? Sophie's surpassed herself.'

'Fabulous,' I agreed.

We were silent for a moment, listening to the laughter coming from the others, as Joe moved onto his favourite story about the time he'd interviewed Peter Kay.

'You must be missing London?' he said eventually.

'Not really,' I replied truthfully. 'I miss Joe when he's not here, of course, but that's it.'

He looked across at Joe, who was now mopping tears of laughter from his eyes. 'It must have been hard for him, raising you alone and building a career. Quite a lot for a young man to deal with.'

'Yes, but he never once complained. Well, not to my face. Anyway, he wasn't quite alone. He took on Mrs Travers to help, when we moved to London. She really looked after me. I love her to pieces. She made leaving Yorkshire bearable. I wasn't too happy about moving to London, you see, but Joe had got a great offer and couldn't turn it down.'

'London takes some getting used to.'

'It was the loneliest place on earth at first. I begged him to move back to Knaresborough. The day he told me he'd sold our house there, I went crazy. It was Gran and Grandad's house, you see, and when we moved south, Joe rented it out for a couple of years. I assumed it would always be there for us to go back to one day. I couldn't believe he'd got rid of it. He had a real rebellion on his hands for a while.'

Gabriel smiled. 'I was very lucky,' he admitted. 'I grew up in a lovely house in Whitby, where my parents still live. I had a very happy, secure childhood. I suppose I took it for granted. It's what I wanted for Lexi. Unfortunately, things didn't turn out that way.'

'I know how you feel,' I said. 'All I wanted was for Amy to have what I didn't. It was the most important thing in the world to me, but I guess we don't always have a choice.'

He hesitated. 'Amy's father — are you and he—?'

'Over? I think we probably are. He's still sunning himself with Miss-Grin-and-Bare-'Em. If he wanted to be with me, he would be, wouldn't he?'

'I don't know. Believe me, I'm the last person to offer advice about relationships.' He nodded over at his mother, who was sitting, enthralled, chewing absently on a potato as she listened to Joe. 'I always thought I'd have a marriage like theirs. They've been together for over fifty years. They've had their ups and downs but, basically, they're rock solid.'

I decided it was now or never. 'You were lucky growing up around here. What did you think to Wetherby?'

He looked a bit thrown by the question. 'What do you mean?'

'Sophie mentioned you used to live in Wetherby. Did you like it there?' I couldn't look at him, keeping my eyes firmly on my plate and thinking that I really would have to get the lamb recipe from Sophie. It was quite delicious.

'Well, I can't say I remember. We were only there a year. I was two when we moved back to Whitby, so I wouldn't know.'

I stared at him, shocked. 'A year? Are you sure?'

He looked at me strangely. 'Of course. Why?'

'Oh, just — just, Sophie gave me the impression you were there longer.'

He shrugged. 'No. Mum missed her friends too much. Luckily, Dad swallowed his pride and made up with my grandfather, and we all returned home.'

'And you never went back?'

'Why would we? No, to be honest, Dad was glad to make my mum's homesickness an excuse. He missed all his friends here, too. He doesn't wander far from home. Never has.'

Sophie looked across at us and smiled. 'Gosh, look at you two with your heads together. I hope you're not criticising my cooking!'

'Far from it,' Gabriel assured her. 'It's lovely.'

'It is, actually,' admitted Mrs Bailey, slightly grudgingly. 'Are you sure you made it yourself?'

'Yes, Mother,' said Sophie rolling her eyes.

I barely heard them as they began to banter with each other. My mind was whirling with the new information I'd just received. I'd worked out that Gabriel was thirty-eight, five years older than me. If his father had left the Leeds area when he was only two, there was no way Raphael Bailey could be my father.

I tried to make sense of my feelings as I digested that fact. I was back to where I'd started when I arrived in the village, with no idea who my father was and no more leads to follow. I looked round the table, listening to this lovely family teasing and laughing, and felt a pang of loss. They weren't my family. Sophie wasn't my sister. Lexi wasn't my niece.

'I reckon it's time for dessert,' said Archie. 'We've all finished, and you're sitting here, yakking. I don't know, Sophe, thought you were the perfect hostess? Get that pudding on the table.'

'Cheeky!' she said, standing up and pushing her chair away. 'It's chocolate trifle, by the way. I hope that's all right with everyone? I warn you, it's packed full of Lightweights units.'

Everyone assured her they didn't give a monkey's about the Lightweights units.

I saw Joe looking at me, his eyes anxious, and tried to clear my head. I was being assaulted with so many emotions I hardly knew what to do with myself. I'd been so sure that this man was the father I'd been searching for, but now I had to accept that I'd been on the wrong track entirely. I looked across at Gabriel, seeing him now as if for the first time. He wasn't my brother.

I felt an overwhelming sense of relief, and finally I realised the truth.

I'd been looking for an angel and I'd found one, but not the one I'd searched for. It was Gabriel I'd discovered, not Raphael — because I knew now, for sure, that my feelings for him weren't those of a sister for a brother. I thought about him constantly and had done for ages, probably since the day I rounded the corner and saw him standing on King's Row with Amy in his arms. I think I'd felt my ovaries ping at that moment but had deliberately ignored those feelings, for obvious reasons. With a start, I remembered Rhiannon's words on that first day in Kearton Bay.

'Maybe you're already on the path to finding what you seek, even if you don't know that you're seeking it.'

She'd been so right. Was Gabriel who I'd been sent to find? Was my mother guiding me towards a very different angel? But then, Gabriel hadn't shown the slightest interest in me, even though he'd never suspected that we may be related. I was on a hiding to nothing. He was a total enigma and showed no inclination to reveal anything of himself to me, and why would he? I was just some sad woman who'd landed on Hannah's doorstep to escape a disastrous marriage. Why should he care?

They all began to pass plates around, and the dining room was filled with the sound of clashing crockery, gossip and laughter. I reached over for Gabriel's plate, and his eyes met mine. For a second, I stared straight into them and I saw something ... what? Before I could begin to analyse it, the shutters came down again and he was his usual impassive self. What was wrong with this man? I had no idea, but I wanted to know. I wanted to whip away the mask he insisted on wearing to the world. But how could I when I didn't know the reason for it?

Chapter 20

I woke up the next morning feeling like a different person. I wasn't Raphael Bailey's daughter. With that shadow no longer hanging over me, life suddenly felt much brighter, even though I was no closer to finding out who was my real father.

'Maybe you'll never know,' Rose said with a sigh. 'I can't think of a single person called Raphael around here, apart from that one, so it strikes me that he probably buggered off years ago and never came back. I'm sorry you didn't find what you came for.'

We were sitting in Pinky's. Rose had opened up for a few hours, but there was no one else in there. It was quite cold and windy today, totally different to yesterday's glorious sunshine, but even so.

'How do you keep going, Rose?' I asked her. 'You must struggle even more in the winter months, when most of the tourists have gone home. How do you manage?'

She shrugged. 'With great difficulty. It's only my second year, don't forget. Last year, I still had some savings from the house, and that tided us over. This year — well, let's just say, it's going to be tight.'

'I wonder how the other cafés manage?' I mused. I'd been in one or two of them, and they were always busy. Then again, they had more traditional decor and — I hated to admit it — much tastier food.

Rose seemed of the same opinion. 'They do better than here. Their grub's better, and, if I'm being really honest, I don't think this pink theme's too popular.'

'So, why don't you change it?'

'With what? Brass buttons?' She sighed. 'Not everyone's in your position, Eliza. Some of us don't have celebrity husbands and uncles to hand out the dosh.'

I looked at her in surprise, and she reached out and squeezed my arm. 'Sorry, pet. That came out all wrong. I'm not having a go at you, honest. Just a bit stressed when I think about the future.'

I was silent as what she'd said sank in. I'd been feeling more and more uneasy about my financial situation. With Harry clearly calling time on our marriage, I realised that I'd no right to continue spending his money and, more importantly, I didn't want to. Everyone around me was struggling financially, and here I was, buying whatever I wanted, with no thought for the cost. I realised I'd been totally spoilt. With Joe earning so much and Harry making good money, I hadn't had to think about finances for years.

I thought about Zoe. Sophie had a low opinion of her because she'd never earned a penny of her own money but had leeched off Gabriel, spending his salary as fast as he could earn it. Was that really the sort of woman I wanted to be?

I focused on Rose when I realised she was still talking.

'Bloody café. Don't know why I bother.'

'But you enjoy it? It's what you wanted?'

'What? Running a café? Hardly. That was Jimbo's idea, not mine. I went along with it 'cos I thought it would be a laugh. Turns out I'm not cut out to run a café. Who knew?'

'So, why don't you sell up? Do something else?'

'Because it's hardly a thriving business, is it? And I'd have to find something with living accommodation, too, which isn't always easy, not to mention another job. And, anyway, prices have gone up so much here, with the demand for holiday lets, and there's no way I want to leave Kearton Bay. I may not like running the café, but I love this village. I'm stuck.'

Rose had helped me out from the minute I met her and all the time she had these worries hanging over her. Well, at least there was one thing I could do.

'Will you let me do some baking for you? I'd be happy to supply the café for as long as I'm here.'

'What? Aw, bless you, thanks, but I couldn't pay you.'

I thought about my own new situation. 'Look, I don't want payment for the work. If you can just cover the cost of the ingredients, I'd be happy to help, the way you've been helping me. Oh, come on, Rose, we're friends, aren't we? And, anyway, I need something to take my mind off the fact that I'm back at square one.'

'I know. It sucks,' she admitted. 'Well, if you're sure you want to? I'd be grateful. Anything that brings in a few more customers is fine by me. Cheers, Eliza.'

I should have been thanking her. The fact was, I was marking time. I'd no reason to stay in Kearton Bay any longer. Harry was in the South of France with Melody, and there was no point kidding myself that he had any desire to drag himself away from her collagen lips, even if he'd managed to break the suction, and my father obviously wasn't in the area any more. There was no way someone else called Raphael could live round here without Rose knowing about it. My mission was redundant, and I should really think about going back to Chiswick and sorting out my life.

Yet, just the thought of it made me feel desperately sad, and I was looking for any reason to stay in the village. The awful thing was, I knew why and I'd a horrible feeling I was facing yet another lost cause.

****

I'd spent all day baking, and the farmhouse kitchen was a bit of a mess. Hannah surveyed the assortment of baking tins, mixing bowls and spoons scattered on the draining board of the sink and put her hands on her hips. 'I hope you're going to clear this away, madam,' she said.

I was most indignant. 'Of course I am. I always do.'

'Is this all for Rose, then? By heck, there's enough to keep her going for weeks. You do know she only gets two customers a day?'

'Well, that's what we're trying to change,' I said. 'I've made three different types of cake, some muffins, a couple of quiches and some scones. That should do for now. We'll see how it goes. Rose is going to do some special offers. She's putting notices up in the window. Hopefully, it will draw more people in, and once they taste the food, they'll spread the word.'

'It would probably help if she got rid of all that awful pink,' said Hannah. 'I went in there once last year with Lexi. I tell you, it nearly made me bring me dinner back up. What was she thinking?'

'She is terribly keen on pink,' I said with a laugh. 'Although, she's realised it was a mistake. I wish I could help her. She's helped me enough.'

'Oh. With what?'

Hannah looked at me curiously, and I hesitated, unsure whether to confide in her about my real reason for being in Kearton Bay. Then I heard Lexi in the yard and decided against it. I didn't want them to find out that, initially, my friendship had been a deliberate ploy to gain more information from them, especially now, when they mattered so much to me.

'If it hadn't been for Rose, I would never have joined Lightweights, so I'd never have met Lexi and then I'd never have met you,' I told her, dropping a kiss on her cheek. 'I have a lot to thank her for.'

She caught my hand and held it. 'I love having you here,' she told me. 'You and Amy. You know that, don't you?'

'Despite the mess?' I asked her, waving my arm in the direction of the sink.

She smiled. 'Aye. Even then.'

The feeling was mutual. Hannah was a blunt, no-nonsense kind of woman in the same mould as Mrs Travers. She'd taken me in and given Amy and me a home. She'd helped me when the story broke about Harry, and she'd given me something real and solid to hold onto, when everything else around me was chaos. I owed her a lot and I hugged her to me, grateful beyond words.

She patted me on the back then held me at arm's length as she looked at me closely. 'So, you've given up on that idiot husband of yours then?'

I swallowed. 'I think he gave up on me, Hannah. The fact that he's sunning himself on a beach with that bimbo kind of gives it away.'

'But you wouldn't take him back?'

Take him back? I hardly thought that was an option.

'Harry's with Melody,' I said. 'He doesn't want me.'

'But if he did,' she persisted. 'If he came back and said he wanted to put things right, what would you do?'

I didn't see why she was so keen to find out. What was the point in playing this *what if* game? I shrugged. 'It won't happen. What are you getting at, Hannah?'

She lowered herself into a chair with a sigh. 'Men like Harry, they have a way with them. They know how to twist things, manipulate 'em, like. I know how they work, love. If he got bored with that curly-haired trollop, and my guess is he will, he'd head home to you and expect you to take him back and be glad of the chance.'

She gazed out of the window across the yard. 'There are other men out there who would never treat you so badly. Good men — men who'd do everything in their power to make you happy. You understand?'

I felt myself redden. What was she trying to tell me?

She leaned forward, holding out her hand, and I took it and sat in the chair beside hers. 'He's a good man,' she told me.

'Who is?'

'You know who I mean,' she said. Her blue eyes may have faded but the look she gave me was sharp enough. I knew there was no point in playing dumb.

'He may be,' I told her quietly, 'but it doesn't change anything, does it?'

'Oh? Why?'

'Because, for a start, I know nothing about him. What happened to Lexi's mother? Why is he working on a farm, when he's a qualified doctor? There's a rumour in this village that he was struck off. If that's the case, what did he do that was so bad?'

She shook her head. 'Do you believe that?'

'I don't know. How can I possibly tell? What's the story with him, Hannah?'

'I told you ages ago, ask him. It's his story alone to tell. Sometimes, you have to decide who you can trust and who you can't. Make sure you pick wisely.'

Well, that was helpful. Not.

'Anyway…' I sighed. 'It doesn't matter. He's never said anything to me that makes me think he's interested. To be honest, he rarely says anything to me at all.'

She was still for a minute then she stood up and wandered over to the sink, where she filled up the bowl, despite my protests. She washed up in silence, and I took a tea towel and began to dry the dishes.

'My Albert told me he loved me once. On the day he proposed,' she said eventually, as I stood drying the last spoon, and she took up a dish cloth and began to wipe down the draining board.

'Only once?' I said, shocked.

'I expect Harry told you all the time.'

I nodded. 'Yes. He did.'

'Aye. He would. My Albert, he brought me flowers every Saturday morning for our entire married life,' she finished. 'No one could have loved me more.'

She shuffled off into the living room, leaving me staring after her, the wet tea towel hanging limply from my hand.

****

Rose looked doubtful when I arrived at Pinky's with all the food.

'It's really good of you, and I do appreciate it,' she told me. 'But what if I don't sell it? It would be a crying shame if it went stale 'cos I couldn't shift it.'

'I'm sure Fuchsia and Cerise would help eat it, if you don't,' I said. 'But you should have a little faith. Have you done the posters?'

She pointed to the window, and I went back outside, wondering how I'd missed the huge sheet of paper that was stuck to the glass, proclaiming the special offer of free tea or coffee with every scone or slice of cake purchased.

'Generous,' I said.

'Desperate,' she replied, rolling her eyes. 'Still, we'll see how this goes, eh?' She glanced at the clock. 'Five to five. Nearly time to close. See what tomorrow brings. You off straight back to the farm?'

I shook my head. 'I'm going to see Rhiannon. Hannah's minding Amy, and I thought I'd pop in for a chat since I've hardly spoken to her since I left the pub.'

Rhiannon and I were sorted, and a part of me wondered if she really did have magic powers. She seemed to have guessed what was going to happen to me here long before it had, and I suppose I was hoping she might have some more premonitions for me. I sure as hell could use a heads up.

'I'll come with you,' said Rose. 'Give me five minutes to lock up. I'll clear away when I get back, and the girls can cook for themselves tonight. Bugger it.'

Ten minutes later, we entered The Hare and Moon and came face to face with the ever-delightful Michelle.

'What can I get you?' she asked, looking me up and down with undisguised disdain.

'We're just here to see Rhiannon. Is she around?' asked Rose, since I was silent.

'Upstairs. Go on up.'

I hesitated. What if she was entertaining again? I thought briefly of Marty but dismissed the idea. She wouldn't go down that road again, I was certain. Anyway, it was too late now, as Rose was already pushing open the door to the stairway, and I could do nothing to stop her without good reason. I followed her, my fingers tightly crossed that we wouldn't walk in on anything unsavoury.

Rhiannon was in the kitchen, thank God. Her face lit up when she saw us.

'How lovely! I do love it when I get unexpected visitors. Would you like a coffee? Or shall we be frightfully naughty and open the wine?'

We all agreed on the wine. She cracked open a bottle and took some glasses from the cupboard.

'So, is this a social call? Or is there a reason behind your visit?' she asked me. I swear she knew exactly what was on my mind.

The trouble was, how to say it with Rose in the room? I took a large slug of wine and decided it was time to be honest with them both. Needless-to-say, Rhiannon was surprised to learn that I was here to find an angel, and Rose was quite hurt that the angel I'd found had turned out to be Gabriel.

'Can't believe you kept that quiet. Why didn't you tell me?'

'Be fair, Rose,' I said, 'I thought he was my brother for long enough. I didn't realise what was building up inside me until I knew he wasn't. That's when I finally recognised the feelings I had.'

'I don't see it myself.' She shrugged. 'Gabriel? I mean, he's all right, but he's a bit buttoned-up. Like he's got a poker up his arse, most of the time. All closed off, like.'

'Don't be horrible,' I said. 'He's bloody gorgeous. Although,' I admitted, 'I know what you mean about being closed off. Wish I knew why and how to help him.'

'"I saw the angel in the marble and carved until I set him free",' murmured Rhiannon.

'Eh?' Rose looked confused.

'Michelangelo,' she said, smiling at me.

I understood what she was saying, but how to go about carving?

'I really don't know what to do.' I stared beseechingly at her, as if she would produce a magic wand and make everything all right.

She seemed quite thoughtful. 'I do wish you'd come to me sooner,' she said. 'I could have helped you, and things would have been sorted much faster, without all this dreadful angst.'

I felt hope rising. 'Really? I knew it! You said to me, that first day we met, that I was already on the path to finding what I was seeking, even if I didn't know I was seeking it, remember? You knew I was meant to find Gabriel, even then, didn't you?'

She looked at me steadily for a moment, then smiled. 'I rather think you're discovering something much more important,' she said. 'Maybe both you and Gabriel are. And maybe you can help each other with that.'

I felt totally bewildered. What did she mean by that?

'The universe is unfolding as it should,' she assured me. 'But I think I can give it a little nudge in the other matter.'

'What are you on about?' asked Rose, a little sulkily.

'Eliza's father, of course. This is a small village with a long history. Someone will know who he was, and I have just the man to help you. Come with me.'

****

To say I felt some trepidation, as Rhiannon led us towards her bedroom, was an understatement of epic proportions. Who the hell did she have in there now? She knocked lightly, as Rose stared at me in astonishment. I shook my head and found that my fingers were tightly crossed again. Rhiannon opened the door slightly and peered into the room.

'Are you decent, poppet? Only, I have some people here who need your help.'

God knows what the poor bloke in the bedroom made of that, but he must have been agreeable, because she beamed at us both and then ushered us inside.

I couldn't have been more surprised if I'd found Prince Harry in there. Rose and I gaped in astonishment at the bed, where, looking extremely sheepish amongst the multitude of cushions and pillows, sat Will.

I'm not sure who blushed the deepest red. Well, yes, I do. Will beat us by quite a margin, but to say Rose and I felt awkward would be like saying Mo Farah could run a bit.

'Bloody hell,' said Rose. 'I wasn't expecting that.'

Rhiannon wandered over to the bed and began to straighten the duvet, as Will arranged the cushions as best he could, to hide his naked chest.

He peeped out at us over a pillow, his eyes full of apologies. 'I'm terribly sorry,' he said. 'I would have dressed if I'd known.'

I said nothing. What do you say in situations like that? Funnily enough, I'd never come across it before. Rhiannon seemed totally relaxed. She sank onto the bed beside him and patted the duvet for us to come and join her. Rose and I looked at each other, and she shrugged, flopping down next to Rhiannon. I looked around and my eyes fell on a tub chair in the corner. I pulled it over and sat down. I figured the bed was crowded enough.

'Eliza, I don't know if you've met Will Boden-Kean?' said Rhiannon. 'Will, this is Eliza.'

'Awfully pleased to meet you,' said Will, holding out his hand. I shook it, too stunned to speak.

'Well, this is all very nice,' said Rose. 'So, how long's this been going on, then? I dunno, nothing but secrets being exposed today.'

Rhiannon smiled. 'Not long. It's all quite new and terribly exciting,' she said.

Will looked up at the ceiling as if praying for assistance. I couldn't say I blamed him.

'Anyway, darling, the reason I've brought the ladies into the room is because Eliza really needs your help.'

Will looked at me. 'If I can be of any assistance, of course I'd be happy to help,' he said.

I couldn't help smiling. Bless him, even caught in this compromising position he was politeness itself. I sat, trying not to look at him, as Rhiannon explained all about my mission to find my father. He seemed genuinely interested, which was pretty big of him, given the circumstances.

'Goodness, how thrilling,' he said, when she'd finished.

She clapped her hands. 'I know! I do wish she'd told me from the beginning. What fun it would have been to investigate.'

I couldn't help thinking how well-matched they were. There may have been fifteen years, or so, between them but they were similar in a lot of ways. Anyway, at least he wasn't married. They were doing nothing wrong or immoral, as far as I could see. And if they were, well, that was their business and certainly nothing I wanted to know about.

Will was thoughtful, stroking his chin. Eventually, he looked up at me and his eyes were full of compassion. 'Are you quite sure you want to know, Eliza? I mean, sometimes it's better not to, don't you think? Things don't always work out the way we plan. I wouldn't want to cause any harm to anyone.'

'What do you mean, harm? How can it harm me?'

'I wasn't just thinking of you,' he said gently.

'So, you do know?'

'I think I do, yes. There was another Raphael in the village. It was quite a few years ago now, but I do just remember him. As the major landowners in this area, my family forged strong links with the villagers over the centuries, and it was always made clear to me that I should learn about the local families and take an interest in them. I recall, quite well, the story of another Raphael and what became of him, but I urge you to think carefully. There are other people to consider. If I tell you, you should take time to decide what to do with this information. Will you promise me you'll do that?'

I nodded, my stomach doing somersaults, as I realised I was about to finally learn who my father was.

Will sighed. 'Very well. If you're sure.'

'Bloody hell, Will,' said Rose impatiently. 'She's sure, she's sure. We're all sure. Spill, for God's sake.'

And so, he did.

Chapter 21

Rose invited me in for coffee, but I refused. I'd followed her to her door without thinking, my mind so full of my new discovery and its implications.

'Oh, come on, you've had a bit of a shock. We all have. Why don't you take an hour or so to digest it all? Bugger the café. I'll clear it up later.'

'No thanks, Rose. I could do with a bit of a walk, I think. Clear my head.'

A walk? Hell, a trek through the Andes wouldn't clear the mess that was swirling through my poor skull.

She peered at me with anxious eyes. 'What are you going to do?'

'I really don't know. I just can't get my head around it all. It never occurred to me.'

'Well, why would it? Him, of all people? Look, are you sure you won't come in? I'm a bit worried leaving you on your own.'

I shook my head. 'I'll be fine. Going to take a slow walk back to the farm, and I'd rather be alone, to be honest.'

She hugged me. 'If you're sure? If you need me, just pick up the phone, okay?'

I smiled. 'Thanks, Rose. I will. Let me know how you get on with the cakes tomorrow.'

She pushed open the side door next to the café and shrugged. 'Doesn't seem so important now, does it? But, yeah, I will. Promise.'

I walked away, deep in thought, my hands in my pockets. Will had been anxious when I left, worried that he'd done the wrong thing, but I'd assured him that he'd been right to tell me. I'd needed to know. The question was what, if anything, did I do with that information now?

I walked slowly up Bay Street, my mind whirling. As I reached the top and the street levelled out, I walked over to the bench in front of the railings and sat gazing out over the sea. It suddenly occurred to me that I'd walked up the hill without stopping, apart from when I said goodbye to Rose, and I wasn't gasping for air. My weight loss had levelled off, and I certainly wasn't thin, but I was much healthier and fitter. Even my skin had improved with all the fresh air, exercise and less make-up, and now I'd finally found out the identity of my father, there was nothing left for me to accomplish here. It was time to go home.

And where was home? The large semi in Chiswick that I'd shared with Harry and Amy? I didn't think so, somehow. That no longer felt like a place I wanted to be. It had too many painful memories.

I stared out over the ocean, wondering what on earth I was going to do next. From within my bag, I heard sleigh bells, and for a moment, I couldn't think what the sound was. Then I realised that my mobile phone was ringing, and I pulled my bag off my shoulder and began rummaging around for it.

I answered it without even looking at the screen, my mind so preoccupied with other matters.

'Eliza? Thank God. Darling, I've got a surprise for you. I'm on my way to see you right now. I should be there in about half an hour.'

It was a good job I was sitting down. It was Harry.

****

Hannah couldn't believe it when I told her. 'He's coming here? Now? Well, of all the bloody cheek!'

I couldn't disagree with that. Harry hadn't even given me chance to refuse. Having found out where I was staying, he'd hung up before I could argue. What the hell was he playing at? I hadn't even known he was back in England, and I doubted that Joe or Mrs Travers had known, either. They would have warned me.

As I'd walked home, I'd briefly contemplated calling Joe. I had such a lot to tell him, and of all the people in the world, Joe was the one I always turned to, but then I decided against it. I knew if I'd told him what was going on, he would immediately have headed up to Kearton Bay to be there for me, and I didn't want that. It was time to take care of myself.

'You should have told him to bugger off,' said Hannah, still seething that my errant husband had dared to contact me.

'Believe me, I would have done if he'd let me get a word in edgeways. He just demanded to know where I was, told me he was on his way and hung up. I don't know, Hannah. Maybe it's best he does come here, anyway. We have a lot to discuss.'

'You do?' She pursed her lips, and I could see she was dying to say more but she managed to restrain herself and shuffled into the living room to read a story to Amy instead.

Harry arrived just after seven, and if I'd expected him to crawl in looking all apologetic and bashful, I couldn't be more wrong.

'Fuck me, this place is the back of beyond,' he said, as I opened the kitchen door. 'What the hell are you doing here? Don't they have hotels in Yorkshire?'

I glared at him in disgust. 'Come in, Harry.' I ushered him inside, where Amy and Hannah were waiting.

'Princess!' he said on spying his daughter, who was sitting at the kitchen table colouring in a picture of Mickey Mouse. She looked up at him curiously, gave him a shy smile, and then continued work on her masterpiece.

Harry looked a bit annoyed, though what he expected I can't imagine, given that he rarely bothered to so much as speak to her at home. I thought about her reaction when Joe had arrived, and it made me want to weep.

Harry wasn't going to give up easily, though. He picked her up and cuddled her, keeping an iron grip on her, though she leaned away from him, her body rigid as she waved her wax crayon desperately at the table. He kissed her, despite her protests, and told her he had presents. I'm ashamed to say she stopped resisting him and looked at him with sudden interest. He smiled triumphantly and handed her back to me.

'I won't be a sec,' he announced and disappeared back into the yard, reappearing a minute or two later with a large carrier bag. Amy, mercenary child that she was, wriggled off my knee and ran straight over to him.

'This is Hannah,' I said, introducing them to each other while Amy began tearing off the wrapping paper, uncovering a toy guitar, some books and a doll.

Hannah struggled to hide her contempt as Harry flashed her his award-winning smile, but he didn't seem to notice.

'I've so missed you,' he said, stroking my hair. 'Goodness, darling, your roots need doing. I'll pay for you to have a few beauty treatments when we leave. I don't expect they have any decent salons around here.'

'I suppose you want a cup of tea,' Hannah said grudgingly.

'God, no,' Harry said. 'I loathe the stuff. I wouldn't say no to a coffee, though — unless it's that ghastly instant trash, in which case I won't bother.'

'You won't be bothering, then,' Hannah said with some satisfaction.

'Oh.' Harry looked rather shocked. He whispered in my ear, 'How do you stand it here? It's positively prehistoric.'

I felt my lip curl in disgust. 'Upstairs, Harry,' I told him. 'We need to talk.'

'Upstairs, eh? Well, if you insist,' he said, giving me a wolfish grin. He grabbed my hand and pulled me towards the hallway door. 'Come on, darling. We've a lot of catching up to do.'

I wrenched my hand away, and he looked at me in surprise. 'Are you all right?'

I don't know how I didn't punch him, but I forced myself to keep calm. 'Go on up,' I muttered.

Hannah looked at me with anxious eyes. She'd worried when I'd appeared in the kitchen wearing all the old war paint that I hadn't bothered with for weeks. It was only when I saw her face that I'd even realised what I'd done. It had been an automatic reaction. Harry hated to see me without make-up, and I'd switched to default mode, but I'd quickly reassured her that it meant nothing. I hoped she realised she'd no need to worry as I followed him upstairs.

He was in my room, sitting on my bed with his bag thrown on the floor, before I'd even reached the landing. I guessed he'd seen the door open and recognised one of my jackets hanging on the wardrobe door but, bloody hell, he had a nerve!

'Stop it, Harry,' I protested, as his lips covered my neck in kisses, and he began to unbutton my shirt. 'What do you think you're doing?'

'Are you saying you don't want it?' he murmured. 'I don't believe you. I know how much you've missed me, just like I've missed you.'

'The difference is,' I said, 'that you've been filling the gap — literally — with that slapper you're living with.'

Harry drew back. 'For fuck's sake! Why do you always have to spoil things? I was looking forward to this all day, and now you've absolutely ruined the mood.'

'Well! Of all the flaming cheek!'

I'd ruined *his* mood? What about him and the fact that he was having rampant sex with a glamorous big-breasted blonde?

Harry sat on the edge of the bed, looking like a petulant child.

'You just don't get it, do you?' I demanded. 'Have you any idea how hard it is—'

'It was,' he interrupted. 'It's kind of gone limp now.' He turned his head and grinned at me. 'Sorry, darling. I'm a total clod, sometimes. I really have missed you, though, you must believe that, and I've been so looking forward to being with you again. Nobody does it for me like you do.'

'Are you completely bonkers? Last I heard, you were living it up in the South of France with Melody.'

He rolled his eyes in horror. 'Don't! It's been a bloody nightmare. Sodding paps everywhere. I got back this morning, and they were actually outside our gate, can you believe? I was out of there pretty sharpish, I can tell you. I went to my mother's, but I couldn't stand it there for long, so I thought I'd come up here and surprise you.'

'Surprise me? Are you absolutely nuts?'

He looked puzzled, so I guess he *was* absolutely nuts. Anyone normal would have understood my point of view, without having to have a picture drawn for them.

He began to unpack his bag, throwing shirts and boxer shorts onto the bed and then wondering aloud where they were all going to go in this tiny excuse for a bedroom.

'What on earth are you doing here?' he asked. 'It's hardly The Ritz, is it? More, debtors' gaol, let's be honest. The sooner we're out of here, the better,' he decided, folding a t-shirt and opening one of my drawers to put it in.

His arrogance took my breath away. 'What about Melody?'

'She's in the States. She really does have a selfish streak, you know. I mean, it was all her doing that we ended up in France. She let slip to one of her cousins, and I'm convinced she did it on purpose. Next thing I know, the papers have been tipped off and we're on a plane. Very convenient that she'd just bought a holiday home there, I must say. Anyway, we had a huge row, and she told me she was going to New York to see a friend and think things over, and I may as well go home and deal with everything myself. Bloody cheek.'

I wanted to say something, but my mouth seemed to have locked in an open position. I just stared at him instead. I felt myself beginning to tremble and fought to stay in control. I wasn't going to let him get to me ever again.

'I must say, I wasn't expecting there to have been quite so much fuss. My mother showed me the papers. She's kept every single one. I'd no idea it would be such a big story. Melody's younger sister told us that we were trending on Twitter for days. She said they were quite rude about me, but she may just have been saying that, out of spite. She's fancied me for ages and I kept turning her down. Melody would kill her if she knew.'

He paused for breath, and I felt my throat tighten. I wasn't sure that I was breathing properly. There didn't seem to be enough air.

'Anyway, darling, let's not talk about Melody. That's definitely over. I have a surprise for you. How do you fancy a holiday?'

'What are you talking about?' I managed to whisper. 'You said you didn't love me any more.'

'Oh, I know. I'm sorry about that. I didn't mean it. I was trying to be kind. I thought, if you believed that, it would make it easier for you to get over me.'

He was trying to be kind?

'Anyway, what about this holiday? Let's go somewhere expensive, before I start filming the new series.'

'The — the new series?'

'*Twice as Nice*. Brilliant news on that front. Martin rang me the other day. He's thrilled with the publicity. Conveniently seems to have forgotten that bullshit he was spouting, about the recession and scrapping the programme. Expects our ratings to go through the roof, and I'll be demanding a pay rise if they do, that's for sure. I was wondering if you'd like to go to that little place just outside Rome where we stayed just before we got engaged? Show the world it's all behind us.'

'Show — show the world?' I could hardly speak. He meant show the reporters. No doubt about it. This was yet another set up.

'Yes. I don't see any reason to hang about. I brought your passports with me so we don't even have to go home first. We could fly from Leeds/Bradford. I checked availability. There's a flight tomorrow evening which would be perfect.'

I shook my head in confusion. There was something wrong, something he wasn't telling me. 'What's going on, Harry?'

'Going on?'

'Why are you really here?'

'I told you. I want to take you and Amy away on a proper family holiday. Is there anything wrong with that?'

'Of course there is! We're not a family any longer! You and Melody saw to that. Why have you fallen out?'

'It was just a stupid argument, but the point is, it's over. What does it matter?'

I folded my arms, trying to breathe calmly even though my chest felt quite tight, and I was feeling increasingly dizzy. 'If you don't tell me what's going on, I won't go anywhere with you at all, that much I can promise you. If you want anything from me, you can be honest with me. It will be a first.'

He stopped folding clothes and sat down heavily on the bed beside me. 'I suppose you're going to find out eventually,' he muttered. 'The press have got hold of another story. It's going to be in the Sunday papers.'

'What kind of story?'

He looked suddenly scared. 'You have to understand, it meant nothing.'

'What meant nothing?'

'It was ages ago. She was just a stupid girl who came onto me. It was a few meaningless shags. I'd forgotten all about them, and I expect she had, too, until the publicity with Melody reminded her and she saw pound signs. Sold her story — stupid kiss-and-tell. You know the type.'

I tried to take a deep breath but couldn't manage it. 'Are you telling me Melody wasn't the first?'

'It meant nothing, like I said.'

'When?'

'Does it matter?'

'When, Harry?'

He sighed. 'About three or four years ago, I suppose. I don't know.' He grabbed my hand. 'You have to understand, darling, we were going through a difficult time. You were heavily pregnant with Amy, and we hadn't been — well, you know — for a while, and all you seemed to talk about was the baby, and I felt a bit…well, pushed out, I suppose.'

Pushed out? So, when that space hopper photograph of me had been taken, he'd been in the midst of an affair with some unknown girl? And I'd blamed Melody for all this mess, believing that if it hadn't been for her, Harry would never have strayed. Had there been others? How could I ever be sure?

'I need some fresh air,' I mumbled and left the bedroom.

I could hear Harry's indignant protests as I ran down the stairs, but nothing would have made me turn back. I had to get out. I was starting to panic. There was no air in the house, and my tears were threatening to overwhelm me.

By the time I reached the front door, they were streaming down my face. All the pain I'd thought was finally under control was breaking loose. Without even considering where I was going, I ran across the yard towards the barn, where I stood helplessly, unsure of where to go. I'd even messed that up.

I sank onto my knees on the mud by the barn door and covered my face with my hands, as sobs wracked my body. Everything was such a mess. He'd been my happy-ever-after. I'd believed in him, in us. All this time, I'd blamed Melody, convinced that it was her who'd led him astray, but I'd been fooling myself. How many more women had there been? Our entire marriage had been a sham.

I sobbed as I thought of Amy. She'd been landed with the same kind of excuse for a father as I'd had, because I knew now, for sure, that mine had abandoned my mother when she needed him most, not because he'd had no choice, but because he'd been weak and selfish and didn't give a damn about her, or about me. All my stupid fantasies had been just that — an illusion that I'd wanted to believe because the alternative was so painful.

There was no such thing as happy-ever-after.

I didn't know what to do any more. I'd been so focused on finding out where I came from, but now I knew, where could I go from there? The future was suddenly empty and completely terrifying.

I couldn't stop crying. I tried to gulp in enough air but there didn't seem to be an adequate supply, even out here. I could hear screaming coming from somewhere. It took me a long, long time to realise it was coming from me.

From somewhere far off I heard Harry calling my name. I didn't want him to see me. I couldn't bear any more. Then I felt his arms around me, and I began to struggle.

'Leave me alone. Go away.' I gasped, but his arms continued to hold me, and I was pulled against him, where my head rested on his chest while my sobs continued unabated for several minutes.

He stroked my hair softly and, gradually, I began to calm down, and my crying started to ease off. I could feel his heart beating beneath my ear, and slowly, I raised my hand and rested it over the soothing pulse, letting it comfort me. It quickened under my touch.

I breathed him in, a delicious and vaguely familiar mix of sandalwood, patchouli and mandarin oil. I realised that the blue cotton I was leaning into was now soaked through with my tears. Had Harry been wearing a blue cotton shirt?

I felt him kiss the top of my head softly and wondered how someone so tender could behave so appallingly, and as I wondered, I felt his hand gently cup my chin and raise my face to his, and I was looking up, as I somehow knew I would be, into Gabriel's eyes. He was looking down at me with such compassion that my breath caught in my throat. I stared at him in wonder for a moment, my eyes drawn to his mouth, which suddenly looked so tempting, so softly kissable that I had to force myself to look away.

'I'm so sorry,' I murmured, trying to sit up as I anxiously rubbed my face.

He gently wiped my tears away then helped me as I struggled to stand.

'I really am sorry. I must seem like a lunatic. Your shirt, it's all wet,' I said, pointing to the tear stain in embarrassment.

'It really doesn't matter. None of it matters.'

We looked at each other, not knowing what to say, and I felt fresh tears spill down my cheeks. 'I can't — I don't—'

He moved towards me, his arm outstretched. 'Eliza, I—'

'There you are! Fuck me, you gave me a fright.' Harry was beside us. He pulled me to him and stared at Gabriel in surprise. 'Who are you? Eliza, what the hell was all that about?' he demanded, not waiting for Gabriel's reply.

I shrugged, unable to answer as tears choked me yet again.

'For God's sake, what's wrong with you?'

'I think she needs to lie down,' said Gabriel. 'Let's get her back indoors. She's obviously in great distress.'

'And you're a doctor, are you?' said Harry sarcastically.

I looked at Gabriel. He swallowed and then squared his shoulders. 'Yes, I am,' he said, and I felt my heart swell with pleasure and pride.

Harry looked suitably crushed. 'Oh. Oh, well, all right. Come on, Eliza. Bed for you, I think.'

He turned me round and began to lead me back towards the farmhouse. He seemed somewhat put out to find Gabriel following us. 'It's okay, thanks,' he said over his shoulder. 'I can take it from here.'

'I want to make sure she's all right,' Gabriel replied.

His voice brooked no arguments, and Harry obviously realised that he wasn't going to go away, so he said nothing more but got me into the house, where Hannah was waiting, her face grey with worry.

'I'll get her upstairs and put her to bed,' he said, pushing me none-too-gently out of the kitchen and into the hall, with Hannah shuffling behind us.

She watched us as we made our way up the stairs, and I heard her asking Gabriel what had happened. I didn't hear his reply. Harry got me into bed and drew the curtains, eyeing me nervously as if worried that I was going to start screaming again.

'It's all right, you can go,' I told him, but he shook his head.

'I'll just sit here and make sure you're okay. Just for a little while.'

It wasn't like him to be so concerned, I thought, then realised he probably didn't want to go downstairs and face Gabriel. I closed my eyes. Gabriel. What had he been doing there? I hadn't realised he was still on the farm. How embarrassing. I closed my eyes, feeling again the tenderness of his touch, seeing once more the compassion in his eyes and the soft, tempting curve of his lips. I remembered how safe I'd felt, as he held me in his arms and I breathed in the scent of his aftershave while he gently stroked my hair.

It had been a day of total confusion and revelations. I needed to make sense of it all. I just wanted Harry to go away, so I could go over it all in my mind. And then I slept.

****

Harry Jarvis didn't look too impressed when he walked into the living room to find Gabriel sitting in an armchair, with Amy perched on his knee as she told him all about Jeeves and Wooster. Gabriel didn't care. How he had the nerve to turn up here, after all he'd done, was beyond him.

He and Hannah glanced at each other, and Hannah said, 'I'll just take Amy into the kitchen. Time for her supper.'

She struggled to her feet and held out her hand for the little girl, who took it and climbed down from Gabriel's knee, following Hannah meekly into the kitchen without a second glance at her father.

'Er, thank you for your help out there,' said Harry awkwardly. Gabriel stared up at him in silence and Harry sat down on the sofa and shook his head. 'That was seriously scary stuff,' he admitted. 'What do you think brought it on?'

He drew back in alarm, as Gabriel almost snarled at him. 'What brought it on? What the hell do you think brought it on, you gutless moron?'

Harry gaped at him in shock. 'Fuck me, you country doctors are far ruder than the ones in London. Who do you think you're talking to?'

'A lying, cowardly cheat, who abandoned his wife and child for his colleague? Of course, I may be wrong. If so, feel free to enlighten me.'

Harry went pale, and Gabriel watched as a gamut of emotions crossed his face. Then Harry squinted at him suspiciously. 'Are you shagging my wife?'

Gabriel leapt to his feet.

Harry held up his hands and leaned back, alarmed. 'Okay, okay, you're not. I'm sorry. It's just that you seem to know a lot about me, and you seem to be upset about Eliza.'

'Do not,' said Gabriel coldly, as he sat down again, his hands trembling, 'judge me by your standards, Mr Jarvis. This is a small village. Everyone knows everyone's business here, and everyone cares. We've all grown fond of Eliza, and of Amy. Your — your wife — has become a close friend of my daughter and has been good to Hannah. She was in real distress out there, and it upset me to see her in that state. Anyone with a shred of decency would feel the same.'

'Yes, well.' Harry sighed and ran his fingers around his shirt collar before burying his head in his hands. 'Jesus, what a fucking mess.'

Gabriel surveyed him for a moment then asked, 'Have you left her for good?'

Harry laughed mirthlessly. 'Which one? The way things stand I have no idea who I'm supposed to be with. Melody's found out that I had an affair a few years ago and she's got the cheek to be annoyed she's not the first. Flounced off to New York in a huff to think things over, no thought for me, or what I'm going through.'

Gabriel thought he'd quite like to punch Harry Jarvis. His fists were clenched so tightly that his knuckles were white.

'If you want to be with Melody so badly, why don't you leave Eliza alone? All this uncertainty is playing havoc with her nerves, surely you can see that now? She needs to face up to it and start to rebuild her life.' He watched Harry through narrowed eyes. 'Of course, that could be the reason you're not letting go.'

'What do you mean?'

'Could it be that you don't want her to get over you? That you'd rather have her hanging on in the background? It's always nice to have an insurance policy, after all, in case things don't work out with the new woman. Plus, it's a lovely boost to the ego, having two women wanting you.'

'Don't be ridiculous,' snapped Harry. 'This is a fucking nightmare. The sooner it's sorted, the better. You have no idea how much strain I'm under.'

'Poor you,' said Gabriel.

'Exactly! Oh, I know you think I'm having the time of my life, but it's not true. It was just supposed to be a bit of fun. How was I to know it would develop into something so serious? Melody Bird, the girl with the worst reputation in show business, and that's saying something. How could I possibly predict that she'd actually fall in love with me?'

'Well, I could see that it's rather unlikely,' said Gabriel.

'All right, have your little digs at my expense,' said Harry. 'Don't sit there pretending to be such a paragon of virtue. You're a man. Don't tell me you've never done anything wrong? Never let anyone down?'

Gabriel bit his lip. 'No,' he said eventually. 'I can't say that, in all honesty. Nevertheless, for everyone's sake, you need to decide.'

'I love Eliza,' said Harry. 'She's sweet and kind and caring, and we have a daughter, for God's sake.' He sighed. 'But then Melody…' He shook his head helplessly. 'She's like no one I've ever met before. I know she's been around the block a few times, but she's so exciting, so challenging. We hang around with the same people, have the same interests. Eliza's such a homebody.'

'Shameful,' said Gabriel.

'I'm not saying it's a bad thing,' protested Harry. 'I'm just saying that maybe it's not for me. Maybe she's just too nice for someone like me. Hell, I don't know.'

Gabriel stood up and turned to leave. 'I must be going. I'm late for dinner,' he said.

'What were you doing here, anyway?' asked Harry curiously.

'I work here.'

'Work here? I thought you said you were a doctor?'

'I was — once. Now I work here.' He forced himself to speak calmly to Harry, although it was an effort to be civil.

'Well, of all the bloody nerve! I could sue you for fraud.'

'Fraud? I haven't even treated her. All I've done is have a man-to-man chat with you, as Eliza's friend.'

'I told you confidential information.'

'Yes, so confidential that most of it's been in all the papers.' He began to walk towards the door, too sickened to stay in the same room as Harry Jarvis any longer. 'You should let her go,' he told him, 'she deserves better than you.'

Harry called to him, as he walked into the kitchen. 'It's hardly my fault that she's still in love with me. What do you want me to do? Break her heart all over again? If I left her, she'd be devastated. Eliza's my wife and she wants it to stay that way. Remember that.'

Gabriel hesitated for a moment, his eyes closed. Then he took a deep breath and walked away.

Chapter 22

I slept solidly right through till seven the next morning, which was quite an achievement considering the day I'd had. I didn't even hear Harry get into bed with me that night, and I was pretty annoyed when I woke to find him lying on his side next to me, his head resting on one hand as he scrutinised me for signs of hysteria.

'Are you all right?' he asked.

'Oh, hell,' I said, blushing to my hair roots as I remembered what I'd done. I struggled to sit up, realising in dismay that I was completely naked — because I didn't remember getting undressed. Surely, he hadn't had the cheek to—? What was I thinking? This was Harry. Of course he had the cheek. Pulling the duvet up around me to cover my modesty — a little too late I feared — I wondered how I'd got myself into such a state over someone who wasn't worth it.

'Eliza, it's fine, don't worry,' Harry soothed, obviously under the impression that I was feeling apologetic. 'That fake doctor last night made it quite clear that stress was to blame.'

Gabriel! I almost groaned aloud as I recalled that it had been *that fake doctor* who'd calmed me down and stopped me from wailing like a banshee. What on earth would he think of me?

'Oh, God,' I said. 'Amy? She didn't see all that?'

'Amy's absolutely fine,' said Harry. 'She was downstairs telling your knight in shining armour all about Joe's pigs, while I was putting you to bed.'

I studied him curiously. There was a definite edge to his voice. Did he think there was something between me and Gabriel? Was there? I remembered the expression in Gabriel's eyes last night, as he looked down at me, and I shivered suddenly as I recalled the compassion in his face. I looked over at Harry, whose eyes showed only annoyance and a trace of anxiety. He was obviously worried that I'd flip out again.

'I don't know what happened,' I began. 'It just seemed to come out of nowhere. I think I just needed to let it all out.'

'Apparently so,' said Harry, climbing out of bed and revealing himself to be as naked as I was. 'We don't need to talk about all that. It's over and done with now. We move forward today.'

He yawned. 'I'm absolutely starving. All this drama has taken it out of me. I'm going to get a shower. Do you think you could fix me some breakfast, sweetheart?'

I shook my head. 'There isn't a shower,' I said, and, knowing how much he loved them, I was, for the first time since arriving at the farm, glad of the fact.

He looked appalled. 'What on earth do you mean, no shower? Everyone has a shower.'

'Not here,' I said, 'Unless you want to go and stand in the yard and I'll hose you down,' I added with a smirk.

Harry shook his head in despair. 'How can you stand it here, Eliza?' he asked. 'This place is the pits. I mean, it's shabby and old, there are no showers, no central heating, the place stinks of animals—'

'It does not!' I protested. 'It may be shabby, but it's very clean.'

'Yes, but the chickens outside smell, and when you have the windows open, I get a definite whiff, and there's a lingering odour of dog coming from somewhere.'

'That'll be Tessa,' I said.

'Tessa?'

'Gabriel's dog.'

'Oh, him again. What is it with that bloke, pretending to be a doctor? I tell you, I soon put the fear of God up him when I threatened to report him for fraud. How dare he pretend to be a medical professional when he's just a farmhand?'

'He's not a farmhand,' I said angrily. 'He's a craftsman, and he *is* a doctor. He's just taking a break from the job for a few months.'

'Sure he is. I don't trust him as far as I can throw him.'

'He's a good man,' I muttered. 'Don't judge him by your standards.'

I saw anger flicker across his face for a moment. 'I'm sorry. I was just jealous. I thought there was something between you,' he said.

I glared at him. 'Well there isn't.'

'I know that now, of course,' he said. 'I made the mistake of asking him if you were having an affair.'

My head shot up in alarm. 'You did what? How could you?'

'Oh, don't worry. He couldn't deny it fast enough. Anyone would think I'd insulted him. Obviously, you're not his type.'

He smiled, leaning over the bed and stroking my face. He still wasn't dressed, and I saw bits of him dangling on the duvet that I never wanted to see again. Now I'd have to wash the bedding.

'You are *my* type, though,' he murmured. 'Are you going to pack? I've reserved our flights. I managed to book that little hotel we stayed at, all those years ago. We can rekindle the flame.'

The very idea nauseated me. One thing I knew for certain, I was going nowhere with him. I reached for my dressing gown and pulled it on, trying to stay covered up as I did so, not wanting Harry to see me naked any more. Those days were over.

I stood up and caught sight of myself in the mirror. I hadn't washed before going to bed last night, obviously, and a painted doll stared back at me. The thick foundation only seemed to emphasise my dull skin, and faded eye shadow, smudged eyeliner and three coats of waterproof mascara couldn't hide the fact that my eyes were still swollen from last night's crying, and the sadness in them was evident. I'd lost my sparkle. I didn't recognise the girl I used to be.

I ran my hand through my dry, over-bleached hair, hating the way it felt, hating the way it looked. Who was I? How had I become this person that I didn't even know? I wanted the old Eliza back, the girl I used to be, the girl I'd begun to rediscover

over the last few weeks.

'Harry,' I said slowly, 'I think we need to talk.'

****

Hannah was already up, and she gave me a big hug as I walked into the kitchen. I clung to her, delighting in the embrace of my paternal grandmother.

'How are you feeling, love?' she asked me.

'Like a fool,' I replied truthfully.

How could I tell Hannah the reality of the situation? How to break it to her that her son, Albert Raphael Lang, who'd been named after his father, and the doctor who'd saved both his and his mother's lives, had fathered a child and abandoned both the baby and its mother to fate, leaving the country without ever telling his own mother that she had a grandchild somewhere in the world? Will had been right. The shock could be too much for her. She'd already had one heart attack, and I didn't want to bring on another.

'Aye, well, there's no one can blame you for that little turn.' Hannah finally released me and pulled out a chair for me as if I were an invalid. She filled the kettle up with water and flicked the switch. 'Truth is, anyone would have a good cry after what you've been through. I'm amazed it took so long. You're stronger than you look.'

'Hardly,' I said. 'I must have looked like a complete idiot. I don't know what everyone must think of me.'

She caught my eye, and I flushed and turned away, wondering if she knew I was thinking of Gabriel.

'He's a trained doctor,' she said softly, confirming my suspicions. 'He's seen it all before and far worse. He didn't think badly of you at all. He saved all his scorn for that husband of yours.'

'Really?' I looked up at her. 'What happened?'

'He just told him what he thought,' she said with a grin. 'Couldn't hear too much, I was in here with Amy, but what I could make out was satisfying.'

230

No wonder Harry had looked annoyed. Knowing my husband, he wouldn't have taken kindly to any criticism, especially from another man, and one who'd ridden to my rescue like "a knight in shining armour". I half smiled to myself at the thought, and Hannah patted my arm eagerly.

'Right fond of you is Gabriel,' she said. 'That much is obvious to anyone.'

I remembered Harry's opinion on that matter. He'd implied Gabriel had looked insulted when it was suggested we were having an affair.

'Hannah,' I said suddenly. 'What did Zoe Bailey look like?'

She frowned. 'Why?'

'Just curious.'

She considered for a moment then nodded. 'Come with me.'

She headed into the living room, and I followed anxiously. She shuffled over to the battered old sideboard and pulled open the drawer, fumbling around before pulling out a photograph album.

'Should be one of her in here,' she said. 'Sure of it.' She sat on the sofa, and I sat beside her, eager for a glimpse of the mysterious Mrs Bailey, yet dreading it at the same time.

'There are a lot of the Baileys in here,' she said, flicking the pages.

'Why?' I asked in surprise.

'Our family and theirs go back a long way. Gabriel's grandad saved my life, and my boy's. I named him after him, as a thank you. Albert Raphael Lang. Not that he turned out to be much of a bloody angel.'

I almost laughed at the irony of it all. If she'd told me all this weeks ago, I wouldn't have had all this agony of uncertainty.

'When Gabriel was little, he used to hang around the farm and help Eddie out sometimes. His dad used to drop him off in the school holidays when he went to work, get him out of Wendy's way. He was a serious little fella, even then. I used to want to see him scrape his knees and fall out of a tree, or something. He was always trying to do the right thing, bless him.'

I swallowed, as she pointed at a picture of a stocky-looking man, standing beside a little boy with dark, curly hair and a solemn expression, holding a lamb in his arms. There was no mistaking those eyes, even then. I felt a swell of love for him and an overwhelming desire to see him laugh. Those dimples didn't come out to play nearly often enough.

'Who's the man?' I asked curiously. It certainly wasn't Dr Bailey.

'That's my Albert,' she said softly, and my breath caught as I gazed down at my grandfather's kindly, weather-beaten face.

'He looks — he looks lovely,' I said.

She squeezed my hand. 'He was. None better. Don't let Harry blind you to the fact that there are some truly good, decent men in this world, love. Here's a picture of two of the finest.'

'I see that,' I said.

She beamed at me. 'I knew you would. Now, let me see...ah, here we go. Oh. It's a wedding photo. Does it matter?'

'No. Why should it?'

But it did. It hurt me to see him standing there beside the woman he'd obviously loved enough to marry. 'My God, they were so young!'

'Still in their teens, I think. Just gone to medical school, when she told him she were expecting, and I tell you, I'm not the only one who thinks it was done deliberate. If you'd seen the way she carried on when she found out he were going away to study, weeping and wailing and threatening to kill herself ... honest to God. Never seen the like. Sophie wanted to do the job for her.' She chuckled. 'Next thing we knew, Lexi was on the way, and they were standing in church signing their lives away.'

I was burning with curiosity. What had gone wrong? And where was Zoe Bailey now?

Hannah turned the page. 'There you go. That's a better one. Clearer, like. Now that shows her for what she is, I reckon.'

I felt my spirits sink. Zoe was beautiful. She was standing by one of the donkeys, her arm around a little girl who was sitting on its back. There was no mistaking Lexi. The red hair gave her away, and it was a characteristic shared with her mother. Zoe had the same long, glossy red hair and creamy skin but, unlike Lexi, she was tiny and supermodel thin. She wore lots of make-up and jewellery, and, despite standing in a paddock, she was wearing a short skirt and skyscraper heels. She was certainly not a flannelette-pyjamas-and-Eeyore-slippers type of girl. So, this was what Gabriel was attracted to.

'You all right, love?'

I nodded, and Hannah sighed, putting an arm around me as she turned the pages. We snuggled together on the sofa, my head on her shoulder, while she told me how busy the farm used to be, her voice thick with emotion.

'That was my lad, Albert,' she told me, pointing to a photograph of a young boy with dark hair and a broad grin. I stared at my father, feeling a mixture of longing, sadness, curiosity and contempt for the man who'd treated his family and his girlfriend so badly. 'Different he were then, till he left school. He used to look after the horses. Two beautiful horses, we had. Oh, and look, that's Harlequin, his favourite cow. He gave them all names, you know. And there's our flock of geese.' She started to laugh and put her hand to her mouth as the laughter gave way to a coughing fit.

'Bugger,' she said when it finally eased. 'Can't even have a laugh these days. Them geese were the very devil. I remember the day they chased young Gabriel round the farmyard. Sounds awful, but me and Eddie, we couldn't do nowt for laughing.'

'Well, this is all very cosy.'

Harry's voice was strained, and Hannah looked at him in surprise. He was carrying his bag and glared at me, as I sat happily browsing through old photographs, clearly not mourning his imminent departure as he'd no doubt expected.

'Do you want a drink before you leave?' I asked.

Hannah's mouth dropped open. 'You're leaving?'

'Oh, didn't she tell you? Eliza has decided our marriage is over. Just like that.'

Hannah shut the photo album and sighed with relief. 'Well, thank God for that.'

'I beg your pardon?'

'I said, thank God for that. I was beginning to think she'd never come to her senses.'

Harry scowled at her before turning his gaze on me, his eyes beseeching. 'Eliza, think about this. Is this really what you want? If I go now, there's no turning back.'

'I'm aware of that, Harry, but really, there's been no turning back since you jumped into bed with Melody Bird.'

He paused for a moment, obviously not sure whether to argue his case some more. Pride eventually won. 'Screw you, then,' he said. 'You'll regret it. You'll come crawling back before the week's out. You wait and see.'

He turned and left the house, slamming the door behind him.

Hannah looked at me. 'So, that's that, then?'

'That's that,' I said. Then I put my head on her shoulder again and cried.

She wrapped her arms around me, as I let the tears fall. It wasn't the hysterical outburst of last night. I cried quietly, sadly, my tears rolling slowly down my cheeks as my mind went over all the hopes I'd had, all the promises we'd made. My happy-ever-after was over. What would happen to me and to Amy now?

'You'll be fine, lovey,' Hannah reassured me, stroking my hair softly. 'Best shot of him. Onwards and upwards, you'll see.'

Chapter 23

'Happy birthday!'

I rubbed my eyes and squinted up in shock. Nope, I wasn't dreaming. Joe was standing by my bed holding Amy, a big grin on his face as he held out a parcel to me with his other hand. Amy clutched some birthday cards to her chest, and there were more parcels at the end of the bed.

'Joe! When did you get here?'

'First thing this morning,' he said. 'Nothing like a lovely long drive to start the day.'

'You look so tired,' I said. I looked at my watch. Ten to eight! Bloody hell, what time had he set off?

'I'm fine, and never mind all that. It's your birthday. Come on, girl. Open your cards and pressies.'

Thanking God I'd bothered to put a nightie on last night, I sat up and reached out for Amy. She threw her arms round my neck and smothered me in kisses.

'Happy birthday, Mummy.'

'Thank you, angel. Nothing I want more than cuddles from my two favourite people,' I said, smiling up at Joe.

'Come on, get on with it,' he urged me, and I took the presents from him and from Amy, who clapped her hands in excitement as I tore the wrapping paper from them.

'Joe, it's beautiful,' I said, admiring the silver charm bracelet that I'd once remarked I liked. 'You remembered.'

'Of course,' he said. 'I've only put four charms on it, but you can have fun collecting the ones you want.'

There was a little girl, a teapot, a cupcake, and a pig on the bracelet.

'They represent Amy, Mrs Travers, you and me,' smiled Joe. 'The pig's for Jeeves and Wooster. I wanted to get you a silver Malteser but, surprisingly, they don't make them.'

'They're lovely,' I said. 'The four of us all together. Family.'

We smiled at each other. Whatever happened in the future, I knew I had a lot to be thankful for.

'Next present, Mummy,' said Amy, as I fastened the bracelet on my wrist and held it out to admire.

'All right, sweetie, give me a chance.' I laughed and picked up a parcel that bore a gift tag stating, *Happy Birthday, Mummy, love from Amy*, clearly in Joe's writing. Underneath that, however, my little girl had drawn three kisses. It was a work of art.

Opening the parcel, I found a CD of my favourite band and a box of Maltesers. I laughed and thanked them both. The next present was from Mrs Travers, and I was surprised to find that she'd bought me a brand-new pair of Eeyore slippers.

'But she hates them!' I laughed.

'Yeah, but she knows you love them,' said Joe, 'and she said if you were going to insist on wearing them, then at least she could get you some that looked halfway decent.'

'Hmm, I suppose mine are looking a bit tatty,' I admitted. 'Bless her, that's so sweet of her. I'll call her later. What a fabulous birthday. I couldn't ask for anything more.'

'One more pressie,' said Joe, handing me another parcel.

'From Hannah.' I swallowed, gazing down at my first present from my grandmother. It was a beautiful photograph frame and, inside it, she'd put the picture of my grandfather and Gabriel as a little boy. I refused to give way to tears, aware that Joe would have no idea why on earth I would want a photograph of either of these men.

'That's so kind,' I said.

'She asked me to get you this, too,' said Joe quietly, and handed me a small box. I opened it to find another charm for my bracelet — a little silver angel. It was too much, and I stifled a sob.

Joe rubbed my shoulder. 'She told me all about it, love. About Harry, and how you finally saw sense. I'm so proud of you. And she told me about the other thing, an' all. You know.'

He obviously didn't want to mention it in front of Amy. I looked up at him and nodded. He didn't have to say the name. Hannah had bought me a little angel, believing my future lay with Gabriel, but she was wrong. I'd seen Zoe, I knew what he liked, and I certainly didn't fit the mould. He wasn't in the slightest bit interested in me, and who could blame him?

Anyway, for all I knew, he was still a married man. That had only occurred to me in bed last night, as I'd lain in the darkness, going over every little look and gesture that he'd made towards me, trying to decipher what was going on in his head. It was lovely of Hannah, but I doubted I'd ever wear the angel charm.

'You're all so kind,' I said at last. 'I don't know what I've done to deserve you all.'

'Don't be daft,' said Joe briskly. 'Come on, open your cards.'

There were cards from Hannah, Joe, Amy, several from friends in London, who were mutual friends of Joe, and my Australian great-uncle. There was no card from Harry or any of his family, not that I'd been expecting anything.

Hannah had made us all a fabulous hearty breakfast. I kissed her and thanked her for the presents.

'Oh, away with you.' She smiled. 'It's the photo that makes it. The frame's nothing. Just wanted you to remember you should never lose faith. There's an angel waiting for you, you mark my words. Just like my Albert.'

'Hannah, you've become like family,' I said seriously. 'I honestly can't imagine life without you now.' I wished with all my heart I could tell her that she really *was* my family, but I knew I couldn't just blurt it out. I had to make sure she could cope with the shock, and I needed to pick the right moment.

Hannah's eyes were suspiciously bright. 'Sit down and eat your breakfast. Enough of all this soppy talk.'

Lexi appeared in the doorway at that moment, Tessa by her side, as usual, and looked around at us all sitting at the table. 'Well, this is a feast,' she said, taking in the plates piled high with bacon, eggs, sausages, tomatoes and mushrooms. 'Do you always eat like this? Hello, Joe. You here again? Wonder you don't just move in.'

'Cheeky bugger,' said Joe, laughing. 'Come in, Lexi. You hungry? There's plenty to go around.'

'No, it's fine, I had some Weetabix,' said Lexi. Then she shrugged. 'Oh, what the heck. I wouldn't mind an egg sandwich, Hannah, if that's okay?'

'Sit yourself down, love,' said Hannah fondly. 'Coming right up.'

'And a nice juicy sausage for this beauty, eh?' Joe beamed, as Tessa abandoned Lexi and headed straight towards him, sitting adoringly at his feet as he stroked her head.

Lexi sat down, and I saw her looking round at us. There was something wrong. She looked nervous. Eventually, she cleared her throat.

'Er, I don't know whether I ought to say, or not,' she began, 'but the thing is, well, something's happened, and maybe it's better coming from me now than finding out about it later on.'

My heart flipped. What now?

Lexi chewed her lip nervously.

'What is it?' asked Joe. 'Come on, love. Get on with it.'

'Eddie brought a paper into work this morning. He's collecting tokens for those free DVDs,' she explained. I waited, though I had a horrible feeling I knew what was coming next.

'The thing is,' said Lexi, 'there's an interview in it with that Melody Bird woman, all about her and Harry. She reckons she's forgiven him for his other affair and that they're massively in love and are talking marriage.'

'That's big of her,' growled Joe. 'It was Eliza he cheated on, not her. What's she got to forgive? Bet Harry doesn't even know she's talked to the papers.'

'Er, the thing is, there's a picture of them together in her hotel room in New York, lounging on the sofa looking all soppy. Apparently, she's been offered some work over there, and he's flown out to join her.'

Everyone looked at me.

Joe slammed his knife and fork down with a clatter. He uttered a word I'd never heard him use before, then apologised immediately.

'I'm sorry,' said Lexi miserably. 'I just didn't want Eliza to walk into the shop and see copies of it all over the counter. Someone's bound to mention it to her. You know what everyone's like in the village, and they're sure to think she already knew.'

'It's all right, Lexi,' I said at last. 'It's not your fault. You did the right thing.'

'Oh, Eliza,' said Hannah sorrowfully, as she handed Lexi her sandwich, 'what a thing to happen. Today of all days.'

'Why, what's special about today?' demanded Lexi.

'It's Eliza's birthday,' Joe said, watching me with undisguised anxiety. He'd heard all about my hysterical outburst from Hannah and had demanded to know why I hadn't called him. Now he was probably worrying that I was about to go into meltdown again.

'Oh, no!' wailed Lexi. 'I'm so sorry. I wouldn't have said a word if I'd known.'

I realised they were all watching me nervously and thought how lucky I was to have so many people who were concerned about me.

'Look, it's fine. Don't worry about it. It's not as if I didn't know they would get back together,' I said. 'Harry's a born liar, and nothing he does surprises me any more. Honestly, I'm through with crying for him. Now, shall we get on with this breakfast? Nothing worse than cold bacon and eggs.'

Joe winked at me approvingly. 'Too right,' he said. 'Except maybe a cold egg sandwich,' he added, looking in disgust at Lexi's plate. 'How you can eat that when you could have bacon and sausages, I'll never know.'

'How you can eat bacon and sausages when you own Jeeves and Wooster, I'll never know!' retorted Lexi.

'Jeeves and Wooster? You wouldn't fill one pork pie with those two.' He laughed, and they began a light-hearted argument about eating meat and keeping micro pigs. I watched them gratefully. I knew they were exaggerating their conversation to take the spotlight from me and I loved them for it.

There was a lull in the conversation when Joe went to fetch his bag from the car, so I casually asked Lexi if her father was in his workshop already.

She looked evasive. 'He, er, had some stuff to do,' she said. 'He might be in this afternoon, but then again, he might not. I said we'd cope.'

'Oh, right.' What stuff was that, I wondered, wishing I had the nerve to pry further.

Joe came in from the yard, shoving his phone back in his pocket.

'Work?'

He shook his head. 'Rose. I've just invited her to the pub tonight for your birthday bash. I'm putting a stash of cash behind the bar, and we're going to get wasted.'

I wasn't sure, though.

'Don't be so daft,' Hannah told me. 'Amy will be tucked up in bed, and it's about time you went out and let yourself go a bit.'

'Is it really a good idea?' I said gloomily. 'Everyone will have seen the papers by now, and they'll be staring and asking questions. It's a bit embarrassing.'

'Don't see why it's embarrassing for you,' Lexi said. 'It's that husband of yours that should be embarrassed. You've done nothing to be ashamed of.'

'Exactly,' said Joe. 'If anything, you should hold your head high. It's Harry who should be hiding away in shame.'

'All right, all right.' I laughed. 'I'll go and get changed. I suppose it's not every day a girl turns thirty-three. What about you, Lexi? Are you coming tonight?'

'I have plans,' she said mysteriously, 'but you might catch me at the pub at some point. I'd better go and help Eddie, or he'll be in a mood with me all day. See you later, guys. Maybe.'

She winked and headed out of the door. No doubt she was going to be with Derry that evening. I wondered if she'd any idea that Will was sleeping with his mother? Come to that, I wondered if Derry knew? I wasn't the only one whose life was a tangled web.

Chapter 24

The bar was already full when Joe and I arrived. Rose, dressed in a bright pink sweater dress, with a wide black belt and a pink floppy bow in her hair, was already sitting at a table. She raised her glass as we approached and called out loudly, 'Happy birthday, Eliza!'

Everyone in the bar turned and began to call, 'Happy birthday!'

'Congratulations!'

'Many happy returns!'

Talk about embarrassing. I gave them a quick wave and slunk into my seat next to Rose, muttering about how mortifying all the attention was.

Rose laughed. 'Don't be daft. Make the most of it. Life doesn't have too many occasions where you're the centre of attention for all the right reasons.'

'And now you know how I feel,' Joe pointed out. 'This is a normal night out for me.'

Rose handed me a present.

'You shouldn't have bothered, Rose. I know how things are.'

'Yeah, well, in a way you've paid for it yourself. Those cakes and scones you're making for me are just flying off the counter.'

'I'm glad. I'll do some more tomorrow.'

Meggie called over to me, 'Don't forget my marshmallows, Eliza! I was slimmer of the week after all. Priorities, please.'

'Are you going to be at Lightweights this week, Eliza?' asked another woman. 'Only, I was wondering if you could make me some of those strawberry and cream ones? Present for me daughter, you understand, not for me.'

'Blimey,' said Joe. 'You're a one-woman industry.'

Rose had got me a bottle of Angel perfume. 'Oh, Rose. You really shouldn't have.'

'Away, man.' She put her arm round me. 'I've had the best few weeks of my life, since you arrived, Eliza. It's been dead exciting doing our undercover mission, and that perfume's to say, ta very much for giving me something else to think about apart from bills and sodding quiche.' She leaned over and whispered in my ear, 'And it's for Gabriel, too. You never know. He may be your angel, after all!'

I tried to smile. She and Hannah had had similar ideas, but they didn't know what I knew about his reaction to Harry's suggestion. Plus, now I'd seen Zoe's photograph, I knew I may as well give up on that fantasy. I couldn't be the painted doll any longer. I had to be myself again.

Rhiannon came over and handed me a small package. 'Happy birthday, Eliza,' she said.

'What's this?' I asked in surprise.

'Blimey, you're doing well for presents,' said Joe. 'Open it.'

I did and found a small silver pendant with a pink stone set in it.

'Rose quartz,' she told me. 'It helps heal emotional hurts and opens you to love. I thought it appropriate.'

I didn't know what to say. I felt so blessed to have so many lovely people around me who'd taken the time to choose gifts that really meant something. I remembered all the bottles of Chanel No 5 I had sitting at home, which seemed to be Harry's standard present to me, and the expensive watch I hadn't wanted, and even the engagement ring that Harry had insisted upon because it looked flashier than the simple solitaire I'd chosen that was a tenth of the price. I felt so emotional that I could barely speak.

'Are you all right?' asked Rose.

I nodded. 'Yes. Thank you, Rhiannon. It means a lot. You're all so kind.' I managed a smile. 'I'm afraid I'm getting too old for this birthday lark now.'

'Good heavens,' said Rhiannon. 'How old are you?'

'Thirty-three,' I confessed.

'I'll be forty-two on my next birthday,' said Rhiannon. 'I fully intend to celebrate wildly and shall continue to do so when I reach my hundredth birthday.'

'Rhiannon love,' said Joe approvingly, 'you're my kind of woman. Come on, girl, let's get the booze flowing. It's party time!'

****

Sophie and Archie had gone to Helmston to see a play. Archie didn't want to go, but Sophie had insisted.

'I dunno why,' he muttered to Gabriel before they left. 'She won't enjoy it. She's only going 'cos she thinks it's something she can brag about to the Lightweights girls, like they give a monkey's.'

'You know Sophie,' said Gabriel with a smile. 'You never know, you may enjoy it.'

'*The Vagina Monologues?* I sincerely doubt it.' Archie looked appalled. 'I may be able to persuade her to go to the cinema, instead. I'll even sit through a sodding love story to avoid all those women yakking about their bits.'

He had Gabriel's deepest sympathy, as they set off for Helmston. Oliver had begged a lift from them as he was meeting some friends in town. Pandora and Tallulah were at the stables. They often stayed late in the summer months, cleaning tack and hanging round with Georgia. It was going to be a quiet evening for a change.

Gabriel thought about his day and the meeting he'd had that morning. There was such a lot to think about. It made his stomach churn, yet, at the same time there was a sudden longing, an interest there that he hadn't felt for a long time. Could he possibly risk it?

Lexi came downstairs, dressed in a vest top and a short skirt that showed off her endless legs.

'Are you going out again?' he asked, as she grabbed her bag from the side of the sofa. 'You're never in these days. I can't keep up with you.'

Lexi smiled. 'You miss me, Poppa Bear?' she asked, kissing him on the forehead.

He clasped her hand. 'Probably more than I should.' he admitted. 'It's hard to accept that I have a daughter with a better social life than mine.'

'You should get yourself out and about then,' she said. 'Seriously, Dad, the way it's going you'll end up like Flynn.'

He sighed. 'Poor Flynn.' He hardly went out of the house apart from to work. Gabriel realised that if he wasn't careful, he could end up the same way, though he always had Sophie to drag him out to events, and she wasn't one to take no for an answer. He wondered how Archie was getting on.

'Don't worry about me,' he reassured Lexi. 'I'll be fine. I've got lots to do. Just get off and enjoy yourself. Where are you going?'

'Oh, just to see Georgia. You know, hang out.'

'Bit overdressed for the stables, aren't you?'

'Dad, she doesn't live in a loosebox.' Lexi laughed. 'She does have a house. We'll probably watch a film, have a few drinks and a gossip.'

'You'll probably bump into Pan and Tally, then. They're at the stables.'

Lexi shrugged. 'Doubt it. They get on with their own thing. Me and Georgia leave them to it. By the way,' she added, as she sat on the sofa and watched him curiously, 'have you heard about Eliza?'

Gabriel looked at her in alarm. 'What about her? She's all right?'

He hadn't told anyone about her breakdown, but he'd wondered if she was all right since that night. He'd asked Hannah about her several times but had kept away from her himself. There was no point in rubbing salt in the wound.

Lexi looked surprised at the question. 'Yes, she's fine. Well, except there's been another story in the papers. I mean, I know you don't read the tabloids, but I thought you might have heard. Anyway, that prick of a husband of hers and his tart have given an interview all about their deep and abiding love, and how they nobly fought their passion, but it just overwhelmed them and that they're destined to be together. There are pictures of them draped over each other. It's sickening.'

'Oh, my God. And Eliza knows?'

'Well, yeah,' admitted Lexi. 'I told her. Only because I didn't want her to have it sprung on her. Thought she'd better be prepared.'

He raked his hands through his hair, imagining how devastated she'd be feeling, having read all that.

'Pretty awful for her.' Lexi sighed. 'Especially with today being her birthday.'

'It's her birthday?'

'Yep.'

'Did Harry send her anything?'

'No way. Not so much as a card. Not surprising, really. She sent him packing, after all.'

'Do you think she really meant it?'

'Judging from the cool way she took today's news, I would say so. Joe's praying it means that, anyway. He's desperate for her to move on. Harry's so not good for her.'

'No,' said Gabriel, remembering his own encounter with the man. 'He certainly isn't.'

'Anyway, Dad, I'm off, so I'll love you and leave you.' Lexi stood up and kissed him on the cheek. 'Don't wait up, now, will you!'

'I'm hardly likely to, am I?' He smiled. 'I do have other things to think about, you know.'

She grinned. He knew perfectly well that he wouldn't sleep a wink until she was safely home again, and he knew she knew it, too.

****

I'd had a fabulous evening. Rose, Joe, Meggie and Ben had sat with me all night, and I'd had birthday hugs and good wishes from Bernie and Eddie, who'd come in for a game of darts, from several of the Lightweights girls, who were on their way into

Helmston to see a film, and from Marty and Milly Henderson, of all people. They'd come in for a quick drink after the shop closed and spent most of the time gazing into each other's eyes and holding hands, to my relief and amusement. Evidently, Rhiannon's unorthodox marriage therapy had had a positive effect on them. It had been an evening of fun and laughter, and for a few short hours I'd put all the horrible stuff out of my mind and just enjoyed the evening.

At half past ten, Joe and I reluctantly decided that we ought to be getting back to Hannah and said a fond goodnight to everyone in the pub. Winding our uneven way back down the road towards the farm, our arms wrapped round each other, we giggled tipsily about birthdays from other years, remembering my childhood and the various treats that Joe had organised for me, some more successful than others.

As we neared the farmhouse door, Joe stopped and pointed at something on the step. 'What's that?'

I looked down at where he was pointing and bent to pick up the object. 'It's the cake tin I took round for Lexi,' I said, surprised.

Joe opened the kitchen door and flicked on the light.

As we stepped into the kitchen, I prised off the lid and peered inside. 'Oh, Joe, look!'

Joe gazed into the tin rather woozily and then looked up at me, his eyes wide. 'Ooh, it's a cake.'

'It is. It *is* a cake. It's a birthday cake.' I wondered if I was more drunk than I'd realised. I tottered to the kitchen table and placed the tin on it, staring at the cake in astonishment.

'Who got you a cake, then?' demanded Joe.

'I don't know. Father Cakemass?'

For some reason, we found this hilarious and snorted with laughter. Hannah came into the kitchen and looked in surprise at the two of us, as we stood, swaying slightly, pointing at a tin on the table and exclaiming in delight.

'By heck, you two have had a few, haven't you?'

'Hannah, Hannah, look,' said Joe, 'Eliza's got a birthday cake.'

Hannah grinned. 'Has she really? Let's have a look at it, then.'

She walked over to the tin and peered inside. 'Dear God.'

For some reason, she looked quite shocked, as if she'd been expecting something else. She reached in and eased the cake out of the tin, placing it carefully on its plate on the table. The three of us stared at it with a mixture of disbelief and wonder.

It was a rather thin cake, made twice as thick by the amount of butter icing that had been piled on top of it and between the two layers. But what caught my eye and made me smile in delight was the fact that, nestling in the fluffy butter cream on the top of the cake, was what appeared to be a whole packet of Maltesers, positioned carefully to form a large letter E.

'Oh, how lovely.' I gave a contented sigh. 'My first birthday cake since ... well, since I was seven. What a lovely girl she is.'

'Eh?' Hannah looked at me in surprise. 'Who?'

'Lexi!'

'Lexi?' Joe snorted with laughter. 'Lexi couldn't bake a cake to save her life. Mind you, looking at it, I suppose...'

'Why would you assume it was Lexi?' said Hannah.

'Well, it's obvious, isn't it? I took that very tin round for her on her birthday, with a cake I'd made for her, and now she's returned the favour. And look, she knows all about my Malteser addiction. She's gone to all that trouble for me. What an angel.'

'Aw, bless,' said Joe. 'Wait till I see her. She's my little star.'

Hannah was watching us with pursed lips, looking eerily like Mrs Travers. She didn't seem to approve of our drunken state.

'Hannah, don't be mad with us,' I wailed. 'Look, it's my birthday, and I've never seen a more beautiful cake.' My eyes began to fill with tears.

'Me neither,' said Joe, nodding his head in agreement. 'It's better than a royal wedding cake.'

Hannah's eyes widened. 'Blimey O'Reilly, how many have you had? So, would you both like a slice?'

'Jesus, no,' said Joe, hastily backing away from the table. 'It looks like a frisbee.'

'Eliza?'

But I couldn't answer. I turned and rushed to the downstairs toilet, my hand over my mouth, on my way to throw up every drop of drink I'd just consumed.

****

I slept on and off for most of the next morning, and I'm ashamed to say that I didn't even wake up to give Amy her lunch. I woke at quarter to one, feeling very embarrassed, but at least my headache had gone. I was surprised to see Joe still there, but he assured me I'd been present when he made the calls, excusing himself from work.

'How are you feeling now?'

'Probably better than I look,' I admitted. 'How about you?'

'Not bad at all,' he said cheerfully. 'I think a greasy fry-up did the trick.'

'Where's Amy?'

'Having a nap. She had a busy morning, cleaning the hen house with Lexi.'

'Where is Lexi? I need to thank her for the cake.'

He laughed. 'She's on the beach with the donkeys, but she'll be back in around half an hour. Don't worry about thanking her. You did that already — several times.'

'Did I?' I tried to remember, and something stirred in the recesses of my mind — a vague memory of a hug, and Lexi assuring me that it had been no trouble at all. 'Oh, yes, I did. Have you tasted it yet?'

'You must be joking. Lexi wanted me to have a slice earlier, but I said we had to wait for you, it being your cake, an' all. Please think of an excuse why I can't eat it.'

'You should have told her you're lactose intolerant, or something,' I said. 'Anyway, stop being mean and have a taste. You might enjoy it.'

'You do remember how it looked? I can't see it tasting like anything I'd want to eat,' he said with a sigh.

'Where's Hannah?'

His forehead creased. 'She's gone to have a lie down. Said she was feeling tired.'

'Hannah?' I'd never heard her admit to feeling tired before. 'Is

248

she all right? Should I check on her?'

'If you like. She's been in there about an hour.'

I stood up and went into Hannah's room. She was tucked up in bed, sound asleep. I stood looking at her for a few moments, wondering again when it would be the right time to tell her that she was my grandmother. Now that I had Joe here, it was probably time to break the news to him, too. I hadn't wanted to tell him over the phone. It wasn't the sort of thing you could say by mobile, and I wanted to discuss it properly with him and ask his advice about how to break it to Hannah. I bent forward and gave her a peck on the forehead then I went back into the kitchen and sat at the table.

'Joe, I really need to talk to you about something.'

He looked at me enquiringly. 'Oh? Well, I'm—' He broke off as Lady Gaga's *Pokerface* echoed round the kitchen. 'Sorry. Excuse me.'

He headed out into the yard, and I watched him from the window. He was frowning and seemed to be arguing with someone. He raised a hand in greeting as Lexi and Eddie led the donkeys into the yard, back from their shift on the sands. I put the kettle on in preparation for them all. It was another fifteen minutes before he came back inside, during which time I'd already finished a strong coffee and poured cups of tea for Joe, Lexi and Eddie.

'Everything all right?'

'Yeah. Just people checking I'd be at work tomorrow.'

'I wish they'd leave you alone for a change,' I muttered.

'Sorry, love. You wanted to talk to me about something?'

The door flew open and Lexi barged in, flopping herself down on the chair next to mine. 'Remind me never to have kids,' she said.

'Bad day?'

'You should have seen all the toffee apple stuck in Blackberry's mane. Took me ages to brush it out. And I'm sick of posing for photographs, while the proud parents insist I stand next to the donkey while their precious child beams for the camera like they're Zara Phillips.'

Joe laughed. 'Annoying, isn't it?'

'It doesn't usually bother you,' I said. 'You're used to it by now, surely? Is something else wrong?'

She shrugged, and Joe looked at her, then at me.

'I think I'll take Eddie his cup of tea,' he said, and picked up his mug, collecting Eddie's as he passed it.

As he headed outside, Lexi sighed. 'It's Derry.'

'What's he done? He's not finished with you?'

She scowled. 'He's refusing to have sex with me.'

I bit my lip, trying not to smile.

'It's not funny,' she said. 'He's decided he wants a proper relationship with me, that there's more to us than sex, so he's put a ban on it to prove it. He says we've to get to know each other properly, and be boyfriend and girlfriend and go on dates, and all that rubbish. You should have seen us last night, sitting in Rhiannon's living room, watching television! Television! I mean, I could do that at home with my dad any night of the week.'

My stomach lurched at the mention of her father, and I tried to focus on Lexi.

'Maybe he's got a point. How will you know if it can work, if you don't give it a try?'

She sipped her tea. 'It won't work, Eliza. I already know that. I'm not interested.'

'Is it just Derry? Maybe if you found someone you had more in common with?'

'I don't want a relationship, full stop. It's not worth the hassle. Feelings get involved, people get hurt, abused. Who needs it?'

'It doesn't have to be like that,' I said. 'Some relationships are wonderful. Look at Albert and Hannah.'

'Yeah, back in the dark ages,' she muttered. 'People are different now. They don't care what the other person wants. They're all selfish, and when things don't go their way, it turns nasty. I don't want to go down that road. Not ever.'

'I don't agree,' I said quietly. 'I think marriage, when it works, is the most wonderful thing in the world.'

'How can you say that?' she demanded. 'After Harry and all his carrying on?'

'How can you say it isn't?' I asked. 'You've never been married, or even given a relationship a chance.'

She was silent. I was dying to ask her more about her mother. Dare I push her? Would it be fair? 'Lexi, your mother—'

She shook her head. 'My mother was an idiot. She believed what she wanted to believe and put up with all sorts because he told her he loved her. She paid a heavy price for that. Believe me, she's no role model to me.'

I suddenly felt very cold. What did she mean? What price? I didn't understand any of it.

'What do you mean about—'

'Can't believe I slept through like that.' As Hannah shuffled into the kitchen, Lexi looked at her in surprise.

'You were asleep? Since when do you sleep during the day?'

I sighed, realising I'd missed yet another opportunity.

'I know, don't tell anyone, for God's sake,' said Hannah. She looked at the kettle and nodded at me. 'Wouldn't say no to a cup of tea, love. What do you think?'

'Of course. Sit down.' I stood up and headed over to the cupboard to collect another mug, knowing that, once again, the subject was closed.

Chapter 25

Rose grinned in delight as I pushed open her kitchen door with my shoulder, my arms full of tins and boxes. 'You're a star!' she cried, rushing to help me and carefully taking half of the load.

'Ooh, these look great,' she added, as we placed them on the worktop and she peered into a few of them. 'These will go down a treat. You have to let me pay for them.'

I shook my head. 'Honestly, I don't want anything, Rose. You paid for the ingredients, and that's enough. Anyway, you've done me a favour. God knows, I need something to take my mind off all it all. I mean, could it get any worse?'

Rose looked at me thoughtfully. 'Right, we'll get these sorted, and then we'll have a coffee and a chat.'

'I'm parked on Bay Street. I can't really stay.'

'Bollocks. You're making a delivery. You're allowed to park there if you're delivering goods.'

'I don't think that includes stopping for coffee,' I said. 'Besides, you haven't got time. You'll be opening up in an hour.'

'Bugger it,' said Rose. 'I'll make time. I doubt I'll be flooded with customers at nine, anyway.'

She called up the stairs to her daughter. 'Cerise, are you nearly ready? If you miss that bus, you'll be late!'

'I won't be a minute,' Cerise called down.

'Where's she going?' I asked, as we carried our load through to the café, aware that we were well into the summer holidays now and there was no school to attend.

'Revision club. Signed up for extra tuition,' said Rose proudly. 'Little gem, she is. Determined to make something of herself. Not like Fuchsia. She's spent the last few days in her bedroom, chatting on Facebook, and sulking 'cos I told her she had to give me half her benefit money, whenever she finally gets some. God knows how long it will take before that's sorted out, and even then, there's no guarantee she'll bother to sign on every time.'

I hesitated. 'Rose, look, if you need money, I can always help you out. Please don't feel you can't ask. I'm not loaded, but I can spare a few quid.'

Rose took the cake boxes from my arms and placed them on the counter, then she put her hands on my shoulders and looked straight at me. 'You're the best mate ever,' she said. 'But I don't want your money, pet. All this—' she waved an arm at the groaning counter, '—is more than enough. I can never thank you enough.'

'Don't be daft. And it's my money, in case you're wondering. Not Harry's.'

She looked at me enquiringly.

I blushed. 'I had a long think about that stuff you said, about me relying on my rich husband and uncle. You were right. I don't want to be another Zoe. I need to sort out my future, and I will do, as soon as I'm done here, but in the meantime, I paid a visit to a jeweller in Helmston and did a deal.'

'What kind of deal?'

'I sold my watch, and wedding and engagement rings.'

'You did what? Why?'

I shrugged. 'Truth is, Rose, I've no money of my own. I had a pretty lowly career before I married Harry and I never earned much at all.'

'But the jewellery? The clothes? The holiday cottage? How did you even support yourself for the last few months?'

Confession time. 'The jewellery and clothes were presents, and everything I've bought since I got here has been paid for with a credit card that Harry gave me.'

'Everything? You paid for everything with Harry's money?'

'I didn't give it a thought until I heard about Zoe — the way she bled Gabriel dry and didn't earn a penny for herself. I started to think about the way I was living, and I felt ashamed. That's when I started asking for money to cover ingredients, and then — well, after Harry and I finished, I sold my watch and rings to get some money.'

I saw her face and reassured her. 'It wasn't difficult, honestly. They mean nothing to me now. Mind you, I think the jeweller must have thought it was Christmas. He'd have made one hell of a profit after what he gave me for them, but at least it means I've got a bit to live on now. Hannah wouldn't take any board money, but I've given Eddie the cash for the feed bill. Apparently, it's been outstanding for ages, so that's a big help to them, and he told me the electricity bill's due, so I'm putting some aside for that, but I can spare a bit for you, if you need it.'

'No, honestly, but I do appreciate it. I just can't believe that you're as broke as I am now.' She rolled her eyes. 'We're a right pair! Come on, let's get these ready for sale, and we can sit and have a catch up.'

Cerise popped her head round the café door as Rose poured our coffees. 'Bye, Mam, bye Eliza,' she called, then hitched up her schoolbag and headed out through the front door.

'Bless her. Wish the other one was more like her,' Rose said, looking upwards at the ceiling in despair.

Five minutes later, we were sitting at a table, sipping coffee and eating chocolate biscuits. 'Not even nine, and I've had too many units already today,' she said with a sigh.

'As if you ever count them.' I laughed. 'I bet you don't even know what a unit is.'

'I don't,' she admitted. 'Can't be arsed with all that. So long as I'm not so fat that I can't walk to the pub, I'm fine. Don't tell Sophie that, for God's sake. You going to the meeting tonight?'

I nodded. 'Got to. I've got a lot of orders to give out. Need to break it to them all that if they want anything else doing, they're going to have to pay.'

She shook her head in wonder. 'I dunno how you do it. You must be knackered. And strikes me, they'll be willing to pay.

Those low-calorie sweets are keeping most of them on the straight and narrow, so to speak. Are you going to keep up with the desserts and the weekly prize?'

I laughed. 'I wouldn't dare stop!'

She nodded. 'They love their marshmallows, don't they? Can't believe the demand. Well, I'll go if you are. I wasn't going to bother, but I suppose it's a night out. Now, come on, lady. Tell me what's wrong.'

'What makes you think anything's wrong?'

'Oh, come on, don't play that game. We both know you'll tell me in the end, so let's cut out the middle bit and get to the point.'

She was right, so I did as I was told and poured out all my troubles. I told her about glamorous Zoe, about Lexi's weird remark that her mother had paid a heavy price for her marriage, and about Gabriel steering well clear of me since my meltdown. Then I told her about Hannah not being well, and that I'd been unable to find a moment to talk to Joe to tell him my news and didn't know how to broach the subject with Hannah, especially now she wasn't herself.

'Blimey, I thought I had problems,' she mused. 'Okay, well, Joe will be back again, and you can talk to him then. Hannah's a bit off-colour, but she'll bounce back. She always does. Then, you can sit her down and tell her the truth about who you are. I reckon she'll be over the moon. Anyone can see she already thinks the world of you. Now, as for the other stuff — well, okay, I'll grant you it all seems a bit dodgy, but as for Gabriel avoiding you … Didn't Lexi say he had meetings the other day?'

I nodded. 'Exactly. What meetings would Gabriel have?'

'Well, who knows? He could have been seeing a bank manager, or maybe he's after renting a stall at Helmston market? Or maybe he was house hunting? Come on, it could've been anything.'

I supposed she was right.

'Then again, I suppose he could have been at a brothel spending his last fifty quid on a dominatrix. The quiet ones are always the worst.'

'Bloody hell! Thanks very much.'

She laughed. 'See? It could be worse. Look, you know as well as I do that he'd never do anything like that. So what if you haven't seen much of him? You said he was working late the night you went doolally. Maybe he's got a big order in and is having to finish it? And if he's taken the odd day off, he'll have to catch up anyway. I think you're reading too much into all this, to be honest.'

'Really?'

'Definitely.'

'But what about the photograph?'

'What about it?'

'You didn't see her. She's beautiful, Rose.'

She smiled at me. 'So are you.'

I pulled a face. 'Yeah, right. Anyway, she's so glamorous and tiny — almost Rhiannon standard.'

'Stop fishing for compliments.' She grinned at me then squeezed my hand. 'I think your self-esteem is at rock bottom. Just because you've seen one photograph of his ex-wife, looking all made-up and glam, doesn't mean that's what Gabriel wants in a woman. Christ, Michelle looks like a drag queen most of the time, and he avoids her the way I avoid the Lightweights diet sheet. Give him a chance. Have you ever thought of asking him?'

'Asking him what?'

'About his past, his marriage, his career change. Making small talk?'

'It's hardly small talk,' I protested. 'More an interrogation. And no, I couldn't.'

'Why not? Better to hear it from the horse's mouth, I reckon.'

'Because it's none of my business. What right have I got to ask him anything? He doesn't care about me, one way or the other, and just because I've got a stupid crush on him, doesn't give me the right to pry into his personal life.'

She raised an eyebrow. 'A stupid crush? Is that what this is?'

As my face burned, I sighed. 'Maybe not. But nothing is ever going to come of it, and, let's face it, I need to tie up all the loose ends around here and then head back to London. I've got a marriage to end and a house to sell, and a new life to plan.'

She looked dismayed. 'Are you serious? About going back to

London, I mean?'

'I have to. I have to sort my life out, once and for all.'

'And when you've done that?'

I stared into my empty coffee cup. 'I don't know.' I looked at my watch and sat up straight. 'It's nine o'clock. You need to be opening up,' I said. 'I'd better get back to Whisperwood and take Amy off Hannah's hands. Fingers crossed, I haven't got a parking ticket.'

'So begins another dreary day. Better unlock the door and let the heaving crowds in.' Rose gave a heavy sigh.

I looked around. 'Where's my bag?'

'I think you left it in the kitchen. Go and get it while I unlock the door,' she said.

I scraped back my chair and headed into the kitchen, looking around for my bag. It was lying on the worktop, and I picked it up, pausing a moment to flick through my mobile phone. Joe had text me to say he'd got into a lot of bother over missing a meeting yesterday morning, and that Mrs Travers had got on the phone and given the man in question a whole load of grief for having a go at him. She'd raged that Joe had never let him down before and that everyone was entitled to take time off if they had personal issues to deal with. Apparently, she hadn't let slip that the personal issue in question was a giant hangover. He added that Mrs Travers missed me and sent her love.

I sent a quick text back to say that I couldn't wait to see her again, and that, the way things were going, I would probably be back in London within a week or two, anyway, then I put the phone away, hitched my bag over my shoulder, and headed towards the café to say goodbye to Rose.

I don't know what made me hesitate when I heard Sophie's voice, but something told me to hang back and listen. She was talking to Rose, and I could hardly believe what she was saying.

'Complete mess, it was. Honest to God, you wouldn't believe it. I said to Archie, it's worse than the flaming kids. We only went out to see *The Vagina Monologues*. Have you seen it, Rose? Truth to tell, I only saw the first half hour. Archie didn't think it was all it's cracked up to be — pardon the pun. I was enjoying it, but he found it all very embarrassing and it wasn't fair, so I agreed to go to the cinema instead. We saw that new Will Smith film. He's a bit of all right, isn't he?

'Anyway, like I said, we saw the film and then we headed home for a nice glass of wine and a bit of relaxation before bedtime, and what do we walk into? Bloody Beirut, that's what! I said to him, "Gabriel, how can you make such a mess from one little cake? I hope to God it was worth it." Then he showed me this cake and, well, what can I say? Looked like an iced biscuit and bet it tasted like cardboard, but, bless him, it was the first thing he's ever made in his life. Never imagined I'd see the day when Gabriel baked a cake. So funny, but quite revealing, don't you think?'

'But I thought Lexi made the cake?' said Rose.

'No, he asked her to say that she had. Didn't want Eliza to know it was from him. I tell you, Rose, if that doesn't prove what I've been saying all along, I don't know what does.'

'You think he likes her?'

'Likes her?' I heard Sophie laugh. 'Yeah, that's one way of putting it. And she likes him, too. You should have seen the way she was looking at him at my dinner party. Stevie bloody Wonder would have spotted how lovesick she was. Honestly, I could bang their heads together.'

'He's never said anything to Eliza.'

'Well, he wouldn't, would he?' There was a pause and then Sophie gave a big sigh. 'I really hope this ends well. I couldn't bear it if he went through any more. He's been making such progress lately.'

'Progress?'

'Yes. It's been a slow process, Rose. One step forward and two steps back, some days. There were times we thought he'd never get there but, I dunno, lately he seems to have got a grip on it all. Seems more determined to sort himself out. We'll see. Anyway, I must go. I've got to take Pandora into town. Making the most of the time I have left with her before university. I'll see you later.'

I heard the clicking of her heels on the tiled floor, then the café door opened and closed. I waited a moment then stepped into the café. Rose looked at me. She didn't have to ask if I'd heard any of that, it was obviously written all over my face.

'Gabriel made the cake?' I said, bewildered. 'But why?'

'Why do you think, you idiot?' She put her hands on her hips and stared at me in exasperation. 'Right, if you don't go and see him, and sort this out once and for all, I'm going to drag you there by your bleached blonde hair. Get it?'

I nodded. She was right. It was time to face up to Gabriel.

****

'Lexi's on her way back,' Hannah said, as I popped my head round the living room door. 'Seems poor Wispa's a bit lame. She's bringing him home and putting a poultice on him.'

She looked at me curiously, obviously seeing something odd about my expression. I wasn't surprised. I was only amazed she hadn't heard the butterflies flapping around in my stomach from across the yard.

'You okay?'

'Are you all right with Amy for ten minutes?' I asked her.

'Of course I am, but why—'

I didn't answer her, heading upstairs two steps at a time. I went into the bathroom and looked in the mirror, wincing at my roots, which were highly visible and looked awful. I needed to go to the hairdresser and fast, but there was no time now. If I didn't confront Gabriel today, I never would, and if Lexi was on her way back already, I may not have long to say what I had to say. The only make-up I had on was a coat of mascara and a slick of clear lip gloss, and, for a moment, it crossed my mind to get out my make-up bag and apply my usual war paint, but then I pulled myself together. I'd gone down that road with Harry and look where it had got me. If Gabriel wanted me, then he had to put up with the real me.

Squaring my shoulders, I headed downstairs and told Hannah that I'd be in the workshop with Gabriel, if she needed me. She couldn't have looked more surprised if I'd said I'd be in Narnia, but she said nothing, the twinkle in her eyes saying it all.

My stomach churned as I headed across the yard to the workshop. I could hear the high-pitched whining of the electric saw, and as I opened the door, the volume increased, assaulting my ear drums and making me wince. The smell of sawdust hung in the air and my nose itched at the bits of wood dust floating around.

Gabriel was at the work bench, goggles over his beautiful eyes, deep in concentration. I watched him as he worked, my heart thudding as I waited for him to finish and realise that he had company. I followed the movement of his forearms as he worked, noting the strong hands that were hardened by manual labour. There were scrapes and little cuts on his knuckles, and a plaster on one of his fingers. I remembered when he'd cradled my face in them and felt shivery. I wondered if I'd ever feel those hands on me again.

He switched off the saw and stood back, removing the goggles and lifting the wood for inspection. Then he turned, and, spotted me standing there. He swallowed and stepped back, almost dropping the wood, before he recovered himself and gave me a weak smile. 'Eliza. Sorry, I didn't see you. Is everything all right?'

I took a deep breath and walked towards him. He watched me with anxious eyes and raised an eyebrow in query, as I took the wood from his hands and placed it on the bench.

'Not really,' I said. 'I have a problem.'

'Problem?'

'It's Lexi.'

He looked at the open door and half-turned towards it, but I grabbed his arm and he looked at me in astonishment. 'What is it? What's happened?'

'Your daughter told me a fib, Gabriel.'

I saw his mouth open and close as he scrutinised me, probably checking I wasn't about to flip again.

'She told me that she'd made me that cake,' I continued. 'Turns out, it wasn't her at all.'

The colour drained from his face. 'Ah.'

We were both silent for a moment, then I shook my head.

'Why? Why did you ask her to tell me she'd baked it?'

He shrugged his shoulders, looking around him at just about everything except me. I couldn't help myself. I reached out and touched his cheek, feeling the muscle contract slightly beneath my fingers. 'Why did you bake that cake for me, Gabriel?'

'I wanted you to have a birthday cake. You'd had such a rotten time of it lately, and you said you'd never had a cake since your mother died. I wanted to do something nice for you.' He gave a short laugh. 'Not that it turned out very nice. It looked pretty awful, and no doubt tasted worse.'

He was right actually, but there was no way I was going to admit to it. 'It was lovely,' I told him. 'And the Maltesers — you even remembered the Maltesers.' And they really *had* tasted good.

'Yes, well, your addiction's hardly a secret,' he said, an embarrassed smile on his face. He still wouldn't look at me and I didn't know what else to do to move the conversation on.

I dropped my hand and glanced around the workshop. There was an assortment of rabbit hutches, hen houses, and dog kennels in various stages of development. In one corner was something bigger, covered with a sheet.

I nodded towards it. 'What's that?'

He followed my gaze, and I saw him swallow. 'Just something I've been working on in my spare time.'

'Can I see?' I wasn't sure why it mattered, but something told me it did.

He nodded reluctantly and led me over to the corner. 'It's not quite finished yet, but it will be ready in a day, or two. It's nothing really,' he said, removing the sheet.

It was a rocking horse — a delicately-carved, dapple-grey rocking horse, with a black mane and tail.

I looked at him, stunned. 'It's beautiful!'

His shoulders dropped. 'I've been waiting for the saddle and bridle to arrive, but there was a delay. Otherwise, I'd have given it to her days ago,' he mumbled.

'Whose is it?'

He looked at me in surprise, as if it was obvious. 'I made it for Amy.'

Gasping, I looked again at the stunning creation before me. 'You made this for Amy?'

'I thought she'd like it. I made one for Lexi, years ago. She loved it. It was her favourite toy. I thought maybe Amy would like one, too.'

'Oh, Gabriel.'

I could barely see him for the tears swimming in my eyes. All I could think about was my grandfather, Albert, who'd brought Hannah flowers every week until the day he died.

I moved towards him, my hand reaching out to touch his lips. He caught hold of it before I could make contact and held it, staring into my face, the struggle evident in his eyes as he fought his emotions. I heard the breath catch in his throat and felt the pressure on my fingers as he squeezed them. Suddenly I was in his arms, and his lips pressed down on mine. I staggered backwards and slammed against the wall, felt him hard against me and smelled the divine essence of patchouli and sandalwood mixed with the scent of sawdust. I lifted my hands and dragged my fingers through his dark curls, closing my eyes, as his hands cupped my face, and his lips scorched into mine.

I could barely breathe, but nothing would have made me leave him. Then I reeled in shock, bereft as he pulled away from me and shook his head.

'I'm sorry.'

'Don't be sorry,' I whispered, putting my mouth to his again. For a second, his teeth gently nipped my lower lip, before he released me and stepped back.

'What is it? What's wrong?' I asked, confused. He wanted me, I knew he did. There was no mistaking that from where I was standing.

'It wouldn't be fair,' he said. 'You're not ready—'

'I'm ready, trust me,' I said, my fingers tracing the sharp edges of his cheekbones. 'Don't you understand? I love you.'

Where the hell had that come from? Yet I knew it was true and I needed him to believe me. I saw a flare of hope in his eyes. 'Gabriel, please...'

He stared at me and I could almost hear his mind formulating a response. I waited, certain that his next words would change my life forever.

'Dad! Dad, help!'

It took us both a moment to realise that it was Lexi calling, and another moment to register the fear in her voice. Then Gabriel ran out of the workshop, with me close behind him, passion replaced in the blink of an eye with sheer terror.

Chapter 26

'Oh, God, please not Amy,' I prayed. There was no mistaking the panic in Lexi's voice.

Gabriel ran to his daughter and grabbed her by the shoulders. She gabbled something at him, tears rolling down her cheeks. He turned and ran into the farmhouse, as I reached Lexi.

'What is it? For God's sake, what's happened?'

'Hannah,' sobbed Lexi. 'She just gasped and fell to the floor. I think she's dying, Eliza.'

I grabbed her hand, and we ran into the house. Gabriel was already on his knees beside Hannah, doing chest compressions on her still body.

'Lexi, call an ambulance,' he ordered. 'Tell them she's not breathing. Quick!'

She nodded and took out her mobile, her hands shaking so much she almost dropped it. I listened, stunned, as she frantically explained the situation to the operator.

Amy sat by Hannah's feet, looking confused. She repeatedly urged her to get up and stop being silly. I took my little girl's hand and pulled her away.

Gabriel breathed into Hannah's mouth twice then listened carefully for signs of breathing.

'Why is Gabyel kissing Hannah?' asked Amy curiously. Gabriel shook his head and began the chest compressions again.

'Come on, Hannah,' Amy said, 'Wake up. Gabyel kiss you like Sleeping Beauty.'

I could feel the fear choking me and made a weird sound in my throat.

Amy looked at me in alarm. 'Mummy, Hannah asleep?' I nodded my head dumbly at my confused daughter.

'The ambulance is on its way,' Lexi said, putting her phone away. 'Don't worry, Amy, she's just playing a silly game. Why don't we go into the lounge and I'll put *Peppa Pig* on for you?'

Amy nodded silently, and Lexi took her hand and led her into the lounge.

'Lexi, come straight back,' said Gabriel breathlessly as he continued the compressions, and she nodded at him.

I couldn't stop shaking. 'Is she going to be all right?'

He didn't answer but his eyes were full of doubt. As he breathed into my poor grandmother again, I watched her chest, praying for any signs that she was fighting back, that Gabriel's efforts weren't in vain.

After a few minutes, Lexi hurried into the kitchen and knelt at the other side of Hannah. 'Okay, Dad. I'll take over now. Rest a while.'

I watched in amazement as Gabriel straightened, and Lexi began chest compressions as if she'd been doing them all her life.

'How does she know what to do?'

Gabriel slumped into the kitchen chair and wiped his forehead with the back of his arm. 'She's a doctor's daughter, but then, you knew that, didn't you?'

I stared at him, aware that I'd never commented on his revelation to Harry that night and he must have wondered why, but it hardly seemed the time to go into that now.

He shrugged. 'I taught her years ago. Everyone should know this stuff,' he said.

I felt completely useless. Thank God they were both there. I dreaded to think what would have happened if I'd been here on my own with Hannah and Amy.

Time seemed to drag as Gabriel and Lexi took turns working on Hannah with no response from her. Oh, God, where was the ambulance?

As if reading my thoughts, Gabriel glanced at his watch. 'Eliza, can you go outside and wait on the road for the ambulance? I don't want to risk them missing the turnoff. Just in case, okay?'

I glanced at Hannah. Lexi was breathing into her, and the two of them seemed to have the situation under control. I was of no use here. I nodded and left the house, heading across the yard and running down the track.

I was only a couple of hundred yards, or so, down it when I saw the ambulance rounding the bend. I waved my arms and began to run back in the opposite direction. It followed me and pulled over into the yard, as I stood, trying to get my breath back. Two paramedics jumped out, and I gabbled something about Hannah being unconscious and not breathing, and that a doctor was with her. I'd quite forgotten that he no longer practised.

They rushed into the kitchen, with me running behind them. Gabriel carried on working on Hannah, while they asked questions and began to set up their machine. He was telling them about her medical history, and I grabbed Amy's hand as she wandered back into the kitchen.

Lexi pulled us both into the hallway. 'We need to get out of the way,' she said. 'They'll be using a defibrillator. Amy doesn't need to see this.'

I marvelled at her maturity. I could hear Gabriel talking quietly to the paramedics, and I looked into Lexi's eyes to see if she could hear what was being said. It was obvious that things weren't good. Lexi pushed her knuckles into her mouth as she waited for any sign of life from my grandmother. The paramedics began to put pads on Hannah's body, and Gabriel, still working on her, turned his head towards the three of us.

'Lexi,' he murmured.

She nodded and pulled Amy and me into the living room, closing the door behind us.

The three of us sat in silence as the clock ticked on. Amy didn't understand what was happening, but she knew that there was something very wrong. I pulled her onto my knee, rocking her gently, trying to soothe her. Lexi was in the armchair, staring into the grate. It seemed like forever before the door opened, and Gabriel stood before us.

Lexi and I stood up and moved towards him, too afraid to ask the question.

'They've stabilised her enough to get her to the hospital. I'll follow them down there.'

'I'm coming, too,' I said.

'It's okay, I'll look after Amy,' Lexi said, with greater nobility than I could have mustered. 'Call me as soon as you know anything, won't you?'

'Of course, darling,' said Gabriel, kissing her forehead. 'The minute we find out.'

The journey to the hospital seemed to take forever, and Gabriel was watching anxiously that the ambulance didn't have to pull over on the way, which would apparently mean they were using the defibrillator again. Thankfully, they didn't stop, which he hoped was a good sign.

Hannah was rushed away from us as soon as we arrived, and all we could do was wait. We sat in the corridor, feeling helpless. Gabriel squeezed my hand.

'I'm so glad you're here,' I whispered. 'What you did back there — you were amazing. You and Lexi. I'm so proud of you.'

'It was nothing,' he said. 'I was just doing what I was trained to do.'

'I mean it, Gabriel. What you do — it matters. Being a doctor matters. It's what you were meant to do, anyone can see that. If Hannah makes it, it will be because of you. Whatever happens, I can never thank you enough. I'll never forget it.'

He put his arm around me, and we sat huddled together, each lost in our own thoughts.

****

Lexi had put Amy to bed and was sitting in the living room, nursing a cup of cold coffee, when her father and I arrived home.

'I thought you were going to ring me?' she demanded but then paled. She could, no doubt, see the expression in our eyes. Gabriel had wanted to tell her the news in person, and now he did so, softly, hesitantly, his voice full of sadness.

'Oh, no,' she whimpered.

'I'm so sorry.' He wrapped his arms around her, and Lexi sobbed on his shoulder, as I sank into the chair and put my head in my hands, tears rolling unchecked down my face.

'She didn't suffer,' said Gabriel gently. 'She wouldn't have known anything about it.'

Lexi wiped her eyes. 'She's with Albert now,' she said. 'They're together again.'

'I'll make us some tea,' I said. 'It's what they recommend for shock, isn't it? Hot tea with lots of sugar?'

They didn't reply, and I headed into the kitchen, filled the kettle with water and stared out of the window at the darkness of the farmyard. Eddie had put the hens and the donkeys away, and everything was safely shut up. We'd called into his house briefly on the way home from the hospital to break the news. He'd said nothing but had gripped the edge of the table so tightly I thought he'd snap his fingers. As we'd walked away down his garden path, we'd heard a crash of breaking china. Hannah had been like a mother to him.

Staring into the blackness, I cursed myself for not telling Hannah that she was my grandmother. I'd wasted so many opportunities, and now it was too late. She'd died never knowing that she had a granddaughter and a great-granddaughter.

'Are you all right?' Gabriel was behind me. I wiped away the tears that were scalding my cheeks and reached for some mugs.

'Eliza?' He took hold of my shoulders and turned me to face him. I was trembling and couldn't stop. 'I'm so sorry,' he murmured.

'For what?' I asked, my voice breaking with emotion.

His eyes darkened, and I saw the battle he was fighting and didn't understand.

'For everything,' he said eventually, and pulled me towards him.

I leaned into him and let the tears fall, not caring any more what he'd said in the workshop, not wanting to know why he thought we weren't ready. All I knew was that I needed him, and I wanted to be held.

We stood like that for a long time, not saying a word. His hands stroked my hair and, occasionally, he would kiss the top of my head. I wrapped my arms around his waist and rested against him, listening to his heart beating comfortingly beneath my ear.

Eventually, we pulled apart, and I made the tea in silence, then we went back into the living room, where Lexi was sitting with her arms wrapped around herself, lost in her own thoughts.

'Thank you,' she said, taking her cup from me and sipping the hot liquid, probably without even tasting it. Gabriel sat beside her, watching her, his face anxious.

I sat staring into my cup for a long time. I'd telephoned Joe from the hospital, and he'd sounded much more upset than I'd expected. He was driving up immediately to be with me, and I would have to break the news that I was burying my own grandmother. I thought about my father. He was somewhere in Australia. Would he want to come back for her funeral, even if someone could track him down? I supposed the farm belonged to him now. He would probably want to sell it off, and it would be bought for development into homes suitable for holiday accommodation and second-homers from the city, the sort that Gabriel so hated, and would be left to stand empty most of the year.

The heart had gone from Whisperwood Farm and I couldn't imagine it ever feeling like a home again.

Neither Lexi nor Gabriel went home that night. We stayed up, shell-shocked and clinging together in our grief. Sometimes, one or the other of us slept for a while, and there were endless cups of tea made that rarely got drunk. We'd remember something Hannah had said or done, which made us laugh or cry. Gabriel told us about the younger Hannah that Lexi and I never knew; of a woman who worked hard on the farm and in the house, who was kind to everyone around her, a vibrant, strong woman who ruled the roost. It wasn't difficult to imagine. Hannah may have been old and frail when I met her, but she'd shown me many times what a compassionate, wise and determined woman she was.

We talked briefly about the future of the farm, and of Albert, and I knew I couldn't tell them who I was. Their scorn for him was palpable, and I didn't want them to think less of me because I carried his genes. I felt too raw, too vulnerable to cope with it all.

We watched the dawn break over the farmyard, and Gabriel and Lexi fed the animals, while I got Amy dressed and made breakfast for the four of us.

And so began our first full day in a new world — a world without Hannah in it.

Chapter 27

The service was as good as these things could ever be. The vicar, Ernest Cawthorne, had known Hannah for many years and gave a beautiful eulogy that brought forth tears of both joy and sadness. She was laid to rest in St Hilda's churchyard beside Albert, in a plot she'd reserved many years ago, when she lost the love of her life. I watched as her coffin was lowered into the ground, finding some comfort in knowing they were together again.

Joe seemed to be taking it very hard. I glanced across at him, watching him as he made small talk with the vicar and other villagers, and noticed how ill he looked. Something would have to be done about him. He was seriously worrying me.

Rhiannon and Rose were amazing. I'd never had a sister, but I was beginning to feel that now I had two. They carried me through those first dark days, in a way that no one else could. Even Gabriel and Joe couldn't reach into the darkest corners of my grief because they didn't know the full truth of what I'd lost. Those two women, those beautiful souls, knew it all; they knew how much it hurt, and supported me through it, letting me cry and rage and mourn without judgement or meaningless platitudes. I didn't want to hear that Hannah was in a better place when I still had so much to say to her, and both women seemed to understand that.

'Life is a mixture of light and shade,' said Rhiannon. 'It hurts, Eliza, but we can't have the good times without the bad. You'll come through this, I promise, and we're here to help you.'

Rose was even more succinct. 'Life can be fucking shit,' she said gloomily. She had such a way with words.

Sophie meant well but her overbearing sympathy was a bit much, as she kept telling me what a tragedy it all was, and how worried she was about the farm's future, as if such a thing hadn't occurred to me.

Archie took me to one side and informed me that Albert had been tracked down. Apparently, someone had come forward with a contact address for him.

'I've left a message for him to get in touch. As soon as he does, I'll let you know, and we'll discuss the future then, Eliza.'

I nodded, realising that he was gently reminding me that I would have to move out pretty soon. I was all too aware of that fact and thought about little else.

Will came over and took my hand. 'I'm so sorry, Eliza. I was so fond of Hannah. It's a terrible shame.'

'Thank you,' I murmured, anxiously watching Lexi, who sat hunched on the sofa, Derry beside her, his arm draped casually across her shoulders. Rhiannon wandered over, glass in hand. She stood beside us and nodded over at her son and his girlfriend.

'Have you spoken to Lexi, darling?' she asked Will.

He blushed. 'No. I mean, well, she has Derry. I don't think she needs me.'

Rhiannon and I exchanged glances.

'Look at them, Will,' Rhiannon said gently. 'Really look at them.'

He turned reluctantly. I looked, too, and saw what I hoped Will could see. Lexi was totally disconnected from Derry. They were sitting together but there was no sense of them being a couple. It wasn't working. They just didn't fit.

'He's not for her,' said Rhiannon. 'He wants to be, but he never will. You do see that?'

Will turned back to her, his eyes lit with a sudden flame of hope, and I marvelled at Rhiannon's generosity and understanding.

'Rhiannon,' he murmured, a little anxiously, 'I think maybe it's time—'

'Absolutely, darling.' She smiled. 'But it was awfully good fun while it lasted.'

****

When people began to drift away I found Joe and took his arm.
'Can we talk, Joe?'
'Of course, love.'
'In private. Let's go upstairs.'
I led him up to my bedroom and closed the door, and we sat together on my bed. I felt sick with nerves, but I knew that I may not get another chance to tell him the truth. He was heading back to London within the hour, and I couldn't let him go without knowing the secret I'd been carrying.

I took his hand and quietly I began to explain about the conversation I'd had with Will, and how Hannah had unknowingly confirmed the truth, when she showed me the photo of my father and revealed his middle name, and the reason he'd been given it.

'When did you find this out?' he asked, his voice choked.

'It was the day before Harry came,' I said. 'Quite an eventful time.'

'Jesus.' He shook his head, squeezing my hand. 'You had all that to carry on your own. Why didn't you tell me?'

'Because I didn't think it was something I could say over the phone. I wanted to tell you in person.'

'Why didn't you tell Hannah?'

Wasn't it obvious? 'How could I? She was ill, and the last thing I wanted was to finish her off.' I felt tears welling up. 'Not that it would have made a difference, as it turned out, and if I had told her, at least she'd have died knowing she had family.'

Joe pulled me to him and his voice caught. 'Oh, love, I'm so, so sorry. I don't know what to say to you.'

'It's okay. It's not your fault, and it's done now. Nothing we can do about it. Look, Joe, while I've got you to myself, is everything all right?'

'What do you mean?'

'You look awful. Are you sure you're okay?'

'Me? I'm fine, love. Don't you worry about me.'

'But I do worry.'

He smiled and ruffled my hair. 'I'm okay, just a bit knackered. But I promise you, I'm going to take a holiday soon. Maybe you and Amy could come with me? We could take Mrs Travers, too. A proper family holiday, what do you say?'

I nodded. 'I think that would be lovely. I'll hold you to it.'

'Deal. Now, I'm going to have to make a move, love. I'm sorry to leave you all alone. Are you going to be all right?'

'I'll be fine, Joe.'

As we said our goodbyes in the yard, some twenty minutes later, surrounded by other people, I looked across at Gabriel. He was standing a little apart from everyone else, and he turned his head, almost as if he knew I was watching him, and gave me a gentle smile. My heart fluttered, and I knew, whatever I'd told Joe, I didn't want to be alone that night.

He held out his hand to me as I made my way to him.

'Will you stay with me tonight?' I asked him.

Gabriel hesitated, obviously unsure what it was I was asking. I wasn't sure myself. All I knew was that I wanted him to be with me.

'I don't want to be alone,' I murmured, and he squeezed my fingers.

'Of course. I'll run Lexi home and pick up some things and I'll be straight back,' he promised.

We stood together, watching as Joe's car left the farmyard and people began to say their goodbyes to each other, preparing to leave. They came over as they left, thanking us for our hospitality and giving us their condolences once again. We nodded and smiled and thanked them, standing together with our fingers entwined. To me, it already felt that we were one.

****

Gabriel was back within half an hour of taking Lexi home, and we spent a quiet evening clearing away the remains of the wake and putting the house back in some sort of order.

He sat with Amy and read her a story, after I'd bathed her and changed her into her pyjamas, and when she finally fell asleep, he carried her upstairs and put her gently to bed.

We stood there, watching her sleep, the sleep of innocents.

'It's been a long day for her,' he murmured.

I nodded. 'For all of us.' I took his hand in mine and squeezed it. 'Thank you for staying with me.'

'No problem.'

He looked awkward, and I didn't blame him. I felt distinctly uncomfortable. I wasn't sure what he was expecting, and I didn't even know for certain what I wanted. We'd had one real kiss, and that had been interrupted for the worst possible reason. I didn't know how to move things on from there.

He led me out of Amy's room, and we closed the door quietly behind us, heading back downstairs in silence. I sat beside him on the sofa, and we watched a film, although I didn't take much of it in. I was too aware of his arm around me, of every muscle twitch, every slight sound, every breath he took. I wanted to lay my head against him and draw comfort from the warmth of him, but I was taut with nerves and didn't dare move.

Eventually, he stood up and asked me if there was anything else that I wanted to watch. I shook my head.

He turned the television off and then crouched before me, taking both my hands in his. 'Why don't you go upstairs and get ready for bed? I'll do a quick check round the farm, make sure everything's okay, and lock up in here. You've had an exhausting day. Let me take care of you now.'

I nodded, grateful beyond words, and headed upstairs. I heard him outside as I cleaned my teeth in the bathroom and felt a warm glow inside me as I listened to him rattling the barn door and checking all was secure for the night.

I climbed into bed and lay there, clutching the duvet to me and trembling, despite the warm August air. I heard him come back inside and lock the kitchen door, and I cast a nervous glance around the bedroom.

The lamplight had given it a cosy, rather romantic atmosphere.

It wasn't the most luxurious room, but it was the best I could do. I heard him climbing the stairs, and my stomach flipped over as he went into the bathroom. I gripped the duvet, wishing he would hurry up and we could get the awkward bit over with.

After what seemed forever, he closed the bathroom door and his footsteps crossed the landing. He stopped outside my door, and I heard a gentle tap. I couldn't manage anything more than a squeak, but he must have heard me, as he opened the door a little and peeped round.

'Everything's secure,' he whispered. 'I'll be in the room across the landing. Sweet dreams, Eliza.'

'Okay. Thank you.'

I stared in dismay, as he closed the door and headed to the spare bedroom. My heart sank, and I felt sick with disappointment. Well, that answered my question as to what it was I'd really wanted. I felt a sudden sense of rejection and shuffled down into the bed, burying my face in the pillow as I tried not to cry. It had been a horrible day, and I needed to feel someone's arms around me. I needed Gabriel's arms around me. I needed him beside me. I wanted him.

I could hardly believe what I was doing, as I climbed out of bed and pulled on my dressing gown. What was I thinking? What had happened to me? I wasn't the sort of woman who would quietly leave her bedroom and head across to a man's, hoping for a bit of …comfort. Well, the papers had said I was being "comforted by friends", and it was about time I proved them right about something.

My heart was beating out a rhythm so loud I could have tangoed across the landing, except my legs had turned to jelly, and I didn't know how I managed to make it at all. My courage almost failed me, but something drove me on. There was something awfully exciting about the whole thing, despite the terror.

Maybe it was the novelty of having to make the first move. I'd never had to behave in such a wanton fashion before. Goodness knows, I only had to flick back my hair and Harry would leer at me and inform me that was quite enough foreplay, so I'd never felt the need to take the lead before. I wouldn't have thought I was capable of it. Yet, there I was, my head stuck to the bedroom door, trying desperately to pluck up the courage to walk inside the room and seduce the man of my dreams. Well, it was blindingly obvious he was far too much of a gentleman to take advantage of me in my vulnerable state. Just my luck.

I couldn't hear anything, but there was no way he could have fallen asleep that quickly. Not unless he suffered from narcolepsy, or something, and, surely, he wouldn't work with dangerous machinery if he did? I began to wonder about insurance for that sort of thing and shook my head. If I wasn't careful I'd talk myself out of this, and I didn't want to be talked out of it. Or maybe I did?

The immediate effect on my insides as I contemplated this only confirmed the truth. There was no way I was heading back to bed alone that night.

Steadying myself, I opened the door and peered round. He was sitting on the edge of the bed, his hands at his sides, staring at the carpet and seemingly deep in thought. I shouldn't think for a moment that the carpet was that interesting. It was all brown and beige swirls and had definitely seen better days. I was one hundred per cent certain that he was thinking of me. I'm a whole lot more appealing than a seventies carpet, even if I do say so myself.

His head shot up as I pushed the door fully open and stood before him.

'Are you all right?'

I didn't answer. I took his hand and pulled him from the bed, leading him back into my own room, as if I was some seasoned seductress and not the nervous, insecure woman with liquefied insides that I really was.

He stared at me as I shut the bedroom door behind us, and I saw the look of amazement in his eyes as I began to unbutton his shirt. My fingers trembled, and I thought for a moment how awful it would be if he demanded to know what the hell I thought I was doing and threatened to sue me for sexual harassment. Then suddenly I saw a different look flare in those eyes, and I just knew it was going to be all right. I forgot all about my embarrassment and any awkwardness as a hunger took over that I hadn't felt in years.

He was almost apologetic when he produced a condom from his pocket.

'I hope you don't think I was expecting ... I mean, I wasn't making any assumptions ... it was just...'

'Oh, shut up,' I said, rather rudely, come to think about it, smothering his attempts at explanations with kisses. He'd hoped for the same thing I had. It made me feel highly desirable, a strange feeling I couldn't remember having before.

When I finally released him, there was a gleam in his eye.

'Bossy, aren't you? What am I getting myself into?'

'Why don't you find out?'

He gave me a delicious smile that made bubbles fizz up inside me like Willy Wonka's fizzy lifting drink. 'Don't worry. I intend to.'

He wasn't kidding. You know, physically it had always been good with Harry. He knew what he was doing and could always hit the spot, so to speak. But this was completely different. Gabriel showed me a tenderness I'd never experienced before.

I was conscious of the contrast between my body and Zoe's, and as I felt his gentle fingers on my stomach, I immediately breathed in and hoped he wouldn't linger, but he did. Actually, he lingered everywhere, really taking his time and stroking and kissing me with such delight and wonder that, before I knew it, I'd forgotten all about my chubby thighs and rounded stomach and, under his loving touch, completely lost myself in the moment.

He murmured into my ear, teasing and making exquisite promises, his skin damp against mine, his breathing quickening as he looked deep into my eyes. I gazed back at him, overcome with emotion, as I saw his love for me expressed so clearly in those turquoise depths that there was no need for words. It was enough. He was telling me all I needed to know.

Afterwards, he lay by my side, his arms around me as I listened contentedly to his breathing. Eventually we fell asleep, wrapped up in each other's arms.

When I woke briefly in the early hours of the morning I felt him stir beside me, and then he held me close and kissed the top of my head, and I let sleep reclaim me, understanding at last that Rhiannon had been quite right. Through him, I had found myself again.

Chapter 28

I woke the next morning to find the space where Gabriel had slept empty. After climbing out of bed, I dragged on my pyjamas and made my way downstairs, feeling a momentary dread that I'd find a note, or worse, nothing at all. I pushed the thought away. He wasn't like that. He was far too honourable.

He was in the kitchen. Amy was sitting at the table eating Weetabix, and he was whistling as he buttered toast then took the milk from the fridge. When he saw me his face lit up, and my heart leapt, knowing that what had happened between us had mattered as much to him as it had to me.

'I was just making your breakfast. I was going to surprise you,' he said.

I went to his side and he kissed me, not seeming to notice, or care, that I didn't have a scrap of make-up on and hadn't even brushed my hair.

'Thank you,' I murmured.

He smiled. 'It's only toast,' he said. 'I wasn't sure what you usually had first thing in the morning.'

'I meant, for everything,' I said.

He stroked my face. 'I could say the same to you,' he told me. 'You have no idea. Now, come on, sit yourself down and let's eat. I must go soon, I'm afraid. I've got to be somewhere today. Lexi's offered to have Amy, give you a break, so I'll drop her off at mine and bring her back to you later, if that's okay?'

I nodded. I was curious to know where he had to be so early in the morning, but I was sure that, when the time was right, he would tell me. We sat together, the three of us, enjoying breakfast, and then I dressed Amy, and Gabriel took her outside to water the donkeys and feed the hens, despite my protests that I could do all that myself.

He left me at about ten to eight, kissing me gently at the door, before scooping Amy into his arms and strapping her into the seat that he'd removed from my Fiesta and fastened into his own car.

I waved to them as they left the farm, then closed the door, feeling an overwhelming contentment. I smiled to myself, sure that Hannah would be delighted at the turn of events. I just wished she could have been there to see it.

I felt a pang of regret and loss. Life was always bittersweet, it seemed, and everything had to be paid for, one way or the other. I hoped that, by now, I was finally in credit.

****

My heart sank when I saw Archie's car pull up into the farmyard that afternoon. I was alone. Eddie was coming round later to feed and check on the donkeys, but we'd decided not to take them out at all that week. It just didn't seem right. Besides, as Eddie pointed out, they were no longer anything to do with us. Legally, any profits we made would go straight to Hannah's son, and none of us particularly wanted to hand any more cash over to him. I was still wondering if I should confess that he was my father. Would it change the way they felt about me? I knew I would have to tell Gabriel, at least, but I was dreading seeing the look of disappointment in his face. I knew he despised Albert Lang and hoped he'd believe that I'd inherited none of his traits.

I'd just attached the angel charm to my bracelet and was admiring it, holding it up to the window to see it better in the light, when I saw the car in the yard.

'Come in, Archie,' I said, my voice trembling as I stepped aside and let him into the kitchen. He sat down at the table and put his briefcase on his knee. He looked deadly serious, definitely in business mode. I tried to stop my knees from shaking but didn't fully succeed.

'Would you like a drink?'

He shook his head. 'No thanks. Sit down, Eliza, please.'

That sounded bad. I sank onto the chair, my nails digging into my palms. 'Is it the farm? Is it going up for sale?'

He looked surprised. 'For sale? Oh, no, no. This is a bit delicate, I'm afraid.' He sighed and put his briefcase on the floor. 'Thing is, Eliza, I'm not sure where to start. This isn't my usual way of working and it's all a bit awkward.'

'You're worrying me now,' I said, trying to smile. 'Why don't you just come straight out and tell me?'

He nodded. 'Probably best. A little while ago, Hannah asked me to come here for a meeting,' he said. 'I was surprised, to say the least, but I came, and we had a long chat, actually. This is difficult.'

I waited, feeling bewildered. What had Hannah wanted to see a solicitor for?

'Thing is, Eliza, I have some big news for you and I'm not sure how you're going to take it. I wasn't going to say anything, but then I thought, well, she obviously intended you to know at some point because of what she did, so I know I'm carrying out her wishes by telling you the truth. The thing is — the thing is, Hannah was your grandmother. Albert, her son, he was your father.'

I stared at him, astonished. 'She knew?'

His mouth dropped open. '*You* knew?'

I nodded, my mind reeling from the fact that Hannah had known I was her granddaughter. How? And when?

'How did you find out?' demanded Archie.

I explained about my mission and Will's revelation.

He leaned back in his chair and let out a sigh of relief. 'Thank God for that. I was worried you'd flip out when you heard the truth. Why didn't you tell her?'

'She hadn't been well, and I wanted to make sure she was up to hearing it. I didn't want to give her a huge shock,' I said. 'I was waiting for the right moment but, well—'

He nodded. 'It never came. Such a shame.'

'But I don't understand,' I said. 'How did Hannah know I was her granddaughter? And why didn't she tell me?'

'As far as I know,' he said, 'it was because of Joe.'

'Joe?' What the hell did Joe have to do with it?

'Yes. You see, Albert had never said a word about having a child to his parents. He was a rotten apple, Eliza. God knows where he got it from, 'cos it wasn't from those two, I can assure you. He kept going off chasing dreams, leaving home, insisting he was going to make his fortune. He always came back eventually, broke and jobless. Then one day he came home, and he had money. He was driving a car and splashing the cash around like an idiot. Only came back to show off, never dreamed of giving his mum and dad anything to help them out. Anyway, he was soon broke again and no wonder.

'A year or so later, he was back, another wad of cash being flashed around. Albert, his dad, was worried sick that he was thieving. Hannah always said the worry of it killed him. He was always scared the police were going to show up and arrest him. Anyway, not long after Albert died, young Albert informed his mother that he was emigrating to Australia. He had a job lined up there and money to take with him, and he was going to start a new life.

'Hannah was beside herself. I mean, how had he managed any of that? Eddie had had enough by that stage, so he collared Albert and threatened to beat the living daylights out of him if he didn't tell them where all this was coming from. I reckon he'd have gone through with it, an' all, and been glad to do so. I'm sorry to say, Eliza, your dad was a bit of a coward, and he soon told them.'

He paused, and I leaned forward in an agony of impatience. 'Well? Told them what?'

'He told them about you. He told them that Hannah had a grandchild, that she was fourteen years old, and that her mum was dead. He said that he'd never met you, but that he'd known your mum had a younger brother, and when Joe Hollingsworth started to make headlines he'd recognised the name. He'd got in touch with him and threatened to apply for custody of you. Joe had paid him off. Seems once wasn't enough, and Albert had pushed his luck a few more times. Eventually, Joe got sick of it and told him that if he came near him again, he'd call the police, so Albert told him that if he gave him one last massive payoff, he'd leave you alone. Joe fixed it with some relative of his in Australia to give him a job, and then he paid him a last lot of cash to go out there with.'

He looked at me, obviously seeing the shock on my face. 'Are you all right, love? Do you want me to go on?'

I nodded dumbly, and he continued.

'Well, of course, Hannah didn't know what to do. She didn't think she'd be welcomed by Joe, after everything Albert had done, and with him making a name for himself on television, she daren't approach him. Only she and Eddie knew at the time, and she decided it would have to stay that way. She used to watch everything he was on and read all the papers and magazines that had any interviews with him, just hoping to see a photo, or read something about you and how you were doing. She knew when you married Harry, and she even watched the programmes he was on, just to feel close to you.' He laughed. 'She never liked him, though. Said he was a smarmy git, and she was sure you could do better for yourself than that.'

He saw that I wasn't laughing and cleared his throat. 'Anyway, when you arrived in the village, and Gabriel told her you were Harry's wife, she was over the moon. Kept pestering Lexi to bring you round to meet her. Lexi thought it was 'cos she was a fan of *Twice as Nice*. When you turned up that first day, she was overcome. Seems you were wearing her ring, an' all — that little silver amethyst that you've got on your little finger? It was Hannah's. She thought she'd lost it. I'm guessing Albert had given it to your mum?'

I looked down at the ring and swallowed hard. This had been Hannah's ring? My God, how low could my father stoop? My poor mother had been well and truly duped. Poor Mum. Poor Hannah. But Joe? Joe had known all this time? All the long years when I'd wondered who my father was, he hadn't said a word but had paid the man to stay away from me. He'd even contacted my great-uncle in Queensland and got him to employ him to keep him away. I'd come to Kearton Bay looking for someone he knew wasn't there. How could he do that to me?

'The thing is, love, and what I wanted you to know more than anything was that Hannah loved you. Not just because you were her granddaughter, but because she got to know you as a person, and she thought the world of you. Hannah didn't leave the farm to her son in her will. She left it to you. She wanted you to have it, Eliza, with the proviso that the donkeys would be Eddie's property and would remain at Whisperwood till the end of their days.'

I gaped at him. 'The farm's mine?'

'It is. Mind you, it's going to take quite a bit of money to bring it up to standard, but I'm sure that won't be a problem.'

He smiled at me, and I wondered why everyone seemed to be under the impression that I was loaded. My estranged husband might be, and my uncle certainly was, but the last time I checked my bank balance, I was pretty much broke and not about to go begging for handouts.

'What about Albert? What will he say when he finds out?'

'He already knows. He got back to me yesterday. It was Joe who came forward with your great-uncle's contact details, and he told me Albert's address. He wasn't happy about it, but what could he do? There's no question that Hannah was of sound mind, and she had two witnesses to the will.'

'Witnesses?'

'Bernie and his son, Robbie. They were here when I turned up. Seems she'd thought it all through.'

I was baffled. 'So, where was I when all this was going on?'

'You'd gone into Helmston for the afternoon. You told Hannah you were going shopping.'

I remembered. It was the day I'd gone to find a jeweller to sell my watch and rings to. How ironic.

'So — so my father knows I'm here?'

Archie sighed. 'He does, darling, yes, but I'm afraid he showed no inclination to come back and meet you. He's got a new wife and a good life in Australia. He probably won't be coming back to England — at least, that's the impression he gave me.'

I swallowed. So, my father wasn't interested in me in the slightest. Well, was I really surprised?

'The main thing,' I said to Archie at last, 'is that Hannah died knowing I was her granddaughter. That's what was upsetting me, her not knowing. I feel better about that, at least.'

'I'm glad about that,' he said, getting to his feet. 'I'll be dropping off a copy of the will, and there are some papers to sign, but that can all wait for now. I know you've had a shock, but I must be going, love. I have a meeting with Sir Paul, and he doesn't like to be kept waiting. Are you sure you're all right?'

I nodded. 'I'm fine, Archie, thank you.'

As he left the farmhouse I picked up my mobile phone and looked at it for a long moment. Then I scrolled through the phone book until I found Joe's number. I was far from fine, and this couldn't wait a moment longer.

Chapter 29

'Morning, love. How are you feeling today?' Joe's voice was gentle down the line. 'Everything okay?'

I gripped the phone tightly, feeling an anger that was totally unfamiliar to me. 'No, actually, it's not okay. I had an interesting chat with Archie earlier. It seems Hannah knew all along that I was her granddaughter, and the reason she knew was because of you. Any idea why?'

There was a silence. I waited, praying there'd been some misunderstanding. He'd never let me down before.

'I'm guessing you know the full story, then?' His voice was quiet, and I realised, for the first time, that what Archie had said was true.

'How could you do that to me?' I said, my voice breaking. 'You, of all people! You paid my own father off and sent him to Australia out of the way, then you let me come here looking for him, when you knew all the time that he wasn't even in the same country.'

'Now, hang on,' he said, 'I tried to stop you. I told you that the chances of him being there were practically zero —'

'*Practically* zero! They were *absolute* zero, thanks to you and my dear Uncle George in bloody Queensland. You let me chase around looking for clues like I was in sodding Scooby Doo, and you let me go on thinking that Raphael Bailey was my father! All that scrabbling around, trying to find out about Sophie and Gabriel and Lexi, digging into their past, prying into their personal lives, and all the time you knew he had nothing to do with me.'

'How was I going to stop you? I kept trying to steer you away from it all, but you wouldn't listen to me. Please, love, see it from my point of view. How on earth could I tell you the truth?'

'Very easily, Joe,' I said. 'You just had to open your mouth and let the words come out.'

'Eliza, please, it wasn't like that. You can't think I wanted this to happen? I was just trying to protect you, that's all.'

'Yes. By paying off my father never to come near me again, and then letting me make a complete idiot of myself looking for him in this village. If you'd told me, Hannah and I would have had time to get to know each other. That's the worst part of it. You knew she was my grandmother. When I told you what I'd discovered, you were just acting, pretending to be surprised. She knew who you were all along, too. Did she tell you that she knew who I was?'

He hesitated for a long moment, then he quietly murmured, 'Yes. The first time I went up. I was nervous about meeting her, wondering how she'd react to me paying for her son to move away, and then there was the worry that she'd be just like him. How was I to know he wasn't cut from the same cloth as her? I had a long chat with her the night I told you about Harry going abroad with Melody. We laid our cards on the table and got things sorted.'

'How nice for you both,' I said. 'Yet, neither of you thought I needed to know?'

'You were dealing with all that stuff with Harry, and Hannah wanted you to get that sorted out first. She thought you had enough to cope with. She wanted to break it to you when you were in a frame of mind to cope with it.'

'I'd have coped with it, just fine! You knew that.'

'Truthfully, love, I wasn't sure I did. You were in a bit of a state. We were all worried about you. She wanted things to settle down, and she also wanted to get to know you without any pressure. She wanted you to like her for who she was, not just because you felt you ought to. She intended to tell you very soon. She told me about Gabriel making you that cake — apparently, he'd asked her for a recipe — and she said she felt things were moving in the right direction. She was hopeful that, once you'd got on track with your life, she could be part of it. I'm sorry.'

'It's all too late, though, isn't it?' I couldn't keep the bitterness from my voice.

'Do you want me to come back? We can't talk over the phone. Let me come up there, and we'll talk properly. I need to explain to you, put it right.'

'I don't think that's a good idea,' I said.

'What do you mean?'

'I mean, I don't want to see you, Joe. Right now, I don't even want to speak to you. You were the one person I thought had always been honest with me, but now, well, I don't know what to think about you any more.'

'You can't mean that?'

'I'm sorry, Joe. I can't do this,' I said and ended the call. Throwing my phone onto the sofa, I sank down beside it, my head in my hands as I howled. I felt so much sadness and regret and frustration, and I sat there for ages, rocking backwards and forwards, letting the tears fall, and thanking God that Lexi had got Amy for a few hours. The last thing she needed was to see me in such a state. It seemed my account wasn't in credit yet, after all.

****

If Gabriel thought I looked a mess, when he arrived back at the farm later that afternoon, he very gallantly said nothing. I knew perfectly well how bad I looked, having glanced in the mirror as I heard the kitchen door open and winced at my swollen eyes, matted hair and blotchy face. He ushered Amy into the room and took one look at me before making me a strong coffee.

Amy settled in front of a DVD and, apparently exhausted, fell asleep within ten minutes.

'Lexi took her to the beach,' he explained, watching her fondly. 'She had her running up and down, chasing a ball, building sandcastles, crabbing, playing rounders. She's absolutely tired out, bless her.'

'Lexi's a star,' I said.

'I think it was for her benefit, too,' he admitted. 'Took her mind off things.'

He looked at me, his concern evident. 'What's happened, Eliza?'

I sighed and sat beside him on the sofa. He put his arm around me, and I leaned against him, weary to my bones. 'It's a long story,' I said. 'Do you really want to know?'

He kissed the top of my head. 'Of course I want to know — if you want to tell me?'

So I did. Bit by bit, I told him everything Archie had said, and about my reason for coming to Kearton Bay, and what I'd discovered about Joe. He said nothing, letting me pour it all out.

'You don't seem too surprised,' I said eventually.

'I have a confession to make,' he admitted. 'This is going to sound awful, and, in the light of what you've just told me about Joe, you may be angry with me.'

'Oh, God,' I said. 'I'm not sure I can take much more. What now?'

He sat up and faced me, his hands holding mine. 'I knew who you were a long time ago. From the day you first came up to the farm, in fact. Hannah told me. She called Eddie and me into the kitchen, and we had a long talk. She was certain that your arrival in Kearton Bay wasn't a coincidence and that you were looking for your father.'

'You knew? Bloody hell, is there anybody who didn't?'

'Eddie and I were worried. I'm sorry, Eliza, I have to confess that I didn't trust you. When I found out you were married to Harry Jarvis, of all people, I'd already begun to suspect your motives for being up here, but when I realised who you were, well, I worried that you were after the farm, and that you were going to break Hannah's heart.'

'You thought that?' I recalled Eddie's warning to me that he didn't want to see Hannah hurt. It was all making sense now.

'I didn't even know who she was,' I said. 'I wish I had. We may have had time together as grandmother and granddaughter.'

'I know that now,' he said, 'but at the time I was convinced that you knew Albert was your father.'

'Hardly,' I said grimly. 'I didn't have a clue.'

'So, how were you expecting to find him? You must have known something about him other than that he came from around here?'

'Just that his name was Raphael, which wasn't even strictly true. He used his middle name, probably to impress my mother. I suppose Albert wouldn't have had the same impact,' I said. 'I was looking for a Raphael, and, of course I found one very quickly. Just the wrong one.'

He frowned at me, puzzled. 'The wrong one? Do you mean my father?'

I hesitated, but there seemed no point in keeping any more secrets. None of it mattered now, anyway.

'When I found out he was called Raphael, I wondered — and then I heard he'd once lived in Wetherby. My father met my mother in Leeds, so I thought it all pointed to it being him. It all went a bit James Bond, to be honest. I was doing this secret mission, trying to find out all about him, and work out if he was actually my father.'

'Wait a minute.' He pulled away from me and stood up, staring down at me. 'Are you telling me that when you befriended Sophie and Lexi, it was to get information from them?'

I blushed. 'Well, initially, yes. I had to be sure, you see—'

He turned away, his hands raking through his hair. 'So, all that stuff with Lightweights, getting Lexi to babysit, the cake? Oh, my God, the cake was a ploy to befriend her?'

'Of course not,' I protested. 'By then, I'd really got to know her and like her. The cake was exactly what I said it was.'

He wasn't even listening. 'You used my daughter to get to my father? How far were you willing to go, Eliza?'

What was he talking about? Why was he being so weird? 'Don't be so dramatic! I love Lexi. I've known for ages we weren't related, but it didn't exactly make me back off, did it?'

'When? When did you know?'

'At Sophie's dinner party. When you told me that you'd left

Wetherby before your second birthday, I realised your father couldn't be the man I was looking for.'

'So, all that time before, when I was —' He broke off and shook his head.

'When you were what? When you were *what*, Gabriel?'

'I have to go.'

'What do you mean, you have to go? Go where?'

I reached for his hand, but he backed away from me. 'You thought I was your brother. That's why you — and I thought… Oh, God, I knew it! That's the worst part of this. I knew it and I still—'

'What are you talking about? Gabriel, you've got this all wrong!'

He shook his head and strode out of the room. The door slammed, and I sank back down onto the sofa, wondering what the hell had just happened.

Why wouldn't he listen to my side of the story? After everything we'd been through, how had everything gone so badly wrong?

I would have cried, but I think I'd run out of tears. Funnily enough, all I could think of was how much I'd love to have Hannah sitting beside me right now, assuring me that all would be well and telling me to put the kettle on.

****

Gabriel couldn't sleep. Sitting on the edge of his bed, he stared into the darkness. Was it really only yesterday that he'd spent the night with Eliza, holding her in his arms and feeling that, at last, life was truly worth living once more? It had taken so much for him to get that far, and now he'd messed it all up again. He knew he'd overreacted. He'd known it even as he drove his car out of the farmyard, leaving her behind, stunned and tearful. How could he do that to her? He felt overwhelmed with shame.

Deep inside, he knew that her motives had been good ones. She wasn't the sort of woman to use people. She wasn't Zoe.

At the thought of his ex-wife, he groaned and buried his head in his hands. How could he have been so stupid? To drive Eliza away after everything they'd been through. She deserved better than that, for God's sake, and he'd no idea how to put things right.

The truth was, he'd been looking for something to go wrong, expecting catastrophe at any moment, and he'd leapt on Eliza's confession as further evidence that he was destined to be alone and unhappy.

Sophie had had his future all mapped out, of course. She'd been floating on air since he'd arrived home that morning, his face alight with happiness.

'I knew you two were made for each other,' she'd told him, and he'd laughed, whirling her round in a joyful hug. She would be furious when she found out he'd blown it again. In Sophie's book, it was all so simple.

'She'll be heading back to London,' she'd warned him, 'soon as that funeral's over with, you mark my words. You need to tell her how you feel, convince her to stay before it's too late.'

But the voice in his head had howled in derision. How could he ask Eliza to stay? How could he make her give up the life she was used to in London, to live in the village with him? He'd tried to force Zoe to live a life that she hated and look how that had turned out. He was still struggling with the guilt he felt for her.

Poor Zoe. He wished he could have made her happy, but instead he'd ruined her life. He'd blamed himself for her overspending and her affair, knowing she was frustrated and bored and battling depression, and had agreed against his better judgement to move to London, where he hoped she would find the kind of life she wanted. Instead, her spending had escalated, wasting money they didn't have on the latest handbags and expensive perfume — the same kind of perfume that Eliza wore. Eliza, with her rich, successful husband and beautiful Chiswick home, and designer clothes and accessories.

If he told her how much she meant to him, she may stay, but then what? He couldn't do the same to her, watching her anger and bitterness grow, seeping between them like poison and turning their feelings to resentment.

But she'd told him she loved him, and her eyes, her touch, her kisses had reinforced those words, giving him hope that she could actually mean it. He'd been afraid that she was latching onto him, using him as a way of coping with Harry's betrayal, but last night had convinced him she was genuine. What if giving up her lifestyle destroyed that love? Was it better to leave with the memory of one perfect night? How could he take the risk of giving his heart away again?

He shivered, knowing that it was too late. He'd already given his heart away. It had leapt into her palm the day he found her crying by the barn and she had laid her hand upon it, as it abandoned him and made a new home with her. Now it was up to her what she did with it.

He got up and walked to the window, where he pulled back the curtains and looked out over the churchyard and fields behind The Old Vicarage. Dawn was already breaking. In a few hours, he would be at work, and he had no idea how he was going to get through the day. He climbed back into bed and lay, one arm folded beneath his head, staring up at the ceiling as the first light crept into his room.

Chapter 30

Rose handed Amy a straw and fixed her with a stern look. 'No bubble volcanoes today, miss, okay?'

Amy gave her a sly grin and nodded. 'Promise.'

'Hmm, I'll believe that when I see it,' said Rose. 'By, butter wouldn't melt with that one.'

Amy began to sip at her milk shake, and Rose turned to me. 'So, a bit of a fiasco all round.'

'You could say that.'

She leaned back in her chair and sighed. 'I dunno, Eliza. What a bloody mess.' She sat up straight, tucking her wayward hair behind her ears and shrugged. 'Right, well, we need to sort it all out,' she said. 'Sitting here moping won't fix things. We need to make a plan.'

'Oh, no, not another mission.' I groaned at the thought. 'I've had more than enough to last me a lifetime.'

'Not exactly a mission,' she promised, but her eyes held that familiar gleam. 'We need to go through all your problems, one by one, and come up with a solution. So, what's the first thing that needs fixing?'

'Where do I start?' I said. 'Joe and I aren't speaking. Mrs Travers rang me last night, and she's not pleased with me either. My marriage is kaput. Sophie and Lexi probably know all about everything now and hate me, and as for Gabriel—'

I swallowed and shook my head, unable to finish the sentence. It was too painful to even think about Gabriel.

Rose growled at Amy, who'd produced a truly wondrous cascade of bubbles, which was now flowing onto the table. 'What did I say? Good job I didn't trust you,' she said, producing a wad of serviettes from her pocket and beginning the mopping-up process.

Amy beamed at her angelically. 'Sorry, Rose.'

'You will be, if you do it again. Drink it properly, and I'll let you have a cupcake.'

'Okay.'

Rose looked at me and tilted her head to one side, frowning at my obvious despair. 'Come on, Eliza. It can all be fixed. Joe, for example. All you need to do is ring him and talk to him properly. You must realise that he had your best interests at heart?'

'Of course I do,' I said gloomily. 'Now. That's the problem. I was such a bitch to him, Rose, and he didn't deserve it. Mrs Travers was furious with me. She told me that my father wasn't interested in me at all, but he wanted money to stay away. He'd threatened to apply for custody, and Joe was afraid he'd get it — not that he'd really want it.'

'Poor Joe. He must have been scared stiff.'

'That's not the worst of it. At the time, he was only just starting to get decent money. Albert was demanding too much for him to find. That's why he sold Grandad's house, to pay Albert off. And I gave him so much grief about it, throwing temper tantrums and accusing him of all sorts because I didn't want to let the house go. He must have wanted to throttle me.'

'He loves you,' she said gently. 'He'd do anything for you.'

'I know.' I felt tears welling up, so the stocks had obviously been replenished.

'I have to apologise,' I said. 'I just don't know if it would be better to go down there and do it in person.'

'To London?'

'Let's face it, Rose, it's time. I have to deal with my divorce and figure out what I'm going to do with the rest of my life. There's no point in putting it off any longer.'

'But you said you wanted to stay here,' she protested. 'And what about the farm? What are you going to do about it?'

I sighed. 'I have no idea. It needs so much work doing to it, and I don't have a clue how I'm going to fix it.'

'So, it's just going to be another millstone round your neck. What about Joe? If you won't take money from Harry, what about him?'

I shook my head. 'I don't want to be that woman any more. I was so busy condemning Zoe, and it was such a shock when I realised I was doing exactly the same thing. Well, not exactly the same. I didn't want all this designer stuff in the first place, but even so. So, you see, I really do have to sort things out and start to build a new life for Amy and myself.'

'But you wouldn't sell the farm?'

'Of course not. I'd be too afraid what would happen to it, but I may have to rent it out or something. I can't afford to live there, and even if I could, it would be too awkward round here, now that Sophie, Lexi and — and the family — won't want to know me. I have Joe and Mrs Travers in London, people who love me. I need to go home.'

'Right, well, if that's how you feel.'

'I'm going to miss you,' I said.

She smiled, in spite of herself. 'Not half as much as I'll miss you, pet. And I still think you're wrong. Go back and sort stuff out, by all means, if that's what you have to do, but sort stuff out here first before you go. You and Gabriel, you're not just going to let it go?'

'He thinks I was lying about everything. He really believes I was only interested in them all because of Raphael.'

'Well, be fair, you were. At first, anyway.'

'But that was right at the beginning. I felt uncomfortable with the whole thing very quickly, you know I did.'

'Rose? Upcake now?'

Rose sighed and headed to the counter, grabbing a cupcake for Amy. I looked around. The café was empty again.

'Seems my cakes weren't as much of a draw as we hoped.'

'Oh, they were, pet. I sold out. This cupcake's mine, God help her,' she added, as she handed Amy the cake. 'Let's face it, there are enough cafés in this village already, and I'm not going to make enough to keep me going over the winter.'

'Then, what are you going to do?'

She shrugged. 'I dunno. Something will come up. Look, why don't you go and see Gabriel now and sort things out with him? Tell him the truth.'

'He won't listen.'

'Make him listen! He's probably calmed down now, anyway, like you have with Joe. It was just the shock, and he probably feels a bit stupid. I bet he's wondering how to go about making it all up with you right now.'

'You think?'

'Guaranteed.' She hesitated a moment then smiled. 'Tell you what, I'll have Amy for a few hours, while you go and get it all done. Why not go home and make yourself beautiful first, and then head round there and knock him dead.'

'Hardly. Look at the state of me!' Then I thought about it. 'Are you sure you wouldn't mind? I'd like to get my hair done and my nails sorted out first. I could do with a confidence boost before I go round there.'

'And you *will* go and see him?'

'Promise,' I said.

'Off you go, then,' she said. 'Take as long as you like. I'll have Amy all day, if needs be. And, Eliza—' she added, as I stood up.

I turned around. 'Yes?'

'Don't take no for an answer.'

****

Denise was sweeping up hair, when I walked in. 'Hiya, not come for a haircut, have you?'

'I was hoping you could fit me in,' I said.

Denise glanced around her empty shop and laughed. 'Well, I'm rushed off my feet, as you can see, but for you, anything.'

She motioned me to a chair and went to fetch an apron, which she wrapped around me. After collecting a towel and her scissors, she began to comb through my hair, asking how much I wanted trimming off. 'Not being funny, love, but your roots are a proper state again. Did you want them doing?'

I thought about it carefully and shook my head. 'I'm fed up with being a blonde, Denise. I fancy going back to my natural colour. Do you think you can do that?'

Denise looked thrilled. 'Ooh, lovely. No problem.'

She produced a colour chart and began to point out the colours that would be best for me to choose, given the amount of bleach in my hair.

'By rights,' she admitted, 'you ought to have a strand test first. That'll take forty-eight hours.'

'I haven't got time,' I said. 'Just go for it.'

'On the condition that, if it goes green, you won't sue me,' she said. I hoped she was joking, but I agreed anyway. I was feeling reckless suddenly.

She began to mix up some dye in a plastic bowl.

'The funeral went well,' she said, eventually, as she began to dab paste onto my hair. 'Lovely service. You did Hannah proud.'

'Thank you, I thought so, too. The vicar was good.'

'Yeah. Doddery old bugger, but he did know Hannah quite well, and I've got to admit, he said some nice things.'

I looked up as the door opened and silently groaned as Michelle entered the shop. That was all I needed, and I couldn't even make my escape.

'Hello, Michelle. Usual?'

'Yeah, if that's okay?'

'I'm just doing Eliza's hair first. You can wait, or you can come back in about half an hour?'

Michelle looked at me and smirked. 'I'll wait,' she said.

I tried not to look bothered, but I was seething. I was at a total disadvantage. No one looks glamorous with their hair plastered in dye.

Denise worked in amiable silence for a while, occasionally asking me if I was going anywhere special, or if I'd booked any holidays. I gave non-committal answers. I didn't want to explain about going back to London. I'd had enough of that conversation.

Michelle flicked through a magazine, pretending to be absorbed in the celebrity gossip, but I knew she was listening keenly to our conversation.

'So, will the farm be sold, then?'

'I'm — I'm not sure,' I said.

'Bet you a tenner Albert Lang won't hang around. Eddie asked Will if he'd buy it, but Sir Paul said no.'

'How on earth do you know that?' I asked in amazement.

'Me mam does Bernie's washing. He told her that Sir Paul and Will had a massive row about it,' she said. 'Bernie said he told Will not to bother, but Will wouldn't listen. I like Will,' she admitted with a sigh. 'I'd give him one.'

Bernie would have known there was no need for Will to ask, but, of course, he would have been unable to say why. Poor Will. I was glad that at least Denise could see his charms, even if Lexi seemed oblivious to them.

'I'm sure he'd be delighted to hear it,' I said. 'I think he must get lonely at that big old house.'

'God, yeah, it would freak me out living there,' admitted Denise. 'It's a shame about the farm. Wonder who'll buy it? Bloody townies, no doubt. No offence, like.'

'None taken,' I assured her.

'What'll happen to the animals?'

'I don't know,' I said uncomfortably. 'I expect the owner will figure something out.'

'I hope they don't get murdered, or nothing. I suppose that means Lexi's out of a job, then. Poor little bugger.'

'Maybe she can come to some arrangement with the new owner. She, Eddie and — and Gabriel.'

I saw Michelle's eyes flicker at the mention of his name. I couldn't blame her. My stomach did a cartwheel just at the thought of him.

'Huh, I don't give a toss what happens to that creep,' said Denise.

'I'm sorry?'

Michelle put down her magazine. 'Stop chatting bubbles, Den. He's not a creep,' she said.

Denise tutted. 'That's all you know. I feel sorry for Lexi, being stuck with him for a father. No wonder she's sneaking around shagging Derry Bone. Even being kind of related to the witch would be better than being related to that bastard.'

Michelle and I both stared at Denise's reflection in shock. Michelle found her voice first. 'What the hell are you on about?'

'Jesus, don't you know about him? He's a fucking wife batterer.' Denise dabbed the last bit of dye onto my hair and piled it all up on the top of my head. 'Do you want a cup of tea while you're waiting?'

I gaped at her, unable to answer.

Michelle shrugged. 'That's bullshit. Stupid rumours.'

Denise pulled up a chair and sat beside me. 'No, it isn't. It's a fact. I know, because my auntie used to clean for the people who lived next door to them in Helmston. He used to work at the Castle Street Practice, but after all this kicked off, well, that was the end of his career, and quite right, too.'

'Bollocks,' said Michelle. I couldn't have put it better myself.

Denise ignored her. 'Anyway, my Auntie Edna, she was cleaning the day it all kicked off. 'Course, she'd heard the rumours about him before. Well, everyone knew their marriage was a sham. That Mrs Bailey, she was shagging around with some posh bloke, and Dr Bailey was furious. The neighbours used to tell my Auntie Edna about all the rows they used to hear through the walls. It was really bad. They said it was bringing house prices down. Anyway, one day, they see her in the garden, and she's got a black eye. No shit. And she tells them she walked into the door. I mean, as if! Everyone uses that excuse, don't they? Well, it seems that, after that, she sported quite a few cuts and bruises, and poor Lexi was in a right state. Started truanting from school and getting into bother. The whole family just collapsed. Dr Bailey had financial trouble, too — been overspending. The bailiffs turned up one day and took some stuff from the house. My auntie said the neighbours were furious. Well, it was a nice class of street till the Baileys moved in, you see?'

I felt sick. Was this some kind of hallucination brought on by hair dye fumes? Denise was prattling on, obviously unaware of the traumatic effect she was having on her client.

'Then one day, my auntie's cleaning the windows, and she sees all this commotion. The police had arrived, and they marched in and dragged Dr Bailey out in handcuffs. Gospel honest truth. And poor Lexi's screaming and crying at the gate, as they shove him in the police car, and poor Mrs Bailey's trying to pull her back indoors, and she turns around and my auntie sees her face. Jesus! Looked like she'd gone ten rounds with Mike Tyson. I tell you, how that bastard got away with it, I'll never know. He should have gone to jail, never mind just being struck off. Just 'cos he's posh, I reckon.'

She tutted again in disgust, and I fought off my overwhelming nausea to murmur, 'Maybe it wasn't that family? Maybe your auntie's got him mixed up with someone else?'

Denise shook her head emphatically. 'No chance. See, she saw him clearly that day he got arrested, and she almost collapsed in shock when she saw him again the other day. We were in Helmston shopping, and he was coming out of the very surgery where he used to work. She was that upset, we didn't even stay after that. She had a flashback, you see, and all she could think about was poor Mrs Bailey's face. I tell you, love, he's a bad 'un. Anyway, are you sure you don't want a drink while I stick you under the dryer? I'm gagging for a cuppa.'

I shook my head dumbly, and Denise shrugged. 'Okay, well, I'm having one. I'll check on you in ten minutes or so. What about you, love?'

Michelle nodded. 'Yeah, white with two sugars, please.'

She looked at me as Denise headed into the back room. 'Blimey. Who'd have thought it, eh? Seems the perfect man isn't so perfect, after all.'

I could barely think straight. I felt as if I was trapped in some kind of nightmare. The Gabriel I knew was a gentle, kind and loving man. He wasn't capable of hitting a woman. I chewed my thumb nail, trying to make sense of it all. Whatever Denise said, whatever Michelle thought, I didn't believe it. There had to be an explanation for it all.

I stared at my reflection in the mirror, remembering our night together, the way he'd held me, the tenderness and gentleness he'd shown me, and I knew that, if I was certain of anything in this world, it was that Gabriel Bailey wasn't the person Denise had just described.

I would stake my life on it.

Chapter 31

The dining room of The Hare and Moon was almost full. Derry and Rhiannon headed backwards and forwards between the kitchen and the tables, carrying Jack's lovingly crafted dishes to the diners. To Gabriel's relief, Michelle was safely tucked behind the bar in the other room. He wasn't in the mood for an evening out and was already regretting agreeing to Sophie's request.

'Busy in here tonight, isn't it?' asked Oliver.

Gabriel looked around. In a table at the corner, Eddie and Bernie were sitting, deep in conversation. Eddie caught his eye and half raised a glass to him, nodding. He looked odd, nervous almost. Gabriel nodded back and turned back to Oliver, who was prodding him with a menu.

'I've picked what I want, Gabriel. What about you?'

'Is everyone else ready to order?' He hadn't even looked at the menu, yet, though he wasn't particularly hungry.

'Not till Archie gets here,' said Sophie. 'Oh, speak of the devil.' She beamed as the door of the dining room was pushed open and her husband entered.

Archie put down his briefcase and kissed her on the cheek. 'Bit out of the blue, love. Are we celebrating something?'

'Fool!' She laughed. 'If the twins' 'A' level results aren't worth celebrating, I don't know what is.'

'Hmm, I suppose they did okay,' he said, taking a seat beside her and winking at the rest of the family. 'Who's paying?'

'Well, you are, of course,' she said. 'What a question.'

'Thought so.' He laughed. 'Well, let's have a look at the menu, then, eh?'

Pandora was watching Gabriel. 'Have you done something to Rhiannon?' she asked.

He frowned. 'Not that I know of. Why?'

'She's giving you some very odd looks, that's all.'

'She's a very odd person,' said Sophie. 'Now, I fancy the scampi. What does everyone else want?'

'Sounds good to me. What about you, Gabriel?'

'I'll buy mine and Lexi's, Archie.'

'No, you won't. When Lexi gets her degree, you can take us all out. Deal?'

'Deal. What are you having, Lexi?'

'Vegetable lasagne,' said Lexi, putting down her menu and peering at Rhiannon curiously. 'Pan's right, Dad. Rhiannon's giving you some very funny looks.' She looked round and frowned. 'You know what? So is Eddie. What have you done?'

Gabriel raised an eyebrow. 'Done? I haven't done anything.'

'Well, something's going on,' said Archie. 'Eddie's coming over.'

Gabriel looked up in surprise as Eddie approached the table.

'Is everything all right, Eddie?'

Eddie cleared his throat. 'Was going to ask you the same thing, mate. Don't want to pry, like, but I just wondered if you knew what was happening with Eliza?'

'What do you mean?'

'Well, I mean, with her leaving so sudden, like.'

Everyone stared at him. 'Leaving? Where's she gone?'

'Back to London, I'm guessing. I'd gone into Helmston to the saddler's, and when I got back, her car had gone, and the farmhouse were all locked up. Got home to find she'd posted the keys through me door and left a note, asking me to take care of the place and saying she'd be in touch.'

'And she didn't say anything else?' demanded Sophie.

'Nope. I were hoping you'd know,' he said. 'Obviously, you don't. Sorry, mate,' he muttered, before heading back to join Bernie.

Lexi looked at Gabriel, her face showing her shock. 'Why would she go like that? I thought you — I mean, I hoped—'

'I hope you haven't been a naughty boy, Gabriel.' Oliver laughed until Pandora nudged him, hard, and he glared at her.

'Shut up, Oliver,' said Tally. She reached over and patted Gabriel's hand. 'Are you all right?'

He said nothing, totally bewildered.

Sophie waved Rhiannon over. 'Did you know Eliza had cleared off back to London?' she demanded.

Rhiannon squeezed Gabriel's shoulder. 'Eddie did mention it. It's a frightful shame. I didn't get to say goodbye, and I'd grown extremely fond of her, and of Amy.'

'But why? Why did she go?'

'I'm not sure. I was rather hoping that you'd tell me. I suspect Rose will know, if anyone.' She turned back to the bar. 'I'm so sorry, darling,' she told Gabriel.

'You must know something,' Sophie insisted, fixing her gaze on her brother. 'Everything was going perfectly. Did you two have an argument?'

He felt the loss of her piercing through him, the pain leaving him almost unable to speak. 'I — I've totally messed this up, Sophie.' He picked up his spoon, staring at his distorted reflection in its bowl.

'Maybe you should tell us everything,' said Sophie.

Archie frowned. 'It's his business, Sophe. He might not want to tell us everything.'

'A problem shared is a problem halved,' she reminded him. 'Go on, love, tell us what went wrong.'

Gabriel told her about the last conversation he'd had with Eliza, his voice slow and hesitant as he recalled the way he'd reacted to her confession.

Archie took a mouthful of beer and shook his head. 'Oops,' he said eventually.

'Oops? Bloody oops?' Sophie was stunned. 'Is that all you can say?' She glared at Gabriel. 'Are you saying that you accused her of lying all this time?'

'Be fair,' said Oliver. 'She did admit that she deliberately joined

Lightweights and hired Lexi as a babysitter to get information about Grandad.'

'And are you telling me,' demanded Sophie, 'that, if you'd been in her situation, you wouldn't have done the same?'

'Dunno,' Oliver admitted. 'Would you?'

'Too right,' she said. 'I'd have moved heaven and earth to find out who my father was. Fancy growing up never knowing, always wondering who he was and why he'd abandoned her. How would you feel if your dad had done that to you? Can you imagine it? If you thought that you'd found him and just needed proof, would you have behaved any differently? Would you, Gabriel?'

He wouldn't have, he had to admit it. He loosened his tie, shame and guilt, his old companions, making their presence felt once again.

'Dad,' said Lexi, 'you don't really believe that it was all a lie?'

'Of course he doesn't,' said Sophie.

Lexi shook her head. 'Well, I certainly don't. I got to know her really well, and I think she liked me. We got on. She was fun, and she cared about me, about all of us. Maybe at the beginning it was a ploy, but once she got to know us... She made me that cake because she wanted to do something nice. No hidden agenda.'

'She hadn't known about Albert for long,' said Archie. 'Will told her only recently. But when exactly did she find out you weren't related, Gabriel?'

'At the dinner party,' he admitted.

'So a while ago then. You know, I'm not being funny, but didn't she spend the night with you recently? And who did she turn to when Hannah died, eh? Who did she want beside her at the worst time of her life? I reckon she'd well and truly fallen for you, mate.'

Gabriel couldn't speak. He felt sick.

'Well, of course she'd fallen for you, head over heels. Anyone could see that,' said Sophie in disgust. 'You only had to look at her face when you were around. Are you telling me that was faked, too?'

He shook his head, his face stricken.

'The trouble with you, Gabriel, is you've been expecting her to let you down the whole time. You're scared stiff to trust her, and you seized on this to prove that you were right all along that you could never be happy.'

Having already admitted that to himself, he could hardly argue.

'I see your friend's done a bunk.'

He looked up, dismayed to see Michelle standing there. He hadn't even noticed her enter the dining room. 'I'm sorry?'

'I bet you are.' She smirked.

Sophie glared at her. 'Bugger off, Michelle. We're not in the mood for your shenanigans tonight.'

'Charming,' she said. 'Think you're so bloody clever, don't you?'

Rhiannon rushed over to the table. 'Michelle, hush. Is there a problem?'

'Yes, there is,' said Sophie. 'This little madam's bugging us. Clear off, Michelle, I won't tell you again.'

'Oh, you won't? And is it up to you?' demanded the barmaid.

Lexi finally snapped. 'Look, will you just get the message? My dad's not interested in you!'

'Lexi—'

'No, Dad, it's time she was told straight. He doesn't want you, and he never will, so just piss off and leave him alone.'

Michelle gave a bitter laugh. Rhiannon took hold of her arm, but she shrugged it off.

'Leave him alone? Don't you worry, Miss High and Mighty, I wouldn't touch your father with a bargepole. Not after what I've heard about him today.'

'All right, I think you've said enough,' said Rhiannon, trying to steer her away, but Sophie grabbed Michelle's arm and pulled her back.

'No you don't! What did you mean by that?'

'Heard all about him and his nasty bullying ways,' said Michelle. She put her hands on the table and leaned towards Gabriel, and he reeled back from the spiteful expression in her eyes. 'Think you're all so perfect, don't you? But turns out you've been hiding one dirty little secret. I know all about you and your handiwork. Think it's clever to beat up women, do you? The police should have thrown away the key, if you ask me.'

'Michelle!'

'Only telling the truth, Rhiannon. And you,' she spat at Lexi, 'should be ashamed of yourself. Living with this cruel bastard after what he did to your poor mother. Proper mashed her face up, didn't he? How many times did he beat her, eh? Did you see him do it? Did you stand by and let it happen?'

Lexi covered her face with her hands, and Gabriel leapt to his feet.

Michelle tilted her chin in a challenge. 'Go on, then. Hit me, an' all. It's what you do, isn't it? No wonder you were struck off.'

Gabriel gripped the edge of the table, his jaw muscle pulsing as he struggled to control his anger. 'You know nothing about it. No one who knows me would believe such a disgusting lie.'

'Really?' Michelle sneered at him. 'Well, your dear *friend* seemed to believe it, didn't she? Don't see her anywhere around here, now, do you?'

He flinched as if she'd punched him in the stomach. 'Eliza? What do you mean?'

'I mean, dear Eliza was with me when we heard all about it. Never seen anyone look so horrified in all my life. Seems she believed every word, because, from what I hear, she's already cleared off back to London. So, there you go. I believe that's what they call karma. You finally got to pay the price, after all. Enjoy your meal.'

There was a general pushing back of chairs and a lot of angry shouting, and someone was trying to call for calm, but Gabriel wasn't really aware of it. He stood, feeling the pain sear through him, knowing for certain that he'd lost Eliza for good. He'd believed the worst of her and now she was returning the favour. It was over, and the worst thing was, he'd never even given it a chance to begin.

****

Fuchsia answered the door, her face sullen when she saw Gabriel standing there. 'Oh, it's you. Did you have to bang that loud? I was trying to watch telly, thanks very much.'

'Is your mother in?' Gabriel had no time for niceties. He heaved a sigh of relief as Rose appeared at the door, her face giving nothing away.

'Oh, it's you,' she said, exactly as her daughter had done. 'Bugger off, Fuchsia, and turn that sodding telly down. Getting on my wick.'

She turned back to him and folded her arms. 'What can I do for you?'

'Eliza, she's gone back to London, hasn't she?'

'Yes.'

'What did she say about me?'

'Nothing.'

'Rose, please. I appreciate that she's your friend and you're protective of her, but I need to know. What did she say?'

'I told you, nothing. I'm not kidding. Look, Gabriel, to be honest, I don't think she had time to stand here and waffle about you. She had more important things to worry about, don't you think?'

He frowned. 'What do you mean?'

'Well, Joe, of course. Haven't you seen the news?'

He shook his head. 'No. Why, what's happened?'

'Jesus. She got a phone call this afternoon from Harry. Joe's had a heart attack. He's in hospital. Dunno how bad he is, but she was in a right state. Came back here, collected Amy, and left.'

Gabriel leaned against the door frame, his legs suddenly weak. 'I had no idea. Poor Eliza. I'll go online when I get home, see what news there is. Thank you. I'm sorry to have troubled you.'

He began to walk away along Water's Edge, heading towards Archie, Sophie and Lexi, who were standing on Bay Street, waiting for him.

'Gabriel!'

He turned back.

Rose was standing on the path. 'What you said to her, you were out of order. You know that, don't you?'

He nodded silently.

'She spent ages desperately trying to prove that she *wasn't* related to you, not that she was. She didn't want you to be her brother. If you can't understand or forgive her for that, then you don't deserve her, anyway.'

She walked back into the house, slamming the door behind her.

Gabriel hesitated for a moment, then crossed the path and stood at the end of the patio by the fence, gazing down over the beck, at the moonlight glinting on the water. He remembered the day Eliza had arrived in the village and they'd stood together on the little bridge, looking down at this very stream, and he'd fought off the strange feeling that had begun to take seed in him even then. He'd been a prize idiot.

But she hadn't told Rose anything about the disgusting things she'd heard about him, and she'd left, not because of them, but because Joe was ill. Maybe there was still a chance, after all?

He pulled out his phone and stared at it for a moment, then put it back in his pocket. This wasn't something that could be resolved by phone. This was something that had to be done face to face. And before he could do that he had something else to sort out first.

For so many years he'd drifted away from who he was — trying to make Zoe happy, keep life stable for Lexi. Somewhere along the way, he'd lost sight of himself and what he wanted. But now he knew who he was. He knew what he needed to do. If he was going to get Eliza back, he was going to do it properly, and that was going to take some time. He could only pray that she would wait for him.

Chapter 32

As I pulled into the Chiswick street that had been my home for the last eight years, I realised I wasn't even aware of how I'd got there. So many thoughts had been swirling round my head as I drove that I must have made the journey on automatic pilot. I stepped out of the car feeling strangely detached. I had so many memories of this place, some of them extremely happy ones, yet now it didn't feel like home to me. It was just a house in a street, in the city, and whatever happened, I knew I would never live there again. If Joe was really bad, I would move in with him, to care for him. *Please let him be alive*, I prayed. *Don't let him be taken as well, especially not now, before I get the chance to tell him how much I love him, and how sorry I am for what I said.*

Harry looked subdued when he opened the door and let me in.

'You didn't take long,' he said. 'Amazing how quickly you can get back here when it suits you. What the hell have you done to your hair?'

'Shut up, Harry,' I said, taking Amy's jacket off.

'Charming,' said Harry.

'Have you heard any more?'

'Just what I told you on the phone. He's had a heart attack and Mrs Travers is with him. She'd been trying to ring you for ages. Must have been desperate, to ring me. How come you weren't answering?'

I didn't want to admit to him, of all people, that I'd been in the hairdresser's while poor Joe had been fighting for his life. 'It doesn't matter. Just take care of your daughter while I visit him, will you?'

Harry nodded sullenly and told me the name of the hospital. 'I'm sure he'll be fine. Don't worry.'

I was alarmed, upon reaching the hospital, to find a posse of journalists waiting outside.

'That's his niece, isn't it?' asked one, and they all surged forwards, thrusting microphones at me and calling for information.

'I'm sorry, I really don't know anything at the moment,' I said. 'I probably know less than you.'

I pushed my way through them and entered the hospital, almost running down the corridor to the reception and demanding to know where Joe was.

He was in a private room, and when I cautiously opened the door I almost wept with relief. He was propped up in bed, attached to a machine that was monitoring his heart rate. Mrs Travers was sitting in a chair beside him. They both turned their heads to look at me as I entered, and I smiled nervously at Joe. His eyes were bright with tears as he held out his arms to me. I hugged him gently.

'I thought you were — I'm so sorry, Joe. It took me ages to get here. I'm so sorry for what I said to you. I'm such a cow,' I said, unable to hold back my sobs.

'Don't be daft,' he murmured, stroking my hair. 'I asked for it, keeping you in the dark like that. Should never have kept it from you. Tried to protect you, but it all backfired, didn't it? I should have known you could cope. My fault not yours.'

'No, it was mine,' I said.

'Oh, for God's sake, blame me, and let's get on with our lives,' said Mrs Travers. 'You two are bonkers. It wasn't you who caused his heart attack, anyway, if that's what you're thinking. Which I know you are.'

'It can't have helped,' I said sadly.

'Doubt it had much to do with it, at all,' she said. 'He works too hard, doesn't he? And he smoked like a chimney till his last doctor's appointment, not to mention all those blooming ready meals he kept shovelling down his neck. I've said it to him, over and over again. Didn't I say to you, your lifestyle would be the death of you?' she demanded.

Joe pulled a face. 'Yes, you did, many times,' he agreed. 'Personally, I think it was the constant bloody nagging that did for me, but there you go. I love your hair, Eliza. You're beginning to look like your old self. We always liked it better dark, didn't we, Mrs Travers?'

She nodded approvingly. 'You've lost weight, an' all. I've not seen you looking this well for a long time. How are things going with this Gabriel bloke?'

'Never mind all that. What have the doctors said?' Pulling up a chair, I sat beside Joe, gripping his hand as if I was never going to let it go.

'Just a mild heart attack. I've been lucky,' he said.

'A warning, the doctor said,' pointed out Mrs Travers. 'Time for you to slow down and start looking after yourself.'

'Oh, shut up.' Joe laughed.

'No, she's right, Joe,' I said. 'You do need to slow down and take care of yourself. You're always so busy taking care of everyone else's needs, mostly mine. I'm sorry. I've been such a drain on you.'

Joe dropped my hand and glared at me. 'Don't you ever let me hear you say that again. You, Eliza, have been the light of my life since the day you were born. Look...' He took hold of my wrist and nodded at the bracelet that he'd bought me for my birthday, just a few short weeks and a whole lifetime ago. 'See? That's us. Family. In it together. I'm nothing without you, girl. You remember that.' He smiled. 'And I see you have an angel on there now. Even better.'

'Are you sure you're going to be all right?' I asked, changing the subject. 'There won't be any long-term damage?'

'They're doing tests,' he said, 'but it's looking good.'

'Anyway, maybe now you'll start listening to us and slow down,' said Mrs Travers.

Joe sighed and nodded. 'You're right. I don't want to go through all this again. Things have got to change, and I promise I'll do something about my lifestyle.'

Mrs Travers leaned forward and kissed him lightly on the cheek. 'About bloody time,' she said tearfully. 'If I'd known it took being ill to make you listen, I'd have poisoned you weeks ago.'

****

Joe made good progress. He insisted that the doctors were only keeping him in as long as they did because he was a private patient.

'If I was on the NHS, they'd have chucked me out days ago,' he assured us.

Mrs Travers and I weren't convinced. Joe was monitored for a few days and subjected to various tests designed to find out how much damage had been done. We were relieved to be told that only a small section of heart muscle had sustained damage in the attack and Joe should make a full recovery. He was prescribed several new tablets and given advice about diet and exercise and maintaining a healthy lifestyle.

'And it's everything I've been telling you for years,' said Mrs Travers with some satisfaction. 'I could have saved you all this palaver, if you'd only listened.'

Joe was discharged and left hospital to face a crowd of reporters, all eager to ask him how he was feeling.

'How do you think?' he asked, baffled. 'I've just had a heart attack. Can't smile wide enough, me.'

We all went back to his house. I was staying there and had been since collecting Amy from Harry after my first hospital visit. Harry had been furious, expecting that I was going to move back in and things would get back to normal. So much for his overwhelming love for Melody and their extravagant wedding plans.

'I have a lot of thinking to do,' I told him, 'and I can't do it with you breathing down my neck. Besides, Joe needs me, and he's my priority right now.'

Mrs Travers had made a hearty stew full of vegetables ready for his return. It was lovely, but I had to admit — only to myself, of course — that it wasn't as tasty as Hannah's chicken stew. There were dozens of bouquets arriving at the house, and hundreds of get well cards and messages poured in every day. It was weeks before Joe got around to opening them all and he was quite overwhelmed.

'Aren't people good?' he kept saying, shaking his head as he opened yet another lovely card from a fan. He paused and then handed it over to me. 'You might like to read this one,' he said.

I took it, and my hands shook as I read the heartfelt message from Sophie, Archie, Pandora, Oliver, Tallulah, Gabriel and Lexi. I handed it back, saying nothing.

'Are you going to tell me what's going on?' asked Joe. 'Only, you've barely mentioned him since you got here, and I'm not daft. I know you're trying to spare me any worry, but I'm not about to keel over, so come on, spill.'

Hesitantly, I told him what had happened.

He listened, saying nothing until I'd finished, then sighed. 'I dunno. There's nowt so queer as folk,' he said. 'So, do you believe all this stuff about him being a wife batterer?'

'Of course not!' I said immediately.

He raised an eyebrow. 'Not a little bit? Not even the slightest doubt?'

I shook my head. How to explain to Joe that the man who had held me so tenderly would be unable to hit a woman? I knew it, deep within me. There was no question in my mind that it was all a misunderstanding. I wasn't sure how, and I couldn't offer any explanation for what Denise's aunt had seen, but, somehow, I knew that he wasn't the man they thought he was. I didn't need evidence for that.

'Well, seems to me, if that's the case, that you're well and truly in love with this man. So, what the hell are you doing here?'

'To be with you, of course!' I said with some indignation.

'Don't fib. I left hospital weeks ago. I'm definitely on the mend. You can leave me here with Mrs Travers, and I solemnly swear I'll keep living. Why haven't you so much as rung him?'

'Didn't you hear what I told you? He thinks I lied to him about everything, and he's angry with me. Thinks he can't trust me, and

I can't really blame him, can I?'

'Oh, what rubbish,' said Joe. 'Look, what I kept from you was a much bigger secret, and you blew up at me, didn't you? Didn't want to see me, or even speak to me for a while, but you calmed down. You forgave me.'

'Of course I did,' I said. 'I love you.'

'And *he* loves *you*,' said Joe. 'He must do, to risk the ridicule he'd get for that bloody cake. Anyway, what about the rocking horse for Amy? Why do that, if not for you? You know he loves you, right?'

I remembered that one, precious night we'd had together when I'd known, without question, that he loved me. Could those feelings really have gone away? I thought about Harry. How many times had he said he loved me and then lied to my face, sleeping with Melody behind my back, making a total fool of me? Gabriel had never said he loved me, but every day he'd tried to show me. He'd never lied to me. He didn't make false promises.

'I'm sure he does,' I admitted eventually. 'But why hasn't he got in touch with me? He's had weeks, and there hasn't been a word in all that time.'

'Have you been in touch with him?'

'Well, no, but it wasn't me who caused the argument.'

'Good grief,' said Joe. 'You're thirty-three not thirteen. If you love this fella, and I'm a hundred per cent certain that you do, go and get him.'

I felt a thrill run through me at the thought, but it was tinged with fear. What if he said no? What if he hadn't forgiven me? Was it better to live with uncertainty than find out for sure it was over?

'I'll get in touch with him soon,' I said, feeling Joe's eyes boring into me. 'Just give me a chance to pluck up the courage.'

He sighed. 'Okay, love. But don't wait too long, eh? Life's so short. If I've learned anything in the last couple of weeks, it's that you should make the most of every day.'

He put the pile of cards onto the sofa next to him and looked at me. 'I've got a bit of thinking to do myself, love. Looks like we both have some big decisions to make, eh?'

Chapter 33

I didn't sleep well that night, as I tried to think of reasons for Gabriel's silence. I knew Joe was right. He'd snapped at me and probably regretted it, but if that was the case, why hadn't he at least phoned me? It had been over a month since I'd last seen him, and my heart ached for him. I knew I would have to do something soon, but I was nervous. How to make an approach? Could I risk being rejected by him, having my biggest fear confirmed — that Gabriel and I were over and there was no going back?

I climbed out of bed and wandered, as I did frequently, to the window, where I gazed up at the moon. I tried to take comfort from the words Lexi had spoken so long ago. The same moon shone over Kearton Bay. I wasn't so far away from him, after all.

Joe was already up when I went downstairs, tired but resigned to the fact that I wasn't going to get any more sleep. He was sitting at the table, drinking tea, and I slumped into a chair opposite him, dropped my head in my hands and peered at him wearily.

'You look lovely,' he said with a grin. 'Cuppa?'

'I'll make it,' I said, but he stood and waved his hand at me.

'I'm perfectly capable of making you a cup of tea. Stop fussing. Anyway, I'm glad you're awake. Have you given any more thought to what you were saying yesterday?'

I gave a bitter laugh. 'I've thought about nothing else. I know I have to make a move soon, because if I don't, he may just forget about me, but I'm scared, Joe. What if he tells me to go away? What if he hasn't forgiven me?'

'Then he's not worth having,' said Joe, taking a mug from the cupboard and dropping a teabag into it. 'But you seem pretty certain that he *is* worth having, so I doubt that he didn't forgive you weeks ago.'

'I just don't understand why he hasn't called,' I said.

'Only one way to find out,' he said, handing me the mug of tea. 'And you know what that is.'

'Yes, all right. I know. Anyway, what about you?' I asked. 'What are you doing up so early?'

'Been doing a lot of thinking,' he admitted. 'What would you say if I told you I was going to retire?'

I nearly spat my tea out. 'Retire? You? I don't believe it.'

'Well, maybe retire is a bit strong,' he said, considering. 'I don't intend to buy a cardigan and sit by the fire doing Sudoku every day but, certainly, I'm thinking of giving up my show. I'm fed up with the constant chasing around and barely seeing anyone I care about. I want to do things that interest me and stop wasting time on things that don't. This house, for instance.'

I looked at him in surprise. 'This house? I thought you loved it?'

'I love it as far as London houses go, but the truth is, I want something totally different. I stayed here because it was close to work, but you know I've always hankered to go back home, and I really want a different way of life. I don't know. Maybe I'll take a look at going back to Knaresborough, or that area. Buy a bit of land for Jeeves and Wooster, get some bigger pigs, chickens, grow my own veggies. Finish that book, and maybe write another. My editor's loved the stuff I've sent in so far, seems to think I've got talent. I've enjoyed writing, just struggled to fit it in. Maybe I could start writing fiction. I'd like to have a go at a good murder mystery.'

I gaped at him. Was this really Joe Hollingsworth talking? 'Are you serious?'

'Absolutely. I'm going to put this place on the market and start looking for another property.'

'What about Mrs Travers?'

'She can come with me. I'm hardly going to abandon her, am I?'

I shook my head. 'Good luck with that one. You know she'll never agree to living in the north.'

'She will, if she knows it will mean saying goodbye to me, otherwise,' he said confidently.

I laughed. 'I'll bet you fifty quid she won't,' I said. 'And I don't think you'll go, anyway. It's just talk. You'll never give up work.'

'Oh, really?' Joe headed into the living room, returning within minutes with his laptop bag. 'I'll prove it to you. I'll start looking now.'

I sipped my tea, watching in amusement as he logged on and started browsing the web for Yorkshire properties for sale.

'Some lovely places here,' he remarked, and I laughed and went over to the toaster, shoving two slices of bread into it.

'Prices are so low, even in that area. I mean, compared with what I paid for this place. Amazing.'

'I still don't believe you,' I said, taking the butter out of the fridge.

'Do I care?' He shrugged. 'Told you, when I was visiting you at Hannah's, I never felt more relaxed, more alive. I want that feeling all the time. I've done London. I've achieved all my work ambitions. I have the top-rated chat show in Britain, so where would I go from there? I just want some time to enjoy my life before it's too late.'

I watched him thoughtfully. 'You're serious, aren't you?'

'Totally.' He sat up straight suddenly and looked at me in surprise. 'Eliza, did you know Pinky's is up for sale?'

I rushed to his side. 'You're kidding? Rose never said a word!'

I looked at the screen. It was Pinky's, all right, with seven photographs of the kitchen and the café area, and Rose's flat above in all its chaotic glory. I'd only spoken to Rose two days ago, and she hadn't said a word. Why?

'I knew she was having financial problems.' I murmured. 'I just didn't realise how bad it was.'

'It's October,' Joe mused. 'I guess she knew she wouldn't see it through the winter. I'm amazed she made it through summer, from what I saw when I visited. Poor Rose.'

The toaster popped, and I automatically began to butter the toast, deep in thought. It wasn't just a business Rose would be losing. It would be her home, too. Where would she go?

'I can't let this happen,' I said. I sat at the table and took a bite of my toast, my mind racing. 'She won't be able to stay in Kearton Bay if she loses Pinky's, and she was so scared of having to leave the place. She did everything she could to help me with my problems, and I just whined on at her, not paying much attention to all her worries. She must have been frantic.'

Joe patted my hand. 'What can you do about it, love?'

I chewed my toast, turning all the possibilities over in my mind. I didn't have any money of my own to help, and I didn't want to ask for any handouts. Then I began to think about what assets I did have, and my heart sank.

'There's always the farm,' I said.

Joe looked shocked. 'You wouldn't sell the farm?'

'I don't want to. Hannah left it to me, and I really want it to be Amy's one day, but if I sold the place, I could help Rose out.'

'But you know what could happen to the farm, if you let it go. It doesn't bear thinking about. Whisperwood can't go the way of all the other places in the village. It has to retain its charm.'

'And its leaking roofs and rotten windows and ancient plumbing,' I said wryly.

Joe laughed. 'It could be beautiful. It just needs a lot of love.'

'And a lot of money,' I pointed out, 'which I don't have.'

We were silent for a moment, then we stared at each other, hardly daring to put our thoughts into words.

'It would make sense,' said Joe eventually.

'And it wouldn't really feel as if I was selling it,' I said.

'And, of course, it would be Amy's one day, that goes without saying,' he added.

'And the money could buy Pinky's,' I said.

'And you could still live there, no question.'

'What about Eddie?'

'He'd be the perfect man to help me set the place up. I'll need all the help I can get.'

We began to laugh.

'It's the perfect solution,' said Joe, and I nodded.

'The only thing is,' he said suddenly, 'with you deciding to divorce Harry, the farm is going to be caught up in the legal proceedings. I mean, lawyers wrangling over who owns what, and division of property, and all that stuff.'

I thought for a moment then I stood up, carrying my empty plate and mug to the sink. 'I think I need to call Rose,' I said, 'and then I have to visit Harry.'

****

Harry wasn't happy. I'd let myself in with my key, which annoyed him. 'If you're not going to live here any longer, you should have knocked,' he told me grumpily.

I ignored him and walked into the lounge, sitting calmly on the sofa.

'You haven't even taken your shoes off. Those heels could scratch the floorboards. You can be so slovenly, my mother's right about that.'

I ignored him. I had more important things to think about than his bloody mother's opinion of me.

'Would you like a drink?'

'Thank you, but no.'

'So, what *do* you want?' he asked.

'I've just come here to clear things up, once and for all. About the divorce, I mean.'

Harry's eyes widened. 'Divorce? Are you serious? Look, I admit it, I was an idiot. You don't understand what it's like. Television can be a lonely business, and Melody was there, and she understood the pressures, and knew the same people that I did and talked the same language. It was no reflection on you. I just found myself getting deeper and deeper into something I didn't want.'

'Didn't want? You were all over the newspapers with your arms wrapped round each other, telling the world how loved up you

322

were and how much you wanted to be together!'

'That was all Melody. I only went to New York in the first place, because you threw me out. If you'd gone to Italy with me, as I'd suggested, none of this would have happened. Look, if I were truly serious about her, I'd be living with her now, wouldn't I? Not staying here on my own. Eliza, listen to me, none of it was my doing. She's so forceful. What Melody wants, Melody gets, and I got dragged along with her, but I promise you, things will be different.'

I shrugged. 'It's too late. I don't want to be married to you. I'm consulting a solicitor about a divorce today. I wanted to tell you in person before the forms landed on your doorstep.'

'You heartless bitch! I suppose this is to do with your fake doctor friend? I knew there was more to it than neighbourly concern. I bet you've been shagging him all along, haven't you? Well, I won't sign them,' he said, folding his arms and doing his sulky child impression again.

'Sign them, don't sign them. Sooner or later, I'll get my divorce. Let's face it, you've given me enough grounds, and it's not going to be hard to prove, is it? I've still got copies of all those tabloids your little affair featured in. Not to mention the issue of *All the Goss*, where the delightful Sindy talks about your passionate relationship when I was pregnant with Amy.'

'Fuck it,' said Harry. 'Well, you can divorce me, but you're not getting any of my money. Let St Joe keep you instead.'

'That's what I wanted to talk to you about,' I said.

He gave me a smug look. 'I knew it. I hope you're not expecting me to give you handouts any longer. You won't get another penny from me.'

'Putting aside the fact that you still have a daughter to support, I'm not asking for handouts. I have a proposition for you.'

'Really? This should be good.'

I tried to ignore his sneer and told him calmly all about my unexpected inheritance.

'You mean that old crone was your grandmother? And that dump is yours? Good luck with that.'

'The point is, Harry,' I said, 'if we argue about money, the legal bill is going to go up and up, and all for nothing. The only people to benefit will be our solicitors. What's the point?'

'So?'

'So, I was thinking, what if we come to some arrangement privately? With no financial wrangling and no custody battle, the divorce will be quick, easy and much cheaper.'

'And what, exactly, are you asking?'

'A fair monthly contribution to Amy's upbringing, and a simple, quick division of property.'

'How simple?' He was obviously suspicious.

'You get the house and everything in it, apart from my own personal belongings and Amy's things, obviously, and I get the farm.'

He tilted his head, thinking. 'How much do you think the farm's worth?' he asked eventually.

'Less than half what we paid for this place,' I said.

He looked astonished that I was aware of the fact. 'Then, what's in it for you?'

I explained about Rose and selling the place to Joe.

He smirked. 'So, if I refuse, this could really be a fly in the ointment,' he said.

My heart sank. 'Why would you refuse? You've got a good deal. If it goes to court, I'd probably get half of everything. Financially, you'd lose out, and for what?'

'Might be worth it to annoy Joe, and anyway, why the fuck should I make things easy for you, so you can go off and live with the fake doctor? That's what you're planning, isn't it? That's what this is really about?'

I glared at him. How could he be so petty and selfish, after everything he'd done? Just as I was wondering what I could do to change his mind, the doorbell rang.

'Wait there,' he instructed as he left the room. I heard angry voices, and then the door was pushed open, and Harry was back, looking petrified, with the woman herself. Finally, for the first time since I'd discovered their affair, I was face to face with Miss-Grin-and-Bare-'Em.

She stood before me and looked me up and down, then glared

at Harry.

'So, what did you expect?' he demanded. 'That she'd be stark naked?'

I pulled a face. 'Hardly. What's this about?'

'I told Melody you were coming here this morning to discuss things, and I made the mistake of thinking she'd trust me. Obviously, that's too much to ask.'

'Do you blame me?' she demanded. 'You buggered off to Yorkshire the minute I went to America, and you supposedly started divorce talks, but nothing happened. I don't believe a word you say.' She turned to me, her eyes bright. 'Harry says you're finally getting a divorce. Is that true?'

I didn't see why I was under any obligation to answer her questions. Bloody cheek.

Harry looked distinctly shifty. His eyes kept flicking between Melody and me, and he kept wetting his lips, a sure sign that he was nervous. I watched him, curiosity aroused. What was going on?

'Melody seems to be under the impression that I'm lying to her. I told her that I only went to Yorkshire to ask for a divorce, but she doesn't believe me.'

He looked at me, and there was undisguised pleading in his eyes. I couldn't believe the nerve of the man. He could sod off. I wasn't going to cover for him, no way.

'It's all sorted now, darling,' he told her. 'Eliza has agreed to a divorce. You'll be able to see the papers in a few days. The only snag is, she may be naming you as co-respondent.'

'I don't care about that,' said Melody. 'It's hardly a surprise to anyone, is it?'

He rushed to the drinks cabinet and poured her a glass of wine. He offered me one, too, but I shook my head, enjoying watching him squirm.

Melody pushed his arm away as he offered her a glass, and I caught the scent of a familiar perfume. Chanel No 5. So, Melody wore it, too. Of course, and by buying it for me, Harry was ensuring that I would never question its scent lingering on him. I should have guessed.

'I hate that wine,' she told him.

'But it's my favourite! You said you loved it, too.'

'Of course I did. That was when I was trying to persuade you that we were compatible. Now I don't give a shit.'

Finally, some honesty from Melody Bird, I thought.

'Please, darling, don't be like this. We were getting on so well.'

'Yes,' she said, sitting down and taking off her coat. 'We were. Until I found out that, the minute I headed to New York, you rushed straight up to North Yorkshire to see your wife.'

He winced and took a large glug of wine.

'How do I know that I can trust you? I'm sure Eliza thought *she* could but look what you did to her.'

Well, that was rich. Still, she had a point.

'Eliza, please tell her that I was trying to get a divorce all along,' pleaded Harry.

No chance, mate, I thought. This is where I finally get my revenge.

'Is that true, Eliza?'

Melody looked at me, and I saw something in her eyes that made me hesitate. There was a defiant expression in her face, and she was trying not to appear as if she cared, but, beneath that tough exterior, I saw something which shocked me. Fear. It mattered to Melody. *Harry* mattered to Melody. The idea that she'd actually fallen in love with him had never occurred to me, but I realised as I looked at her that she had, and her future depended on my answer.

'It took me a long time to come to terms with everything,' I said carefully, 'but now that I have, I realise it's all turned out for the best. Harry and I were never compatible. I think you and he make a much better couple. I'm ready to end our marriage now.'

Harry gave me a look of profound gratitude, tinged with obvious surprise. It hadn't been difficult in the end. The way I saw it, they deserved each other, and the fact that Melody had fallen for such a selfish, self-obsessed, vain, shallow liar was her lookout. They could go off on their exotic holidays and live the glamorous celebrity lifestyle he'd always wanted. He was free.

Melody closed her eyes briefly then she turned to Harry and

took his hand. 'I'm sorry, Harry.'

'Don't worry about it, sweetheart,' he said, his voice as smooth as treacle. 'And Eliza and I have come to an arrangement about our finances. Eliza has agreed that this house will be mine, and a little property she's inherited in Yorkshire will be hers. Apart from the financial arrangements for Amy, we're all agreed. The divorce should be through very soon.'

I looked at him in surprise. Seemed my good deed had been rewarded, thank God.

'I can't tell you how glad I am to hear that. The sooner we start living together, the better, don't you agree?'

'Absolutely, darling,' he said. 'This is my proper grown up relationship. Till death us do part, I swear.'

Don't mind me, I thought, getting ready to leave. Harry caught my arm, as I picked up my bag. I turned to him in surprise.

'Eliza, I'm — I'm sorry for the way I behaved. You didn't deserve it.'

I was stunned. 'Thank you. That means a lot.'

'You will let me see Amy?'

It was the best thing he could have said to me. I felt weak with relief. 'Of course, whenever you want to. Amy needs her father. She always will.'

He nodded, smiling faintly, and Melody obviously decided she needed to re-stake her claim on him.

'Well, that's all settled, then. I'm so happy,' she told him, turning to me with a look of triumph on her face, 'because I have some rather wonderful news for you. Harry, my darling, I'm pregnant. We're having a baby.'

'Oh, fuck,' said Harry.

Boy, was I glad I was around to hear her drop that little bombshell. I waved at the radiant Melody and the dumbstruck Harry and bid the not-so-happy couple a not-so-fond farewell.

Chapter 34

It struck me, as I looked down on Kearton Bay that dark October evening, that maybe I should have set off from London much earlier in the day. Now I was going to have to face that long, twisting descent with only the moon to guide me.

Way below me, its light made a glittering path across the dark body of ocean, leading from the horizon towards the shore, where a huddle of roofs and chimneys and a distant church spire were the only manmade shapes visible against the dark sky.

I braced myself, wondering how the brakes on my little Fiesta would cope with the steep decline. There was only one way to find out. I began to edge forward, my heart pounding with trepidation, knowing that this nerve-wracking drive down to the village wasn't the scariest thing I had to face.

I was heading to the farm to clean it up and get it ready in preparation for the arrival of Joe and Amy. Mrs Travers wouldn't be joining us, though. After a long and emotionally-charged discussion, she'd told us that she'd decided she was ready to retire.

'But you can retire to Kearton Bay,' Joe had protested. 'We wouldn't expect anything from you, except to relax and enjoy yourself.'

'Enjoy myself? Up there, with that funny lot?' she'd demanded, rolling her eyes at how ludicrous the idea was. 'Truth is, love, I've wanted to tell you for a long time, but the way things were, I didn't like to add to your troubles. My sister's asked me to move in with her, and I've said yes.'

'But she gets on your nerves!' I'd said, shocked at her revelation.

'Yeah — always has, always will. But she's still me sister, and Margate, well, it feels like the kind of place I could be happy. Now I know you two are sorted, I feel it's the right time for me, an' all.'

We were upset, and we were going to miss her, but in all honesty, I knew she'd made the right choice. She would never have settled in Yorkshire, and Joe finally accepted that she was serious and sent her on her way, with much love and thanks, a big fat cheque, and promises to visit regularly.

He was going to bring Amy to me in a few days' time, after I'd done what I was here to do. I had a business meeting with Rose the following day, and there was something else I had to sort out, too.

Rose and I had talked many times on the phone in the last few weeks. She and I had so many plans. Pinky's was closed now for the winter, and we already knew that we wouldn't be re-opening it. There were enough cafés in the village and, besides, neither of us really wanted to run a café. My idea was to open a gourmet marshmallow shop. They'd proved so popular with the Lightweights ladies I was pretty sure we would have a year-round custom base for them, and we were going to launch a website and sell them online, too.

We also planned to buy a little hand cart and stock it with our products, hiring it out to weddings and birthday parties. I knew we could work well together, and I was sure we could make the business pay. Pinky's was going to be renamed and totally refitted, with the kitchen updated and the café part converted into a shop. Rose would keep her home, and we would both have an income to support our children.

I'd bought half the business from her, but the flat was still all hers, and we were even hopeful that we would be able to employ Fuchsia at some point soon, which would maybe put a smile on her face. With the money I'd made from selling the farm, buying just a half share in the business had left me enough money to start looking for a cottage in the area, too. It wouldn't be a grand place, but it would be home, and I didn't care how small it was, or how squashed in by neighbours, as long as it had enough room for four people and a dog. That, I hoped, was going to be essential.

The future looked hopeful. There was only one thing I still had to tackle, and I'd given that matter a great deal of thought, too.

I looked up at the moon as it guided me home and sent a silent message to my angels. Mum and Hannah would surely be watching over me now, as I headed towards what could be the most important meeting of my life. I really hoped they could help me. I had a feeling I was going to need it.

I still hadn't heard a word from Gabriel, and I was afraid I'd blown it with him for good, yet something inside kept telling me that it couldn't be over, not like this. There was still so much to say, and I couldn't give up without giving it one last shot. I couldn't imagine life without him. There had to be a way of making him see that, okay, I was stupid and had gone about everything in my usual ridiculous fashion, but I'd been totally genuine in my affection for his family, and I couldn't be more sincere about my feelings for him. I just knew that we could make each other happy, if he'd only give us the chance.

My eyes widened as I came to the junction opposite The Kearton Arms. I had to be seeing things. It just wasn't possible. Talk about déjà vu. Across the road, heading towards Bay Street, was a crowd of people dressed in beautiful black Victorian style clothing. Goths. But why?

I reached for my mobile phone as a thought occurred to me, and the date displayed on the home screen confirmed my suspicions. October thirty-first. Hallowe'en — or Samhain, as Rhiannon had referred to it once in a conversation we'd had about her beliefs. The Whitby Goth Weekend must be due to start, too.

It was weird, like events were turning full circle. This time, however, the Goths were heading down Bay Street, not up it, and I hesitated, wondering where they were heading. Should I follow them? I looked to my left, which was the road to Whisperwood Farm. Then I looked right, which was the way to

The Hare and Moon and the sea. I got out of the car and stood there, undecided.

Up above me, the moon smiled down upon me, and I remembered the silvery path it traced to the shoreline. I knew where I had to go. I parked the car on The Kearton Arms car park, ignoring the sign that clearly stated that it was for customers only and other vehicles could be clamped, and began to walk down Bay Street, my calf muscles pulling at the unfamiliar work after so many weeks on flat London streets.

I passed the ice cream bar, the gift shop, the tourist information building; I passed the outdoor clothing shop, The Mermaid Inn and the fish and chip shop, and crossed the little stone bridge, glancing fondly up at Water's Edge and wondering if Rose was at home or had headed towards wherever it was I was going; I passed the old police station, pulling my coat collar up to protect me from the cold night air and tucking my hands into my pockets, my fingers folding around my mobile phone, the only thing I'd brought with me from the car. Rounding the final bend in the road, I saw the sea before me, the moon beckoning me ever forward, her shimmering rays lighting the way to the sea wall, where I could see the silhouettes of dozens of figures.

As I headed towards The Hare and Moon, voices carried towards me on the crisp, clear air — the chattering and laughter of my friends and neighbours. I saw the glow of candles, some carried in people's hands, others tucked inside hollowed-out pumpkins.

Families sat at the tables and on the benches by the slipway, and I saw Rose with Cerise and Fuchsia, sitting with a tall, dark-haired man I didn't know, sipping drinks and laughing, their worries evidently eased and their bond strengthening. I saw Rose look up and catch sight of me, and I saw her half rise and then sit again. She turned her head, and I followed her gaze to where he was standing at the edge of the sea wall, staring out across the ocean. I saw Sophie and Archie just behind him, saying something to him, and Sophie mopping her eyes, and Archie slapping him on the back, and then I saw him fumble in his pocket. I saw him bow his head, and I wondered, just for a moment, what he was doing. And then I heard sleigh bells. And I knew.

****

'But how long has it been going on?' demanded Sophie. 'And why didn't you tell us?'

'You're a dark horse, mate,' said Archie. 'Kept that very quiet. Mind you,' he added, glancing across at his wife, 'I can't say I blame you.'

'I couldn't face letting you all down again,' said Gabriel. 'I needed to be certain that it was going to work out.'

'And it did?'

'He took to it like a duck to water,' said Flynn. 'They were delighted with him at the Castle Street practice. Offered him a permanent job. Highly relieved he turned them down in favour of Ivy House.'

'You ought to be careful,' said Sophie. 'That's twice you've spoken without being prompted, to my knowledge. You'll be getting a reputation.'

She laughed at his stricken face and put her arm through his. 'Only teasing, Flynn. I'm so grateful to you, I can't tell you. Whoever would have thought you'd manage to persuade him to take up medicine again? I'd given up trying.'

'I needed a partner, and I wanted my old colleague to be the one. Couldn't face interviewing, to be honest,' he mumbled.

Gabriel laughed. 'Glowing recommendation there, Flynn.'

'So, how long have you been planning it?' repeated Sophie. 'And how did you manage to keep it so quiet?'

'A few months, and it wasn't too difficult. Lexi knew, of course, and she covered for me. I just kept my suit in the car and dropped her off at the farm before heading to Helmston. I was only locuming one or two days a week, so I still managed to get plenty of woodwork done and not draw too much attention to myself.'

'But Castle Street, of all places! Why would you put yourself through that?'

332

'To exorcise the ghosts,' he admitted. 'I figured if I was going to do this, I had to do it properly. I needed to reassure myself that I could cope, and I did. It was much easier than I thought it would be. Like taking off a starchy suit and putting on my comfy jeans. Funny really, because it was actually the other way around.'

'And you're going to be a partner?'

'He'll be on a salary for six months, or so,' said Flynn, 'then, yes, we'll talk about a partnership.'

'Thank God for that,' said Sophie. 'Dad will be so pleased you're getting yourself sorted at last.'

'I think this calls for a drink,' said Archie. 'Flynn, come with me to the bar?'

They headed inside The Hare and Moon, and Sophie looked up at her brother. 'So, now you're finally sorting out your professional life, what about the other matter?'

He put his arm around her shoulders. 'You never give up, do you?'

'Unlike you. What's going on in your head, Gabriel? I know how devastated you were the night that Eliza left, yet you never rang her to put your side of the story. Even when you heard about Joe and you knew why she'd had to rush home, you still never called her. You never tried to convince her to come back and give it another try. Why?'

He shook his head. 'I couldn't.'

'But you love her. You do, don't you? Why can't you say it? You've left her believing that you're some kind of wife-battering thug. Why didn't you defend yourself? And what now? Are you just going to pretend she never happened?'

'Sophie, trust me. I could never pretend she never happened. Everything that I'm doing now has happened because of Eliza, and I'm going to do all I can to make sure she knows how much she means to me.'

Sophie's eyes brightened. 'You're going to contact her? Get her to come back?'

'I'll do my best,' he promised. 'Somehow, I'm going to make her see that I'm not the monster she believes me to be. I don't know how, yet. I'm hoping for some divine inspiration,' he admitted, looking up at the moon and remembering another night when he'd silently asked for help and the universe had answered his prayer, sending him a fairy queen to enslave him forever. Could he dare hope that his prayers would be answered again?

'I knew you'd see sense,' she whispered tearfully. 'I'm going to help Archie with the drinks.'

She disappeared into the bar, and Gabriel held out his hand as Lexi appeared at his side.

'You told them then?'

'I did.'

'Bet Sophie's thrilled to bits.'

'She is. And what about you? Did you tell Derry?'

She sighed. 'Yeah. It wasn't so bad. He was a bit upset, but he knew I was right. We've just got nothing in common, and I'm not interested in him any more, not like that. Thanks for being so understanding, Dad.'

He ruffled her hair. 'Not at all. You should have told me ages ago. I can't think why you thought I'd mind. I'd far rather you had some fun while you're young than get tied down to the wrong person before you even know who you are.'

'Like you did?'

'Perhaps,' he admitted. 'But I'll never be sorry for that, Lexi. If Zoe and I hadn't got together, I would never have had you, and you've made my life worth living.'

'And now you've got Eliza, too.' She smiled.

'Well, not yet. I have to tell her the truth, and God knows if she'll even listen to my side of it. She may believe the rumours and then, well, I don't know what I'll do.'

'She won't,' said Lexi.

'You seem very sure?'

'I am. You and Eliza, you — well, you fit together, somehow. I mean, you were both kind of lost when you met, and somehow you found yourselves, and each other. Now you're both complete, but you can be even stronger together. Does that make sense?'

'Lexi,' said Gabriel, shaking his head in wonder, 'I honestly couldn't have put it better myself.'

They looked up as Rhiannon, Archie, Sophie and Flynn headed out, drinks in their hands, trailing a bashful Will behind them.

'Look who we bumped into,' said Archie, grinning at Lexi.

'Hi, Will,' she said.

Will smiled. 'Hello, Lexi.'

'Will's got a question for you,' said Rhiannon. She nodded at Will. 'Go on, ask her. She won't bite.'

Lexi looked at Will curiously. 'Well? What is it?'

'I, er, I was wondering if you'd be interested in coming to work at Kearton Hall? Just on a part-time basis, initially, but with a view to expanding your role.'

'What do you mean? On the farm?'

'No, no.' He shook his head. 'Father has accepted that, for the estate to survive, he has to open the house up to the public, not just the gardens, as we currently do. Bernie and I have persuaded him that it needs to be a real tourist attraction, and we want people who know and care about the place to help us. I understand you're doing a degree in the arts, and I was wondering if you'd be interested—'

'Yes!'

He blinked, his face turning so pink it was even visible in the moonlight.

'Yes?'

'I'd love to work at Kearton Hall. It would be my dream job. Thank you so much.'

'Really?' He could hardly wipe the smile off his face.

'How splendid!' said Rhiannon, clapping her hands. 'I just know she'll be perfect for the job, and the two of you will work together so well. Maybe you should both take a seat somewhere and discuss it,' she added, nudging Will gently.

Will looked at Lexi.

She grabbed his arm and began to drag him away. 'Come on, then. Let's discuss my working terms and conditions,' she said.

Archie turned to Gabriel and laughed. 'That's all Will's birthdays and Christmases come at once,' he said.

Gabriel smiled, and Sophie tutted impatiently. 'Never mind all that. Did you hear what I told you about Eliza?'

Archie exchanged glances with his brother-in-law. 'So, you and Eliza, eh?'

Gabriel nodded. 'Yeah.'

'Nice one. Here's your pint.'

Sophie rolled her eyes. 'Men! I don't know why we bother. I suppose it will be another six months before you do anything about it.'

'Actually,' said Gabriel, 'Lexi made me realise that Eliza and I are meant to be together, and I don't want to waste any more time. I need to act now.'

Rhiannon touched his cheek, her eyes twinkling. 'Samhain,' she told him, 'is exactly opposite Beltane on the wheel of life. Did you know that?'

Sophie sighed. 'Oh, Rhiannon, not now.'

Gabriel shook his head. 'No, I didn't, Rhiannon.'

'Summer's end,' she told him softly. 'A new year, and a time for reflection. Did you know that right now, the veil between the two realms is at its thinnest? Tonight, the dead are able to visit the living.'

She looked up at the sky, and he followed her gaze, their eyes fixing on the luminous moon, the shining light in the dark heavens.

'Maybe tonight, of all nights, is the time to act. There may be a guiding hand to help you on your way.'

She turned to Flynn, her face wreathed in smiles. 'Now, Flynn, darling, shall we have a drink together? You know, it's rather crowded inside. Shall we take a seat out here? I do believe there's an empty bench opposite the MacLeans.'

She slipped her arm through his and began to lead him towards the side of the slipway where Rose, Fuchsia and Cerise were sipping drinks and chatting amiably to each other for the first time in months.

Sophie tutted, watching their progress for a moment, then turned back to Gabriel. 'So, what are you going to do?'

'I'm going to call her and ask her if I can come down to London to talk to her.'

'London?' Sophie screwed up her nose in disgust. 'You hate

London. You said it was the worst experience of your life, living there.'

'It doesn't matter. I've got to see her. I'm going to call her.'

'What, now?'

'Right now,' he confirmed, handing her his glass.

He saw tears spilling from her eyes, threatening the security of her mascara. She dabbed at them with her other hand.

Archie clapped Gabriel on the back. 'Good luck, mate. Sophie, stop blubbing. This is what you wanted, for God's sake!'

'Tears of joy, don't worry,' she assured him, turning away as Gabriel took out his mobile phone and began to scroll down, looking for Eliza's number.

He hovered over her name for a moment, feeling a nervous flutter. It was now or never. He pressed call and waited, holding his breath until the dial tone sounded in his ear.

From somewhere behind him, he heard sleigh bells. For a second, he couldn't think straight, and then realisation dawned as he heard Sophie's gasp. For a moment he gazed up at the moon, his face alight with wonder, then he turned, the phone still ringing, until Sophie gently took it from his hand and ended the call.

'Eliza.'

'Hello, Gabriel,' she said.

Chapter 35

Gabriel led me down the slipway and onto the beach, guiding me across the sand, still wet from the outgoing tide, and towards a large slab of limestone and shale that made a handy bench. It was rather slimy with seaweed, but he didn't seem to care, and I wasn't going to argue. His hand was in mine. It was enough.

We sat in silence for a few minutes, neither of us knowing what to say.

'You do know they'll all be watching us?' I said eventually, more out of desperation to break the silence than from any real concern.

'Well, Sophie will be trying. Archie will be heading her off,' he said with a faint smile.

I looked at him. He was so beautiful, but there was that expression in his eyes again, the one I'd come to know and dread. The shuttered, closed off look. I longed to reach out to him and stroke that guarded face and tell him everything was going to be all right, but I didn't know what he wanted from me. Had he forgiven me? Would he ever understand why I'd behaved the way I had?

'Gabriel I'm so sorry,' I said desperately, hardly daring to look at him. 'What I did — I know how sneaky and deceitful it was, and I can't make any excuses for it.'

He turned to me, a stunned expression on his face. '*You're sorry?*'

'I really am. All I can say is, after Lexi's birthday, I was desperate to find out that you and I weren't related. I really didn't want you to be my brother. I cared about you so much, and not just you. I cared about Sophie and Archie and Lexi. I'd really grown to love them, and the last thing I wanted was to destroy your family. Well, not the last thing. Maybe the second to last thing,' I admitted, in the interests of honesty.

He was silent for a moment, then he took hold of my hand and held it gently. I felt a shiver run through me, and a strange sensation that I didn't think was entirely due to me sitting on wet seaweed.

'I know what Denise told you,' he said quietly. 'Michelle took great delight in informing me. Is that why you didn't contact me?'

I looked at him blankly. 'What?'

'Eliza, I know you've been told that I hit Lexi's mother, and that I was struck off. You have to believe me, it's not true. Any of it.'

My God, was that what was worrying him? I reached out to him, and he took hold of my hand, as I ran my fingers down those sharp cheekbones, tracing the contours of his face.

'Of course it's not true. I couldn't figure out why you'd give up medicine to build rabbit hutches, but that could have been for all sorts of reasons. I never thought you capable of hitting a woman, Gabriel.'

'Not even for a moment?'

I shook my head. 'When Denise told me, I was shocked, but only that people could believe that about you. I don't know how those rumours got started, but I'm one hundred per cent certain there's an explanation for it. I know you'd never do that.'

'How do you know? How do you know it isn't true?'

'Because you're not that person,' I said slowly. 'You're a good man, and besides, you adore Lexi more than anything in this world. You'd never do anything to hurt her, or the woman who gave her to you.'

His eyes glistened with tears. 'That's all I needed to know. It means more to me than you could ever imagine. I owe you such a big apology, Eliza. It wasn't you I was really doubting when I left you that day. I just couldn't believe things could be so right.

That night we spent together — it was incredible, but I felt so, so—'

'Overwhelmed? I know I did. It was an amazing night.'

He shrugged. 'It was perfect. I was so nervous. I'd wanted to touch you for such a long time, but I was out of practice. It had been a while.'

'I know.'

He winced. 'Great.'

'No, no! I didn't mean that!' I felt the familiar burning sensation on my face. 'I meant, I knew you'd split up with Zoe ages ago, and I knew there hadn't been anyone else. God, I didn't mean — I wasn't saying — I mean, you were completely fantastic. Amazing.'

'Keep talking. I'm desperate for reassurance.'

I peered at him. 'You're having me on, aren't you?'

He laughed. 'Yes. But you look so beautiful when you're blushing and, luckily, you blush a lot. It's one of the reasons I love you so much.'

My eyes widened. 'What did you say?'

He took my face between his hands and kissed me, a gentle kiss full of tenderness.

'I love you,' he said, as we broke apart and smiled at each other. 'I'm so, so sorry. I should have told you that before. I wanted to—'

'But you did!' I broke in. 'Why do you think I wouldn't give up? You told me you loved me over and over again, in every action. It was in every touch, every look. It's what's carried me through all these weeks. But there were other things — the cake you made for me and remembering the Maltesers, the rocking horse for Amy, telling me I looked beautiful when I know I looked like a space hopper. Harry told me he loved me all the time, and it meant nothing. I wanted him to show me, not tell me, but he never did. You did, Gabriel, and I loved you for it. You're just like my grandad.'

He looked baffled by that, unsurprisingly.

'It doesn't matter. Look, Gabriel, I came to find you because I love you, too, and I couldn't give up on us, no matter what you thought of me. I think we're good together. We — we fit. Don't we?'

He looked over toward where the moon glistened on the horizon. 'My mother used to tell me that the sun loved the moon so much that he died every night just to let her breathe. I used to think it was a ridiculous story, but I understand it now.'

'Are you getting soppy?'

'Yes. Under this cool exterior I'm a surprisingly emotional man.'

'I knew it!' I said. 'The angel in the marble! I kept on carving and now you're free.'

'You say the strangest things,' he said. 'I wonder if I'll know what you're talking about half the time? It could be a very puzzling existence.'

'Are you willing to take the chance?'

'I don't seem to have a choice. I don't think I can live without you.'

He pulled me to him, and we clung together for a while, drained as if we'd fought a huge battle. Then he gently kissed the top of my head and sat up straight. 'There are things you need to know.'

'Really? Isn't it enough to know that we love each other?'

He shook his head. 'If this is going to work, darling, we must have a clean slate. No more secrets. I've had enough of them to last me a lifetime.'

I nodded, glowing with happiness that he'd called me darling. 'Go on.'

Slowly, hesitantly, he told me of his marriage to Zoe, of the increasing arguments, her affair, the massive over-spending and the miserable years in London.

'We had bailiffs coming to the door eventually,' he confessed, clearly still embarrassed. 'We ended up losing almost everything. I sold the house in London and we moved back to Yorkshire, partly because it was so much cheaper, and we needed the money, but mostly because I couldn't stand being in London any longer. I hated it from the first, and so did Lexi. She was getting bullied at school and I just wanted to bring her home. Zoe knew she'd pushed it too far and tried to behave for a while, but it all started again.'

'Why didn't you just leave her?' I said.

He sighed. 'Believe me, I wanted to. At first, when Lexi was still at school, she said that, if I left, she'd make damn sure I'd never get to see her, and I believe she meant it. I couldn't lose Lexi, so I waited. I thought, when she left school, we'd both go, but by then Zoe had met Hugh Appleton. Things took a turn for the worse, and Lexi wouldn't leave her. She was terrified for her and begged me to stay. I couldn't abandon them, could I? And, as it turned out, Lexi was right to be terrified.'

His voice faltered, and I squeezed his arm reassuringly. 'Gabriel, you don't have to do this.'

'I do. You deserve the truth.' He took a deep breath. 'Appleton was rich, which was just how Zoe liked them. They carried on in front of us quite openly. It was the worst time of our lives. Lexi's grades at school had been pretty appalling — unsurprisingly — and she'd enrolled at college, hoping to re-sit her exams, but it was pointless. She was worried sick. Couldn't concentrate, wasn't eating, wasn't sleeping. She knew what was going on, you see. It was a while before I spotted it.

'One night, Zoe came home with bruises on her arm. She told me it was an accident, but I didn't believe her. It started to happen regularly. Lexi had known Appleton was hitting her, but Zoe was so stupid and so easily bought by him that she wouldn't stop seeing him, and she told Lexi to keep it quiet. I wanted to call the police when I found out, but she said she would deny everything. Then one night, she didn't come home till the early hours of the morning. Oh, Eliza, if you'd seen her! It broke my heart. She just expected me to clean her up and treat her injuries, but I rang the police. Zoe went crazy. She rang Appleton, and he told her to keep her mouth shut. He said he loved her and that he'd only done it because he was jealous that she was still with me, and that he wanted to marry her and start a new life with her abroad. Everything she wanted to hear.'

He shivered. 'So, when the police arrived, she told them I'd done it. They wouldn't listen to me, or to Lexi.' He hung his head, his face wracked with pain. 'Lexi was hysterical, screaming at them that I hadn't done it. They put me in handcuffs and arrested me, dragged me into the car, while all the time she was begging them to leave me alone. They threw me in a cell for the night and spent most of the next day questioning me.'

'Oh, Gabriel.' I didn't know what to say. I stroked his fingers, and he shrugged.

'Have you ever been really scared, Eliza? I mean, really, really scared? That night in the cell, I was truly terrified. I didn't know where Appleton was, what he'd be doing to Zoe, how Lexi was coping, what would happen to her. I kept thinking that, while I was stuck in there, Appleton could take her somewhere I'd never find her. What if he beat her, the way he was beating her mother? They were the longest hours of my life.'

'But they didn't charge you?'

He rubbed his forehead. 'No. A witness came forward who'd seen a man hitting Zoe outside the bar where she worked. She wouldn't name him, but she swore that it wasn't me, and they finally listened to me and let me go. They questioned Zoe, and she admitted lying but refused to name her attacker. It was just my word against hers, and since I hadn't actually seen the assault, they couldn't do anything. They could have charged her with wasting police time, but I think they thought she'd suffered enough. Anyway, I begged her to stay and to give up Appleton. I was worried sick about what would happen to her, but she just packed her bags and left. A few weeks later, I got divorce papers through the post and then she moved to Paris with that thug. I haven't seen her since. I'm not even sure she's still alive.'

'Oh, God, I'm so sorry,' I murmured. 'But you did everything you could for her. Far more than most men would have done.'

His eyes were full of sadness. 'I let her down. You see, I never loved her, and I couldn't pretend. I thought I was doing the honourable thing, but I should never have married her. She didn't really love me, either. It was a way out of a pretty miserable existence with her parents, that's all. I tried to make her happy, but it wasn't enough. Anyway, by the time I was arrested, she was in so much debt that I was working just to pay it all off. I knew the neighbours were whispering, putting two and two together and making five. It dragged on like that for almost a year. Then, one day, I heard a woman in the reception, refusing an appointment with me because I was a wife-beater. I went to see the practice manager, and he admitted they'd had quite a few cancellations and complaints. Lexi and I had a long talk. She told me there was gossip and rumours and she'd had to defend me from all sorts of lies. We were both so depressed, and I knew we had to do something.

'So, I handed in my notice, sold the house, paid off the mortgage and all Zoe's debts with the proceeds, and we moved back to Kearton Bay. Sophie and Archie took us in. I don't know what Lexi and I would have done without them. I was pretty raw, to be honest. I just wanted to hide away. I'd always been good at woodwork, and Hannah offered me the use of her workshop. I just started helping around the farm and building hutches to make a living. It wasn't a grand plan, or anything. I didn't want to face people, or risk anyone pointing the finger at me again. It took me so long to come to terms with it all.'

'But you have?'

'I'm getting there. Thanks to you.'

'Not thanks to me, Gabriel. You've done it all yourself. I don't know how you've come through it all, but you have.'

'You made me want to move on. You have no idea ... especially after Hannah died.' He squeezed my hand. 'What you said about my job mattering. I realised you were right, and I knew it was what I wanted to do, more than anything.'

'And do you think you can face going back to it?'

'I am. I'd been doing locum work a couple of days a week at my old practice, just to help out and see if I could bear it. Then, after Hannah died, well, I knew I wanted to do it again full time. That's why I didn't contact you. I wanted to sort myself out first, make sure that I'd something to offer you. I was calling you to tell you my news. I've been lucky. I'm starting work at Ivy House with Flynn in a week's time, and there's a possible partnership in it for me.'

'So that's where you kept disappearing to,' I said. 'I thought you were avoiding me. I'm so glad for you.'

He kissed me again then rubbed my hands. 'You're freezing.

Shall we head up back to the pub? I think we should continue this talk indoors, don't you?'

I nodded, suddenly realising how cold I was, and we stood up and began to walk back towards the slipway, his arm draped over my shoulder.

'You look stunning, by the way,' he said, looking at my dark hair with undisguised approval.

'Thank you. I decided that the bleach and the make-up belonged in the past, and I'm putting the past behind me.'

'I think I'm finally doing the same,' he said.

'And what about the future?' I asked, hopefully. 'What does that hold for you?'

'A job, a home, peace of mind? You?' We stopped at the bottom of the slipway, and he turned to face me, his eyes piercing into mine. 'What do you think, Eliza? Seriously. Could my future be with you?'

'Of course,' I said. 'It's all I want. Though, I must warn you, I can't iron to save my life.'

'I can,' he said, his dimples reappearing as he smiled down at me. 'I'll make you a deal. I'll do all the ironing, if you promise I'll never have to bake another cake. Deal?'

'Deal,' I said. 'Though I think you're a sad loss to the baking world. You could have been the next Mary Berry.'

His smile faded, his expression turning suddenly anxious. 'Could you really be happy here? Could you really give up London and the celebrity life? I'm not a television presenter. I'm a country GP — or, at least, I will be. I'll never have the kind of money that Harry has. It wasn't enough for Zoe, and I couldn't bear to make you unhappy, too.'

'Luckily for you, I'm not Zoe,' I told him. 'Besides, there's something I haven't told you. You're not the only one planning a new career, Dr Bailey. Let me tell you all about a little venture called Mallow Magic.'

I gave him the gist of it, but the details had to wait for another time, as he seemed to decide that my lips were more useful for other things than talking and, to be honest, I had to agree with him.

Above us, we could hear cheering and whooping from our friends and neighbours, but Gabriel didn't seem to care, and I wasn't going to stop him. I did have a slight wobble when I heard Sophie call out to us not to stop because she was going to take our photo, but Gabriel just wrapped his arms around me tighter and kissed me harder. Against my lips, I felt his own curve into a smile, as Sophie's wail could be heard echoing across the sands.

'Oh, Archie, how do you work the sodding camera on this thing?'

****

"Reader, I married him."

I used to think, when I came to the end of a romantic novel like *Jane Eyre*, that was that — a happy ending. Then I married Harry and that illusion was shattered. It took me a long time to realise that it's not the marriage that guarantees the happy ending. I mean, it's so obvious I can't think why I hadn't figured it out before. To get your happy ending you don't just have to get married, you've got to marry the right person. Stands to reason, really.

I came to Kearton Bay looking for an angel, and I found him. Just not the one I thought I was looking for. Turns out, Gabriel was my angel all along, my hero, and the love of my life. And you know what? I have a really good feeling that, this time, we're both going to live happily ever after.

The End

To find out more about Sharon Booth
and to sign up to her newsletter
visit her website
www.sharonboothwriter.com

Acknowledgements

Firstly, thank you to my long-suffering family, who must have forgotten what I looked like during the writing of this book. Love you all lots, and I'm so grateful for your interest and patience.
I've had a great deal of support from the writing community — particularly from Valerie-Anne Baglietto and Lizzie Lamb. Also, Sue Johnson, who read the many different versions of the first chapter and helped me decide where to start the story.
I'm particularly grateful to the Romantic Novelists' Association. Without its New Writers' Scheme, I very much doubt that you would be reading this book now. My special thanks to the anonymous reader, who read this novel when it was called *Angel in the Marble* and gave me such wonderful advice.
My thanks to Julie Belfield and Jennie Dunn, who worked wonders on the manuscript, with their brilliant editing and proof-reading skills, and to Berni Stevens for the lovely cover. Thank you, also, to my beta-readers, Jo Bartlett, Liz Berry, Cheryl Eggleton, Julie Heslington, and Julia Richardson.
I want to say an extra special thank you to three people. Firstly, Jo. Without you, I have no idea if, or how, this book would have been published at all. Thank you for your belief in *Angel*, your "can do" attitude, and for sharing with me your astounding knowledge.
Huge thanks and massive hugs to Alys West and Jessica Redland, for all the afternoons spent in coffee shops, eating cake and pouring out our ideas, problems, and anxieties. And laughing. A lot. Somehow, nothing seemed too difficult after those meetings. It may have been the cake, of course, but I think it far more likely that it was your friendship and understanding, and your unfailing encouragement, that made everything seem possible.
Where would I be without you? Here's to the next cakefest!
Finally, love and gratitude to Emma Crook and your kind. Oh, I really hope you know why.

Sharon xx

More from Sharon Booth

A Kiss from a Rose (Kearton Bay Book 2)

Rose Maclean's new beginning in Kearton Bay didn't go quite as expected, but now she has a new career and things finally seem to be improving.
But Rose's life never runs smoothly for long. With money tight, space in her tiny flat at a premium, and her eldest daughter, Fuschia, behaving even more strangely than usual, the last thing she needs is to spend more time with her mother. Mrs Maclean is straight-talking and hard to please, but when she becomes the unexpected victim of a crime, Rose has no choice but to take her into her already cramped home.
Reduced to sleeping on the sofa, dealing with her mother's barbed comments, and worrying endlessly about her teenage daughters, Rose is desperately in need of something good to happen.
Flynn Pennington-Rhys is the quiet man of Kearton Bay. He lives alone in a large, elegant house, and works as a GP in the village. Thoughtful, reliable, but a bit of a loner, Flynn is the last person Rose expected to fall for. Then a drunken kiss at a wedding sets them on a path that neither could have predicted.
But Flynn has his own issues to deal with, and when events take an unexpected turn, it seems Rose may not be able to rely on him, after all.
Will the quiet man come through for her? Will her daughters ever sort themselves out? And will Rose ever get her bedroom back from her mother, or is she destined to spend the rest of her life on the sofa?

Once Upon a Long Ago (Kearton Bay Book 3)

Lexi Bailey doesn't do love. Having seen the war zone that was her parents' marriage, she has no interest in venturing into a relationship, and thinks romance is for fairy tales. As far as she's concerned, there's no such thing as happy ever after, and she's not looking for a handsome prince.
For Will Boden-Kean, that's probably a good thing. He hardly qualifies as a handsome prince, after all. He may be the son of a baronet and live in a stately home, but he's not known for his good looks. What he is known for, among the residents of Kearton Bay, is his kind heart, his determination to fund Kearton Hall — and his unrequited love for Lexi.
While Lexi gazes at the portrait of the Third Earl Kearton, and dreams of finding the treasure that is reputed to be hidden somewhere in the house, Will is working hard to ensure that his home survives. When he goes against Lexi's wishes and employs the most unpopular man in the village, she begins to wonder if he's under a spell. Will would never upset her. What could possibly have happened to him?
As plans take shape for a grand ball, Lexi's life is in turmoil. With a secret from Will's past revealed, a witch who is far too beautiful for Lexi's peace of mind, and a new enchantress on the scene, things are changing rapidly at Kearton Hall. Add to that a big, bad wolf of a work colleague, a stepmother in denial, and a father who is most definitely up to no good, and it's no wonder she decides to make a new start somewhere else.
Then she makes a discovery that changes everything — but time is running out for her. Is it too late to find her happy ending? Will Lexi make it to the ball? Will Buttons save the day? And where on earth did that handsome prince come from?

www.ingramcontent.com/pod-product-compliance
Lightning Source LLC
Chambersburg PA
CBHW051208190726
48288CB00006B/1865